**Praise for #1 *New York Times* bestselling author
Debbie Macomber**

"Debbie Macomber tells women's stories in a way
no one else does."
—*BookPage*

"Macomber is a skilled storyteller."
—*Publishers Weekly*

"No one writes stories of love and forgiveness like
Macomber."
—*RT Book Reviews*

**Praise for *New York Times* bestselling author
Shannon Stacey**

"This contemporary tale is full of the love (and
requisite family high jinks) that readers have come
to expect from Shannon Stacy. The chemistry
between Emma and Sean positively sizzles."
—*RT Book Reviews* (4½ stars) on *Yours to Keep*

"Stacey's gift for writing easily relatable characters
will hook readers and leave them eagerly waiting
for the next installment."
—*Publishers Weekly* on *Heat Exchange*

Debbie Macomber is a #1 *New York Times* bestselling author and a leading voice in women's fiction worldwide. Her work has appeared on every major bestseller list, with more than 170 million copies in print, and she is a multiple award winner. Hallmark Channel based a television series on Debbie's popular Cedar Cove books. For more information, visit her website, www.debbiemacomber.com.

New York Times and *USA TODAY* bestselling author **Shannon Stacey** lives with her husband and two sons in New England, where her two favorite activities are writing stories of happily-ever-after and driving her UTV through the mud. You can contact Shannon through her website, shannonstacey.com, where she maintains an almost daily blog, visit her on Twitter, Twitter.com/shannonstacey, and on Facebook, Facebook.com/shannonstacey.authorpage, or email her at shannon@shannonstacey.com.

To find out about other books by Shannon Stacey or to be alerted to new releases, sign up for her monthly newsletter at bit.ly/shannonstaceynewsletter.

DEBBIE MACOMBER

WHITE LACE AND PROMISES

(H) HARLEQUIN® BESTSELLING AUTHOR COLLECTION

ISBN-13: 978-1-335-14511-6

White Lace and Promises

Copyright © 2018 by Harlequin Books S.A.

The publisher acknowledges the copyright holders of the individual works as follows:

White Lace and Promises
Copyright © 1986 by Debbie Macomber

Yours to Keep
Copyright © 2011 by Shannon Stacey

Recycling programs for this product may not exist in your area.

HARLEQUIN®

Printed in U.S.A.

www.Harlequin.com

CONTENTS

WHITE LACE AND PROMISES

Debbie Macomber

To Maggie Osborne
With deep respect and affection

One

Maggie Kingsbury ground the gears of her royal-blue Mercedes and pulled to a screeching halt at the red light. Impatient, she glanced at her wristwatch and muttered silently under her breath. Once again she was late. Only this time her tardiness hadn't been intentional. The afternoon had innocently slipped away while she painted, oblivious to the world.

When Janelle had asked her to be the maid of honor for the wedding, Maggie had hesitated. As a member of the wedding party, unwelcome attention would be focused on her. It wasn't until she had learned that Glenn Lambert was going to be the best man that she'd consented. Glenn had been her friend from the time she was in grade school: her buddy, her co-conspirator, her white knight. With Glenn there everything would be perfect.

But already things were going badly. Here she was due to pick him up at San Francisco International and she was ten minutes behind schedule. In the back of her mind, Maggie realized that her tardiness was another symptom of her discontent.

The light changed and she roared across the intersection, her back tires spinning. One of these days she was going to get a well-deserved speeding ticket. But not today, she prayed, please not today.

Her painting smock was smudged with a full spectrum of rainbow colors. The thick dark strands of her chestnut hair were pinned to the back of her head, disobedient curls tumbling defiantly at her temples and across her wide brow. And she had wanted to look so good for Glenn. It had been years since she'd seen him—not since high school graduation. In the beginning they had corresponded back and forth, but soon they'd each become involved with college and had formed a new set of friends. Their texts and emails had dwindled and as often happens their communication became a chatty note on a Christmas card. Steve and Janelle had kept her updated with what had been going on in Glenn's life, and from what she understood, he was a successful stockbroker in Charleston. It sounded like a job he would manage well.

It surprised Maggie that in all those years, Glenn hadn't married. At twenty-nine and thirty they were the only two of their small high school graduation class who hadn't. Briefly she wondered what had kept Glenn away from the altar. As she recalled, he had always been easy on the eyes.

Her mind conjured up a mental picture of a young Glenn Lambert. Tall, dark, athletic, broad shouldered, thin—she smiled—he'd probably filled out over the years. He was the boy who lived next door and they had been great friends and at times the worst of enemies. Once, in the sixth grade, Glenn had stolen her diary and as a joke made copies and sold them to the boys in their class. After he found her crying, he had spent weeks trying to make it up to her. Years later his patience had gotten her a passing grade in chemistry and she had fixed him up with a date for the Junior-Senior prom.

Arriving at the airport, Maggie followed the freeway signs that directed her to the passenger-pickup area. Almost immediately she sighted Glenn standing beside his luggage, watching the traffic for a familiar face. A slow smile blossomed across her lips until it hovered at a grin. Glenn had hardly changed, and yet he was completely different. He was taller than she remembered, with those familiar broad shoulders now covered by a heather-blue blazer instead of a faded football jersey. At thirty he was a prime specimen of manhood. But behind his easy smile, Maggie recognized a maturity—one he'd fought hard for and painfully attained. Maggie studied him with fascination, amazed at his air of deliberate casualness. He knew about her inheritance. Of course he knew; Steve would have told him. Involuntarily, her fingers tightened around the steering wheel as a sense of regret settled over her. As much as she would have liked to, Maggie couldn't go back to being a carefree schoolgirl.

She eased to a stop at the curb in front of him and leaned across the seat to open the passenger door. "Hey, handsome, are you looking for a ride?"

Bending over, Glenn stuck his head inside the car. "Muffie, I should have known you'd be late."

As she climbed out of the vehicle, Maggie grimaced at the use of her nickname. Glenn had dubbed her Muffie in junior high, but it had always sounded to Maggie like the name of a poodle. The more she'd objected the more the name had stuck until her friends had picked it up. The sweet, innocent Muffie no longer existed.

After checking the side-view mirror for traffic to clear, she opened her door and stepped out. "I'm sorry I'm late, I don't know where the time went. As usual I got carried away."

Glenn chuckled and shook his head knowingly. "When haven't you gotten carried away?" He picked up his suitcase and tucked it inside the trunk Maggie had just opened. Placing his hands on her shoulders, he examined her carefully and gave her a brief hug. "You look fantastic." His dark eyes were somber and sincere.

"Me?" she choked out, feeling the warmth of many years of friendship chase away her earlier concerns. "You always could lie diplomatically." Maggie had recognized early in life that she was no raving beauty. Her eyes were probably her best feature—dark brown with small gold flecks, almond shaped and slanting upward at the corners. She was relatively tall, nearly five foot eight, with long shapely legs. Actually, the years hadn't altered her outwardly. Like Glenn's, the changes were more inward. Life's lessons had left their mark on her as well.

Looking at Glenn, Maggie couldn't hide the feeling of nostalgia she experienced. "The last time I looked this bad I was dressed as a zucchini for a fifth-grade play."

He crossed his arms and studied her. "I'd say you were wearing typical Muffie attire."

"Jeans and sneakers?"

"Seeing you again is like stepping into the past."

Not exactly. She didn't stuff tissue paper in her bra these days. Momentarily, she wondered if Glenn had ever guessed that she had. "I've got strict instructions to drop you off at Steve's. The rehearsal's scheduled at the church tonight at seven." This evening he'd have the opportunity to see just how much she had changed.

Of all the people Maggie knew, Glenn would be the one to recognize the emotional differences in her. She might have been able to disguise them from others, but not from Glenn.

"With you chauffeuring me around there's little guarantee I'll make the wedding," Glenn teased affectionately.

"You'll make it," she assured him and climbed back into the car.

Glenn joined her and snapped the seat belt into place. Thoughtfully he ran his hand along the top of the dashboard. "I heard about your inheritance and wondered if it'd made a difference in your life."

"Well, I now live in a fancy beach house, and don't plan to do anything with the rest of my life except paint." She checked his profile for a negative response and finding none, she continued. "A secretary handles the mail, an estate planner deals with the finances, and there's a housekeeper and gardener as well. I do exactly as I want."

"Must be nice."

"I heard you haven't done so shabbily yourself."

"Not bad, but I don't lounge around in a beach house." He said it without censure. "I've had dealings with a lot of wealthy people the past few years. As far as I can see, having money can be a big disappointment."

The statement was open-ended, but Maggie refused to comment. Glenn's insight surprised her. He was right. All Great-aunt Margaret's money hadn't brought Maggie or her brother happiness. Oh, at first she had been filled with wonderful illusions about her inheritance. But these days she struggled to shroud her restlessness. To anyone else her lifestyle was a dream come true. Only Maggie knew differently.

"Money is supposed to make everything right. Only it creates more problems than it solves," she mumbled and pulled into the flow of traffic leaving the airport. Glenn didn't respond and Maggie wasn't sure he heard her, which was just as well, because the subject was one she preferred to avoid.

"It's hard to imagine Steve and Janelle getting married after all these years." A lazy grin swept across his tanned face.

Maggie smiled, longing to keep things light. "I'd say it was about time, wouldn't you?"

"I've never known two people more right for each other. The surprising part is that everyone saw it but them."

"I'm happy for those two."

"Me, too," he added, but Maggie noted that Glenn's tone held a hint of melancholy, as if the wedding was going to be as difficult for him as it was for her. Maggie couldn't imagine why.

"Steve's divorce devastated him," Maggie continued, "and he started dating Janelle again. The next thing I knew they decided to march up the aisle." Maggie paused and gestured expressively with her right hand.

Glenn's eyes fell on Maggie's artistically long fingers. It surprised him that she had such beautiful hands. They looked capable of kneading the stiffest clay and at the same time gentle enough to soothe a crying child. She wore no rings, nor were her well-shaped nails painted, yet her hands were striking. He couldn't take his eyes from them. He had known Maggie most of her life and had never appreciated her hands.

"Are you going to invite me out to your beach house?" he asked finally.

"I thought I might. There's a basketball hoop in the gym and I figured I'd challenge you to a game."

"I'm not worried. As I recall the only slam dunk you ever made was with a doughnut into a cup of coffee."

Hiding her laugh, Maggie answered threateningly, "I'll make you pay for that remark."

Their families had shared a wide common driveway, and Maggie had passed many an hour after school playing ball with Glenn. Janelle and Steve and the rest of the gang from the neighborhood had hung around together. Most of the childhood friendships remained in place. Admittedly, Maggie wasn't as trusting of people nowadays. Not since she had inherited the money. The creeps had come crawling out of the woodwork the minute the news of her good fortune was out. Some were obvious gold diggers and others weren't so transparent. Maggie had gleaned valuable lessons from Dirk Wagner and had nearly made the mistake of marrying a man who loved her money far more than he cared for her.

"I don't suppose you've got a pool in that mansion of yours?"

"Yup."

"Is there anything you haven't got?" Glenn asked suddenly serious.

Maggie didn't know where to start, the list was so long. She had lost her purpose, her ambition, her drive to succeed professionally with her art. Her roster of friends was meager and consisted mainly of people she had known most of her life. "Some things," she muttered, wanting to change the subject.

"Money can't buy everything, can it?" Glenn asked so gently that Maggie felt her throat tighten.

She'd thought it would at first, but had learned the hard way that it couldn't buy the things that mattered most: love, loyalty, respect or friendship.

"No." Her voice was barely above a whisper.

"I suppose out of respect for your millions, I should call you Margaret," Glenn suggested next. "But try as I might, you'll always be Muffie to me."

"Try Maggie. I'm not Muffie anymore." She smiled to take any sting from her voice. With his returning nod, her hand relaxed against the steering wheel.

She exited from the freeway and drove into the basement parking lot of Steve's apartment building. "Here we are," she announced, turning off the engine. "With a good three hours to spare."

While Glenn removed his suitcase from the car trunk, Maggie dug in the bottom of her purse for the apartment key Steve had given her. "I have strict instructions to personally escort you upstairs and give you a stiff drink. You're going to need it when you hear what's scheduled."

With his suitcase in tow, Glenn followed her to the elevator. "Where's Steve?"

"Working."

"The day before his wedding?" Glenn looked astonished.

"He's been through this wedding business before," she reminded him offhandedly.

The heavy doors swished closed and Maggie leaned against the back wall and pulled the pins from her hair. It was futile to keep putting it up when it came tumbling down every time she moved her head. Stuffing the pins in her pocket, she felt Glenn's gaze studying her. Their eyes met.

"I can't believe you," he said softly.

"What?"

"You haven't changed. Time hasn't marked you in the least. You're exactly as I remember."

"You've changed." They both had.

"Don't I know it." Glenn sighed, leaned against the side of the moving elevator and pinched the bridge of his nose. "Some days I feel a hundred years old."

Maggie was mesmerized by him. He was different. The carefree, easygoing teen had been replaced by an introspective man with intense, dark eyes that revealed a weary pain. The urge to ask him what had happened burned on her lips, but she knew that if she inquired into his life, he could ask about her own. Instead she led the way out of the elevator to the apartment.

The key turned and Maggie swung open the door to the high-rise that gave a spectacular view of San Francisco Bay.

"Go ahead and plant your suitcase in the spare bedroom and I'll fix us a drink. What's your pleasure?"

"Juice if there's any."

Maggie placed both hands on the top of the bar. "I'll see what I can do." Turning, she investigated the contents of the refrigerator and brought out a small can of tomato juice. "Will this do?"

"Give it to me straight," he tossed over his shoulder as he left the living room.

By the time he returned, Maggie was standing at the window holding a martini. She watched him take the glass of juice from the bar and join her.

"Are you on the wagon?" she asked impulsively.

"Not really. It's a little too early in the afternoon for me."

Maggie nodded as a tiny smile quirked at the corners of her mouth. The first time she had ever tasted vodka had been with Glenn.

"What's so amusing?"

"Do you remember New Year's Eve the year I was sixteen?"

Glenn's brow furrowed. "No."

"Glenn!" She laughed with disbelief. "After all the trouble we got into over that, I'd think you'd never forget it."

"Was that the year we threw our own private party?"

"Remember Cindy and Earl, Janelle and Steve, you and me and…who else?"

"Brenda and Bob?"

"No… Barb and Bob."

"Right." He chuckled. "I never could keep the twins straight."

"Who could? It surprises me he didn't marry both of them."

"Whatever happened to Bob?"

Maggie took a sip of her martini before answering. "He's living in Oregon, going bald, and has four kids."

"Bob? I don't believe it."

"You weren't here for the ten-year reunion." Maggie hadn't bothered to attend either, but Janelle had filled in the details of what she'd missed.

"I'm sorry I missed it," Glenn said and moved to the bar. He lifted his drink and finished it off in two enormous swallows.

Mildly surprised at the abrupt action, Maggie took another sip of hers, moved to a deep-seated leather chair, sat and tucked her long legs under her.

Glenn took a seat across from her. "So what's been going on in your life, Maggie? Are you happy?"

She shrugged indolently. "I suppose." From anyone else she would have resented the question, but she'd always been able to talk to Glenn. A half hour after being separated for years and it was as if they'd never been apart. "I'm a wealthy woman, Glenn, and I've learned the hard way about human nature."

"What happened?"

"It's a long story."

"Didn't you just get done telling me that we had three hours before the rehearsal?"

For a moment Maggie was tempted to spill her frustrations out. To tell Glenn about the desperate pleas for money she got from people who sensed her soft heart. The ones who were looking for someone to invest in a sure thing. And the users, who pretended friendship or love in the hopes of a lucrative relationship. "You must be exhausted. I'll cry on your shoulder another time."

"I'll hold you to that." He leaned forward and reached for her hand. "We had some good times, didn't we?"

"Great times."

"Ah, the good old days." Glenn relaxed with a bittersweet sigh. "Who was it that said youth was wasted on the young?"

"Mark Twain," Maggie offered.

"No, I think it was Madonna."

They both laughed and Maggie stood, reaching for her purse. "Well, I suppose I should think about heading home and changing my clothes. Steve will be here in an hour. That'll give you time to relax." She fanned her fingers through her hair in a careless gesture. "I'll see you tonight at the rehearsal."

"Thanks for meeting me," Glenn said, coming to his feet.

"I was glad to do it." Her hand was on the doorknob. "It's great to see you again."

The door made a clicking sound as it closed and Glenn turned to wipe a hand over his tired eyes. It was good to be with Maggie again, but frankly, he was glad she'd decided to leave. He needed a few minutes to compose his thoughts before facing Steve. The first thing his friend was bound to ask him about was Angie.

Glenn stiffened as her name sent an instant flash of pain through him. She had married Simon two months earlier, and Glenn had thought that acceptance would become easier with time. It had, but it was far more difficult than he'd expected. He had loved Angie with a reverence; eventually he had loved her enough to step aside when she wanted to marry Simon. He'd been a fool, Glenn realized. If he had acted on his instincts, he'd have had a new bride on his arm for this trip. Now he was alone, more alone than he could ever remember. The last place he wanted to be was a wedding. Every part of it would only be a reminder of what could have been his, and what he'd allowed to slip through his fingers. He didn't begrudge Steve any happiness; he just didn't want to have to stand by and smile serenely when part of him was riddled with regrets.

Maggie shifted into third gear as she rounded the curve in the highway at twenty miles above the speed limit. Deliberately she slowed down, hating the urgency that forced her to rush home. The beach house had become her gilded cage. The world outside its door had taken on a steel edge that she avoided.

Although she had joked with Glenn about not being

married, the tense muscles of her stomach reminded her of how much she envied Janelle. She would smile for the wedding pictures and be awed at all the right moments, but she was going to hate every minute of it. The worst part was she was genuinely happy for Janelle and Steve. Oh, Janelle had promised that they'd continue to get together as they always had. They'd been best friends since childhood, and for a time they probably would see each other regularly. But Janelle wanted to start a family right away, and once she had a baby, Maggie thought, everything would change. It had to.

Automatically Maggie took the road that veered from the highway and a few minutes later turned onto the long circular driveway that led to her waterfront house. The huge structure loomed before her, impressive, elegant and imposing. Maggie had bought it for none of those reasons. She wasn't even sure she liked it. The two-story single-family dwelling on Eastwood Drive where she had grown up was far more appealing. Even now she couldn't bring herself to sell that house and had rented it for far less than market value to a retired couple who kept the yard and flower beds meticulously groomed. Sometimes during the darkest hour of a sleepless night, Maggie would mull over the idea of donating her money to charity. If possible, she would gladly return to the years when she had sat blissfully at her bedroom window, her chin resting on her crossed arms as she gazed into the stars and dreamed of the future. Childhood dreams that were never meant to come true.

Shaking herself from her reverie, Maggie parked the fancy sport car in front of the house. For this night she would put on her brightest smile. No one would ever know what she was feeling on the inside.

* * *

Janelle's mother looked as if she were preparing more for a funeral than a wedding. Flustered and worried, she waved her hands in five different directions, orchestrating the entourage gathered in the church vestibule.

"Girls, please, please pay attention. Darcy, go right, June, left and so on. Understand?"

The last time anyone had called Maggie a girl was in high school. Janelle, Maggie, the bridesmaids, the flower girl, and the ring bearer were all positioned, awaiting instructions. Maggie glanced enviously to the front of the church where Steve and Glenn were standing. It didn't seem fair that they should get off so lightly.

"Remember to count to five slowly before following the person in front of you," Janelle's mother continued.

The strains of organ music burst through the church and the first attendant, shoulders squared, stepped onto the white paper runner that flowed down the center aisle.

"I can't believe this is really happening," Janelle whispered. "Tomorrow Steve and I will be married. After all the years of loving him it's like a dream."

"I know," Maggie whispered and squeezed her friend's forearm.

"Go left, go left." Mrs. Longmier's voice drifted to them and Maggie dissolved into giggles.

"I can't believe your mother."

"The pastor assured her he'd handle everything, but she insisted on doing it herself. That's what I get for being the only girl in a family of four boys."

"In another twenty years or so you may well be doing it yourself," Maggie reminded her.

"Oops." Janelle nudged her. "Your turn. And for heaven's sake don't goof up. I'm starved and want to get out of here."

Holding a paper plate decorated with bows and ribbons from one of Janelle's five wedding showers, Maggie carefully placed one foot in front of the other in a deliberate, step-by-step march that seemed to take an eternity. The smile on her face was as brittle as old parchment.

Standing in her place at the altar, Maggie kept her head turned so she could see Janelle's approach. The happiness radiating from her friend's face produced a curious ache in Maggie's heart. If these feelings were so strong at the rehearsal, she couldn't help wondering how she'd react during the actual wedding. Maggie felt someone's eyes on her and glanced up to see Glenn's steady gaze. He smiled briefly and looked away.

The pastor moved to the front of the young couple and cracked a few old jokes. Everyone laughed politely. As the organ music filled the church, the bride and groom, hands linked, began their exit.

When it came time for Maggie to meet Glenn at the head of the aisle, he stiffly tucked her hand in the crook of his elbow.

"I never thought I'd be marching down the aisle with you," she whispered under her breath.

"It has all the makings of a nightmare," Glenn countered. "However, I'll admit you're kinda cute."

"Thanks."

"But so are lion cubs."

Maggie's fingers playfully bit into the muscles of his upper arm as she struggled not to laugh.

His hand patted hers as he whispered, "You're lovely."

"Is that so?" Maggie batted her eyes at him, blatantly

flirting with him. "And available. I have a king-size bed too."

They were nearing the back of the church. Glenn's dark eyes bored holes into her. "Are you looking for a lover?"

The question caught Maggie by surprise. The old Glenn would have swatted her across the rump and told her to behave. The new Glenn, the man she didn't know, was dead serious. "Not this week," she returned, deliberately flippant. "But if you're interested, I'll keep you in mind."

His gaze narrowed slightly as he tilted his head to one side. "How much have you had to drink?"

Maggie wanted to laugh and would have if not for a discouraging glare from Mrs. Longmier. "One martini."

The sound of a soft snort followed. "You've changed, Maggie." Just the way he said it indicated that he wasn't pleased with the difference.

Her spirits crashed to the floor with breakneck speed. Good grief, she thought angrily, it didn't matter what Glenn thought of her. He had made her feel like a teenager again and she'd behaved like a fool. She wasn't even sure why she was flirting with him. Probably to cover up how miserable the whole event made her.

Casually, Glenn dropped her arm as they entered the vestibule and stepped aside to make room for the others who followed. Maggie used the time to gather her light jacket and purse. Glenn moved in the opposite direction and her troubled gaze followed him.

A flurry of instructions followed as Steve's father gave directions to the family home, where dinner was being served to the members of the wedding party.

Maggie moved outside the church. There wasn't any

need for her to stay and listen. She knew how to get to the Grants' house as well as her own. Standing at the base of the church steps, Maggie was fumbling inside her purse for her keys when Glenn joined her.

"I'm supposed to ride with you."

"Don't make it sound like a fate worse than death," she bit out, furious that she couldn't do what she needed.

"Listen, Maggie, I'm sorry. Okay?"

"You?" Amazed, Maggie lowered the purse flap and slowly raised her dark eyes to his. "It's me who should apologize. I was behaving like an idiot in there, flirting with you like that."

He lifted a silken strand of hair from her shoulder. "It's rather nice to be flirted with now and then," he said with a lazy smile.

Maggie tore her gaze from his and withdrew her car keys. "Here," she said, handing the key chain to him. "I know you'll feel a whole lot safer driving yourself."

"You're right," he retorted, his mood teasing and jovial. "I still remember the day you wiped out two garbage cans and an oak tree backing out of the driveway."

"I'd just gotten my learner's permit and the gears slipped," she returned righteously.

"Unfortunately your skills haven't improved much."

"On second thought, I'll drive and you can do the praying."

Laughing, Glenn tossed an arm across her shoulders.

They chatted easily on the way to the Grants' home and parked behind Steve and Janelle in the driveway. The four car doors slammed simultaneously.

"Glad to see you still remember the way around town," Steve teased Glenn. The two men were nearly the same height, both with dark hair and brown eyes.

Steve smiled lovingly at Janelle and brought her close to his side. "I hope everyone's hungry," he said, waiting for Glenn and Maggie to join them. "Mom hasn't stopped cooking in two days."

"Famished," Glenn admitted. "The last time I ate was on the plane."

"Poor starving baby," Maggie cooed.

Glenn was chuckling when the four entered the house. Immediately Janelle and Maggie offered to help Steve's mother and carried the assorted salads and platters of deli meats to the long table for the buffet. Soon the guests were mingling and helping themselves.

Maggie loaded her plate and found an empty space beside Glenn, who was kneeling in front of the coffee table with several others. He glanced up from the conversation he was having with a bridesmaid when Maggie joined them.

"Muffie, you know Darcy, don't you?" Glenn asked.

"Muffie?" Darcy repeated incredulously. "I thought your name was Maggie."

"Muffie was the name Glenn gave me in junior high. We were next-door neighbors. In fact, we lived only a few blocks from here."

"I suppose you're one of those preppy, organized types," Darcy suggested.

Glenn nearly choked on his potato salad. "Hardly."

Maggie gave him the sharp point of her elbow in his ribs. "Glenn thought he was being cute one day and dubbed me something offensive. Muffie, however, was better than Magpie—"

"She never stopped talking," Glenn inserted.

"—or Maggie the Menace."

"For obvious reasons."

"For a while it was Molasses." Maggie closed her eyes at the memory.

"Because she was forever late."

"As you may have guessed, we fought like cats and dogs," Maggie explained needlessly.

"The way a lot of brothers and sisters do," Glenn inserted.

"So where did the Muffie come in?"

"In junior high things became a bit more sophisticated. We couldn't very well call her Magpie."

Darcy nodded and sliced off a bite of ham.

"So after a while," Glenn continued, "Steve, Janelle, the whole gang of us decided to call her Muffie, simply because she talked so much we wanted to muffle her. The name stuck."

"Creative people are often subjected to this form of harrassment," Maggie informed her with a look of injured pride.

"Didn't you two…?" Darcy hesitated. "I mean Steve and Janelle obviously had something going even then."

"Us?" Maggie and Glenn shared a look of shock. "I did ask you to the Sadie Hawkins dance once."

Glenn nodded, a mischievous look in his eyes. "She'd already asked five other guys and been turned down."

"So I drastically lowered my standards and asked Glenn. It was a complete disaster. Remember?"

Their eyes met and they burst into fits of laughter, causing the conversational hum of the room to come to an abrupt halt.

"Hey, you two, let me in on the joke," Darcy said. "What's so funny?"

Maggie composed herself enough to begin the story. "On the way home, Glenn's beat-up car stalled. We learned later it was out of gas. Believe me, I wasn't pleased, especially since I'd sprung for new shoes and my feet were killing me."

"I don't know why you're complaining; I took you to the dance, didn't I?"

Maggie ignored him. "Since I didn't have a driver's license, Mr. Wonderful here insisted on steering while I pushed his car—uphill."

"You?" Darcy was aghast.

"Now, Maggie, to be fair, you should explain that I helped push, too."

"Some help," she grumbled. "That wasn't the worst part. It started to rain and I was in my party dress, shoving his car down the street in the dead of night."

"Maggie was complaining so loud that she woke half the neighborhood," Glenn inserted, "and someone looked out the window and thought we were stealing a car. They phoned the police and within minutes we were surrounded by three patrol cars."

"They took us downtown and phoned Glenn's dad. It was the most embarrassing moment of my life. The Girls' Club had sponsored the dance and I was expecting roses and kisses in the moonlight. Instead I got stuck pushing Glenn's car in the rain and was darn near arrested."

"Believe me, Maggie made me pay for that one." Glenn's smiling eyes met hers and Maggie felt young and carefree again. It'd been so long since she had talked and laughed like this; she could almost forget. Almost. The present, however, was abruptly brought to her attention a few minutes later when Steve's cousin approached her.

"Maggie," he asked, crowding in next to her on the

floor, "I was wondering if we could have a few minutes alone? There's something I'd like to ask you."

A heavy sensation of dread moved over her. It had happened so often in the past that she knew almost before he spoke what he would say. "Sure, Sam." As of yet, she hadn't found a graceful way of excusing herself from these situations.

Rolling to her feet, she followed Sam across the room to an empty corner.

"I suppose Steve's told you about my business venture?" he began brightly with false enthusiasm.

Maggie gritted her teeth, praying for patience. "No, I can't say that he has."

"Well, my partner and I are looking for someone with a good eye for investment potential who would be willing to lend us a hundred thousand dollars. Would you happen to know anyone who might be interested?"

Maggie noticed Glenn making his way toward them. As she struggled to come up with a polite rejection to Sam, Glenn stopped next to her.

"Sam," he interrupted, taking Maggie by the arm, "excuse us for a minute, will you?" He didn't wait for a response and led her through the cluttered living room and into the kitchen.

"Where are you taking me?" Maggie asked when he opened the sliding glass door that led to the patio.

"Outside."

"That much is obvious. But why are you taking me out here?"

Glenn paused to stand under the huge maple tree and looked toward the sky. "There's only a half-moon tonight, but it'll have to do."

"Are you going to turn into a werewolf or something?" Maggie joked, pleased to be rescued from the clutches of an awkward conversation.

"Nope." He turned her in his arms, looping his hands around her narrow waist and bringing her against the hard wall of his chest. "This is something I should have done the night of the Girls' Club dance," he murmured as he looked down at her.

"What is?"

"Kiss you in the moonlight," he whispered just before his mouth claimed hers.

Two

Maggie was too amazed to respond. Glenn Lambert, the boy who had lived next door most of her life, was kissing her. And he was kissing her as if he meant to be doing exactly that. His lips moved slowly over hers, shaping and fitting his mouth to hers with a gentleness that rocked her until she was a churning mass of conflicting emotions. This was Glenn, the same Glenn who had teased her unmercifully about "going straight" while she wore braces. The Glenn who had heartlessly beaten her playing one-on-one basketball. The same Glenn who had always been her white knight. Yet it felt so right, so good to be in his arms. Hesitantly, Maggie lifted her hands, sliding them over his chest and linking her fingers at the base of his neck, clinging to him for support. Gently parting her lips, she responded to his kiss. She savored the warm taste of him, the feel of his hands against the small of her back and the tangy scent of his after-shave. It seemed right for Glenn to be holding her. More right than anything had felt in a long time.

* * *

When he lifted his head there was a moment of stunned silence while the fact registered in Glenn's bemused mind that he had just kissed Maggie. Maggie. But the vibrant woman in his arms wasn't the same girl who'd lived next door. The woman was warm and soft and incredibly feminine, and he was hungry for a woman's gentleness. Losing Angie had left him feeling cold and alone. His only desire had been to love and protect her, but she hadn't wanted him. A stinging chill ran through his blood, forcing him into the present. His hold relaxed and he dropped his arms.

"Why'd you do that?" Maggie whispered, having difficulty finding her voice. From the moment he had taken her outside, Maggie had known his intention had been to free her from the clutches of Steve's cousin—not to kiss her. At least not like that. What had started out in fun had become serious.

"I'm not sure," he answered honestly. A vague hesitancy showed in his eyes.

"Am I supposed to grade you?"

Glenn took another step backward, broadening the space between them. "Good grief, no; you're merciless."

Mentally, Maggie congratulated him for recovering faster than she. "Not always," she murmured. At his blank look, she added, "I'm not always merciless."

"That's not the way I remember it. The last time I wanted to kiss you, I got a fist in the stomach."

Maggie's brow furrowed. She couldn't remember Glenn even trying to kiss her and looked at him with surprise and doubt as she sifted through her memories. "I don't remember that."

"I'm not likely to forget it," he stated and arched one brow arrogantly. "As I recall, I was twelve and you were eleven. A couple of the guys at school had already kissed a girl and said it wasn't half-bad. There wasn't anyone I wanted to kiss, but for a girl you weren't too bad, so I offered you five of my best baseball cards if you'd let me kiss you."

Maggie gave him a wicked grin as her memory returned. "That was the greatest insult of my life. I was saving my lips for the man I planned to marry. At the time I think it was Billy Idol."

"As I recall you told me that," he replied with a low chuckle. He tucked an arm around her waist, bringing her to his side. "Talking about our one and only date tonight made me remember how much I took you for granted all those years. You were great."

"I know," she said with a complete lack of modesty.

A slow, roguish grin grew across his features. "But then there were times…"

"Don't go philosophical on me, Glenn Lambert." An unaccustomed, delicious heat was seeping into her bones. It was as if she'd been standing in a fierce winter storm and someone had invited her inside to sit by the cozy warmth of the fire.

"We've both done enough of that for one night," Glenn quipped, looking toward the bright lights of the house.

Maggie didn't want to go back inside. She felt warm and comfortable for the first time in what seemed like ages. If they returned to the house full of people, she'd be forced to paint on another plastic smile and listen to the likes of Steve's cousin.

"Do you ever wonder about the old neighborhood?"

Grinning, Glenn looked down on her. "Occasionally."

"Want to take a look?"

He glanced toward the house again, sensing her reluctance to return. The old Maggie would have faced the world head-on. The change surprised him. "Won't we be missed?"

"I doubt it."

Glenn tucked Maggie's hand in the crook of his arm. "For old times' sake."

"The rope swing in your backyard is still there."

"You're kidding!" He gave a laugh of disbelief.

"A whole new generation of kids are playing on that old swing."

"What about the tree house?"

"That, unfortunately, was the victim of a bad windstorm several years back."

His arm tightened around her waist and the fragile scent of her perfume filled his senses. She was a woman now, and something strange and inexplicable was happening between them. Glenn wasn't sure it was right to encourage it.

"How do you keep up with all this?" he asked, attempting to steer his thoughts from things he shouldn't be thinking, like how soft and sweet and wonderfully warm she felt.

"Simple," Maggie explained with a half smile. "I visit often." The happiest days of her life had been in that house in the old neighborhood. She couldn't turn back the clock, but the outward symbols of that time lived on for her to visit as often as needed. "Come on," she said brightly and took his hand. She was feeling both foolish and fanciful. "There probably won't be another chance if we don't go now."

"You'll freeze," Glenn warned, running his hands down the lengths of her bare arms and up again to cup her shoulders.

"No," she argued, not wanting anything to disturb the moment.

"I'll collect your jacket and tell Steve what we're up to," Glenn countered.

"No," she pleaded, her voice low and husky. "Don't. I'll be fine. Really."

Glenn studied her for an instant before agreeing. Maggie was frightened. The realization stunned him. His bubbly, happy-go-lucky Maggie had been reduced to an unhappy, insecure waif. The urge to take her in his arms and protect her was nearly overwhelming.

"All right," he agreed, wrapping his arms around her shoulder to lend her his warmth. If she did get chilled he could give her his own jacket.

With their arms around each other, they strolled down Ocean Avenue to the grade school, cut through the play yard and came out on Marimar near Eastwood Drive.

"Everything seems the same," Glenn commented. His smile was filled with contentment.

"It is."

"How are your parents doing?" he inquired.

"They retired in Florida. I told them they ought to be more original than that, but it was something they really wanted. They can afford it, so why not? What about your folks?"

"They're in South Carolina. Dad's working for the same company. Both Eric and Dale are married and supplying them with a houseful of grandchildren."

A chill shot through Maggie and she shivered involuntarily. She was an aunt now, too, but the circumstances weren't nearly as pleasant. Her brother, Denny, had also discovered that his inheritance wasn't a hedge against unhappiness. Slowly shaking her head, Maggie spoke. "Do you realize how old that makes me feel? Dale married—I'd never have believed it. He was only ten when you moved."

"He met his wife the first year of college. They fell in love, and against everyone's advice decided not to wait to get married. They were both nineteen and had two kids by the time Dale graduated."

"And they're fine now?"

"They're going stronger than ever. The boys are in school and Cherry has gone back to college for her degree." There wasn't any disguising the pride in his voice.

"What about Eric?"

"He married a flight attendant a couple of years ago. They have a baby girl." His hand rested at the nape of her neck in a protective action. "What about your brother?"

"Denny was already married by the time you moved, wasn't he? He and Lisa have two little girls."

"Is he living in San Francisco?"

"Yes," she supplied quickly and hurried to change the subject. "The night's lovely, isn't it?"

Glenn ignored the comment. "Is Denny still working for the phone company?"

"No," she returned starkly. "I can't remember when I've seen so many stars."

They were silent for a moment while Glenn digested the information. Something had happened between Denny and Maggie that she was obviously reluctant to discuss.

"Do you realize that there's never been a divorce in either of our families?" she said softly with sudden insight. She knew what a rarity that was in this day and age. Nearly thirty percent of their high school class were on their second marriages.

"I doubt that there ever will be a divorce. Mom and Dad believe strongly in working out problems instead of running from them and that was ingrained in all three of us boys."

"We're in the minority then. I don't know how Janelle is going to adjust to Steve's children. It must be difficult."

"She loves him," Glenn countered somewhat defensively.

"I realize that," Maggie whispered, thinking out loud. "It's just that I remember when Steve married Ginny. Janelle cried for days afterward and went about doing her best to forget him. Every one of us knew that Ginny and Steve were terribly mismatched and it would only be a matter of time before they split."

"I wasn't that sure they couldn't make a go of it."

Maggie bristled. "I was, and anyone with half a brain saw it. Ginny was pregnant before the wedding and no one except Steve was convinced the baby was his."

"Steve was in a position to know."

Maggie opened her mouth to argue, glanced up to see Glenn's amused gaze and gingerly pressed her lips tightly closed. "I don't recall you being this argumentative," she said after several moments.

"When it comes to the sanctity of marriage, I am."

"For your sake, I hope you marry the right woman then."

The humor drained from his eyes and was replaced with such pain that Maggie's breath caught in her throat. "Glenn, what did I say?" she asked, concern in her voice.

"Nothing," he assured her with a half smile that disguised none of his mental anguish. "I thought I had found her."

"Oh, Glenn, I'm so sorry. Is there anything I can do? I make a great wailing wall." From the pinched lines about his mouth and eyes, Maggie knew that the woman had been someone very special. Even when Maggie had known him best, Glenn had been a discriminating male. He had dated only a few times and, as far as she could remember, had never gone steady with one girl.

The muscles of his face tightened as he debated whether to tell Maggie about Angie. He hadn't discussed her with anyone over the past couple of months and the need to purge her from his life burned in him. Perhaps someday, he thought, but not now and not with Maggie, who had enough problems of her own. "She married someone else. There's nothing more to say."

"You loved her very much, didn't you?" Whoever she was, the woman was a fool. Glenn was the steady, solid type most women sought. When he loved, it would be forever and with an intensity few men were capable of revealing.

Glenn didn't answer. Instead he regarded her with his pain-filled eyes and asked, "What about you?"

"You mean why I never married?" She gave a shrug of indifference. "The right man never came along. I thought he might have once, but I was wrong. Dirk was more interested in spending my money than loving me."

"I'm sorry." His arm tightened around her as an unreasonable anger filled him over the faceless Dirk. He had hurt Maggie, and Glenn was intimately aware of how much one person could hurt another.

"Actually, I think I was lucky to discover it when

I did. But thirty is looming around the corner and the biological clock is ticking like Big Ben. I'd like to get married, but I won't lower my standards."

"What kind of man are you looking for?"

He was so utterly blasé about it that Maggie's composure slipped and she nearly dissolved into laughter. "You mean in case you happen to know someone who fits the bill?"

"I might."

"Why not?" she asked with a soft giggle. "To start off, I'd like someone financially secure."

"That shouldn't be so difficult."

He was so serious that Maggie bit into her bottom lip to hide the trembling laughter. "In addition to being on firm financial ground, he should be magnanimous."

"With you he'd have to be," Glenn said in a laughter-tinged voice.

Maggie ignored the gibe. "He'd have to love me enough to overlook my faults—few as they are—be loyal, loving, and want children."

She paused, expecting him to comment, but he nodded in agreement. "Go on," he encouraged.

"But more than simply wanting children, he'd have to take responsibility for helping me raise them into worthwhile adults. I want a man who's honest, but one who won't shout the truth in my face if it's going to hurt me. A special man to double my joys and divide my sorrows. Someone who will love me when my hair is gray and my ankles are thick." Realizing how serious she'd become, Maggie hesitated. "Know anyone like him?" Her words hung empty in the silence that followed.

"No," Glenn eventually said, and shook his head for

emphasis. Those were the very things he sought in a wife. "I can't say that I do."

"From my guess, Prince Charmings are few and far between these days."

They didn't speak again until they paused in front of the fifty-year-old house that had been Glenn's childhood home. Little had altered over the years, Glenn realized. The wide front porch and large dormers that jutted out from the roof looked exactly as they had in his mind. The house had been repainted, and decorative shutters were now added to the front windows, but the same warmth and love seemed to radiate from its doors.

Maggie followed Glenn's gaze to the much-used basketball hoop positioned above the garage door. It was slightly crooked from years of slam dunks. By the look of things, the hoop was used as much now as it had been all those years ago.

"I suppose we should think of heading back. It's going to be a long day tomorrow." Maggie's gaze fell from the house to the cracked sidewalk. It hit her suddenly that in a couple of days Glenn would be flying back to Charleston. He was here for the wedding and nothing more.

"Yes," Glenn agreed in a low, gravelly voice. "Tomorrow will be a very long day."

The vestibule was empty when Maggie entered the church forty minutes before the wedding. Out of breath and five minutes late, she paused to study the huge baskets of flowers that adorned the altar, and released an unconscious sigh at the beauty of the sight. This wedding was going to be special. Hurrying into the dressing room that was located to her right, Maggie knocked once and opened the door. The woman from The Wedding Shop was helping Janelle into her flowing lace gown. Mrs. Longmier was sitting in a chair, dabbing the corner of her eye with a tissue.

"Oh, Maggie, thank goodness you're here. I had this horrible dream that you showed up late. The wedding was in progress and you ran down the aisle screaming how dare we start without you."

"I'm here, I'm here, don't worry." Stepping back, Maggie inspected her friend and could understand Mrs. Longmier's tears. Janelle was radiant. Her wedding gown was of a lavish Victorian style that was exquisitely fashioned with ruffled tiers of Chantilly lace and countless rows of tiny pearls. "Wow," she whispered in awe. "You're going to knock Steve's eyes out."

"That's the idea," Janelle said with a nervous smile.

Another woman from the store helped Maggie don her blushing-pink gown of shimmering taffeta. Following a common theme, the maid of honor's and the bridesmaids' dresses were also Victorian in style, with sheer yokes and lace stand-up collars. Lace bishop sleeves were trimmed with dainty satin bows. The bodice fit snugly to the waist and flared at the hip. While the woman fastened the tiny buttons at the back of the gown, Maggie studied her mirrored reflection. A small smile played on her mouth as she pictured Glenn's reaction when he saw her. For years she wore tight jeans and sweatshirts. She had put on a dress for the rehearsal, but this gown would amaze him. She was a woman now and it showed.

The way her thoughts automatically flew to Glenn surprised Maggie, but she supposed it was natural after their kisses and walk in the moonlight. He had filled her dreams and she'd slept better than she had in a long while.

After their visit to the old neighborhood, Maggie's attitude toward the wedding had changed. She wouldn't be standing alone at the altar with her fears. Glenn, her friend from childhood, would be positioned beside her. Together they would lend each other the necessary strength to smile their way through the ordeal. Maggie realized her thoughts were more those of a martyr than an honored friend, but she'd dreaded the wedding for weeks. Not that she begrudged Janelle any happiness. But Maggie realized that at some time during the wedding dinner or the dance scheduled to follow, someone would comment on her single status. With Glenn at her side it wouldn't matter nearly as much.

From all the commotion going on outside the dressing room, Maggie realized the guests were beginning to arrive. Nerves attacked her stomach. This wasn't the first time she'd been in a wedding party, but it was the most elaborate wedding to date. She pressed a calming hand to her abdomen and exhaled slowly.

"Nervous?" Janelle whispered.

Maggie nodded. "What about you?"

"I'm terrified," she admitted freely. "Right now I wish Steve and I had eloped instead of going through all this." She released her breath in a slow, drawn-out sigh. "I'm convinced that halfway through the ceremony my veil's going to slip or I'll faint, or something equally disastrous."

"You won't," Maggie returned confidently. "I promise. Right now everything's overwhelming, but you won't regret a minute of this in the years to come."

"I suppose not," Janelle agreed. "This marriage is forever and I want everything right."

"I'd want everything like this, too." Maggie spoke

without thinking and realized that when and if she ever married she wanted it to be exactly this way. She yearned for a flowing white dress with a long train and lifetime friends to stand with her.

Someone knocked on the door and, like an organized row of ducklings, the wedding party was led into the vestibule. Organ music vibrated through the church and the first bridesmaid, her hands clasping a bouquet of pink hyacinths, stepped forward with a tall usher at her side.

Maggie watched her progress and knew again that someday she wanted to stand in the back of a church and look out over the seated guests who had come to share her moment of joy. And like Janelle, Maggie longed to feel all the love that was waiting for her as she slowly walked to the man with whom she would share her life. And when she repeated her vows before God and those most important in her life she would feel, as Janelle did, that her marriage was meant to last for all time.

When it was her turn to step onto the trail of white linen that ran the length of the wide aisle, Maggie held her chin high, the adrenaline pumping through her blood. Her smile was natural, not forced. Mentally she thanked Glenn for that and briefly allowed her gaze to seek him out in the front of the church. What she found nearly caused her to pause in midstep. Glenn was standing with Steve at the side of the altar and looking at her with such a wondrous gaze that her heart lodged in her throat. This all-encompassing wonder was what Maggie had expected to see in Steve's eyes when he first viewed Janelle. A look so tender it should be reserved for the bride and groom. The moment stretched out until Maggie was convinced everyone in the church had turned to see what was keeping her. By sheer force of will she continued with short steps toward the front of the church. Every resounding note of the organ brought her closer to Glenn. She felt a throb of excitement as the faces of people she'd known all her life turned to watch her progress. A heady sensation enveloped her as she imagined it was she who was the bride, she who would speak her vows, she who had found her soul mate. Until that moment Maggie hadn't realized how much she yearned for the very things she had tried to escape in life, how much she was missing by hiding in her gilded cage, behind her money.

As they'd practiced the night before, Maggie moved to the left and waited for Janelle and Steve to meet at center front. At that point she would join her friend and stand at Janelle's side.

With the organ music pulsating in her ear, Maggie strained to catch Steve's look when he first glimpsed Janelle. She turned her head slightly, and paused. Her gaze refused to move beyond Glenn who was standing with Steve near the front of the altar. Even when Janelle placed her hand in Steve's, Maggie couldn't tear her eyes from Glenn. The pastor moved to the front of the church and the four gathered before him. Together they lifted their faces to the man of God who had come to unite Steve and Janelle.

The sensations that came at Glenn were equally disturbing. The minute Maggie had started down the aisle it had taken everything within him not to step away from Steve, meet her and take her in his arms. He had never experienced any sensation more strongly. He wanted to hold her, protect her, bring the shine back to her eyes and teach her to trust again. When she had met him at the airport he'd been struck by how lovely she'd become. Now he recognized her vulnerability, and she was breathtaking. He had never seen a more beautiful woman. She was everything he'd ever wanted—warm, vibrant, alive and standing so close that all he had to do was reach out and touch her. He felt like a blind man who had miraculously and unexpectedly been gifted with sight. Maggie needed him. Charleston, with all its painful memories, lay on the other side of the world.

"Dearly beloved, we are called here today to witness the vows between Janelle and Stephen."

The rush of emotion that assaulted Maggie was unlike anything she'd every known. She couldn't keep her eyes from Glenn, who seemed to magnetically compel her gaze to meet his. Their eyes locked and held as the pastor continued speaking. There was no exchange of smiles, no winks, nothing cute or frivolous, but a solemn mood that made that instant, that moment, the most monumental of their lives. Maggie felt a breathless urgency come over her, and an emotion so powerful, so real that it brought brimming tears that filled her vision. In order to keep her makeup from streaking, she held one finger under each eye a hand at a time and took in several deep breaths to forestall the ready flow. The void, the emptiness in her life wasn't entirely due to her money. What she needed was someone to love and who would love her. Desperately, Maggie realized how much she wanted to be needed. Several seconds passed before she regained her composure. The tightening lessened in her chest and she breathed freely once again.

When the pastor asked Steve and Janelle to repeat their vows, Maggie's gaze was again drawn to Glenn's.

He didn't speak, nor did Maggie, but together, in unison, each syllable, each word was repeated in their hearts as they issued the same vows as their friends. When the pastor pronounced them man and wife, Maggie raised stricken eyes to the man of God who had uttered the words, needing the reassurance about whom he had meant. It was as if he had been speaking to Glenn and her, as well, and as if the formal pronouncement included them.

The organ burst into the traditional wedding march and Steve and Janelle turned to face the congregation, their faces radiant with happiness. As the newly wedded couple moved down the aisle, Glenn's arm reached for Maggie's, prepared to escort her. At the touch of his hand at her elbow, Maggie felt a series of indescribable sensations race through her: wonder, surprise, joy. Their eyes met and for the first time that day, he smiled. An incredible, dazzling smile that all but blinded her. Their march down the aisle, her arm on his elbow, added to the growing feeling that that day, that moment was meant for them as well.

Family and friends gathered outside the church doors, spilling onto the steps, giving hearty applause as Steve turned Janelle into his arms and kissed her. A festive mood reigned as Janelle was joyously hugged and Steve's hand was pumped countless times. The photographer was busily snapping pictures, ordering the wedding party to pose one way and then another.

For a brief second the fantasy faded enough to frighten Maggie. What game was Glenn playing with her? No. She'd seen the sincerity in his eyes. But pretending was dangerous, far too dangerous.

"Are you all right?" Glenn whispered in her ear.

Maggie didn't have the opportunity to answer. As it was, she wasn't sure how to respond. Under other circumstances, she would have asked him to drive her to the hospital emergency room. Her daydreams were overpowering reality. This wasn't her wedding, nor was the man at her side her husband. She had no right to feel sensations like these.

The next thing she knew, Glenn had disappeared. Maggie hardly had time to miss him when a shiny new Cadillac pulled to the curb. Just Married was painted on the back window. Glenn jumped out and opened both doors on the passenger side. Then, racing up the church stairs, he took Maggie by the hand and following on the heels of Steve and Janelle, pulled her through a spray of rice and laughter as he whisked her toward the car.

Amidst hoots and more laughter, Glenn helped her gather her full-length skirt inside the automobile before closing the door and running around the front to climb in beside her.

Maggie was still breathless with laughter when he flashed her another of his dazzling smiles and started the engine. A sea of happy faces was gazing in at them. Turning her head to look out the side window, Maggie was greeted with the well-wishes of several boys and girls—children of their friends—standing on the sidewalk and waving with all their might. Glenn checked the rearview mirror and pulled into the steady flow of street traffic.

"Maggie, it was just as wonderful as you claimed it would be," Janelle said softly from the back seat.

"Did you doubt?" Steve questioned, his voice thick with emotion.

"I'll have you know, Mr. Grant, that I nearly backed

out of this wedding at the very last minute. The only thing that stopped me was Maggie. Somehow she convinced me everything was going to work out. And it did."

"Janelle, I hardly said anything," Maggie countered, shocked by her friend's admission.

"You said just enough."

"I'm eternally grateful," Steve murmured and from the sounds coming from the back seat he was showing Janelle just how grateful he was that she was his bride.

Glenn's hand reached for Maggie's and squeezed it gently. "You look stunning." He wanted to say so much more and discovered he couldn't. For weeks he had dreaded the wedding and having to stand at the altar with his friend when it should have been his own wedding. The day had been completely unlike anything he'd expected. Maggie alone had made the difference.

"You make a striking figure yourself," she said, needing to place their conversation on an even keel.

Glenn unfastened the top button of the ruffled shirt and released the tie. "I feel like a penguin."

Laughter bubbled up in Maggie. She felt happy, really happy for the first time in a long while. When Glenn held out his arms, she scooted across the seat so that they were as close as possible within the confines of the vehicle.

The sounds of smothered giggles from the back seat assured Maggie that things were very fine indeed. They stopped at a light and Glenn's gaze wandered to her for a brief, glittering second, then back to the road. "Thank you for today," he said, just low enough for her to hear.

"You made our friends' wedding the most special day of my life."

"I...felt the same way about you," she whispered, wanting him to kiss her so badly she could almost taste his mouth over hers.

"Maggie," Janelle called from the back seat. "Will you check this veil? I can't walk into the dinner with it all askew. People will know exactly what kind of man I married."

"Oh, they will, will they?" Steve said teasingly, and kissed her soundly.

Maggie turned and glanced over her shoulder. "Everything looks fine. The veil's not even crooked, although from the sound of things back there it should be inside out and backward."

"Maggie," Steve said in a low and somewhat surprised tone as he studied her, "I expected Janelle's mother to cry, even my own. But I was shocked to see you were the one with tears in your eyes."

"You were shocked?" she tossed back nonchalantly. "Believe me, they were just as much of a surprise to me. Tears were the last thing I expected."

"Count your blessings, you two," Glenn said, tossing a glance over his shoulder. "Knowing Muffie, you should be grateful she didn't burst into fits of hysterical laughter." He glanced over to her and leaned close and whispered, "Actually, they should thank me. It took everything in me not to break rank and reach for you." Glenn hadn't meant to tell her that, but those tears had nearly been his undoing. He had known when he'd seen her eyes bright with unshed tears that what was happening to him was affecting Maggie just as deeply. He had come so close to happiness once, and like a fool, he'd let it slip away. It wouldn't happen again; he wouldn't allow it.

Everything was happening so quickly that Maggie didn't have time to react. Glenn's breath fanned her temple and a shiver of apprehension raced up her spine. They were playing a dangerous game. All that talk in the moonlight about the sanctity of marriage had affected their brain cells and they were daydreaming. No...pretending that this moment, this happiness, this love, was theirs. Only it wasn't, and Maggie had to give herself a hard mental shake to dislodge the illusion.

A long string of cars followed closely behind as the other members of the wedding party caught up with the Cadillac. Watching Glenn weave in and out of traffic, Maggie was impressed with his driving skill. However, everything about Glenn had impressed her today. Fleetingly, she allowed her mind to wander to what would happen when he left on Monday. She didn't want this weekend to be the end, but a beginning. He lived in Charleston, she in San Francisco. The whole country separated them, but they were only hours apart by plane and seconds by phone.

When he turned and caught her studying him, Maggie guiltily shifted her attention out the side window. The way her heart was hammering, one would think she was the bride. She struggled for composure.

Janelle's family had rented a huge Victorian hall for the dinner and dance. Maggie had no idea that there was such a special place in San Francisco and was assessing the wraparound porch and second-floor veranda when the remainder of the wedding party disembarked from the long row of cars that paraded behind the Cadillac.

Wordlessly, Glenn took her by the elbow and led her up the front stairs.

Everything inside the huge hall was lushly decorated in antiques. Round tables with starched white tablecloths were set up to serve groups of eight. In the center of each table was a bowl of white gardenias. A winding stairway with a polished mahogany banister led to the dance floor upstairs.

Being seated at the same table as Steve and Janelle added to the continuing illusion. Somehow Maggie made it through the main course of veal cordon bleu, wild rice and tender asparagus spears. Her appetite was nonexistent and every bite had the taste and the feel of cotton. Although Glenn was at her side, they didn't speak, but the communication between them was louder than words. Twice she stopped herself from asking him what was happening to them, convinced he had no answers and the question would only confuse him further.

When Janelle cut the wedding cake and hand-fed the first bite to Steve, the happy applause vibrated around the room. The sound of it helped shake Maggie from her musings and she forced down another bite of her entrée. The caterers delivered the cake to the wedding guests with astonishing speed so that all the guests were served in a matter of minutes.

Glenn's eyes darkened thoughtfully as he dipped his fork into the white cake and paused to study Maggie. He prayed she wasn't as confused as he. He didn't know what was happening, but was powerless to change anything. He wasn't even convinced he wanted anything different. It was as if they were in a protective bubble, cut off from the outside world. And although they sat in a room full of people, they were alone. Not knowing what made him do anything so crazy, Glenn lifted his fork to her mouth and offered Maggie the first sample of wedding cake. His eyes held her immobile as she opened her mouth and accepted his offering. Ever so lightly he ran his thumb along her chin as his dark, penetrating eyes bored into hers. By the time she finished swallowing, Glenn's hand was trembling and he lowered it.

Promptly Maggie placed her clenched fingers in her lap. A few minutes later she took a sip of champagne, her first that day, although she knew that enough was happening to her equilibrium without adding expensive champagne to wreak more damage.

The first muted strains of a Vienna waltz drifted from the upstairs dance floor. Maggie took another sip of champagne before standing.

Together, Steve and Janelle led their family and friends up the polished stairway to the dance floor.

When he saw the bride and groom, the orchestra leader stepped forward and announced: "Ladies and gentlemen, I give you Mr. and Mrs. Stephen Grant."

Steve took Janelle in his arms and swung his young bride around the room in wide fanciful steps. Pausing briefly, he gestured to Glenn, who swung Maggie into his arms.

Again the announcer stepped to the microphone and introduced them as the maid of honor and best man. All the while, the soft music continued its soothing chords and they were joined by each bridesmaid and usher couple until the entire wedding party was on the dance floor.

As Glenn held Maggie in his arms, their feet made little more than tiny, shuffling movements that gave the pretense of dancing. All the while Glenn's serious, dark eyes held Maggie's. It was as though they were the only two in the room and the orchestra was playing solely for them. Try as she might, Maggie couldn't pull her gaze away.

"I've been wanting to do something from the moment I first saw you walk down the aisle."

"What?" she asked, surprised at how weak her voice sounded. She thought that if he didn't kiss her soon she was going to die.

Glenn glanced around him to the wide double doors that led to the veranda. He took her by the hand and led her through the crowd and out the curtained glass doors.

Maggie walked to the edge of the veranda and curled her fingers over the railing. Dusk had already settled over the city and lights from the bay flickered in the distance. Glenn joined her and slipped his arms around her waist, burying his face in her hair. Turning her in his arms, he closed his eyes and touched his forehead to hers. He took in several breaths before speaking.

"Are you feeling the same things I am?" he asked.

"Yes." Her heart was hammering so loud, Maggie was convinced he'd hear it.

"Is it the champagne?"

"I had two sips."

"I didn't have any," he countered. "See?" He placed the palm of her hand over his heart so she could feel its quickened beat. "From the moment I saw you in the church it's been like this."

"Me too," she whispered. "What's happening to us?"

Slowly, he shook his head. "I wish I knew."

"It's happening to me, too." She took his hand and placed it over her heart. "Can you feel it?"

"Yes," he whispered.

"Maggie, listen, this is going to sound crazy." He dropped his hands as if he needed to put some distance between them and took several steps back.

"What is?"

Glenn jerked his hand through his hair and hesitated. "Do you want to make this real?"

Three

"Make this real?" Maggie echoed. "What do you mean?"

Glenn couldn't believe the ideas that were racing at laser speed through his mind. Maggie would burst into peals of laughter and he wouldn't blame her. But even that wasn't enough to turn the course of his thoughts. He had this compulsion, this urgency to speak as if something were driving him to say the words. "Steve and Janelle are going to make this marriage a good one."

"Yes," Maggie agreed. "I believe they will."

The look she gave him was filled with questions. Surely she realized he hadn't asked her onto the veranda to discuss Steve and Janelle. After Angie, Glenn hadn't expected to feel this deep an emotion again. And so soon was another shock. Yet when he'd seen Maggie that first moment in the church the impact had been so great it was as though someone had physically assaulted him. She was lovely, possessing a rare beauty that had escaped his notice when they were younger. No longer had he been standing witness to his best friends' wedding, but he'd participated in a ceremony with a woman who could stand at his side for a lifetime. Maggie had felt it, too; he had seen it in her eyes. The identical emotion had moved her to tears.

"Glenn, you wanted to say something?" She coaxed him gently, her mind pleading with him to explain. He couldn't possibly mean what she thought.

Remembering the look Maggie had given him when Steve and Janelle exchanged vows gave Glenn the courage to continue. "Marriage between friends is the best kind, don't you think?"

"Yes," she answered, unable to bring her voice above a husky whisper. "Friends generally know everything about each other, whether good or bad, and then still choose to remain friends."

They stood for a breathless moment, transfixed, studying each other, hesitant and unsure. "I'd always believed," Glenn murmured, his voice low and seductive, "that it would be impossible for me to share my life with anyone I didn't know extremely well."

"I agree." Maggie's mind was formulating impossible thoughts. Glenn was leading this conversation down meandering paths she'd never dreamed of traveling with him.

"We're friends," he offered next.

"Good friends," she agreed, nodding.

"I know you as well as my own brothers."

"We lived next door to each other for fifteen years," she added, her heart increasing its tempo to a slow drumroll.

"I want a home and children."

"I've always loved children." There hadn't been a time in her life when the pull was stronger toward a husband and family than it was that very moment.

"Maggie," he said, taking a step toward her, but still not touching her, "you've become an extremely beautiful woman."

Her lashes fluttered against her cheek as she lowered her gaze. Maggie didn't think of herself as beautiful. For Glenn to say this to her, sent her heart racing. She hardly knew how to respond and finally managed a weak "Thank you."

"Any man would be proud to have you for his wife."

The sensations that raced through her were all too welcome and exciting. "I… I was just thinking that a woman…any woman would be extremely fortunate to have you for a husband."

"Would you?"

Her heart fluttered wildly, rocketed to her throat and then promptly plummeted to her stomach. Yet she didn't hesitate. "I'd be honored and proud."

Neither said anything for a timeless second while their minds assimilated what had just transpired, or what they thought had.

"Glenn?"

"Yes."

Her throat felt swollen and constricted, her chest suddenly tight as if tears were brewing just beneath the surface. "Did I understand you right? Did you—just now—suggest that you and me—the two of us—get married?"

"That's exactly what I'm suggesting." Glenn didn't hesitate. He'd never been more sure of anything in his life. He had lost one woman; he wasn't going to lose Maggie. He would bind her to him and eliminate the possibility of someone else stepping in at the last moment. This woman was his and he was claiming her before something happened to drive her from his arms.

"When?"

"Tonight."

She blinked twice, convinced she hadn't heard him right. "But the license, and…"

"We can fly to Reno." Already his mind was working out the details. He didn't like the idea of a quickie wedding, but it would serve the purpose. After what they had shared earlier they didn't need anything more than a document to make it legal.

Stillness surrounded them. Even the night had gone silent. No cars, no horns, no crickets, no sounds of the night—only silence.

"I want to think about it," she murmured. Glenn was crazy. They both were. Talking about marriage, running away this very night to Reno. None of it made sense, but nothing in all her life had sounded more exciting, more wonderful, more right.

"How long do you want to think this over?" A thread of doubt caused him to ask. Perhaps rushing her wasn't the best way to proceed, but waiting felt equally impossible.

A fleeting smile touched and lifted Maggie's mouth. They didn't dare tell someone they would do anything so ludicrous. She didn't need time, not really. She knew what she wanted: she wanted Glenn.

"An hour," she said, hoping that within that time frame nothing would change.

The strains of another waltz drifted onto the veranda and wordlessly he led her back to the dance floor. When he reached for her, Maggie went willingly into his arms. His hold felt as natural as breathing, and she was drawn into his warmth. The past two days with Glenn had been the happiest, most exciting in years. Who would have thought that Glenn Lambert would make her pulse pound like a jackhammer and place her head in the clouds where the air was thin and clear thought was impossible? Twenty-four hours after his arrival, and they were planning the most incredible scheme. Their very best scheme, crazy as it sounded.

"This feeling reminds me of the night we stole out of the house to smoke our first cigarette," Glenn whispered in her ear. "Are we as daring and defiant now as we were at fourteen?"

"Worse," she answered. "But I don't care as long as you're with me."

"Oh, Maggie." He sighed her name with a wealth of emotion.

Her hands tightened around his neck as she fit her body more intimately to the contour of his. Her breasts were flattened to his broad chest; and they were melded together, thigh to thigh, hip to hip, as close as humanly possible under the guise of dancing.

Every breath produced an incredible range of new sensations. Maggie felt drugged and delirious, daring and darling, bold and extraordinarily shy. Every second in his arms brought her more strength of conviction. This night, in less than an hour she was going to walk out of this room with Glenn Lambert. Together they would fly to Reno and she would link her life with his. There was nothing to stop her. Not her money. Not her pride. Not her fears. Glenn Lambert was her friend. Tonight he would become her lover as well.

Unable to wait, Maggie rained a long series of kisses

over the line of his jaw. The need to experience his touch flowered deep within her.

Glenn's hold at her waist tightened and he inhaled sharply. "Maggie, don't tease me."

"Who's teasing?" They'd known each other all these years and in that time he had only kissed her once. But it was enough, more than enough to know that the loving between them would be exquisite.

Without her even being aware, Glenn had maneuvered her into a darkened corner of the dance floor where the lighting was the dimmest. His eyes told her he was about to kiss her and hers told him she was eager for him to do exactly that. Unhurriedly, Glenn lowered his mouth to hers with an agonizing slowness. His kiss was warm and tender and lingering, as if this were a moment and place out of time meant for them alone. Her soft mouth parted with only the slightest urging and her arms tightened around his neck. Trembling in his embrace, Maggie drew in a long unsteady breath. Glenn's kisses had been filled with such aching tenderness, such sweet torment that Maggie felt tears stinging for release. Tears for a happiness she had never hoped to find. At least not with Glenn. This was a wondrous surprise. A gift. A miracle so unexpected it would take a lifetime to fully appreciate.

"I want you," he whispered, his voice hoarse with desire. His breath warmed her lips.

"Yes" she returned, vaguely dazed. "I want you, too."

His arms tightened and Maggie felt the shudder that rocked him until her ribs ached. Gradually his hold relaxed as his gaze polarized hers. "Let's get out of here."

"Should…should we tell anyone?" *No*, her mind shouted. Someone might try to talk them out of this and she didn't want that to happen. She yearned for everything that Glenn suggested.

"Do you want to tell Steve and Janelle?" Glenn asked.

"No."

Tenderly he brushed his lips across her forehead. "Neither do I. They'll find out soon enough."

"It'll be our surprise." She smiled at him, the warm happy smile of someone about to embark on the most exciting adventure of her life. And Maggie felt like an adventurer, daring and audacious, dauntless and intrepid, reckless and carefree. There'd be problems; she realized that. But tonight with Glenn at her side there wasn't anything she couldn't conquer.

Glenn raised her fingertips to his lips and kissed each one. "I'm not letting you out of my sight. We're going directly to the airport."

"Fine." She had no desire to be separated from him, either.

"I'll call a taxi."

"I'll get my purse."

The night air brought a chill to her arms, but it didn't sharpen any need to analyze what they were doing. If Glenn expected her to have second thoughts as they breezed through the streets of San Francisco, she found none. Even the busy airport, with its crowded concourses and people who stared at their unusual dress, wasn't enough to cause her to doubt.

Glenn bought their airline tickets, and she found a seat while he used his cell to make hotel reservations. When he returned, the broad smile reached his eyes. Maggie was struck anew with the wonder of what was happening.

"Well?"

"Everything's been taken care of."

"Everything?" It seemed paramount that they get married tonight. If they were forced to wait until morning there could be second thoughts.

"The Chapel of Love is one block from city hall and they're going to arrange for the marriage license." He glanced at his watch and hesitated. "The plane lands at ten-thirty and the ceremony is scheduled for eleven-fifteen." He sat in the seat beside her and reached for her hand. "You're cold."

"A little." Despite her nerves she managed to keep her voice even. She didn't doubt they were doing the right thing and wanted to reassure Glenn. "I'm fine. Don't worry about me."

Rising to his feet, Glenn stripped the tuxedo jacket from his arms and draped it over her shoulders. "Here. We'll be boarding in a few minutes and I'll get you a blanket from the flight attendants." His dark eyes were full of warmth and he was smiling at her as if they'd been sitting in airports, waiting for planes to fly them to weddings every day.

His strong fingers closed over hers and for the first time she admired how large his hands were. The fingers were long and tapered and looked capable of carving an empire or soothing a crying child. "Are you—" Maggie swallowed convulsively, almost afraid to ask "—are you having any second thoughts?"

"No," he answered quickly. "What about you?"

"None." She was never so positive of anything in her life.

"I'll be a good husband."

"I know." She placed her free hand over the back of his. "And I'll be a good wife."

His returning smile, filled with warmth and incredible wonder, could have melted a glacier.

"My parents are going to be ecstatic." Shocked too, her mind added, but that didn't matter.

"Mine will be pleased as well," Glenn assured her. "They've always liked you."

He bent his head toward her and Maggie shyly lifted her face and met him halfway. His kiss was filled with soft exploration, and they parted with the assurance that everything was perfect.

"After we're married, will you want me to move to Charleston?" Maggie ventured.

"No," he said on a somber note. "I'll move to San Francisco." The time had come to leave Charleston. Glenn wanted to bury the unhappiness that surrounded him there. The brief visit to San Francisco had felt like coming home. With Maggie at his side he'd build a new life in San Francisco. Together they'd raise their family and live in blissful happiness. No longer would he allow the memory of another woman to haunt him.

Maggie felt simultaneously relieved and confused. Her career in art made it possible for her to work anywhere. For Glenn to move to San Francisco would mean giving up his Charleston clientele and building up a new one on the West Coast. It didn't make sense. "I don't mind moving, really. It would be easier for me to make the change. You've got your career."

He slid his hand from her arm to her elbow, tightening his hold. "I'll transfer out here." Turning his wrist he glanced at his watch, but Maggie had the feeling he wasn't looking at the time. "I'm ready for a change," he murmured after a while. "You don't mind, do you?"

Did she? No, Maggie decided, she loved California. "No, that'll be fine. You'll like the beach house."

"I don't doubt that I will."

Their flight number was announced and Maggie returned Glenn's tuxedo jacket before they boarded the plane. The flight attendant came by a few minutes later, after they were comfortably seated, to check their seat belts. She paused and commented that they both looked as if they were on their way to a wedding. Glenn and Maggie smiled politely, but neither of them opted to inform the young woman that it was exactly what they were doing. Maggie feared that if they let someone in on their plan it would somehow shatter the dream. Briefly she wondered if Glenn shared her fears.

The flight touched down on the Reno runway precisely on schedule. With no luggage to collect, Glenn and Maggie walked straight through the airport and outside, where a taxi was parked and waiting.

"You two on your way to a wedding?" the cabdriver asked with a loud belly laugh as he held the door open for Maggie.

"Yes," Maggie answered shyly, dismissing her earlier fears.

"Ours," Glenn added, sliding into the seat next to Maggie and reaching for her hand.

The heavyset cabbie closed the door and walked around to the driver's side. He checked the rearview mirror and merged with the traffic. "Lots of people come to Reno to get married, but then a lot of folks come here to get unmarried, too."

A thundering silence echoed through the close confines of the taxi. "There won't be any divorce for us," Glenn informed him.

The driver tipped back the rim of his cap with his index finger. "Lot of folks say that, too." He paused at the first red light, placed his arm along the back of the seat and turned to look at Glenn. "Where was it you said you wanted to go?"

"Chapel of Love," Glenn said firmly and glanced over to Maggie. "Unless you want to change your mind?" he whispered.

"You're not backing out of your proposal, are you?" The words nearly stuck in her throat.

"No."

"Then we're getting married," she murmured, more determined than ever. "I didn't come this far in a shimmering pink taffeta gown to play the slot machines."

"Good."

"Very good," she murmured, unwilling to let anyone or anything ruin this night.

A half hour later, after arriving at the chapel, Maggie had freshened her makeup and done what she could with her hair. They stood now before the proprietor of the wedding chapel.

"Organ music is fifteen dollars extra," Glenn told her as he reached for his back pocket.

Her hand stopped him. "I don't need it," she assured him with perfect serenity. "I'm still hearing the music from the church."

The impatience drained from his eyes and the look he gave her was so profound that it seemed the most natural thing in the world to lean forward and press her lips to his.

The justice of the peace cleared his throat. "If you're ready we can start the ceremony."

"Are you ready?" Glenn asked with smiling eyes.

"I've been ready for this all night," she answered, linking her arm with his.

The service was shockingly short and sterile. They stood before the justice and repeated the words that had already been spoken in their hearts. The stark ceremony wasn't what Maggie would have preferred, but it didn't diminish any of her joy. This wedding was necessary for legal reasons; their real vows had already been exchanged earlier that day as they stood witnesses for Steve and Janelle. Those few moments in the church had been so intense that from then on every moment of her life would be measured against them. Maggie yearned to explain that to Glenn, but mere words felt inadequate. He, too, had experienced it, she realized, and without analyzing it, he had understood.

Their room at the hotel was ready when they arrived. With the key jingling in Glenn's pocket they rode the elevator to the tenth floor.

"Are you going to carry me over the threshold, Mr. Lambert?" Maggie whispered happily and nuzzled his ear. She felt a free-flowing elation unlike anything she'd ever experienced. That night and every night for the rest of her life would be spent in Glenn's arms.

"I'll see what I can manage," Glenn stated seriously as he backed her into the corner of the elevator and kissed the side of her neck.

Maggie shot him a dubious look. "I'm not that heavy, you know."

"What I suggest we do," he murmured as he nibbled on her earlobe, "is have me lift one of your legs and you can hop over the threshold."

"Glenn," she muttered, breaking free. "That's crazy."

Chuckling, he ignored the question. "On second

thought I could probably manage to haul you piggy-back."

Deftly her fingers opened his tie and she teased his throat with the moist tip of her tongue. If he was going to joke with her then she'd tease him as well. "Never mind," she whispered. "I'll carry you."

The elevator came to a grinding halt and the doors swished open. Glenn glanced around him, kissed Maggie soundly and with a mighty heave-ho, hauled her over his shoulder fireman fashion.

"Glenn…" she whispered fiercely, stunned into momentary speechlessness. "Put me down this instant."

Chuckling, he slowly rubbed his hand over her prominently extended derriere. "You said you wanted me to carry you over the threshold. Only I can't very well manage you, the key and the door all at once."

Using her arms against his shoulders for leverage, Maggie attempted to straighten. "Glenn, please," she begged, laughing until it was difficult to speak and probably just as impossible to be understood.

He shifted her weight when he fidgeted with the key. Maggie couldn't see what was happening, but the sound of the door opening assured her all was well. Her eyes studied the same door as it closed and the narrow entryway as he carried her halfway into the room. The next thing Maggie knew, she was falling through space. She gave a frightened cry until the soft cushion of the mattress broke her rapid descent.

Panting and breathless with laughter, Maggie lay sprawled across the bed. She smiled up at Glenn playfully and raised her arms to her husband of fifteen minutes. Glenn knelt beside her, his eyes alive with passion as he lowered his mouth to hers in a deep kiss that sent her world into a crazy tailspin. She clung to him, her fingers ruffling the thick, dark hair that grew at his nape. Wildly, she returned his kiss, on fire for him, luxuriating in the feel of his body over hers. Unexpectedly, he tore his mouth from hers and lifted his head. Without a word, he brushed the soft wisps of hair from her temple and dipped his head a second time to sample her mouth. When he broke away and moved to the long dresser that dominated one side of the hotel room, Maggie felt a sudden chill and rose to a sitting position.

A bottle of champagne was resting in a bed of crushed ice. With his back to her, Glenn peeled off the foil covering and removed the cork. He ached with the need to take her physically, but feared his building passion would frighten her. Silently, Glenn cursed himself for not having approached the subject sooner. He wanted her, but did he dare take her so soon?

The dresser mirror revealed Glenn's troubled frown and Maggie felt a brooding anxiety settle over her. For the first time she could see doubt in his eyes. The breath jammed in her lungs. No, not doubt, but apprehension, even foreboding. Maggie was feeling it, too. Maybe advancing from friends to lovers in the space of a few hours wasn't right for them. Maybe they should think it through very carefully before proceeding with what was paramount on both their minds. As far as she was concerned there wasn't any reason to wait. They were married. They knew each other better than most newlyweds. The certificate in Glenn's coat pocket granted them every right.

With her weight resting on the palm of one hand, she felt her heart throb painfully. "Glenn," she whispered brokenly, not knowing what to say, or how to say it.

The sound of her voice was drowned by the cork, exploding from the bottle. Fizzing champagne squirted across the dresser. Glenn deftly filled the two glasses and returned the dark bottle to its icy bed.

Handing her a goblet, Glenn joined her on the side of the mattress. "To my wife," he whispered tenderly and touched the edge of her glass to his.

"To my husband," she murmured in return. The bubbly liquid tickled her nose and she smiled shyly at Glenn as she took another sip. "I suppose this is when I'm supposed to suggest that I slip into something more comfortable."

"I'm for that." He quickly stood and strode across the room for the bottle, setting it on the floor next to the bed as he sat down again, avoiding her eyes the whole time.

"However, we both seemed to have forgotten something important." She bit her bottom lip in a gesture of uncertainty and laughter.

He glanced up expectantly. "What's that?"

"Clothes," she said and giggled. They had been so afraid to leave one another for fear something would happen to change their minds that they hadn't even stopped to pack an overnight bag.

"We're not going to need them." In that instant Glenn realized that they weren't going to wait. He wanted her. She wanted him; it was in her eyes and the provocative way she regarded him. "We have two days," he murmured, "and I can't see any need we'll be having for clothes."

He was so utterly serious that laughter rumbled in her throat. Where there had once been anxiety there was expectancy. "Maybe we could get away with that sort of thing on the Riviera, but believe me, they arrest people for walking around nude in Reno."

Smiling, he tipped back his head and emptied his glass. "You know what I mean."

Maggie set their champagne glasses aside. "No," she said breathlessly as she lightly stroked the neatly trimmed hair at his temple. "I think you'll have to show me."

Gently, Glenn laid her back on the bed and joined her so the upper portion of his body was positioned over the top of hers. His arms went around her, pressing her to his hard strength until her breasts strained against him. "I have every intention of doing exactly that."

His lips left hers to investigate her ear before tracing their way back across her cheek and reclaiming her mouth.

Maggie buried her face in the hollow of his throat, drawing in a deep shuddering breath as his busy hands fumbled with the effort to locate the tiny buttons at the back of her dress. Every place his fingers grazed her skin, a glowing warmth spread. Again Maggie opened her mouth to explore the strong cord of his neck, savoring his salty-tasting skin. She heard the harsh intake of his breath when she pulled his silk dress shirt free and stroked his muscular back.

"Oh, Glenn," she whispered when she didn't think she could stand it anymore. Her shoulders were heaving when he lifted his weight from her.

He rolled onto his back and she heard him release a harsh breath. "Maggie." His voice was thick and husky. "Listen, are you sure about this? We can wait."

"I'm sure," she whispered and switched positions so

that now it was she who was sprawled half atop him. "Glenn, I'm so sure it hurts."

"Maggie, oh, Maggie." He repeated her name again and again in a broken whisper. She'd spent a lifetime searching for him when all along he'd been so close and she hadn't known.

His arms crushed her then, and his mouth passionately sought hers with a greedy need that seemed to want to devour her. He took; she surrendered. He gave; she received. They were starved for each other and the physical love their bodies could share. With her arms wrapped securely around him, Maggie met his hunger with her own. When he half lifted her from the mattress she was trembling.

"Glenn," she whispered brokenly. "Oh, Glenn, don't ever let me go."

"Never," he promised, sitting on the edge of the bed with her cradled in his lap. "This is forever." His words were a vow. Carefully, in order not to tear her dress, his fingers released each tiny button at the back of her gown. As each one was freed he pressed his lips to the newly exposed skin.

"Forever," she repeated, and twisted so she could work loose the tuxedo tie and the buttons to the ruffled shirt. She pulled the shirt free of his shoulders and slid her hand down his chest to his tightening abdomen.

"Maggie," he warned hoarsely.

"Love me," she whispered. "Oh, Glenn, make me your wife."

Her fingers clutched frantically at his thick dark hair as he continued to stroke her breast.

All too soon she was on fire for him. Consumed with

desire, lost in a primitive world, aware of nothing but the desperate need he awoke within her.

Moving quickly he laid her upon the mattress and eased his body over hers.

The loving was exquisite and when they'd finished a long moment passed before he gathered her in his arms. He rolled onto his side, taking her with him. Lying cradled in his embrace, their legs entwined, Maggie closed her eyes and released a contented sigh.

"It was beautiful," she whispered, still overcome with emotion.

Glenn kissed the top of her head. "You're beautiful."

"So are you," she added quickly. "Oh, Glenn, we're going to have such a good life."

"Yes," he agreed and kissed her forehead.

Maggie snuggled closer against him and kissed the nape of his neck when he reached down to cover them with the sheet and blanket.

Glenn held her close, kissing the crown of her head until her eyes closed sleepily. Her last thought as she drifted into the welcoming comfort of slumber was of warmth and security.

Maggie woke a couple of times in the darkest part of the night, unaccustomed to sharing her bed. Each time she experienced the unexpected thrill of finding Glenn asleep at her side. No longer was she alone. Her joy was so great that she felt ten years old again, waking up on Christmas morning.

She cuddled him spoon fashion, pressing her softness to his backside. Her body fit perfectly to his. Edging her hand over his muscular ribs she felt his strength and knew that this man was as steady as the Rock of

Gibraltar. She had chosen her life mate well. Content, she drifted back to sleep.

A low, grumbling sound woke her when morning light splashed into the room from the small crack between closed drapes. Sitting up, Maggie yawned and raised her arms high above her head. She was ravenous, and pressed a hand to her stomach to prevent her rumbling from waking Glenn. A menu for room service sat by the phone and Maggie reached for it, studying its contents with interest, wondering if it would wake him if she ordered anything.

Glenn stirred and rolled onto his back, still caught in the last dregs of sleep. Gloriously happy, Maggie watched as a lazy smile grew on his face. Pride swelled in her heart as she realized their lovemaking was responsible for his look of blessed contentment. Maybe she wasn't so hungry after all.

Her long, tangled hair fell forward as she leaned down to press her lips to his. As she drew near, he whispered something. At first Maggie couldn't understand his words, then she froze. Stunned, her hand flew to her breast at the unexpected pain that pierced her. The arctic chill extended all the way to her heart and she squeezed her eyes closed to fight back the burning tears. Choking on humiliation, she struggled to untangle herself from the sheet. Her frantic movements woke Glenn from the nether land of sleep to the world of consciousness.

He turned on his side and reached for her hand. "Good morning," he said cheerfully. At the sight of her stricken face, he paused and rose to a full sitting position. "What's wrong?"

"The name is Maggie," she whispered fiercely, shoving his hand away. "And in case you've forgotten, I'm your wife as well."

Four

Tugging the sheet loose from the mattress, Maggie climbed out of bed. Her hands were shaking so badly that she had trouble twisting the material around her. Glenn had mistaken her for another woman. A woman he had obviously once loved…and apparently still did. Holding it together with one hand she sorted through the tangled mess of clothes on the floor. The tightness in her chest was so painful she could barely breathe. The room swayed beneath her feet and she closed her eyes, struggling to maintain her balance and her aplomb. Everything had been so beautiful. So perfect. How readily she had fallen into the fantasy, believing in each minute with a childlike innocence and trust. She'd been living in a twenty-four-hour dream world. That fantasy had been shattered by the reality of morning and she was shamed to the very marrow of her bones.

Glenn wiped a hand over his face and struggled to a sitting position. He vaguely recalled the contented pleasure of sleeping with a warm body at his side. In his sleep he must have confused Maggie with Angie. He cursed Angie for haunting him in his marriage.

"Maggie, what did I say?"

Straightening, she turned to regard him coolly before speaking. "Enough." *More than enough,* her mind shouted. Clenching the sheet in one hand, her clothes in the other, she marched across the floor, her head tilted at a stately angle. She never felt more like crying in her life. Her pride and dignity remained intact but little else was as it should be.

Once inside the bathroom she leaned against the heavy door, her shoulders sagging. Covering her face with both hands in hurt and frustration, she let the sheet slip to the floor. Equal doses of anger and misery descended on her until she was convinced she'd slump under the force of their weight. She didn't know what do, but taking a bath seemed important.

"Maggie." Glenn stood on the other side of the door, his voice low and confused. "Tell me what I said. At least talk to me."

"No," she shouted, still reeling from the shock. "I don't want to talk. I've heard enough to last me a lifetime." Forcing herself into action, she turned on the faucet and filled the tub with steaming hot water. She had been a fool to believe in yesterday's illusions. The morning had shattered the dream—only she didn't want it to end. Glenn was someone she had thought she could trust. In her heart she knew that he wouldn't be like all the rest.

"Maggie, for the love of heaven give me a chance to explain."

Sliding into the steaming bath, Maggie bit into her bottom lip and forced herself to think. She could demand that they divorce, but she didn't want that and Glenn didn't, either. For twelve hours she had been a happily married woman. Somehow Maggie had to find a way to stretch twelve hours into a lifetime.

In the other room Glenn dressed slowly, his thoughts oppressive. Things couldn't be worse. From the moment Maggie had met him at the airport he had seen how reserved and untrusting her inheritance had made her. Now he had hurt her, and he silently cursed himself for doing the very thing he vowed he never would. He could still see her stricken eyes glaring down at him when he woke. He'd wanted to take her in his arms and explain, but she'd jumped from the bed as if she couldn't get away fast enough. Not that he blamed her. The worst part was that he couldn't guarantee it wouldn't happen again. Angie had been an integral part of his life for nearly two years. He had cast her from his thoughts with an all-consuming effort, but he had no control over the ramblings of his mind while he slept. If only he knew what he'd said. He stroked his fingers through his hair and heaved a disgusted sigh. Whatever it was, he wouldn't allow it to ruin this marriage. Somehow he'd find a way to make it up to Maggie.

The bathroom door opened and Glenn turned anxiously. He studied Maggie's face for evidence of tears and found none. He had forgotten what a strong woman she was and admired her all the more. He vividly recalled the time she was fifteen and broke her arm skateboarding. She'd been in intense pain. Anyone else would have been screaming like a banshee, but not Maggie. She had gritted her teeth, but hadn't shed a tear. He also remembered how the only person she had trusted to help her had been him. The guilt washed over him in dousing waves.

"Can we talk now?" he asked her gently.

"I think we should," she said, pacing because standing in one spot seemed an impossible task. "We need to make some rules in this marriage, Glenn."

"Anything," he agreed.

"The first thing you have to do is stop loving that other woman right now. This minute." Her voice trembled and she battled for control.

Glenn felt physically ill. Maggie was unnaturally pale, her cheeks devoid of color. Her dark, soulful eyes contained a sorrow he longed to erase and yet he knew he couldn't. His thoughts were in turmoil. "You know I'd never lie to you."

"Yes." Glenn might be a lot of things, she knew, but a liar wasn't one of them.

"Maggie, I want this marriage to work, but what you're asking me to do is going to be hard."

A tingling sensation went through her that left her feeling numb and sick. She wouldn't share this man—not even with a memory.

"In that case," she murmured and swallowed, "I've got some thinking to do." She turned from him and started toward the door.

"Maggie." Glenn stopped her and she turned around. Their eyes met and held. "You don't want a divorce, do you?"

The word hit Maggie with all the impact of a freight train. "No," she said, shaking her head. "I may be mad, Glenn Lambert, but I'm not stupid."

The door made an echoing sound that bounced off the walls as Maggie left the hotel room. Glenn felt his tense shoulder muscles relax. It had taken everything in him to ask her about a divorce. That was the last thing he wanted, but he felt he had to know where Maggie stood after what had happened that morning.

The curious stares that met Maggie as she stepped off the elevator convinced her that the first thing she had to do was buy something to wear that was less ostentatious. A wrinkled pink maid-of-honor gown would cause more than a few heads to turn, and the last thing Maggie wanted was attention. In addition, she couldn't demand that her husband give up his affection for another woman and love and care for her instead, when she looked like something the cat left on the porch.

The hotel had a gift shop where she found a summer dress of pale-blue polished cotton, which she changed into after purchasing it. A walk through the lobby revealed that Glenn was nowhere to be seen. With time weighing heavily on her hands, Maggie pulled a ten-dollar bill from her purse. Already the hotel casino was buzzing with patrons eager to spend their money. Standing in front of the quarter slot machine, Maggie inserted the first coin. Pressing the button, she watched the figures spin into a blur and slowly wind down to two oranges and a cherry. Maggie stared at the fifty cents she won in disbelief. She didn't expect to win. Actually, it was fitting that she was in Reno. She had just made the biggest gamble of her life. The scary part was that Maggie felt like a loser and had felt like one almost from the minute she inherited her Great-aunt Margaret's money. She felt the ridiculous urge to laugh, but recognized that if she gave in to the compulsion tears wouldn't be far behind.

Glenn found her ten minutes later, still playing the slot machine. For several moments he stood watching her, wondering how to approach this woman he had

known most of his life. The woman who was now his
wife. There were so many issues facing them that had
to be settled before he left for Charleston. Maggie's inheritance was one thing he wouldn't allow to hang between them like a steel curtain. It was best to clear the
air of that and everything else they could.

A discordant bell clanged loudly and a barrage of cel-
ebratory characters danced across the slot machine. She
looked stunned and stepped back as the machine finished. Without emotion, she cashed out. As she turned,
their eyes clashed. Her breath caught in her throat and
she hesitated, waiting for him to speak first. Like her, he
had purchased another set of clothes, and again Maggie
wondered why she'd never noticed how extraordinarily
good-looking Glenn was. He was a man any woman
would be proud to call her husband. If he'd come to tell
her he wanted out of the marriage, she didn't know what
she would say. The time spent in front of the slot machine had given her the perspective to realize that Glenn
was as shocked by what had happened as she was. She
prayed that he hadn't come for the reason she suspected.
Maggie wanted this marriage. She had been so lonely
and miserable. The previous day with Glenn had been
the most wonderful day of her life. Maybe she was still
looking at the situation through rose-colored glasses,
but the deed was done. They were married now. The
other woman had no claim to him. He might murmur
"her" name in his sleep, but he was married to Maggie.

"Our plane leaves in two hours," he said, stepping
forward. "Let's get something to eat."

Nodding required a monumental effort. Her body
went limp with relief.

The hostess at the restaurant led them to a booth and

handed them menus. She gave Glenn a soft, slightly seductive smile, but Maggie was pleased to notice that he
didn't pay the woman the least bit of attention. Glenn
had never been a flirt. Beyond anything else, Maggie
realized, Glenn was an intensely loyal man. For him to
whisper another woman's name in his sleep had been
all the more devastating for just that reason.

Almost immediately a waitress arrived, poured them
each a cup of coffee and took their order.

"I want you to know that I'll do everything in my
power to do what you asked," Glenn announced, his eyes
holding hers. His hands cupped the coffee mug and there
was a faint pleading note shining from his eyes. "About
this morning; I suppose you want to know about her."

"Yes," Maggie whispered, hating the way his eyes
softened when he mentioned his lost love.

A sadness seemed to settle over him. "Her name is
Angie. We were..." He hesitated. "Engaged. She decided to marry her childhood sweetheart. It's as simple
as that."

"You obviously cared about her a great deal," Maggie said softly, hoping to take some of the sting from her
earlier comments. Talking about Angie, even now, was
obviously painful for him.

He held her gaze without hesitation. "I did care for
her, but that's over now. I didn't marry you longing
for anyone else. You aren't a substitute. This marriage
wasn't made on the rebound. We're both vulnerable for
different reasons. I want you for my wife. Not anyone
else, only you. We've known each other most of our
lives. I like you a great deal and respect you even more.
We're comfortable together."

"Yes, we are," she agreed. So Glenn regarded her

as an old pair of worn shoes. He could relax with her and put aside any need for pretense…as she could. But then she hadn't exactly come into their marriage seeking white lace and promises. Or maybe she had, Maggie didn't know anymore; she was confused.

"We're going to work this out," he said confidently, smiling for the first time that day as he reached for her hand.

"We're going to try," she suggested cautiously. "I'm not so sure we've done the right thing running off like this. We were both half-crazy to think we could make a marriage work on a twenty-four-hour reacquaintance."

"I knew what we were doing every second," Glenn countered gruffly. "I wanted this, Maggie."

"I didn't know if it was right or wrong. I guess only time will tell if we did the right thing or not."

The flight back to San Francisco seemed to take a lifetime. Maggie sat by the window, staring at the miniature world far below. The landscape rolled and curved from jutting peaks to plunging valleys that reminded her of the first few hours of her marriage. Even now a brooding sense of unreality remained with her.

The days were shorter now that winter was approaching, and dusk had settled by the time the taxi pulled up in front of the beach house. While Glenn was paying the cabdriver, Maggie looked over the house where she'd voluntarily sequestered herself, wondering how Glenn would view the ostentatious showplace. Undoubtedly he would be impressed. Her friends had praised the beach house that seemed to lack for nothing. There was a work-out gym, a sauna, a Jacuzzi, a swimming pool and a tennis court in the side yard that Maggie never used. The house held enough attractions to keep even the most discriminating prisoner entertained.

On the way from the airport they had stopped off at Steve's empty apartment and picked up Glenn's luggage. Seeing it was a vivid reminder that he was scheduled to leave in the morning. "What time is your flight tomorrow?" she asked, wondering how long they'd be in Charleston. They had already decided to make their home in San Francisco, but arrangements would need to be made in Charleston.

His mouth hardened. "Are you so anxious to be rid of me?"

"No." She turned astonished eyes to him, stunned at his sharp tongue. He made it sound as though she wouldn't be going with him. She should. After all, she was his wife. She could make an issue of it now, or wait until she was certain she'd read him right. They had already experienced enough conflict for one day and Maggie opted to hold her tongue. Her fingers fumbled with the lock in an effort to get inside the house. "I have to phone my brother," she announced once the door was open.

"Denny?"

"Yes, Denny, or is that a problem, too?"

He ran his fingers through his hair and expelled an angry breath. "I didn't mean to snap at you."

Maggie lowered her gaze. "I know. We're both on edge. I didn't mean to bite your head off, either." They were nervous and unsure of each other for the first time in their lives. What had once been solid ground beneath their feet had become shifting sand. They didn't know where they stood...or if they'd continue to stand at all.

Glenn placed a hand at the base of her neck and gently squeezed it. "My flight's scheduled for three. We'll have some time together."

He didn't plan to have her travel with him! That was another shock. Fine, she thought angrily. If he didn't want her, then she wouldn't ask. "Good," she murmured sarcastically. Fine indeed!

The house foyer was paved with expensive tiles imported from Italy, and led to a plush sunken living room decorated with several pieces of furniture upholstered in white leather. A baby grand piano dominated one corner of the room. As she hung up Glenn's coat he wandered into the large living room, his hands in his pockets.

"Do you like it?"

"It's very nice" was all he said. He stood, legs slightly apart while his gaze rested on an oil painting hung prominently on the wall opposite the Steinway. It was one of Maggie's earlier works and her favorite, a beachscape that displayed several scenes, depicting a summer day's outing to the ocean. Her brush had captured the images of eager children building a sand castle. Another group of bikini-clad young girls were playing a game of volleyball with muscle-bound he-men. A family was enjoying a picnic, their blanket spread out on the sand, shaded by a multicolored umbrella. Cotton-candy clouds floated in a clear blue sky while the ocean waves crested and slashed against the shore. Maggie had spent hours agonizing over the minute details of the painting. Despite its candor and realism, Maggie's beachscape wasn't an imitation of a snapshot recording, but a mosaiclike design that gave a minute hint at the wonder of life.

"This is a marvelous painting. Where did you ever

find it?" Glenn asked without turning around. "The detail is unbelievable."

"A poor imitation of a Brueghel." A smile danced at the corners of her mouth.

"Who?"

"Pieter Brueghel, a sixteenth-century Flemish painter."

"A sixteenth-century artist didn't paint this," Glenn challenged.

"No. I did."

He turned with a look of astonished disbelief. "You're not teasing, are you?" The question was rhetorical. His eyes narrowed fractionally as if reassessing her.

"It's one of my earliest efforts after art school. I've done better since, but this remains one of my favorite."

"Better than this?" His voice dipped faintly as though he doubted her words. "I remember you scribbling figures as a kid, but I never suspected you had this much talent."

A shiver of pleasure raced up her arm at the pride that gleamed from his eyes as he glanced from the painting back to her. "I had no idea you were this talented, Maggie."

The sincerity of the compliment couldn't be doubted. Others had praised her work, but Maggie had felt a niggling doubt as to the candidness of the comments. "Thank you," she returned, feeling uncharacteristically humble.

"I'd like to see your other projects."

"Don't worry, you'll get the chance. Right now, I've got to phone Denny. He'll wonder what happened to me."

"Sure. Go ahead. I'll wait in here if you like."

Maggie's office was off the living room. She hesitated a moment before deciding, then walked to the telephone on a table next to the couch. Her back was to Glenn as she picked up the receiver and punched out the number.

"Denny, it's Maggie."

"Maggie," he cried with obvious relief. "How was the wedding? You must have been late. I tried to get hold of you all day."

It was on the tip of Maggie's tongue to tell him about her marriage, but she held back, preferring to waylay his questions and doubts. She would tell him soon enough.

Her brother's voice softened perceptibly. "I was worried."

"I'm sorry, I should have phoned." Maggie lifted a strand of hair around her ear.

"Did you get the money transferred?"

Maggie sighed inwardly, feeling guilty. Denny knew all the right buttons to push with her. "The money will be ready for you Monday morning."

"Thanks. You know Linda and I appreciate it." His voice took on a honey-coated appeal.

"I know."

"As soon as I talk to the attorney about my case I'll let you know where we stand."

"Yes, Denny, do that." A large portion of Denny's inheritance had been lost in a bad investment and Maggie was helping him meet expenses. She didn't begrudge him the money: how could she when she had so much? What she hated was what it was doing to him. Yet she couldn't refuse him. Denny was her brother, her only brother.

After saying her goodbye, she replaced the receiver and turned back to Glenn. "I gave the housekeeper the weekend off. But if you're hungry, I'm sure I'll be able to whip up something."

"How's Denny?" Glenn ignored her offer.

"Fine. Do you want something to eat or not?"

"Sure." His gaze rested on the phone and Maggie realized that he'd probably picked up the gist of her conversation with Denny. More than she had intended. As a stockbroker Glenn would know what a foolish mistake her brother had made and she wanted to save her brother the embarrassment if possible.

Determined to avoid the subject of her brother, Maggie strolled past Glenn, through the dining room and into the expansive kitchen that was equipped with every conceivable modern cooking device. The double-width refrigerator/freezer was well stocked with frozen meals so that all that was required of her was to insert one into the microwave, push a button and wait.

The swinging doors opened as Glenn followed her inside. He paused to look around the U-shaped room with its oak cabinets and marble countertops. His hands returned to his pockets as he cocked his thick brows. "A bit large, wouldn't you say? One woman couldn't possibly require this much space."

Of course the kitchen was huge, she thought, irritated. She hadn't paid an exorbitant price for this place for three drawers and a double sink. "Yes," she returned somewhat defensively. "I like it this way."

"Do you mind if I take a look outside?" he asked and opened the sliding glass doors that led to a balcony overlooking the ocean.

"Sure. Go ahead."

A breeze ruffled the drape as he opened and closed the glass French door. Maggie watched him move to the railing and look out over the beach below. If she paused and strained her ears, she could hear the ocean as the wild waves crashed upon the sandy shore. A crescent moon was barely visible behind a thick layer of clouds.

Leaning a hip against the counter, Maggie studied his profile. It seemed incomprehensible that the man who was standing only a few feet from her was her husband. She felt awkward and shy, even afraid. If he did head back to Charleston without her, their marriage would become increasingly unreal. Before Glenn turned to find her studying him, Maggie took out a head of lettuce from the refrigerator and dumped it into a strainer, and then placed it under the faucet.

Rubbing the chill from his arms, Glenn returned a few minutes later.

"Go ahead and pour yourself a drink," Maggie offered, tearing the lettuce leaves into a bowl. When he hesitated, she pointed to the liquor cabinet.

"I'm more interested in coffee if you have it."

"I'll make it."

"I'll do it."

Simultaneously they moved and somehow Maggie's face came sharply into contact with the solid mass of muscle and man. Amazingly, in the huge kitchen, they'd somehow managed to collide. Glenn's hand sneaked out to steady Maggie at the shoulders. "You okay?"

"I think so." She moved her nose back and forth a couple of times before looking up at him. "I should have known this kitchen wasn't big enough for the two of us."

Something warm and ardent shone from his eyes as his gaze dropped to her mouth. The air in the room crackled with electricity. The hands that were gripping her shoulders moved down her upper arms and tightened. Every ticking second seemed to stretch out of proportion. Then, very slowly, he half lifted her from the floor, his mouth descending to hers a fraction of an inch at a time. Maggie's heart skipped a beat, then began to hammer wildly. He deliberately, slowly, left his mouth a hair's space above hers so that their breaths mingled and merged. Holding her close, he seemed to want her to take the initiative. But the memory of that morning remained vivid in her mind. And now it seemed he intended to leave her behind in San Francisco as well. No, there were too many questions left unanswered for her to give in to the physical attraction between them. Still his mouth hovered over hers, his eyes holding her. At the sound of the timer dinging, Glenn released her. Disoriented, Maggie stood completely still until she realized Glenn had moved away. Embarrassed, she turned, making busywork at the microwave.

"That smells like lasagna," Glenn commented.

"It is." Maggie's gaze widened as she set out the dishes. What an idiot she'd been. The bell she heard hadn't been her heart's song from wanting Glenn's kisses. It had been the signal from her microwave that their dinner was ready. The time had come to remove the stars from her eyes regarding their marriage.

Maggie noted that Glenn's look was thoughtful when they ate, as if something was bothering him. For that matter, she was unusually quiet herself. After the meal, Glenn silently helped her stack the dinner plates into the dishwasher. "Would you like the grand tour?" Maggie inquired, more in an effort to ease the tension than from any desire to show off her home.

"You did promise to show me some more of your work."

"My art?" Maggie hedged, suddenly unsure. "I'm more into the abstract things now." She dried her hands on a terry-cloth towel and avoided looking at him. "A couple of years ago I discovered Helen Frankenthaler. Oh, I'd seen her work, but I hadn't appreciated her genius."

"Helen who?"

"Frankenthaler." Maggie enunciated the name slowly. "She's probably the most historically important artist of recent decades and people with a lot more talent than me have said so."

Glenn looped an arm around her shoulders and slowly shook his head. "Maggie, you're going to have to remember your husband knows absolutely nothing about art."

"But you know what you like," she teased, leading him by the hand to the fully glassed-in upstairs studio.

"That I do," he admitted in a husky whisper.

No one else had ever seen the studio, where she spent the vast majority of her time. It hadn't been a conscious oversight. There just had never been anyone she'd wanted to show it to. Not even Denny, who, she realized, only gave lip service to her work. She led Glenn proudly into her domain. She had talent and knew it. So much of her self-esteem was centered in her work. In recent years it had become the outpouring of her frustrations and loneliness. Her ego, her identity, her vanity were all tied up in her work.

Glenn noted that her studio was a huge room twice the size of the kitchen. Row upon row of canvases were propped against the walls. From the shine in her eyes, Glenn realized that Maggie took her painting seriously. She loved it. As far as he could see it was the only thing in this world that she had for herself.

He hadn't been pleased by what he'd overheard in her telephone conversation with Denny. He had wanted to ask Maggie about it over dinner, but hesitated. He felt that it was too soon to pry into her relationship with her brother. As he recalled, Denny was a decent guy, four or five years older than Maggie. From the sounds of it, though, Denny was sponging off his sister—which was unusual since he had heard that Denny was wealthy in his own right. It was none of his affair, Glenn decided, and it was best that he keep his nose out of it.

Proudly Maggie walked around the studio, which was used more than any other room in the house. Most of the canvases were fresh and white, waiting for the bold strokes of color that would bring them to life. Several of the others contained her early experiments in cubism and expressionism. She watched Glenn as he strolled about the room, studying several of her pictures. Pride shone in his eyes and Maggie basked in his approval. She wanted to hug him and thank him for simply appreciating what she did.

He paused to study a large ten-foot canvas propped at an angle against the floor. Large slashes of blue paint were smeared across the center and had been left to dry, creating their own geometric pattern. Maggie was especially pleased with this piece. It was the painting she had been working on the afternoon she was late meeting Glenn at the airport.

"What's this?" Glenn asked, his voice tight. He cocked his head sideways, his brow pleated in concentration.

"Glenn," she chided, "that's my painting."

He was utterly stupefied that Maggie would waste her obvious talent on an abstract mess. The canvas looked as though paint had been carelessly splattered across the top. Glenn could see no rhyme or pattern to the design.

"Your painting," he mused aloud. "It's quite a deviation from your other work, isn't it?"

Maggie shrugged off his lack of appreciation and enthusiasm. "This isn't a portrait," she explained somewhat defensively. This particular painting was a departure from the norm, a bold experiment with a new balance of unexpected harmony of different hues of blues with tension between shapes and shades. Glenn had admitted he knew nothing about art, she thought. He wouldn't understand what she was trying to say with this piece, and she didn't try to explain.

Squatting, Glenn examined the large canvas, his fingertips testing the texture. "What is this material? It's not like a regular canvas, is it?"

"No, it's unprimed cotton duck—the same fabric that's used for making sails." This type of porous material allowed her to toss the paint across the canvas; then point by point, she poured, dripped and even used squeegees to spread the great veils of tone. She spent long, tedious hours contemplating each aspect of the work, striving for the effortless, spontaneous appeal she admired so much in Helen Frankenthaler's work.

"You're not into the abstract stuff, are you?" she asked with a faint smile. She tried to make it sound as if it didn't matter. The pride she'd seen in Glenn's eyes when he saw her beachscape and her other work had thrilled her. Now she could see him trying to disguise his puzzlement. "Don't feel bad, abstracts aren't for everyone."

A frown marred his smooth brow as he straightened and brushed the grit from his hands. "I'd like to see some more of the work like the painting downstairs."

"There are a couple of those over here." She pulled

a painting out from behind a stack of her later efforts in cubism.

Glenn held out the painting and his frown disappeared. "Now this is good. The other looks like an accident."

An accident! Maggie nearly choked on her laughter. She'd like to see him try it. "I believe the time has come for me to propose another rule for this marriage."

Glenn's look was wary. "What?"

"From now on everything I paint is beautiful and wonderful and the work of an unrecognized genius. Understand?"

"Certainly," he murmured, "anything you say." He paused to examine the huge canvas a second time. "I don't know what you're saying with this, but this is obviously the work of an unrecognized and unappreciated genius."

Maggie smiled at him boldly. "You did that well."

Five

Glenn muttered under his breath as he followed Maggie out of her studio. Her dainty back was stiff as she walked down the stairs. She might have made light of his comments, but he wasn't fooled. Once again he had hurt her. Twice in one day. The problem was that he was trying too hard. They both were. "I apologize, Maggie. I didn't mean to offend you. You're right. I don't know a thing about art."

"I'm not offended," she lied. "I keep forgetting how opinionated you are." With deliberate calm she moved into the living room and sat at the baby grand piano, running her fingers over the ivory keys. She wanted to be angry with him, but couldn't, realizing that any irritation was a symptom of her own insecurity. She had exposed a deeply personal part of herself. It had been a measure of her trust and Glenn hadn't known or understood. She couldn't blame him for that.

"I don't remember that you played the piano." He stood beside her, resting his hand on her shoulder.

His touch was oddly soothing. "I started taking lessons a couple of years ago."

"You're good."

Maggie stopped playing; her fingers froze above the keys. Slowly, she placed her hands in her lap. "Glenn, listen, the new rule to our marriage only applies to my painting. You can be honest with my piano playing. I'm rotten. I have as much innate rhythm as lint."

Glenn recognized that in his effort to make up for one faux pas he had only dug himself in deeper. He didn't know anything about music. "I thought you played the clarinet."

"I wasn't much better on that, if you recall."

"I don't."

"Obviously," she muttered under her breath, rising to her feet. She rubbed her hands together in a nervous gesture. "It's been a long day."

Glenn's spirits sank. It had been quite a day and nothing like he'd expected. Yet he couldn't blame Maggie—he had brought everything on himself. His hand reached for hers. "Let's go to bed."

Involuntarily, Maggie tensed. Everything had been perfect for the wedding night, but now she felt unsure and equally uneasy. Glenn was her husband and she couldn't give him the guest bedroom. But things were different from what they had been. Her eyes were opened this time, and white lace and promises weren't filling her mind with fanciful illusions.

"Is something wrong?" Glenn's question was more of a challenge.

"No," she murmured, abruptly shaking her head. "Nothing's wrong." But then not everything was right, either. She led the way down the long hallway to the master bedroom, feeling shaky.

The room was huge, dominated by a brick fireplace,

with two pale-blue chairs angled in front of it. The windows were adorned with shirred drapes of a delicate floral design that had been specially created to give a peaceful, easy-living appeal. The polished mahogany four-poster bed had a down comforter tossed over the top that was made from the same lavender floral material as the drapes. This room was Maggie's favorite. She could sit in it for hours and feel content.

If Glenn was impressed with the simple elegance or felt the warmth of her bedroom, he said nothing. Maggie would have been surprised if he had.

His suitcase rested on the thick carpet, and Glenn sighed, turning toward her. "We have a lot to do tomorrow." Frustrated anger filled Glenn at his own stupidity. Everything he had done that day had been wrong. From the moment he had opened his eyes to the time he'd mentioned going to bed. He couldn't have been more insensitive had he tried. He didn't want to argue with Maggie and yet, it seemed, he had gone out of his way to do exactly that. There would be a lot of adjustments to make with their marriage and he had gotten off on the wrong foot almost from the moment they'd started. Maggie was uncomfortable; Glenn could sense that. He could also feel her hesitancy. But he was her husband, and by heaven he'd sleep with her this and every night for the remainder of their lives.

The mention of the coming day served to remind Maggie that Glenn was planning on returning to Charleston alone. That rankled. Sometime during the evening, she had thought to casually bring up the return trip. But with what had happened in her studio and afterward, the timing hadn't been right. Crossing her arms over her breasts, she met his gaze.

"Oh. What are we doing tomorrow?" She couldn't think of anything they needed to do that couldn't be handled later.

"First we'll see a lawyer, then—"

"Why?" she asked, her voice unnaturally throaty. Alarm filled her. Glenn had changed his mind. He didn't want to stay married. And little wonder. She kept making up these rules and—

"I want to make sure none of your inheritance money is ever put in my name." With all the other problems they were facing, Glenn needed to assure Maggie that he hadn't married her for her wealth. If anything, he regretted the fact she had it. Her Great-aunt Margaret's money had been a curse as far as he was concerned. And judging by the insecure, frightened woman Maggie had become, she might even have realized that herself.

"I… I know you wouldn't cheat me." The odd huskiness of her voice was made more pronounced by a slight quiver. Of all the men she had known in her life, she trusted Glenn implicitly. He was a man of honor. He might have married her when he was in love with another woman, but he would never deliberately do anything to swindle her.

Their gazes melted into each other's. Maggie trusted him, Glenn realized. The heavy weight that had pressed against him from the moment she had turned her hurt, angry eyes on him that morning lessened. Surely there'd been a better way to handle that business with her paintings, he thought. She had talent, incredible talent, and it was a shame that she was wasting it by hiding it away.

"After the lawyer we'll go to a jeweler," he added.

"A jeweler?"

"I'd like you to wear a wedding ring, Maggie."

The pulse in her neck throbbed as she beat down a rush of pure pleasure. "Okay, and you too."

"Of course," he agreed easily. His gaze did a sweeping inspection of the room as if he'd noticed it for the first time. It reminded him of Maggie. Her presence was stamped in every piece of furniture, every corner. Suddenly, a tiredness stole into his bones. He was exhausted, mentally and physically. "Let's get ready for bed."

Maggie nodded, and some of her earlier apprehension faded. She wasn't completely comfortable sleeping with him after what had happened. Not when there was a chance he would take her in his arms, hold her close, kiss her, even make love to her, with another woman's name on his lips. "You go ahead, I've got a few odds and ends to take care of first."

Sitting at the oak desk in her office, Maggie lifted her long hair from her face and closed her eyes as weariness flooded her bones. She was tired—Glenn was tired. She was confused—Glenn was confused. They both wanted this marriage—they were both responsible for making it work. All right, there wasn't any reason to overreact. They'd share a bed and if he said "her" name in his sleep again, Maggie refused to be held responsible for her actions.

By the time Glenn returned from his shower, Maggie had gone back to the bedroom and changed into a sexless flannel pajama set that would have discouraged the most amorous male. She had slipped beneath the covers, and was sitting up reading, her back supported by thick feather pillows. Behind her book, she followed Glenn's movements when he reentered the bedroom.

He paused and allowed a tiny smile of satisfaction to touch his lips. He had half expected Maggie to linger in her office until he was asleep and was greatly pleased that she hadn't. Although she looked like a virgin intent on maintaining her chastity in that flannel outfit, he knew that this night wasn't the time to press for his husbandly rights. Things had gone badly. Tomorrow would be better, he promised himself.

Lifting back the thick quilt, Glenn slid his large frame into the king-size bed and turned off the light that rested on the mahogany nightstand on his side of the bed.

"Good night." His voice was husky and low with only a trace of amusement. He thought she would probably sit up reading until she fell asleep with the light on.

"Good night," she answered softly, pretending to read. A few minutes later, Maggie battled to keep her lashes from drooping. Valiantly she struggled as her mind conjured up ways of resisting Glenn. The problem was that she didn't want to resist him. He would probably wait until she was relaxed and close to falling asleep, she theorized. When she was at her weakest point, he would reach for her and kiss her. Glenn was a wonderful kisser and she went warm at the memory of what had happened their first night together. He had held her as if he were dying of thirst and she was a cool shimmering pool in an oasis.

Gathering her resolve, Maggie clenched her teeth. By heaven, the way her thoughts were going she'd lean over and kiss him any minute. Her hand rested on her abdomen and Maggie felt bare skin. Her pajamas might be sexless, but they also conveniently buttoned up the front so he had easy access to her if he wanted. Again she recalled how good their lovemaking had been and how she had thrilled to his hands and mouth on her. Her eyes drooped shut and with a start she forced them open.

Lying completely still she listened, and after several long moments discovered that Glenn had turned away from her and was sound asleep.

An unexpected rush of disappointment filled her. He hadn't even tried to make love to her. Without a thought, he had turned onto his side and gone to sleep! Bunching up her pillow, Maggie rolled onto her stomach, feeling such frustration that she could have cried. He didn't want her, and as unreasonable as it sounded, Maggie felt discouraged and depressed. Her last thought as she turned out her light was that if Glenn reached for her in the night she would give him what he wanted…what she wanted.

Sometime in the middle of the night Maggie woke. She was sleeping on her side, but had moved to the middle of the bed. Her eyes fluttered open and she wondered what had caused her to wake when she felt so warm and comfortable. Glenn's even breathing sounded close to her ear and she realized that he was asleep, cuddling his body to hers. Contented and secure, she closed her eyes and a moment later a male hand slid over her ribs, just below her breasts. When he pulled her close, fitting his body to hers, Maggie's lashes fluttered open. Not for the first time, she was amazed at how perfectly their bodies fit together. Releasing a contented breath, Maggie shut her eyes and wandered back to sleep.

Glenn woke in the first light of dawn with a serenity that had escaped him for months. That morning he didn't mistake the warm body he was holding close. Maggie was responsible for his tranquility of spirit, Glenn realized. He needed Maggie. During the night, her pajama top had ridden up and the urge to move his hand and trace the soft, womanly curves was almost overpowering. Maggie was all the woman he would ever want. She was everything he had ever hoped to find in a wife—a passionate, irresistible mistress with an intriguing mind and delectable body, who surrendered herself willingly. Her passion had surprised and pleased him. She hadn't been shy, or embarrassed, abandoning herself to him with an eagerness that thrilled him every time he thought about it. She was more woman than he'd dared hope and he ached to take her again.

In her sleep, Maggie shifted and her breasts sprang free of the confining top. For an eternity he lay completely still until he couldn't resist touching her any longer. In his mind he pictured turning her onto her back and kissing her until her lips opened eagerly to his. With inhuman patience he would look into those dark beautiful eyes and wait until she told him how much she wanted him.

Groaning, he released her and rolled onto his back, taking deep breaths to control his frantic frustration. He had no idea how long it would be before he would have the opportunity to make love to his wife again. Two weeks at least, maybe longer. Almost as overwhelming as the urge to make love to her was the one to cherish and protect her. She needed reassurance and he knew she needed time. Throwing back the blankets he marched into the bathroom and turned on the cold water.

Maggie woke at the sound of the shower running. Stirring, she turned onto her back and stared at the ceiling as the last dregs of sleep drained from her mind. She had been having the most pleasant erotic dream. One that caused her to blush from the roots of her dark hair to the ends of her toenails. Indecent dreams maybe, but excruciatingly sensual. Perhaps it was best that Glenn was gone when she woke, she thought. If he had been beside her she didn't know what she would have done. She could well have embarrassed them both by reaching for him and asking him to make love to her before he returned to Charleston...alone.

Taking advantage of the privacy, she dressed and hurriedly made the bed. By the time she had straightened the comforter across the mattress, Glenn reappeared.

"Good morning," he said as he paused just inside the bedroom, standing both alert and still as he studied her. "Did you sleep well?"

"Yes," she responded hastily, feeling like a specimen about to be analyzed, but a highly prized specimen, one that was cherished and valued. "What about you?" she asked.

The hesitation was barely noticeable, but Maggie noticed. "Like a rock."

"Good. Are you hungry?" Her eyes refused to meet his, afraid of what hers would tell him.

"Starved."

"Breakfast should be ready by the time you've finished dressing," she said as she left the room. Glenn had showered last night, she remembered; she couldn't recall him being overly fastidious. Shrugging, she moved down the long hall to the kitchen.

The bacon was sizzling in the skillet when Glenn reappeared, dressed in dark slacks and a thick pullover sweater. Maggie was reminded once again that he was devastatingly handsome and experienced, and with a burst of pride, she remembered that he was married to her. At least legally, he was hers. However, another woman owned the most vital part of him—his heart. In time, Maggie trusted, she would claim that as well.

The morning swam past in a blur; such was their

pace. They began by contacting Maggie's attorney and were given an immediate appointment. Together they sat in his office, although it was Glenn who did the majority of the talking. Maggie was uncomfortable with the rewording of her will, but Glenn was adamant. He desired none of her money and he wanted it stated legally. When and if they had children, her inheritance would be passed on to them.

From the attorney's they stopped off at a prominent San Francisco jeweler. Maggie had never been one for flashy jewels. All too often her hands were in paint solvent or mixing clay and she didn't want to have to worry about losing expensive rings or valuable jewels. Knowing herself and her often thoughtless ways, Maggie was apt to misplace a diamond and she couldn't bear the thought of losing any ring Glenn gave her.

"You decide," Glenn insisted, his hand at the back of her neck. "Whatever one you want is fine."

Sensing a sure sale, the young jeweler set out a tray of exquisite diamonds, far larger than any Maggie had dreamed Glenn would want to purchase. Her gaze fell on a lovely marquise and her teeth worried her bottom lip. "I...was thinking maybe something with a smaller stone would be fine," she murmured, realizing that she should have explained her problems about a diamond to Glenn earlier.

He pinched his mouth closed with displeasure, resenting her concern that he couldn't afford to buy her a diamond large enough to weight her hand.

"Try on that one," he insisted, pointing to the marquise solitaire with the wide polished band that she had admired earlier. The diamond was the largest and most expensive on the tray.

Maggie paled, not knowing how to explain herself. The salesman beamed, exchanging pleased glances with Glenn.

"An excellent choice," the jeweler said, lifting Maggie's limp hand. The ring fit as if it was made for her slender finger. But the diamond was so heavy it felt bulky and unnatural. In her mind Maggie could picture the panic of looking for it once it was mislaid... and it would be.

"We'll take it."

"Glenn." Maggie placed her hand on his forearm. "Can I talk to you a minute? Please."

"I'll write up the sales order," the jeweler said, removing the tray of diamonds. "I'll be with the cashier when you've finished."

Maggie waited until the salesman was out of earshot before turning troubled eyes to Glenn. Her heart was in her eyes as she recognized the pride and irritation that glared back at her.

"What's the matter, Maggie?" he growled under his breath. "Are you afraid I can't afford a wedding ring for my wife? I may not own a fancy beach house, but be assured, I can afford a diamond."

Glenn's words smarted and it was all Maggie could do to bite back a flippant reply. "It's not that," she whispered fiercely, keeping her voice low so the jeweler wouldn't hear them arguing. "If you'd given me half a chance, I'd have explained. I'm an artist, remember? If you buy me that flashy diamond, I'll be constantly removing it for one reason or another."

"So? What are you suggesting? No ring at all?"

"No... I'm sorry I said anything. The ring is fine." Maggie backed down, aware that anything said now would be misconstrued. Somehow she would learn to be careful with the diamond. Purchasing it had become a matter of male pride and Maggie didn't want to cause any more problems than the ones already facing them.

"Would a plain gold band solve that?" he asked unexpectedly.

"Yes," she murmured, surprised. "Yes, it would." To her delight, Glenn also asked the jeweler to size a band for her. Maggie felt wonderful when they stepped outside. The question of the ring might have been only a minor problem, but together they had settled it without wounding each other's sensitive pride. They were making progress and it felt good.

They ate lunch in Chinatown, feasting on hot, diced chicken stir-fried with fresh, crisp vegetables. All the time they were dining, Maggie was infinitely aware of two pressing items: the heavy feel of the ring on the third finger of her left hand, and the time. Within hours Glenn would be leaving for Charleston. A kaleidoscope of regrets and questions whirled through her mind. She wanted to go with him, but didn't feel she could make the suggestion. Glenn had to want her along, yet he hadn't said a word. Silence hung heavy and dark between them like a thick curtain of rain-filled clouds. He was going back to his lost love. Dread filled Maggie with each beat of her heart.

Glenn made several attempts at light conversation during their meal, but nothing seemed to ease the strained silence that had fallen over them. A glance at his watch reminded him that within a few hours he would be on a plane for Charleston. He didn't want to leave, but in some ways felt it was for the best. Maggie seemed to assume that she wouldn't be going with him and he was disappointed that she hadn't shown the willingness to travel with him. He might have made an issue of it if he hadn't thought a short separation would help them both become accustomed to their marriage without the issue of sleeping together. Those weeks would give Maggie the opportunity to settle things within her own mind. When he came back to her they would take up their lives as man and wife and perhaps she'd come to him willingly as she had that first night. That was what he wanted.

The drive back to the house and then on to the airport seemed to take a lifetime. With each mile, Maggie felt her heart grow heavier. She was apprehensive and didn't know how to deal with it. She and Glenn had been together such a short time that separating now seemed terribly wrong. Unreasonable jealousy ate at her and Maggie had to assure herself repeatedly that Glenn probably wouldn't even be seeing the other woman. She was, after all, married to another man or so Glenn had told her. But Maggie didn't gain a whit's comfort from knowing that. For the first time in memory, she found herself in a situation where money wasn't part of the solution.

As they left the airport parking garage, Glenn's hand took hers. "I won't be long," he promised. "I'll need to get everything settled at the office, list the condominium with a Realtor and settle loose business ties—that kind of thing. I can't see it taking more than two weeks, three at the most."

"The weeks will fly by," she said on a falsely cheerful note. "Just about the time I clean out enough closet space for you, you'll be back."

"I wouldn't leave if it wasn't necessary," Glenn assured her as they approached the ticketing desk to check in his luggage.

"I know that." Maggie hugged her waist, feeling a sudden and unexpected chill. "I'm not worried about… you know." *Liar,* her mind tossed back.

Their shoes made a clicking sound as they walked together toward security. Maggie had the horrible feeling she was about to cry, which, she knew, was utterly ridiculous. She rarely cried, yet her throat felt raw and scratchy and her chest had tightened with pent-up emotion. All the things she wanted to say stuck in her throat and she found that she couldn't say a thing.

"Take care of yourself," Glenn murmured, holding her by the shoulders.

"I will," she promised and buried her hands deep within the pockets of her raincoat. Even those few words could barely escape.

Glenn fastened the top button of her coat and when he spoke his voice was softly gruff. "It looks like rain. Drive carefully."

"I always do. You'll note that you're here on time." She made a feeble attempt at humor.

Tiny laugh lines fanned out from his eyes. "Barely. I don't suppose you've noticed that by now my flight's probably boarding. Married two days and I'm already picking up your bad habits."

His observation prompted a soft smile. "You'll phone?" She turned soft, round eyes to him.

"Yes," he promised in a husky murmur. "And if you need me, don't hesitate to call." He had written down both his work and home numbers in case she had to get in touch with him.

"You'll phone tonight." It became immensely important that he did. She pulled her hands from her pockets and smoothed away an imaginary piece of lint from his shoulder. Her hand lingered there. "I'll miss you." Even now if he hinted that he wanted her with him, she'd step on that plane. If necessary she'd buy the stupid plane.

"I'll phone, but it'll be late because of the time change," Glenn explained.

"I don't mind.... I probably won't sleep anyway." She hadn't meant to admit that much and felt a rush of color creep up her neck and into her cheeks.

"Me either," he murmured. His hands tightened on her upper arms and he gently brought her against his bulky sweater. With unhurried ease his mouth moved toward hers. The kiss flooded her with a swell of emotions she had tasted only briefly in his arms. She was hot, on fire and cold as ice. Hot from his touch, cold with fear. His kiss sent a jolt rocketing through her and she fiercely wrapped her arms around his neck. Her mind whirled and still she clung, afraid that if Glenn ever released her she'd never fully recover from the fall. Dragging in a deep breath, Maggie buried her face in his neck.

Glenn wrapped his arms around her waist and half lifted her from the floor. "I'll be back soon," he promised.

She nodded because speaking was impossible.

When he released her his gaze was as gentle as a caress and as tender as a child's touch. Maggie offered him a feeble smile. Glenn turned up the collar of her coat. "Stay warm."

Again she nodded. "Phone me."

Glenn claimed Maggie's lips again in a brief but surprisingly ardent kiss. "I'll call the minute I land."

With hands in her pockets for fear she'd do something silly like reach out and ask him not to go, or beg him to ask her to come. "Hurry now, or you'll miss the flight."

Glenn took two steps backward. "The time will go fast."

"Yes," she said, not exactly sure what she was agreeing to.

"You're my wife, Maggie. I'm not going to forget that."

"You're my husband," she whispered and choked back the tears that filled her eyes and blurred her vision.

Then tossing a glance over his shoulder, he hurriedly handed the TSA agent his boarding pass and identity.

Maggie pushed her. "Go on," she encouraged, not wanting him to see her cry. For all the emotion that was raging through her one would assume that Glenn was going off to war and was unlikely to return. Her stomach was in such tight knots that she couldn't move without pain. Rooted to the spot close to security, Maggie stood as she was until Glenn turned and ran toward his gate. When she could, she stepped to the window and whispered, "New rules for this marriage…don't ever leave me again."

The days passed in a blur. Not since art school had Maggie worked harder or longer. Denny phoned her twice. Once to thank her for the "loan" and later to talk to her about the top-notch lawyer he had on retainer. The attorney was exactly who he had hoped would pursue his case, and his spirits were high. Maggie was pleased for Denny and prayed that this would be the end of his problems.

Without Glenn, sound sleep was impossible. She'd drift off easily enough and then jerk awake a couple of hours later, wondering why the bed seemed so intolerably large. Usually she slept in the middle of the mattress, but she soon discovered that she rested more comfortably on the side where Glenn had slept. She missed him. The worst part was the unreasonableness of the situation. Glenn had spent less than twenty-four hours in her home, yet without him the beach house felt like a silent tomb.

As he promised, Glenn had phoned the night he arrived back in Charleston and again three days later. Maggie couldn't recall any three days that seemed longer. A thousand times she was convinced her mind had conjured up both Glenn and their marriage. The marquise diamond on her ring finger was the only tangible evidence that the whole situation hadn't been a fantasy and that they really were married. Because she was working so hard and long she removed it for safekeeping, but each night she slipped it on her finger. Maggie didn't mention the wedding to her parents or any of her friends, and Denny didn't notice anything was different about her. She didn't feel comfortable telling everyone she was married, and wouldn't until Glenn had moved in with her and they were confident that their marriage was on firm ground.

Glenn phoned again on the fifth day. Their conversation was all too brief and somewhat stilted. Neither of them seemed to want it to end, but after twenty minutes, there didn't seem to be anything more to say.

Replacing the receiver, Maggie had the urge to cry. She didn't, of course, but it was several minutes before she had composed herself enough to go on with her day.

Nothing held her interest. Television, music, solitaire—everything bored her. Even the housekeeper lamented that Maggie had lost her appetite and complained about cooking meals that Maggie barely touched. Glenn filled every waking thought and invaded her dreams.

Each time they spoke she had to bite her tongue to keep from suggesting she join him; her pride wouldn't allow that. The invitation must come from him, she believed. Surely he must realize that.

As for Angie, the woman in Glenn's past, the more Maggie thought about the situation, the more angry she became with herself. Glenn hadn't deceived her. They both were bearing scars from the past. If it wasn't love that cemented their marriage then it was something equally strong. Between them there was security and understanding.

The evening of the eighth day the phone rang just as Maggie was scrounging through the desk looking for an address. She stared at the telephone. Instantly she knew it was Glenn.

"Hello," she answered, happily leaning back in the swivel chair, anticipating a long conversation.

"Hi." His voice sounded vital and warm. "How's everything?"

"Fine. I'm a little bored." Maggie was astonished that she could sound so blasé about her traumatic week. "A little bored" soft-pedaled all her frustrations. "What about you?"

Glenn hesitated, then announced, "I've run into a small snag on my end of things." A small snag was the understatement of the century, he thought. Things had been in chaos from the minute he had returned. The company supervisor had paid a surprise visit to him Thursday afternoon and had suggested an audit because of some irregularity in the books. The audit had gone smoothly enough, but Glenn had worked long hours and had been forced to reschedule several appointments. In addition, the Realtor who listed the condominium offered little hope that it would sell quickly.

And worse, Glenn was miserable without Maggie. He wanted her with him. She was his wife, yet pride dictated that he couldn't ask her. The suggestion would have to come from her. Even a hint would be enough. He would pick up on a hint, but she had to be one to give it.

"A small snag?" Her heart was pounding so hard and strong that she felt breathless.

"I've got several accounts here that have deals pending. I can't leave my clients in the lurch. Things aren't going as smoothly as I'd like, Maggie," he admitted.

"I see." Maggie's vocabulary suddenly decreased to words of one syllable.

"I can't let them down." He sounded as frustrated as she felt. A deafening silence grated over the telephone line, and it was on the tip of Glenn's tongue to cast his stupid pride to the wind and ask her to join him.

"Don't worry, I understand," she said in an even tone, congratulating herself for maintaining firm control of her voice. On the inside she was crumbling to pieces. She wanted to be with him. He was her husband and her place was at his side. Closing her eyes she mentally pleaded with him to say the words—to ask her to come to Charleston. She wouldn't ask, couldn't ask. It had to come from Glenn.

"In addition there are several loose ends that are going to require more time than I originally planned." He sounded almost angry, an emotion that mirrored her own frustration.

"I think we were both naive to think you could make it back in such a short time."

"I suppose we were." *Come on, Maggie,* he pleaded

silently. *If you miss me, say something. At least meet me halfway in this.*

The line went silent again, but Maggie didn't want to end the conversation. She waited endless hours for his calls. They would talk for ten minutes, hang up and immediately she'd start wondering how long it would be before he phoned again.

"The weather's been unseasonably cold. There's been some talk of freezing temperatures," Maggie said out of desperation to keep the conversation going.

"Don't catch cold." *Damn it, Maggie, I want you here, can't you hear it in my voice?*

"I won't," she promised. *Please,* she wanted to scream at him, *ask me to come to Charleston.* With her eyes shut, she mentally transmitted her need to have him ask her. "I've been too busy in the studio to venture outside."

"Brueghel or Frankenthaler?" Glenn questioned, his voice tinged with humor. "However, I'm sure that either one would be marvelous and wonderful." He smiled as he said it, wanting her with him all the more just to see what other crazy rules she'd come up with for their marriage.

"This one's a Margaret Kingsbury original," she said proudly. Maggie had worked hard on her latest project and felt confident that Glenn would approve.

"It can't be." Glenn stiffened and tried to disguise the irritation in his voice.

Maggie tensed, wondering what she had said wrong. He hadn't approved of her art, but surely he didn't begrudge her the time she spent on it when he was away.

"Your name's Lambert now," Glenn stated.

"I…forgot." *Remind me again,* she pleaded silently.

Ask me to come to Charleston. "I haven't told anyone yet.... Have you?"

"No one," Glenn admitted.

"Not even your parents?" She hadn't told hers, either, but Glenn's family was in South Carolina. It only made sense that he'd say something to them before moving out west.

"That was something I thought we'd do together."

The sun burst through the heavy overcast and shed its golden rays on Maggie. He had offered her a way to Charleston and managed to salvage her pride. The tension flowed from her as her hand tightened around the receiver. "Glenn, don't you think they'll be offended if we wait much longer?"

"They might," he answered, unexpectedly agreeable. "I know it's an inconvenience, but maybe you should think about flying...."

"I'll be on the first flight out tomorrow morning."

Six

Glenn was in the terminal waiting when Maggie walked off the plane late the following afternoon. He was tall, rugged and so male that it was all Maggie could do not to throw her arms around him. He looked wonderful and she wanted to hate him for it. For nine days she had been the most miserable woman alive and Glenn looked as if he'd relished their separation, thrived on it. Renewed doubts buzzed about her like swarming bees.

Stepping forward, Glenn took the carry-on bag from her hand and slipped an arm around her waist. "Welcome to Charleston."

Shamelessly, Maggie wanted him to take her in his arms and kiss her. She managed to disguise the yearning by lowering her gaze. "I didn't know if you'd be here."

She tried to call to give him her flight number, but his phone had gone directly to voice mail. She'd left a message and then later sent him a text. If he hadn't gotten her message Maggie wouldn't have had a way of getting into Glenn's condominium.

"Of course I'm here. Where else would I be?"

"I'm so glad to see you." *Very glad,* her heart sang.

"How was the flight?"

"Just the way I like 'em," she said with a teasing smile. "Uneventful."

Glenn's features warmed and he grinned at her answer. Captivated by the tenderness in his eyes, Maggie felt her heart throb almost painfully. His eyes were dark, yet glowing with a warm light. Although he hadn't said a word, Glenn's gaze told her he was pleased she was with him.

"Your luggage is this way," he commented, pressing a hand to the middle of her back as he directed her toward baggage claim.

"I didn't bring much."

"Not much" constituted two enormous suitcases and one large carry-on. Maggie had spent half the night packing, discarding one outfit after another until her bedroom floor was littered with more clothes than a second-hand store. She wanted everything perfect for Glenn. She longed to be alluring and seductive, attractive without being blatant about it. She wanted his heart as well as his bed and only she realized how difficult that was going to be if Glenn was still in love with "her."

The more Maggie thought about the other woman who had claimed his heart the more she realized what an uphill struggle lay before her. Glenn wouldn't ever give his love lightly, and now that he had, it would take a struggle to replace her in his heart. Maggie yearned to know more of the details, but wouldn't pry. In the meantime, she planned to use every womanly wile she possessed and a few she planned to invent.

The leather strap of her purse slid off her shoulder and Maggie straightened it. As she did, Glenn stopped in midstride, nearly knocking her off balance.

"Where's your diamond?" he asked, taking her hand. Surprise mingled with disappointment and disbelief. "I thought you said the only time you wouldn't wear it was when you were working. You aren't painting now."

Maggie's mind whirled frantically. She had removed the diamond the morning before the phone call and placed it in safekeeping the way she always did. Then in her excitement about flying out to be with Glenn, she had forgotten to put it back on her finger.

"Maggie?"

Her fingers curled around the strap of her purse. "Oh, Glenn…"

He took her hand and examined the plain gold band that he had bought her with the marquise.

Maggie wanted to shout with frustration. From the moment they'd ended their phone conversation she had been carefully planning this reunion. Each detail had been shaped in her mind from the instant he picked her up until they dressed for bed.

"Maggie, where is the diamond?" he repeated.

"I forgot it, but don't worry… I have it with me." Her voice rose with her agitation. They hadn't so much as collected her luggage and already they were headed for a fight.

"You mean to tell me you packed a seven-thousand-dollar diamond with your underwear?" His voice was a mixture of incredulity and anger.

"I didn't do it on purpose, I…forgot I wasn't wearing it." Somehow that seemed even worse. "And furthermore it isn't in the suitcase, I have it in my carry-on."

Glenn's stride increased to a quick-paced clip that left Maggie half trotting in an effort to keep up. "Glenn," she protested, refusing to run through airports.

He threw an angry glare over his shoulder. "Forgive me for being overly concerned, but I work hard for my money."

The implication being, she thought, that she didn't work and the ring meant nothing to her. Little did he realize how much it did mean.

Maggie stopped cold as waves of anger hit her. Few words could have hurt her more. She was outraged he would say such a thing to her. For several minutes she found herself unable to speak. Nothing was going as she had planned. She'd had such wonderful images of Glenn sweeping her into his arms, holding her close and exclaiming that after the way he'd missed her, they'd never be separated again. He was supposed to tell her how miserable he'd been. Instead, he'd insulted her in a way that would hurt her the most.

Apparently he was angry because she had forgotten to slip on the diamond ring he'd gotten her, finding her casualness with the diamond a sign of irresponsibility. She had the ring; she knew where it was.

Glenn was standing outside the baggage-handling system, waiting for it to unload the luggage from her flight, when she joined him.

"If you'd give me a second I'll…"

"Talk to me after you've gotten your ring, Maggie. At the moment I'm worried about losing an expensive diamond."

"And you work hard for your money. Right? At least that's what you claim. I don't doubt it. It's said that those who marry for it usually do."

Although he continued to look straight ahead, a nerve jumped convulsively in his clenched jaw, and Maggie was instantly aware of just how angry that remark had made him. Good, she meant it to do exactly that. If he wanted to hurl insults at her, then she could give as well as take.

"Can I have my carry-on?"

Without a word, he handed it to her. He studied the baggage conveyor belt as if it were the center of his world. Maggie wasn't fooled. Glenn was simply too outraged to look at her.

Maggie knelt down on the floor and flipped open the lid. Her small jewelry case was inside and the ring was tucked safely in that. With a brooding sense of unhappiness, Maggie located the marquise diamond and slipped it on her finger beside the plain gold band. Snapping the suitcase closed, she stood.

"I hope to hell you didn't mean that about me marrying you for your money."

Maggie regarded him coolly before answering. "I didn't," she admitted. "I was reacting to your implication that I didn't have to work hard for my money."

He exhaled slowly. "I didn't mean it like that."

"I hope not."

They stood side by side, silent for several moments before his hand claimed hers. Right away he noticed the diamond was on her ring finger, and he arched one brow expressively. "You had it with you all the time?"

"Yes."

He groaned inwardly. He had been wanting Maggie for days, longing for her. And now things were picking up right where they'd left off, with misunderstandings and sharp words. He had wanted everything perfect for her, and once again this bad start had been his own doing.

His fingers tightened over hers. "Can I make a new rule for this marriage?" he asked her with serious eyes.

"Of course."

"I want you to wear your wedding set all the time."

"But…"

"I know that may sound unreasonable," he interrupted, "and I'm not even entirely sure why my feelings are so strong. I guess it's important to me that your wedding bands mean as much to you as our marriage."

Slowly, thoughtfully, Maggie nodded. "I'll never remove them again."

Looking in her eyes, Glenn felt the overwhelming urge to take her in his arms and apologize for having started on the wrong foot once again. But the airport wasn't the place and now wasn't the time. From here on, he promised himself, he'd be more patient with her, court her the way he should have in the beginning.

They didn't say a word until the luggage was dispensed. Maggie pointed out her suitcases.

He mumbled something unintelligible under his breath and Maggie realized he was grumbling about the fact she claimed to have packed light for this trip. But he didn't complain strenuously.

The deafening quiet in the car was one neither seemed willing to wade into. Maggie wanted to initiate a brilliant conversation, but nothing came to mind and she almost cried with frustration. Their meeting wasn't supposed to happen this way. She sat uncomfortably next to a man she'd known most of her life and whom, she was discovering, she didn't know at all.

Glenn's condominium was situated just outside historic Charleston with a view of Colonial Lake. Maggie knew little about the area. Her head flooded with questions about the city that Glenn had made his home for a decade, but she asked none. While he took care of her luggage, she wandered into the living room to admire the view. The scenery below revealed magnificent eighteenth-century homes, large public buildings and meticulously kept gardens. The gentle toll of church bells sounded, and Maggie strained to hear more. Charleston was definitely a city of grace, beauty and charm. Yet Glenn was willing to sacrifice it all—his home, his family, his job, maybe even his career to move to San Francisco.

He must have suffered a great deal of mental anguish to be willing to leave all this, Maggie determined, experiencing an attack of doubt. Glenn had told her so little about this other woman, and Maggie had the feeling he wouldn't have told her anything if it hadn't been for the unfortunate scene the morning after their wedding. He was an intensely personal man.

The condominium was far more spacious than what Maggie had assumed. The living room led into a formal dining area and from there to a spacious kitchen with plenty of cupboards and a pantry. A library/den was separated from the living room by open double-width doors that revealed floor-to-ceiling bookcases and a large oak desk. She hadn't seen the bedrooms yet, but guessed that there were three, possibly four. The condo was much larger than what a single man would require. Her eyes rounded with an indescribable ache that came over her when she realized Glenn had purchased this home for Angie.

"Are you hungry?" he asked, halfway into the living room, standing several feet from her.

Maggie unbuttoned her coat and slipped the scarf

from her neck. "No thanks, I ate on the plane, but you go ahead." The lie was a small, white one. The flight attendant had offered her a meal, but Maggie had declined. She'd been too anxious to eat when she was only a few hours from meeting Glenn.

He hesitated, turned, then whirled back around so that he was facing her again. "I regret this whole business with the ring, Maggie."

A shiver of gladness came over her at his offhand apology. "It's forgotten."

Something close to a smile quirked his mouth. "I'm glad you're here."

"I'm glad to be here."

He leaned around the kitchen door. "Are you sure you're not hungry?"

A small smile claimed her mouth. "On second thought, maybe I am at that."

A sense of relief flooded through Glenn's tense muscles. He hadn't meant to make such an issue of the diamond. For days he'd been longing for Maggie, decrying his earlier decision to leave her in San Francisco. They had so few days together that he'd thought the separation would give her the necessary time to adjust mentally to her new life. Unfortunately, it was he who had faced the adjustment…to his days…and nights without her. Now that she was here, all he wanted was to take her in his arms and make love to her. The level of physical desire she aroused in him was a definite shock. He hadn't expected to experience this intensity. All he had thought about since he'd known she was coming was getting her into his bed. He'd dreamed of kissing her, holding her and making love to his wife. She was the woman he'd married and he'd waited a long time for the privileges due a husband. He doubted that Maggie had any conception of how deep his anger had cut when she had suggested that he'd married her for her money. That was a problem he had anticipated early on and it was the very reason he had insisted they see a lawyer as soon as possible.

Working together they cooked their dinner. Maggie made the salad while Glenn broiled thick steaks. Glenn didn't have a housekeeper to prepare his meals and for that matter, Maggie surmised, he might not even have someone in to do the housework. Now that she was here, she decided, she would take over those duties. Surprisingly, Maggie discovered she looked forward to being a wife. Glenn's wife.

Later, while he placed the few dirty plates in the dishwasher, Maggie decided to unpack her bags. She located the master bedroom without a problem and gave a sigh of relief when she noticed that Glenn fully intended that she would sleep with him. It was what she wanted, what she had planned, but after their shaky beginning, Maggie hadn't known what to think. A soft smile worked its way across her face, brightening her dark eyes. Glenn longed for their marriage to work as much as she did, she thought. What they both needed to do was quit trying so hard.

When Maggie had finished unpacking, she joined Glenn in the living room. It amazed her how unsettled they were around each other still. Glenn suggested they turn on the last newscast of the evening. Readily, Maggie agreed. She supposed that this time could be thought of as their honeymoon. They were probably the only couple in America to watch television when they could be doing other…things.

After the news, Glenn yawned. Once again Maggie
was reminded that his daily schedule was set with the
routine of his job. Staying awake until two or three in
the morning, watching a late late movie or reading would
only cause problems the following morning. She would
need to adjust her sleeping habits as well, although she
had become a night person these past few years, often
enjoying the peace and tranquility of the early-morning
hours to paint. Glenn didn't live a life of leisure and she
couldn't any longer, either.

Funny, Maggie thought, that the realization that she
must now live according to a clock didn't depress her.
She was willing to get up with him in the morning and
cook his breakfast and even do the dishes. She didn't
know how long this "domesticated" eagerness would
continue, and vowed to take advantage of it while it
lasted. In the morning, she would stand at the front door,
and send him off to the office with a juicy kiss. But from
the frowning look he was giving the television, Maggie had the impression the goodbye kiss in the morning
would be all the kissing she was going to get.

Glenn's thoughts were heavy. Maggie was sitting at
his side and he hadn't so much as put his arm around
her. He felt as though he were stretched out on a rack,
every muscle strained to the limit of his endurance. It
was pure torture to have her so close and not haul her
into his arms and make love to her. If she could read only
half of what was going through his mind, she would run
back to California, he thought dryly. No, he wouldn't
take her that night. He'd bide his time, show her how
empty his life was without her, how much he needed a
woman's tenderness. Then, in time, she would come to

him willingly and desire him, maybe even as keenly as he did her.

"Don't you think we should go to bed? It's after eleven." Maggie broached the subject with all the subtlety of a locomotive. Sitting next to him was torture. They had hardly said two words all night. The thick, unnatural silence made the words all the more profound.

Smoothly rolling to his feet, Glenn nodded. He hadn't noticed that the news was over. For that matter, he couldn't recall the headlines or anything that had been reported. Not even the weather forecast, which he listened for each night. "I imagine you're tired," he finally answered.

"Dead on my feet," she confirmed, walking with him toward the hallway and the master bedroom. *You're wide awake,* her mind accused. She was on Pacific time and it was barely after eight in San Francisco.

Following a leisurely scented bath, Maggie joined him wearing a black nightshirt that buttoned up the front and hit her at midthigh with deep side slits that went halfway up to her hip. The satin top was the most feminine piece of sleepwear Maggie owned. The two top buttons were unfastened and she stretched her hands high above her head in a fake yawn, granting him a full glimpse of her upper thighs.

Glenn was in bed, propped against thick feather pillows, reading a spy thriller. One look at her in the black satin pajama top and the book nearly tumbled from his hands. Tension knotted his stomach and he all but groaned at the sight of his wife. Still wanting her was torture he endured willingly.

The mattress dipped slightly as she lifted back the blankets and slipped into the bed. Glenn set his novel aside and reached for the lamp switch. The room went dark with only the shimmering rays of the distant moon dancing across the far walls.

Neither moved. Only a few inches separated them, but for all the good it did to be sleeping with her husband, Maggie could well have been in San Francisco, she decided.

"Good night, Glenn," Maggie whispered after several stifled moments. If he didn't reach for her soon she'd clobber him over the head. Maybe she should say something to encourage him—let him know her feelings. But what? *Listen, Glenn, I've reconsidered and although I realize that you may still be in love with another woman I've decided it doesn't matter. We're married. I'm your wife....* Disheartened, Maggie realized she couldn't do it. Not so soon, and not in a condominium he probably bought with "her" in mind.

Glenn interrupted Maggie's dark thoughts with a deep, quiet voice. "Good night." With that he rolled onto his side away from her.

Gallantly, she resisted the urge to smash the pillow over the top of his head, pull a blanket from the mattress and storm into the living room to sleep. She didn't know how any man could be so unbelievably dense.

Maggie fell easily into a light, untroubled slumber. Although asleep, lying on her side, her back to him, she was ever conscious of the movements of the man who was sharing the bed. Apparently, Glenn was having more difficulty falling asleep, tossing to one side and then to another, seeking a comfortable position. Once his hand inadvertently fell onto her hip and for a moment he went completely still. Content now, Maggie smiled inwardly and welcomed the calm. Sleeping with him was like being in a rowboat wrestling with a storm at sea.

With unhurried ease the hand that rested against her bare hip climbed upward, stopping at her ribs. Shifting his position, Glenn scooted closer and gathered her into his embrace. As if he couldn't help himself, his hand sought and found a firm breast. His touch was doing insane things to her equilibrium and she was encompassed in a gentle, sweet warmth. Savoring the moment, Maggie bit into her bottom lip as he slowly, tantalizingly, caressed her breasts until she thought she'd moan audibly and give herself away.

Glenn was in agony. He had thought that he would wait and follow all the plans he'd made for courting his wife. But each minute grew more torturous than the one just past. He couldn't sleep; even breathing normally was impossible when she lay just within his grasp. He hadn't meant to touch her, but once his hand lightly grazed her hip he couldn't stop his mind from venturing to rounder, softer curves and the memory of the way her breast had fit perfectly into the palm of his hand. Before he could stop, his fingers sought to explore her ripe body. Maggie remained completely still, waiting patiently for him to roll her onto her back and make love to her. When he didn't move and she suspected that he might not ease the painful longing throbbing within her, she rolled onto her back and linked her arms around his neck.

"Kiss me," she pleaded.

"Maggie." He ground out her name like a man possessed, and hungrily devoured her lips with deep, slow, hot kisses that drove him to the brink of insanity. Groaning, he buried his face in her hair and he drew deep gulps of oxygen into his parched lungs. Again he kissed her, tasting her willingness, reveling in her eagerness. Her hands rumpled the dark thickness of his hair while she repeated his name again and again. Hungry for the taste of him, Maggie urged his mouth to hers, but his devouring kiss only increased her aching need.

"I want you," he groaned, breathing in sharply.

"Yes," she murmured, kissing the hollow of his throat and arching against him.

"Oh, Glenn," Maggie groaned in a harsh whisper. "What took you so long?" The sensation was so blissfully exultant that she felt she could have died from it.

"Took me so long?" he repeated and groaned harshly. "You wanted me to make love to you?"

Looping her arms around his neck, Maggie strained upward and planted a long, hot kiss on his parted mouth. "How can any man be so blind?"

"Next time, hit me over the head." He arched forward then, and buried himself deep within her.

Maggie moaned. "I will. Oh, Glenn, I will," she cried. He took her quickly, unable to bear slow torture. Their bodies fused in a glorious union of heart with soul, of man with woman, of Maggie with Glenn. They strained together, giving, receiving until their hearts beat in a paired tempo that left them breathless, giddy and spent.

Glenn gathered her in his arms and rolled onto his side, taking her with him. Her head rested in the crook of his shoulder, their legs entwined as if reluctant to release the moment.

Maggie felt the pressure of his mouth on her hair and snuggled closer into his embrace, relishing the feel of his strong arms wrapped securely around her.

Brushing a wayward curl from her cheek, Glenn's hand lingered to lightly stroke the side of her face. Maggie smiled gently up at him, the contented smile of a satisfied woman.

"Do you think you'll be able to sleep now?" she teased.

Glenn chuckled, his warm breath fanning her forehead. "Did my tossing and turning keep you awake?"

"Not really…. I was only half-asleep." Maggie lowered her chin and covered her mouth in an attempt to stifle a yawn. "Good night, Mr. Lambert," she whispered, dragging out the words as she swallowed back another yawn.

"Mrs. Lambert," he murmured huskily, kissing the crown of her head.

Maggie's last thought before slipping into an easy slumber was that she wasn't ever going to allow another woman's ghost to come between them again. This man was her husband and she loved him…yes, loved him with a ferocity she was only beginning to understand. Together they were going to make this marriage work. One hundred Angies weren't going to stand in the way of their happiness. Maggie wouldn't allow it.

Within minutes Maggie was asleep. Still awake, Glenn propped up his head with one hand and took delight in peacefully watching the woman who had become everything to him in such a shockingly short amount of time. She was his friend, his lover, his wife, and he had the feeling he had only skimmed the surface of who and what Maggie would be in his life. His finger lightly traced the line of her cheek and the hollow of her throat. As impulsive as their marriage had been, there wasn't a second when Glenn regretted having pledged his life to Maggie. She was fresh and warm, a loving, free spirit. And he adored her. She had come to him with an ardor he had only dreamed of finding in a woman. She was stubborn, impulsive, headstrong: a rare and exquisite jewel. His jewel. His woman. His wife.

The low, melodious sound of a ballad slowly woke Maggie.

"Good morning, Sleeping Beauty," Glenn said as he sat on the edge of the mattress and kissed her lightly. He finished buttoning his shirt and flipped up the collar as he straightened the silk tie around his neck.

"You're dressed," she said, struggling to a sitting position and wiping the sleep from her eyes. She had wanted to get up with him, but must have missed the alarm.

"Would you like to undress me?"

Leaning against the down pillow, Maggie crossed her arms and smiled beguilingly up at him. "What would you do if I said yes?"

Glenn's fingers quit working the silk tie. "Don't tempt me, Maggie, I'm running late already."

"I tempt you?" He'd never said anything more beautiful.

"If only you knew."

"I hope you'll show me." She wrapped her arms around her bent knees and leaned forward. "It...it was wonderful last night." She felt shy talking about their lovemaking, but it was imperative that he realize how much he pleased her.

"Yes it was," he whispered, taking her hand and kissing her knuckles. "I never expected anything so good between us."

"Me neither," she murmured and kissed his hand. "I wish you'd gotten me up earlier."

"Why?" He looked surprised.

Tossing back the covers, Maggie climbed out of bed and slipped into a matching black satin housecoat that she hadn't bothered to put on the night before—for obvious reasons. "I wanted to do the wifely thing and cook your breakfast."

"I haven't got time this morning." He paused, thinking he'd never seen any woman more beautiful. Her tousled hair fell to her shoulders, her face was free of any cosmetics, but no siren had ever been more alluring.

"Is there anything you'd like me to do while you're gone?" she offered. The day stretched before her and they hadn't made plans.

"Yes, in fact there are several things. I'll make a list." He reached for a pad and paper on his nightstand and spent the next few minutes giving her directions and instructions. "And don't plan dinner tonight," he added. "I phoned my parents yesterday and told them I had a surprise and to expect two for dinner."

Maggie sat on the bed beside him and unconsciously her shoulders slouched slightly. This was the very reason she'd come to Charleston, yet she was afraid. "Will they think we've gone crazy?"

"Probably," he returned with a short chuckle. "But they'll be delighted. Don't worry about it; they know you and have always liked you. Mom and Dad will be happy for us."

"I'm happy, Glenn." She wanted to reassure him that she had no regrets in this venture.

The smile faded from his dark eyes and his gaze held her immobile. "I am, too, for the first time since I can remember. We're going to make it, Maggie."

A grandfather clock in the den chimed the hour and reluctantly Glenn stood. "I've got to leave."

"Glenn." Maggie stopped him, then lowered her gaze, almost afraid of what she had to say. Waiting until the last minute to tell him wasn't the smartest thing to do.

"Yes?" he prompted.

"I'm… Listen, I think you should probably know that I'm not using any birth control."

His index finger lifted her chin so that her uncertain gaze met his. "That's fine. I want a family."

A sigh of relief washed through her and she beamed him a brilliant smile. "I probably should warn you, though, my mother claims the Kingsbury clan is a fertile one. We could be starting our family sooner than you expect."

"Don't worry about it; I'm not going to. When a baby comes, you can be assured of a warm welcome."

Maggie experienced an outpouring of love far too powerful to be voiced with simple words. Nodding demanded an incredible effort.

"I'll leave the car keys with you and I'll take public transportation. If you're in the neighborhood around noon stop into the office and I'll introduce you and take you to lunch."

"Maybe tomorrow," she said, stepping onto her tiptoes to kiss him goodbye. There was barely enough time to do everything she had to and be ready for dinner with his parents that evening.

A minute later Glenn was out the door. The condo seemed an empty shell without him. Maggie wandered into the kitchen with her list of errands, then poured a cup of coffee and carried it to the round table. She pulled out a chair and sat, drawing her legs under her.

The first place she needed to stop was the bank to sign the forms that would add her name to the checking account. When she was there, Glenn had asked her to make a deposit for him.

She glanced at the front page of the paper he had left on the table and worked the crossword puzzle, then finished her coffee and dressed. The day held purpose. If she was going to see his parents it might not be a bad idea to find someplace where she could have her hair done.

With a jaunty step, Maggie found the deposit envelope Glenn had mentioned on the top of his desk. The room emanated his essence and she paused to drink it in. As she turned, Maggie caught a glimpse of a frame sticking above the rim of his wastepaper basket. What an unusual thing to do to a picture, she thought. As an artist, her sense of indignation rose until she lifted the frame from out of the basket and saw the multitude of small pictures with faces smiling back at her. Her breath came to an abrupt halt and the room crowded in on her, pressing at her with a strangling sensation. *So this was Angie.*

Seven

The first thought that came to Maggie was how beautiful Angie was. With thick, coffee-dark hair and intense brown eyes that seemed to mirror her soul, Angie had the ethereal look of a woman meant to be cherished, loved and protected. There was an inner glow, a delicate beauty to her that Maggie could never match. Angie was a woman meant to be loved and nurtured. It was little wonder that Glenn loved her. One glance at the woman who claimed his heart told Maggie that by comparison she was a poor second.

The frame contained a series of matted pictures that had obviously been taken over a period of several months. There was Angie on a sailboat, her windblown hair flying behind her as she smiled into the camera; Angie leaning over a barbecue, wearing an apron that said Kiss The Cook; Angie standing, surrounded by floral bouquets, in what looked like a flower shop, with her arms outstretched as though to signal this was hers. And more…so much more. Each picture revealed the rare beauty of the woman who claimed Glenn's heart.

A sickening knot tightened Maggie's stomach and

she placed a hand on her abdomen and slowly released her breath. Although most of the photos were of Angie alone, two of them showed Glenn and Angie together. If recognizing the other woman's inner and outer beauty wasn't devastating enough, then the happiness radiating from Glenn was. Maggie had never seen him more animated. He seemed to glow with love. In all the years Maggie had known Glenn, she had never seen him look more content. He was at peace with his world, and so in love that it shone like a polished badge from every part of him. In comparison, the Glenn who had arrived in San Francisco was a sullen, doleful imitation.

Pushing the hair off her forehead, Maggie leaned against a filing cabinet and briefly closed her eyes. As early as the night before, she'd thought to banish Angie's ghost from their marriage. She had been a fool to believe it would be that easy. With a feeling of dread, she placed the frame back where she'd found it. Building a firm foundation for their marriage wasn't going to be easy, not nearly as easy as she'd thought. But then, nothing worthwhile ever was. Maggie loved her husband. Physically, he wanted her and for now that would suffice. Someday Glenn would look at her with the same glow of happiness that Angie evoked. Someday his love for her would be there for all the world to witness. Someday...

Glancing at her wristwatch, Maggie hurried from the bathroom into the bedroom. In a few hours she and Glenn were having dinner with his parents, Charlotte and Mel, people she'd known and liked all her life. Family friends, former neighbors, good people. Yet Maggie had never been less sure of herself. Already she had changed outfits twice. This one would have to do, she decided. There wasn't time to change her mind again. As she put the finishing touches on her makeup, Maggie muttered disparaging remarks over the sprinkling of freckles across the bridge of her nose; wanted to know why her lashes couldn't be longer and her mouth fuller. Mentally she had reviewed her body: her breasts looked like cantaloupes, her hips like a barge; her legs were too short, her arms too long. Maggie could see every imperfection. Finally she had been forced to admit that no amount of cosmetics was going to make her as lovely as Angie. She had to stop thinking of Charlotte and Mel as the mother- and father-in-law who would compare her to their son's first choice. She had to force herself to remember them instead as the friends she knew they were.

Perhaps if she'd had more time to prepare mentally for this dinner, she thought defensively. As it was, the list of errands had taken most of the day and Maggie had been grateful to have something to occupy her time and her mind. Instead of concentrating on being bright and witty for her meeting with Glenn's parents, her thoughts had returned again and again to the discarded series of photographs. If she had found those photos, she reasoned, then there were probably other pictures around. The realization that Angie could be a silent occupant of the condominium was an intolerable conjecture.

When Glenn had walked in the door that afternoon and kissed her, Maggie had toyed with the idea of confronting him with the pictures. Sanity had returned in the nick of time. He had obviously intended to throw them away, but surely must have realized that she would stumble upon them. Maybe it was cowardly of her, but Maggie had decided to ignore the fact that the pictures were in the other room, and pretended she hadn't seen them. For the first time since their marriage, things were going right and she didn't want to ruin that.

"Maggie, are you ready?" Glenn sauntered into the bedroom and hesitated when he saw her. "I thought you were wearing a blue dress."

"I...was," she answered slowly, turning and squaring her shoulders. "Do I look all right?"

"You're lovely." He placed a hand on each of her shoulders. "Maggie, I wish you'd stop worrying. Mom and Dad are going to be thrilled for us."

"I know." Absently she brushed her hand across the skirt of her black-and-red-print dress and slowly released her breath. "I've always been Muffie to them and I'm... I'm not sure they'll be able to accept me as your wife."

Glenn's chuckle echoed through the bedroom. "Maggie, how can they not accept you? You're my wife. Mother's been after me for years to marry and settle down. She'll be grateful I finally took the plunge."

"That's encouraging," she mumbled sarcastically. "So you were desperate to placate your mother and decided I'd do nicely as a wife. Is that supposed to reassure me?"

The muscles of his face tightened and a frown marred his wide brow as he dropped his hands to his side. "That's not true and you know it."

Ashamed, Maggie lowered her head and nodded. "I'm sorry, I didn't mean that. My stomach feels like a thousand bumblebees have set up camp. Even my hands are clammy." She held them out, palms up, for him to inspect. "Wait until we visit my parents, then you'll know how I feel."

Slipping an arm around her waist, Glenn led her into the living room. "If you're worried, stick to my side and I'll answer all the questions."

"I had no intention of leaving your side," she returned, slightly miffed.

A faint smile touched his mouth.

The ride to Glenn's parents' did little to settle her nerves. Maggie thought she would be glad when this evening was over. When Glenn turned off the main road and into a narrow street lined with family homes, Maggie tensed. Two blocks later he slowed and turned into a cement driveway.

Before Maggie was out of the car the front door opened and Mel and Charlotte Lambert were standing on the wide porch. Maggie was surprised by how little they'd changed. Glenn's father's hair was completely gray now and his hairline had receded, but he stood proud and broad shouldered just as Maggie remembered him. Glenn's mother was a little rounder, and wearing a dress. As a child, Maggie knew she was always welcome at the Lamberts' kitchen. Charlotte had claimed it was a pleasure having another woman around since she lived with a house full of men. Maggie had dropped over regularly when Dale, the youngest Lambert, was born. She had been at the age to appreciate babies and had loved to help feed and bathe him.

"Muffie!" Charlotte exclaimed, her bright eyes shining with genuine pleasure. "What a pleasant surprise. I had no idea you were in town."

Glenn joined Maggie and draped his arm around her shoulders as he boldly met his parents' gaze. To be honest, he had been dreading this confrontation himself. His parents would be pleased for him and Maggie, and do their best to hide their shock. But his father was bound to say something about Angie when they had a private moment. He might even suspect that Glenn had married on the rebound. He hadn't. Glenn tried not to think of Angie and ignored the nip of emotional pain associated with her name. His parents had loved her and encouraged him to marry her. Their disappointment had been keen when he told them she'd married Simon.

"Are you visiting from California?" Charlotte asked with a faint tinge of longing. "I do miss that old neighborhood. If we had a hundred years, we'd never find any better place to raise our family." Taking Maggie by the elbow, she led her into the house. "What's the matter with us, standing on the porch and talking when there's plenty of comfortable chairs inside."

Maggie tossed a pleading glance over her shoulder to Glenn, hoping he wouldn't leave the explaining to her.

The screen door closed with a bang as they entered the house. The small living room managed to hold a recliner, a sofa and an overstuffed chair and ottoman. In addition, a rocking chair sat in one corner. The fireplace mantel was lined with pictures of the three sons and the grandchildren.

"Mom, Dad," Glenn began, his expression sober as he met their curious faces. His arm slipped around Maggie as he stood stiffly at her side. He didn't know any better way to say it than right out. "Maggie is my wife. We've been married nearly two weeks."

"Married? Two weeks?" Charlotte echoed in a stunned whisper.

Mel Lambert recovered quickly and reached across the room to pump Glenn's hand. "Congratulations, son." Cupping Maggie's shoulders he gently kissed her cheek. "Welcome to the family, Muffie."

"Thank you." Her voice was both weak and weary. This was worse than she'd thought. Glenn's mother stood with a hand pressed over her heart and an absurd look of shock written across her face, which she was trying desperately to disguise.

"You two…are married," Charlotte whispered, apparently having recovered. "This is wonderful news. Mel, you open that bottle of wine we've been saving all these years and I'll get the goblets." Within seconds they had both disappeared.

Glenn took Maggie's hand and led her to the sofa where they both sat. "See, I told you it wouldn't be so bad." His hand squeezed hers and his eyes smiled confidently into hers. He smoothed a strand of hair from her temple with his forefinger in a light caress.

"How can you say that?" she hissed under her breath. "Your mother nearly fainted." To further her unease she could hear hushed whispers coming from the kitchen. The barely audible word "rebound" heightened the embarrassed flush in Maggie's red cheeks. She pretended not to hear, as did Glenn.

Glenn's handsome face broke into a scowl. It was a mistake not to have said something to his parents earlier. His better judgment had prompted him to tell them. But he had made such an issue of the necessity of Maggie and him confronting them together that he couldn't very well change plans. Informing his parents of their marriage had been what it took to get Maggie to join him in Charleston, and he would never regret that.

Mel and Charlotte reappeared simultaneously. Charlotte carried four shining crystal goblets on a silver tray and Mel had a wine bottle and corkscrew in one hand.

"Before leaving California," Mel explained as he pulled open the corkscrew, "Charlotte and I took a drive through the Napa Valley and bought some of the finest wines available. That was thirteen years ago now and we only open those bottles on the most special occasions."

"Let me see, the last time we opened our California wine was…" Charlotte paused and a network of fine lines knitted her face as she concentrated.

Glenn tensed and his hand squeezed Maggie's so tightly that she almost yelped at the unexpected pain. Gradually he relaxed his punishing grip, and Maggie realized that the last special occasion in the Lambert family had been shared with Angie and Glenn.

"Wasn't it when Erica was born?" Mel inserted hastily.

"No, no," Charlotte dismissed the suggestion with an impatient wave of her hand. "It was more recent than that… I think it was…" Flustered, she swallowed and reached for a wineglass to hide her discomfort. "I do believe you're right, dear, it was when Erica was born. It just seems more recent is all."

The tension left Glenn, and even Maggie breathed easier. Mel finished opening the bottle and nimbly filled the four goblets. Handing Maggie and Glenn their wineglasses, he proposed a toast. "To many years of genuine wedded happiness."

"Many years," Charlotte echoed.

Later Maggie helped Charlotte set the table, carrying out the serving dishes while Glenn and his father chatted companionably in the living room. At dinner, the announcement that Glenn would be moving to San Francisco was met with a strained moment of disappointment.

"We'll miss you, son," was all that was said.

Unreasonably, Maggie experienced a flood of guilt. It hadn't been her idea to leave Charleston. She would make her home wherever Glenn wished, but apparently he wanted out of South Carolina.

"We'll visit often," Glenn assured his parents and catching Maggie's eye, he winked. "Especially after the children come."

Mel and Charlotte exchanged meaningful glances, making Maggie want to jump up and assure them she wasn't pregnant…at least she didn't think so.

The meal was saved only because everyone felt the need to chat and cover the disconcerting silence. Maggie did her share, catching the Lamberts up on what had been happening with her parents and skimming over Denny's misfortunes, giving them only a brief outline of his life. In return, Charlotte proudly spoke of each of her three grandchildren, and while they cleared the table the older woman proudly brought out snapshots of the grandkids. Maggie examined each small smiling face, realizing for the first time that these little ones were now her nieces and nephew.

While Maggie wiped off the table, Charlotte ran sudsy water into the kitchen sink. "There was a time that I despaired of having a daughter," Charlotte began awkwardly.

"I remember," Maggie responded, recalling all the afternoons she had sat with Mrs. Lambert.

"And now I have three daughters. Each one of my sons have married well. I couldn't be more pleased with the daughters they've given me."

Maggie's hand pushed the rag with unnecessary vigor across the tabletop. "Thank you. I realize our marriage must come as a shock to you, but I want you to know, Mrs. Lambert, I love Glenn and I plan to be a good wife to him."

The dark eyes softened perceptively. "I can see that, Muffie. No woman can look at a man the way you look at Glenn and not love him." Hesitantly, she wiped her wet hands on her apron and turned toward Maggie. Her gaze drifted into the living room and she frowned slightly. "Are you free for lunch tomorrow? I think we should talk."

"Yes, I'd enjoy that."

Maggie didn't tell Glenn of her luncheon arrangement with his mother until the following morning. She woke with him and put on the coffee while he showered. When he joined her in the kitchen, Maggie had fried bacon and eggs, which was about the limit of her breakfast skills. Learning to cook was something she planned to do soon. Rosa, her housekeeper at the beach house, would gladly teach her. Thoughts of California brought back a mental image of her brother, and Maggie sighed expressively. "I'll need the car again today; do you mind?" Maggie asked Glenn, turning her thoughts from the unhappy subject of Denny.

Glenn glanced up from the morning paper. "Do you want to do some shopping?"

"No... I'm meeting your mother for lunch." With a forced air of calm she scooted out the chair across from him. Her hands cupped the coffee mug, absorbing its warmth. She was worried about letting Glenn know she was meeting his mother. "You don't mind, do you... I mean, about me using the car?"

"No." He pushed his half-eaten breakfast aside, darting a concerned look toward Maggie. "I don't mind." Great! he thought vehemently. He could only imagine what his mother was going to tell Maggie. If Maggie heard the details of his relationship with Angie, he'd prefer that they came from him, not his mother.

"Good." Despite his aloofness, Maggie had the impression that he wasn't altogether pleased. He didn't have to be—she was going and she sensed they both knew what would be the main subject of the luncheon conversation.

"Would you like to meet me at the health club afterward?" Glenn asked, but his attention didn't waver from the newspaper. "I try to work out two, sometimes three times a week."

It pleased Maggie that he was including her. "Sure, but let me warn you I'm terrible at handball, average at tennis and a killer on the basketball court."

"I'll reserve a tennis court," Glenn informed her, a smile curling up one side of his mouth. "And don't bother about dinner tonight. We'll eat at the club."

The morning passed quickly. Since she was meeting Glenn later, Maggie dressed casually in white linen slacks and a pink silk blouse, checking her appearance several times. All morning, Maggie avoided going near Glenn's den. She wouldn't torment herself by looking at the pictures again; stumbling upon them once had been more than enough. For all she knew, Glenn could have tossed them out with the garbage, but Maggie hadn't the courage to look, fearing that he hadn't.

Allowing herself extra time in case she got lost, Maggie left early for her luncheon date with Charlotte. She had some difficulty finding the elder Lamberts' home, and regretted not having paid closer attention to the route Glenn had taken the night before. As it turned out, when she pulled into the driveway it was precisely noon, their agreed time.

Charlotte met her at the door and briefly hugged her. "I got to thinking later that I should have met you someplace. You hardly know your way around yet."

"It wasn't any problem," Maggie fibbed, following the older woman into the kitchen. A quiche was cooling on the countertop, filling the room with the delicious smell of egg, cheese and spices.

"Sit down and I'll get you a cup of coffee."

Maggie did as requested, not knowing how to say that she didn't want to be thought of as company. Charlotte took the chair beside her. "The reason I asked you here today is to apologize for the way I behaved last night."

"No, please." Maggie's hand rested on her mother-in-law's forearm. "I understand. Our news must have come as a shock. Glenn and I were wrong not to have told you earlier."

"Yes, I'll admit that keeping it a secret for nearly two weeks was as much of a surprise as the deed." She lifted the delicate china cup to her mouth and took a sip. Glenn had always been close to his family; for him to have married without letting them know immediately was completely out of character. For that matter, their rushed marriage wasn't his style either. Maggie didn't need to be reminded that Glenn was a thorough person who weighed each decision, studied each circumstance. It was one reason he was such an excellent stockbroker.

"You have to understand," Maggie said, wanting to defend him. "We were as surprised as anyone. Glenn arrived for Steve and Janelle's wedding and everything seemed so right between us that we flew to Reno that night."

"The night of the wedding?" Charlotte did a poor job

of hiding her astonishment. "Why, he'd only arrived in San Francisco…"

"Less than twenty-four hours before the wedding." Maggie confirmed her mother-in-law's observation. "And we hadn't seen each other in twelve—thirteen years. It sounds impulsive and foolish, doesn't it?" Maggie wouldn't minimize the circumstances surrounding their marriage.

"Not that… Glenn's never done anything impulsive in his life. He knew exactly what he was doing when he married you, Maggie. Don't ever doubt that."

"I don't. But I know that Glenn was engaged to someone else recently and that he loved her a great deal."

Obviously flustered, Charlotte shook her head, her face reddening. "You don't need to worry any about her."

"I have, though," Maggie confirmed, being frank and honest. "Glenn hasn't told me much."

"He will in time," Charlotte said confidently. The older woman's brow was furrowed with unasked questions, and Maggie nearly laughed aloud at how crazy the situation must sound to someone else. Glenn and Maggie had grown up fighting like brother and sister, had moved apart for more than a decade and on the basis of a few hours they'd decided to get married.

"I think I always knew there was something special between you and Glenn. He wasn't too concerned about girls during high school. Sports and his grades took up the majority of his energy. But he was at ease with you. If there was something troubling him, it wasn't me or his father he discussed it with; instead he talked it over with you. I suppose a few people will be surprised at this sudden marriage, but don't let that bother you. The two of you are perfect together."

"I won't." Maggie swallowed, the words nervously tripping over her tongue. "Neither of us came into this marriage the way normal couples do, but we're both determined to make it work. I'd been hurt, perhaps not as deeply as Glenn, but for the past few years I've been lonely and miserable. Glenn's still…hurting, but I've staked our future together on the conviction that time will heal those wounds."

"I'm pleased he told you about Angie." The look of relief relaxed Charlotte's strong face.

"Only a little. He loved her very much, didn't he?" Just saying the words hurt, but she successfully disguised a grimace.

"I won't deny it. Glenn did love her," Charlotte answered, then added to qualify her statement, "More than she deserved."

Maggie had guessed as much already. When Glenn committed himself to someone or something there would never be any doubts. He had loved her, but by his own words, he had no intention of pining away the rest of his life because she married another man. With their wedding vows, Glenn had pledged himself to Maggie. At moments like these and the one yesterday when she discovered the photos, this knowledge of his determination was the only thing that kept her from drowning in frustration.

"I think I always knew that Angie wasn't the right woman for Glenn. Something in my mother's heart told me things were wrong for them. However, it wasn't my place to intrude in his life. He seemed to love her so much."

This time Maggie was unable to hide the pain of Charlotte's words. She felt the blood drain from her face and lowered her eyes, not wanting her mother-in-law to know how tender her heart was.

"Oh dear, I've said the wrong thing again. Forgive me." Shaking her head as if silently scolding herself, Mrs. Lambert added, "That came out all wrong. He was happy, yes, but that happiness wouldn't have lasted and I suspect that even Glenn knew that." Charlotte stood and brought the quiche to the table along with two place settings.

"No, please continue," Maggie urged, needing to know everything about the situation she had married into.

Seeming to understand Maggie's curiosity, Charlotte rejoined her at the kitchen table. "Glenn cared enough for Angie to wait a year for her to decide she'd marry him. I've never seen Glenn so happy as the night she agreed to be his wife. We'd met Angie, of course, several times. She has the roundest, darkest eyes I've ever seen. She's an intense girl, quiet, a little withdrawn, exceptionally loyal, and although she's hurt Glenn terribly, I'm afraid I can't be angry with her. Ultimately she made the right decision. It would have been wrong for her to have married Glenn when she was in love with another man."

The irony of the situation was more than Maggie could stand. It was wrong for Angie to have married Glenn in those circumstances, yet he had done exactly that when he married her. Apparently, Charlotte didn't see it that way. For that matter, Maggie was convinced that had she known beforehand, she probably would have married him anyway.

"And she never did take the ring," Charlotte finished.

"The ring?"

"My mother's," the older woman explained. "She

willed it to me as part of my inheritance, and when Glenn graduated from college I opted to make it his. It's a lovely thing, antique with several small diamonds, but of course, you've seen it."

Maggie thrust an expectant look at her mother-in-law. "No… I haven't. Glenn's never mentioned any ring."

Charlotte dismissed the information with a light shrug. "I wouldn't worry about it, you'll receive it soon enough. As I recall, Glenn had it sized and cleaned when he and Angie decided…" Realizing her mistake, Charlotte lowered her gaze and fidgeted with her coffee cup. "He's probably having it resized and is keeping it as a surprise for Christmas. As it is I've probably ruined that. I apologize, Maggie."

The racket slammed against the tennis ball with a vengeance and Maggie returned it to Glenn's side of the court with astonishing accuracy. So he had his grandmother's antique ring that was to go to his wife. She was his wife. Where exactly was the ring? *Slam.* She returned the tennis ball a second time, stretching as far as she could reach to make the volley. Not expecting her return, Glenn lost the point.

Maggie's serve. She aced the first shot, making his return impossible. Fueled by her anger, she had never played a better match. The first two games were hers, and Glenn's jaw sagged open as he went into mild shock. He rallied in the third, and their fourth and fifth games were heated contests.

"I don't recall you ever being this good," he shouted from the other side of the court.

She tossed the ball into the air, and fully extending

her body, wielded the racket forward, bending her upper torso in half.

"There are a lot of things you don't know about me, Lambert," she shouted back, dashing to the far end of the court to return the volley. She felt like a pogo stick hopping from one end of the clay surface to the other with a quickness she didn't know she possessed. At the end of the first set, Maggie was so exhausted that she was shaking. Good grief, she thought, she had a tennis court at the beach house that she never used. This match was a misrepresentation of her skill.

Wiping the perspiration from her face with a thick white towel, Maggie sagged onto the bench. Glenn joined her, taking a seat beside her. "You should have told me you were this good. I've never had to work this hard to win."

Her breath came in deep gasps. "That was quite a workout." She hoped he didn't suggest another one soon. A repeat performance of this magnitude was unlikely. The match had helped her vent her frustrations over the issue of his grandmother's ring—her normal game was far less aggressive.

Taking his mother's words at face value, Maggie decided the best thing she could do was patiently wait. Glenn had originally intended the ring would go to Angie, but he'd married Maggie. When he felt comfortable with the idea he'd present her with the ring, not before. Christmas was less than seven weeks away, and Charlotte was probably right. He'd give it to her then.

Maybe.

Regaining his breath, Glenn leaned forward and placed his elbows on his knees. "What did you and my mother have to talk about?" The question wasn't an idle one. His brows were drawn into a single tense line. All afternoon he had worried about that luncheon date. Maggie had a right to know everything, but he didn't want the information coming from his mother. If anyone was going to tell her, it would come best from him. He had thought to call and talk to his mother, and discreetly explain as much, but the morning had been hectic and by the time he was out of the board meeting, it had been too late.

Wickedly, Maggie fluttered her thick, dark lashes. "I imagine you'd love to know what tales she carried, but I'm not breaking any confidences."

"Did she give you her recipe for my favorite dinner?"

"What makes you think we discussed you?" Maggie tilted her flushed face to one side and grinned up at him, her smile growing broader.

"It only seems natural that the two women in my life would talk of little else." He placed his arm around her shoulder and helped her stand, carrying her tennis racket for her.

Maggie placed her arm around his waist, pleased with the way he linked her with his mother. "If your favorite meal is beef Stroganoff, then you're in luck."

"The luckiest day of my life was when you agreed to be my wife," Glenn murmured as he looked down on her with a haunting look so intense that Maggie's heart throbbed painfully. Her visit with his mother hadn't been easy for him, she realized. He had probably spent the entire day worrying about what she'd say afterwards.

Her voice grew husky with emotion. "What an amazing coincidence, that's my favorite day, too."

The longing in his eyes grew all the more poignant as Glenn weighed her words. If they'd been anyplace else,

Maggie was convinced he would have tossed their tennis rackets aside and pulled her into his arms.

"Come on," she chided lovingly. "If you're going to beat me when I've played the best game of my life, then the least you can do is feed me."

Laughing, Glenn kissed the top of her head and led her toward the changing room and then to the restaurant.

His good mood continued when they reached the condominium. Maggie was bushed, and although she had taken a quick shower at Glenn's club, she couldn't resist a leisurely soak in a hot tub to soothe the aching cries of unused muscles. This day had been their best yet. The tension eased from her sore muscles and her heart. The matter with the ring no longer bothered her. When Glenn decided to give it to her, she'd know that it came from his heart and she need never doubt again.

With her hair pinned up, and a terry-cloth bathrobe wrapped around her, Maggie walked into the living room, looking for her husband.

"Glenn."

"In here." His voice came from the den.

Remembering the photographs inside, Maggie paused in the doorway. Tension shot through her, although she struggled to appear outwardly composed. With monumental effort she kept her gaze from the large garbage can beside his desk.

"What are you doing?" She was exhausted and it was late. She'd have thought that after a workout on the courts he'd be ready for bed.

"I've got a few odds and ends to finish up here. I'll only be a few minutes," he answered without looking up, scribbling across the top of a computer sheet. When he did glance up he was surprised to find Maggie standing in the doorway as if she were afraid to come into the room. "I'd appreciate a cup of coffee."

Maggie shrugged. "Sure."

"Maggie." Glenn stopped her. "Is anything wrong?"

"Wrong?" she echoed. "What could possibly be wrong?" *Just that I'm such a coward I can't bear to look and see if those snapshots are still there,* she chastised herself, turning toward the kitchen.

"I don't know." Glenn's puzzled voice followed her.

The coffee only took a minute to make. Maggie stood in the kitchen, waiting for the liquid to drain into the cup and told herself she was behaving like an idiot.

She pasted a smile on her lips as she carried the mug into his den and set it on the edge of the desk. "Here you go."

"Thanks," Glenn murmured, busily working.

Maggie straightened and took a step backward. As she did, her gaze fell to the empty garbage can. Relief washed over her. He had gotten rid of them. She wanted to dance around the room and sing.

"Glenn." She moved behind his chair and slid her arms around his neck.

"Hmm…"

"How late did you say you'd be?" She dipped her head and nuzzled the side of his neck, darting her tongue in and out of his ear.

Glenn could feel the hot blood stirring within him. "Not long, why?"

"Why?" she shot back, giggling. "You need me to tell you why?"

Scooting the chair around, Glenn gripped her by the waist and pulled her into his lap. A brilliant smile came over her as she slid her arms around his neck.

Glenn's mouth twisted wryly as he studied her. He didn't know what had gotten into Maggie today. First she had surprised him on the tennis court. Then she had behaved like a shy virgin outside his door, looking in as if his office was a den of iniquity. And now she was a bewitching temptress who came to him with eyes that were filled with passion. Not that he was complaining, he'd never get enough of this woman.

Maggie's fingers fumbled with the buttons of his shirt so that she had the freedom to run her hands over his chest. She reveled in simply touching him, and pulled the shirt free of his shoulders. His muscles rippled as she slowly slid her hands upward to either side of his neck. Unhurried, she branded him with a kiss so hot it stole his breath.

"Maggie," he whispered hoarsely, intimately sliding his hands between her legs and stroking her bare thigh. "Maybe I haven't got so much paperwork to do after all."

Smiling dreamily, Maggie directed his mouth back to hers. "Good."

Eight

Two weeks passed and Maggie grew more at ease with her marriage. She realized that a silent observer to their world would have assumed that they had been married for several years. Externally, there was nothing to show that their marriage wasn't the product of a long, satisfying courtship. It didn't seem to matter that Glenn hadn't declared his love. He respected her, enjoyed her wit, encouraged her talent. They were happy...and it showed.

Maggie greeted each day with enthusiasm, eager to discover what lay in store for her. She purchased several cookbooks and experimented, putting her creativity to work in the kitchen. Glenn praised her efforts and accepted her failures, often helping her laugh when it would have been easy to lose patience. In the early afternoons, if there was time, Maggie explored Charleston with Glenn's mother and came to appreciate anew what a wonderful woman Charlotte Lambert was. They never spoke of Angie again.

South Carolina was everything Maggie had known it would be, and more than she'd ever expected. She was thrilled by the eighteenth- and nineteenth-century paintings that displayed regional history in the Gibbes Art Gallery and explored the Calhoun Mansion and the Confederate Museum, examining for the first time the Civil War from the Confederate point of view. One hundred and fifty years after the last battles of the war had been waged, Maggie felt the anguish of the South and tasted its defeat.

Her fingers longed to hold a paintbrush, but she satisfied her urgings with a pen and pad, sketching the ideas that came to her. Charlotte was amazed at her daughter-in-law's talent, and Maggie often gave Glenn's mother her pencil sketches. At Sunday dinner with his family, Maggie was embarrassed to find those careless drawings framed and hanging on the living room wall. Proudly, Glenn's eyes had met hers. They didn't often speak of her art, and Maggie basked in the warm glow of his approval.

For his part, Glenn was happy, happier than he ever imagined he'd be. In the afternoons he rushed home from the office, knowing Maggie would be there waiting for him. Maybe he hadn't married her for the right reasons, maybe what they had done was half-crazy, but, he thought tenderly, he wouldn't have it any different now, and he thanked God every single day that he'd acted on the impulse. Maggie gave his life purpose. In the afternoons she would be there waiting. And the minute he walked in the door, she'd smile. Not an ordinary smile, but a soft feminine one that lit up her dark eyes and curved the edges of her mouth in a sultry way that sent hot need coursing through him. In his lifetime, Glenn never hoped to see another woman smile the way Maggie did. Often he barely made it inside the door before he knew he had to kiss her. He would have preferred to react casually to his desire for her, but discovered that was impossible. Some days he couldn't get home fast enough, using every ounce of self-control he possessed not to burst in the door, wrap his arms around her and carry her into their bedroom. He couldn't touch, or taste, or hold her enough. Glenn felt he'd choose death rather than a life without her. Angie might have possessed his heart, but Maggie had laid claim to his soul.

He wondered sometimes if she had even an inkling of what she did to him physically. He doubted it. If she wasn't pregnant soon, he mused, it would be a miracle. The thought of Maggie heavy with his child, her breasts swollen, her stomach protruding, produced such a shocking desire within him that it was almost painful. The feeling left him weak with wonder and pride. They'd have exceptionally beautiful children.

For the first time, Glenn understood his brothers' pride in and awe of their children. At thirty, Glenn hadn't given much thought to a family. Someday, he had always thought, he'd want children, but he hadn't put faces or names to those who would fill his life. With Maggie he envisioned a tall son and a beautiful daughter. Every man wanted an heir, and now he yearned for a son until some nights he couldn't sleep thinking about the children Maggie would give him. On those evenings, late, when his world was at peace, Glenn would press his hand over her satiny smooth stomach, praying her body was nurturing his seed. A child would cement Maggie and him so firmly together that only death would ever separate them.

Their evenings were filled with contentment. Only rarely did he bring work home, lingering instead in front of the television, using that as an excuse to have Maggie at his side, to watch her. If he did need to deal with some paperwork, she sat quietly in his den, curled up in a chair reading. It was as though they couldn't be separated any longer than necessary and every moment apart was painful.

Maggie enjoyed watching Glenn in his home office more than any other place. He sat with simple authority at his desk while she pretended absorption in a novel, when actually she was studying him. Now and then he would look up and they'd exchange warm, lingering glances that left her wondering how long it would be until they could go to bed.

When they did head toward the bedroom, it was ridiculously early. The instant the light went off Glenn reached for her with such passion that she wondered if he would ever get his fill of her—then promptly prayed he wouldn't. Their nights became a celebration for all the words stored in their hearts that had yet to be spoken. Never shy nor embarrassed, Maggie came to him without reserve, holding nothing back. She was his temptress and mistress. Bewitching and bewitched. Seduced and seducer.

Maggie had assumed that the fiery storm of physical satisfaction their bodies gave each other would fade with time, not increase. But as the days passed, she was pleased that Glenn's constant need equaled her desire for him. Each time they made love, Maggie would lie in his arms thinking that their appetite for each other would surely diminish, and knew immediately that it wouldn't.

In the mornings when she woke to the clock radio, Maggie was securely wrapped in Glenn's arms. He held her close and so tight she wondered how she had managed to sleep. Some mornings Maggie felt the tension leave Glenn as he emerged from the last dregs of slumber and realized she remained with him. It was as though he feared she would be gone. Once assured she was at his side, Glenn would relax. As far as Maggie could tell, this insecurity was the only part of his relationship with Angie that continued to haunt him. One hundred times each day, in everything she did, every place she went, Maggie set out to prove she would never willingly leave him.

Life fell into a comfortable pattern and the third full week after Maggie arrived in Charleston, the condominium sold. Maggie met Glenn at the door with the news.

"The Realtor was by with an offer," she said, draping her arms around his neck and pressing her body to his.

Glenn held her hips and placed his large hands on her hips, as he kissed her. "As far as I can see we should be able to make the move within a week, two at the most," he commented a few minutes later, as he curled an arm around her shoulder and deposited his briefcase in the den.

"A week?" Now that she was here, Maggie would have welcomed the opportunity to settle in South Carolina. California, Denny, the beach house seemed a million miles away, light-years from the life she shared with Glenn here.

"You sound like you don't want to move." He leaned against the edge of his desk, crossing his long legs at the ankles.

"South Carolina is lovely."

"So is California," Glenn countered. "You don't mind the change, do you?"

In some ways she did. Their time in Charleston was like a romantic interlude—the honeymoon they'd never gotten. They were protected from the outside world. No one knew who Maggie was, or cared. For the first time in several years she was a regular person and she loved it. In Charleston she had blossomed into a woman who boldly met a passerby's glance. She explored the art galleries without fear that someone would recognize her. No one came to her with "get rich quick" schemes, seeking naive investors. No one rushed to wait on her or gain her attention or her gratitude. However, Maggie was wise enough to know that those things would follow in time.

"No," she told Glenn soberly. "I don't mind the move."

He turned, sorting through the stack of mail she had set on the desktop, smiling wryly. Maggie wanted to stay in Charleston for the same reasons he wanted to move to San Francisco. They were each looking for an escape to problems they would need to face sooner or later. For his part, Glenn chose the West Coast more for nostalgia than any need to escape. San Francisco felt right and Charleston held too many painful memories.

"Will you want to live at the beach house?" Maggie's one concern was that Glenn might not like her home. Her own feelings toward the house were ambivalent. On some days, it was her sanctuary and on others, her prison. She liked the house; she was comfortable there, but she didn't know that Glenn would be.

"Sure. Is there any reason you'd want to move?"

"No, it's just that…" The telephone rang and Maggie paused as Glenn lifted the receiver.

After a moment he handed it to her. "It's for you."

"Me?" She felt her heart rate accelerate. She'd given specific instructions that she wasn't to be contacted except for her brother. And Denny would only call if he was in financial trouble.

"Hello." Her voice was wispy with apprehension.

"Who was that?"

"Denny, are you all right?"

"I asked you a question first. It's not often I call my sister and a man answers the phone. Something's going on. Who is it, Maggie?"

"I'm with Glenn Lambert."

A low chuckle followed, but Maggie couldn't tell if her brother was pleased or abashed. "So you and Glenn are together. Be careful, Maggie, I don't want to see you hurt again." He hesitated, as though he didn't want to continue. "Are you living with him?"

"Denny," Maggie had been foolish not to have told her family sooner, "Glenn and I are married."

"Married," he echoed in shock. "When did this happen?"

"Several weeks ago."

A short, stunned silence followed. "That's sudden, isn't it? Linda and I would have liked to have attended the wedding."

"We eloped."

"That's not like you."

"It wasn't like either of us. I'm happy, Denny, really happy. You know what it's been like the past few years. Now don't worry about me. I'm a big girl. I know what I'm doing."

"I just don't want to see you get hurt."

"I won't," she assured him.

"Do Mom and Dad know?"

Denny had her there. "Not yet. We're planning to tell them once we're back in San Francisco."

"And when will that be?" His words were slow as if he were still thinking.

"A couple of weeks."

He didn't respond and the silence seemed to pound over the great echoing canyon of the telephone wire. Denny hadn't done a good job of disguising his reservations. Once he saw how good this marriage was for her, she was sure, he'd share her happiness. Her brother had been her anchor when she broke up with Dirk. He had seen firsthand the effects of one painful relationship and sought to protect her from another. Only Glenn wasn't Dirk, and when they arrived back in San Francisco Denny would see that.

"Is there a reason you phoned, Denny?"

"Oh, yeah." His voice softened. "Listen, I hate to trouble you but there's been some minor complications and the lawyer has to charge me extra fees. Also, Linda's been sick and the kids aren't feeling that well, either...."

"How much do you need?"

"I hate having to come to my sister like a pauper. But I swear as soon as everything's straightened out I'll repay every penny."

"Denny, don't worry about it. You're my brother, I'm happy to give you whatever you need. You know that." She couldn't refuse her own brother no matter what the reason.

"I know and appreciate it, sis. I really do."

"You wouldn't ask if it wasn't necessary." She had hoped to make this difficult time in Denny's life smoother but sometimes wondered if she contributed more to the problem. Yet she couldn't say no. "I'll have Shirley write you a check."

Once he had gotten what he wanted the conversation ended quickly. Maggie replaced the receiver and forced a smile to her lips. "That was my brother," she announced, turning back to Glenn.

"Who's Shirley?" he asked starkly.

"My money manager." She lowered her gaze to the lush carpet, feeling her husband's censure. Glenn didn't understand the circumstances that had led to Denny's problems. They had both received a large inheritance. Maggie had received half of her great-aunt's fortune; her parents and Denny had split the other half. Everything had gone smoothly until Denny had invested in a business that had quickly gone defunct. Now his money—or what was left of it—was tied up in litigation.

"Does Denny need her name often?"

"Not really," she lied. "He's been having some cash flow problems lately." As in not having any, her mind added. "We were talking about the move to California when the phone buzzed, weren't we?"

"You don't want to discuss Denny, is that it?"

"That's it." Glenn couldn't tell her anything she didn't already know. She was in a no-win situation with her brother. She couldn't abandon him, nor could she continue to feed his dependence on her.

"Okay, if that's the way you want it." His eyes and voice silently accused her as he turned back and sorted through the mail.

"California will be good for us," Maggie said, hoping to lighten the atmosphere.

"Yes, it will," Glenn agreed almost absently, without looking up. "Before I forget, the office is having a farewell party for me Friday night. We don't have any plans, do we?"

Maggie had met Glenn's staff and seen for herself the respect his management had earned him. One afternoon when she had met him for lunch, Maggie had witnessed anew the quiet authority in his voice as he spoke to his associates. He was decisive and sure, calm and reassuring, and the office had thrived under his care. It went without saying that he was a popular manager and would be sorely missed.

Friday night Maggie dressed carefully, choosing a flattering cream-colored creation and pale blue designer nylons. She had never been one to enjoy parties, especially when they involved people she barely knew. This one shouldn't be so bad though, she reasoned. The focus would be on Glenn, not her.

"Am I underdressed?" she asked him, slowly rotating for his inspection. Not having attended this kind of function previously put her at a disadvantage. She didn't know how the other wives would dress and had chosen something conservative.

Glenn stood, straightening his dark blue silk tie. His warm chuckle filled their bedroom as he examined his wife. "As far as I'm concerned you're overdressed. But I'll take care of that later myself." His eyes met hers in the mirror and filled with sweet promise.

After inserting dangly gold earrings into her earlobes, Maggie joined Glenn in the living room. He was pouring them a drink and Maggie watched her husband with renewed respect. He was tall, athletic and unbearably handsome. Her heart swelled with the surge of love that raced through her. She hadn't been looking forward to the party; in fact, she had been dreading it from the moment Glenn had mentioned it. Early on, she had reconciled herself to being a good stockbroker's wife, and that meant that she'd be attending plenty of functions over the years. It would be to her advantage to adapt to them now. Although he hadn't said anything, Maggie was confident Glenn knew she was determined to make the best of this evening.

They arrived precisely at eight at the home of Glenn's regional manager, Gary Weir. Already the living room was filled with smoke, and from the look of things the drinks had been flowing freely. As Glenn and Maggie walked in the front door, spirited cheers of welcome greeted them. Maggie painted a bright smile on her lips as they moved around the room, mingling with the guests. Everyone, it seemed, was in a good mood. Everyone, that is, except Maggie.

She didn't know how to explain her uneasiness. There wasn't anything she could put a name to and she mentally chastised herself. Glenn's friends and associates appeared to be going out of their way to make her feel welcome. Her hostess, Pamela Weir, Gary's wife, was warm and gracious, if a bit reserved. Yet a cold persistence nagged at Maggie that something wasn't right. Glenn stayed at her side, smiling down on her now and then. Once her eyes fell upon two women whispering with their heads close together. They sat on the far side of the room and there wasn't any possibility that Maggie could hear their whispered conversation, but something inside told Maggie they were talking about her. A chill went up her spine and she gripped Glenn's elbow, feeling ridiculous and calling herself every kind of idiot. Lightly, she shook her head, hoping to toss aside those crazy insecurities.

A few minutes later Glenn was pulled into a conversation with some of the men and Maggie was left to her own devices. Seeing Maggie alone, Pamela Weir strolled over.

"It was such a pleasant surprise when Glenn announced he had married," Pamela said.

Maggie took a sip of her wine. Glenn was involved with his friends and moved to another section of the crowded room. "Yes, I imagine it was. But we've known each other nearly all our lives."

"That was what Glenn was saying." Pamela gave her a funny look and then smiled quickly. "For a long time Gary was worried that Glenn wanted the transfer because of a problem at the office."

Maggie forced a smile. "We decided when we married that we'd live in San Francisco," she explained to the tall, elegant woman at her side. "We were both raised there."

"Yes, Glenn explained that too."

Maggie's throat constricted and she made an effort to ease the strange tension she felt. "Although I've only been in Charleston a few weeks, I'm impressed with your city. It's lovely."

Pamela's eyes revealed her pride in Charleston. "We do love it."

"I know Glenn will miss it."

"We'll miss him."

Silence. Maggie could think of nothing more to comment upon. "You have a lovely home," she said and faltered slightly. "Glenn and I both appreciate the trouble you've gone to for this evening."

"It's no bother. Glenn has always been special to the firm. We're just sick to lose him." The delicate hands rotated the stem of the crystal wineglass. "I don't mind telling you that Glenn is the best manager Gary has. In fact—" she paused and gave Maggie a falsely cheerful smile "—Gary had been hoping to move Glenn higher into management. Of course that won't be possible now."

As with his parents, Maggie was again put on the defensive. Leaving Charleston hadn't been her idea and she didn't like being made the scapegoat. Swallowing back a retort, Maggie lowered her gaze and said, "I'm sure Glenn will do just as well in San Francisco."

"We all hope he does," Pamela said with a note of censure.

Glenn's gaze found Maggie several moments later. She stood stiff and uneasy on the other side of the room, holding her drink and talking to Pamela Weir. Even from the other side of the room, he could see that Maggie was upset and he couldn't understand why. He had known from the beginning that she hadn't been looking forward to this party. He wasn't all that fond of this sort of affair himself. But since the party had been given in his honor, he couldn't refuse the invitation. Maggie's attitude troubled him. Earlier in the evening, he'd stayed at her side, but eventually he'd been drawn away for one reason or another. Good grief, he thought, he shouldn't have to babysit her. The longer he watched her actions with Pamela, the more concerned he became. He noticed Maggie wasn't making eye contact with Pamela and when his supervisor's wife moved away, Glenn crossed the room to Maggie's side.

She lifted her gaze to his and Glenn was shocked at the look of anger she sent him.

"What's wrong?" he asked.

She met his gaze with a determined lift to her chin. She was upset, more upset than she'd been since the first morning of their marriage. Glenn had let her walk into the party, knowing the resentment his co-workers felt toward her because he was leaving. "When we arrived tonight I kept feeling these weird vibes that people didn't like me. Now I know why...."

"You're being ridiculous," Glenn muttered, his hand tightening around his drink. "These are my friends and they accept you as my wife."

Glenn was on the defensive and didn't appear willing to listen to her. "You're wrong, Glenn," she murmured. "They don't like me and with good reason. We'll talk about it later."

Glenn said nothing. The sound of someone banging a teaspoon against the side of a glass interrupted their discussion.

"Attention, everyone," Gary Weir called as he came to stand beside Glenn and Maggie. With dull blue eyes that revealed several drinks too many, Gary motioned with his arms that he wanted everyone to gather around.

Maggie felt like a statue with a frozen smile curving her mouth as she watched the party crowding around them. Glenn placed an arm at her neck, but his touch felt cold and impersonal.

Ceremoniously clearing his throat, Gary continued. "As you're all aware, tonight's party is being given in honor of Glenn and his—" he faltered momentarily, and seemed to have forgotten Maggie's name "—bride." A red blush attacked the cheeks of the supervisor and he reached for his drink and took a large swallow.

"As we know," he said, glancing over his shoulder to Glenn and Maggie, "Glenn has recently announced that he's transferring to California." Gary was interrupted with several low boos until he sliced the air, cutting off his associates. "Needless to say, everyone is going to miss him. Glenn has been a positive force within our company. We've all come to appreciate him and it goes without saying that he'll be missed. But being good sports, we want to wish him the best in San Francisco." A polite round of applause followed.

"In addition," Gary went on, his voice gaining volume with each word, "Glenn has taken a wife." He turned and beamed a proud smile at the two of them. "All of us felt that we couldn't send you away without a wedding gift. So we took up a collection and got you this." He turned around and lifted a gaily wrapped gift from behind a chair, holding it out to Glenn and Maggie.

Clearing his throat, Gary finished by saying, "This gift is a token of our appreciation and well wishes. We'd all like to wish Glenn and Angie many years of happiness."

Maggie's eyes widened and she swallowed hard at the unexpectedness of it. An embarrassed hush fell over the room and Maggie felt Glenn stiffen. Not realizing his mistake, Gary flashed a troubled look to his wife who was mouthing Maggie's name.

To cover the awkward moment, Maggie stepped forward and took the gift from Gary's hand. He gave her an apologetic look and fumbled, obviously flustered and embarrassed.

"Glenn and I would like to thank you, Larry."

"Gary," he corrected instantly, some color seeping back into his pale face.

A slow smile grew across Maggie's tight features. "We both seem to be having problems with names tonight, don't we?"

The party loved it, laughing spontaneously at the way she had aptly turned the tables on their superior.

Laughing himself, Gary briefly hugged her and pumped Glenn's hand.

Not until they were on their way home did Glenn comment on the mishap. "Thank you," he said as they headed toward the freeway.

"For what?"

"For the way you handled that." He didn't need to explain what "that" was. Maggie knew. Rarely in his life had Glenn felt such anger. He had wanted to throw Gary against the wall and demand that he apologize to Maggie for embarrassing her that way. Of course, the slip hadn't been intentional, but it hadn't seemed to matter.

Several times in the past few weeks, Glenn had questioned whether he was making the right decision leaving Charleston. Maggie had blossomed here and seemed to genuinely love the city. Now he knew beyond a shadow of a doubt that leaving was best. Angie would haunt their marriage in Charleston. He had been a fool not to realize why Maggie had been so miserable at the party. The thought that his co-workers would confuse her with Angie hadn't crossed his mind. It seemed impossible that only a few months back he had been planning to marry someone else. These days he had trouble picturing Angie and seldom tried. Angie would always hold a special place in his heart. He wished her a long and happy life with Simon. But he had Maggie now, and thanked God for the woman beside him. He might not have courted her the way he should have, the way she deserved, but he desperately needed her in his life.

He loved her. Simply. Profoundly. Utterly. He'd tell her soon. Not tonight though, he thought or she'd think the mistake at the party had prompted the admission. Glenn wanted to choose the time carefully. For several weeks now, he had realized she loved him. Yet she hadn't said anything. He couldn't blame her. Things would straighten themselves out once they were in San Francisco. The sooner they left Charleston the better. In California, Maggie need never worry that someone would bring up Angie's name again.

"Gary's mistake was an honest one. He didn't mean to embarrass anyone." Without a problem, Maggie excused Glenn's friend.

"I know," Glenn murmured, concentrating on his driving.

They didn't talk again until they were home and then only in polite phrases. They undressed in silence and when they lifted the covers and climbed into bed, Glenn gathered her close in his arms, kissing her softly. He was asleep long before she was and rolled away from her. Maggie lay staring at the ceiling, unable to shake what had happened earlier from her mind. The flickering moon shadows seemed to taunt her. All they had been doing for the past few weeks was pretending. The two of them had been so intent on making believe that there had never been another woman in Glenn's life that the incident tonight had nearly devastated them. That was the problem with fantasies—they were so easily shattered. Maggie didn't need to be told that Glenn had been equally disturbed. Angie was present in their lives; she loomed between them like an uninvited guest.

With a heavy heart, Maggie rolled over and tried to sleep, but she couldn't. Not until Glenn's arms found her and he pulled her into the circle of his embrace. But he had been asleep, and for all she knew, Maggie thought bitterly, he could have been dreaming it was "her" he was holding.

Monday morning after Glenn left for work, Maggie sat lingering over a cup of coffee, working the crossword puzzle. The first thing she should do was get dressed, but she had trouble shaking off a feeling of melancholy. No matter how hard she tried, she hadn't been able to forget what had happened Friday night. They hadn't spoken about it again, choosing to ignore it. For now the puzzle filled her time. Her pen ran out of ink and after giving it several hard shakes, she tossed it in the garbage. Glenn kept a dozen or more in his desk.

Standing, Maggie headed toward his office. One thing they had decided over the weekend was that Maggie would fly ahead of Glenn to California. Like a fool Maggie had suggested it on the pretense that she had several items that required her attention waiting for her. She had hoped that Glenn would tell her he wanted them to arrive together. But he had agreed all too readily and she'd been miserable for the remainder of the day.

Pulling open Glenn's drawer, she found what she needed and started to close the desk drawer. As she did it made a light, scraping sound. Her first inclination was to shove it closed. Instead, she carefully pulled the drawer free and discovered an envelope tucked away in the back that had been forced upward when she'd gotten the pen.

It wasn't the normal place for Glenn to keep his mail, and she examined the envelope curiously. The even, smooth flowing strokes of the handwriting attracted her artist's eye. This was a woman's handwriting—Angie's handwriting. Maggie felt the room sway as she sank onto the corner of the swivel chair, her knees giving out. The postmark revealed that the letter had been mailed a week before Steve and Janelle's wedding.

Perspiration broke out across Maggie's upper lip and she placed a hand over her mouth. Her heart hammered so loudly she was sure it rocked the room. The letter must have meant a great deal to Glenn for him to have saved it. Although she hadn't searched through the condominium, she had felt confident that he'd destroyed everything that would remind him of the other woman. Yet the letter remained.

Half of her wanted to stuff it back inside the drawer and pretend she'd never found it. The other half knew that if she didn't know the contents of the letter she would always wonder. Glenn had told her so little. She was his wife. She had a right to know. He should have explained the entire situation long ago and he hadn't, choosing instead to leave her curious and wondering. If she looked, it would be his own fault, she argued with herself. He had driven her to it.

It was wrong; Maggie knew it was wrong, but she couldn't help herself. Slowly, each inch pounding in nails of guilt, she withdrew the scented paper from the envelope.

Nine

Carefully Maggie unfolded the letter and was again struck by the smoothly flowing lines of the even handwriting. Angie's soulful dark eyes flashed in Maggie's memory from the time she'd seen the other woman's photograph. The handwriting matched the woman.

Dear Glenn,
I hope that I am doing the right thing by mailing you this letter. I've hurt you so terribly, and yet I owe you so much. I'm asking that you find it in your heart to forgive me, Glenn. I realize the pain I've caused you must run deep. Knowing that I've hurt you is my only regret.

Glenn, I don't believe that I'll ever be able to adequately thank you for your love. It changed my life and gave Simon back to me. Simon and I were destined to be man and wife. I can find no other way to explain it. I love him, Glenn, and would have always loved him. You and I were foolish to believe I could have forgotten Simon.

My hope is that someday you'll find a woman

who will love you as much as I love Simon. You deserve happiness. Simon and I will never forget you. We both want to thank you for the sacrifice you made for us. Be happy, dear Glenn. Be very happy.

With a heart full of gratitude,

Angie

With trembling hands, Maggie refolded the letter and placed it back inside Glenn's drawer. If she had hoped to satisfy her curiosity regarding Angie, the letter only raised more questions. Angie had mentioned a sacrifice Glenn had made on her behalf. But what? He was like that, noble and sensitive, even self-sacrificing. Angie's marrying Simon clearly had devastated him.

All day the letter troubled Maggie, until she decided that if she were to help Glenn bury the past, she had to understand it. That night she would do the very thing she had promised she wouldn't: she would ask Glenn to tell her about Angie.

No day had ever seemed so long. She didn't leave the house, didn't comb her hair until the afternoon, and when she did, her mirrored reflection revealed troubled, weary eyes and tight, compressed lips. If Glenn could talk this out with her, their chances of happiness would be greatly increased. He had saved the letter, risked her finding it. Although he might not be willing to admit it, he was holding on to Angie, hugging the memory. The time had come to let go.

With her arms cradling her middle, Maggie paced the living room carpet, waiting for Glenn to come home from work. The questions were outlined in her mind. She had no desire to hurt or embarrass him. She wanted him to tell her honestly and freely what had happened with Angie and why he had stepped aside for Angie to marry Simon.

Yet for all her preparedness, when Glenn walked in the door Maggie turned abruptly toward him with wide, apprehensive eyes, her brain numb.

"Hello, Glenn." She managed to greet him calmly and walked across the room to give him a perfunctory kiss. She felt comfortable, but her cheeks and hands were cold. Earlier she had decided not to mention finding the letter, not wanting Glenn to know she had stooped so low as to read it. However, if he asked, she couldn't… wouldn't lie.

His hands found her waist and he paused to study her. "Maggie, what's wrong, you're as cold as an iceberg."

She felt ridiculously close to tears and nibbled at her lower lip before answering. This was far more difficult than she'd thought it would be. "Glenn, we need to talk."

"I can see that. Do you have another rule for our marriage?"

Absently, she rubbed the palms of her hands together. "No."

He followed her into the living room and took a seat while she poured him a glass of wine. "Do you think I'm going to need that?" He didn't know what was troubling Maggie, but he had never seen her quite like this. She looked almost as if she were afraid, which was ludicrous. There was nothing she had to fear from him. He was her husband, and she should always feel comfortable coming to him.

Maybe she was pregnant. His pulse leaped eagerly at the thought. A baby would be wonderful, exciting news.

A feeling of tenderness overcame him. Maggie was carrying his child.

"Maggie," he asked gently, "are you pregnant?"

She whirled around, sloshing some of the wine over the side of the glass, her eyes wide with astonishment. "No, what makes you ask?"

Disappointed, Glenn slowly shook his head. "No reason. Won't you tell me what's troubling you?"

She handed him the drink, but didn't take a seat, knowing she would never be able to sit comfortably in one position. She was too nervous. Hands poised, her body tense, she stood by the window and looked down at the street far below. "I've been waiting to talk to you all day."

He wished she'd get to the point instead of leaving him to speculate what troubled her. He had never seen her this edgy. She resembled a child who had come to her parent to admit a great fault. "If it was so important, why didn't you phone me at the office?"

"I...couldn't. This was something that had to be done in person, Glenn," she said, then swallowed, clenching and unclenching her fists as she ignored the impatience in his eyes. "This isn't easy." She resisted the urge to dry her clammy palms on the pockets of her navy-blue slacks.

"I can see that," he said gently. Whatever it was had clearly caused her a lot of anxiety. Rushing her would do no good, and so he forced himself to relax as much as possible. He crossed his legs and leaned back against the thick cushions of the chair.

"I thought for a long time I'd wait until you were comfortable about this...this subject. Now I feel like a fool, forcing it all out in the open. I wish I were a stronger person, but I'm not. I'm weak." Slowly she turned and hesitantly raised her eyes to his. "Glenn, I'm your wife. Getting married the way we did may have been unconventional, but I have no regrets. None. I'm happy being married to you. But as your wife, I'm asking you to tell me about Angie."

Maggie watched as surprise mingled with frustration and grew across his face.

"Why now?" Angie was the last subject he had expected Maggie to force upon him. As far as he was concerned, his relationship with the other woman was over. He wouldn't deny that he had been hurt, but he had no wish to rip open the wounds of his pride. And that was what had suffered most. Even when he'd known he'd lost her, he had continued to make excuses to see and be with Angie. Something perverse within himself had forced him to go back again and again even when he had recognized that there wasn't any possibility of her marrying him. For weeks he had refused to let go of her even though he'd known he'd lost her and she would never be his.

Now was the opportunity to explain that she'd found the letter, Maggie thought. But she couldn't admit that she'd stooped so low as to read the extremely personal letter. "I…wanted to know.… It's just that…"

"Is it because of what happened the other night?"

Glenn offered her an excuse that Maggie readily accepted. "Yes."

Glenn's mouth tightened, not with impatience, but confused frustration. Maggie should have put it out of her mind, long ago. No good would come from dredging up the past. "Whatever there was between us is over. Angie has nothing to do with you and me."

"But ultimately she does," Maggie countered. "You wouldn't have married me if your engagement hadn't been broken."

"Now you're being ridiculous. We wouldn't have married if I hadn't attended Steve and Janelle's wedding, either."

"You know what I mean."

"Maggie, trust me. There's nothing to discuss." The words were sharp.

Previously when Glenn was angry, Maggie had marveled at his control. He rarely raised his voice, and never at her. Until now. The only evidence she had ever had of his fury was a telltale leap of muscle in his jaw. He moved from his chair to the far side of the room.

"Glenn," she ventured. "I don't understand why you're so reluctant to discuss her. Is it because I've never told you about Dirk? I would have gladly, but you see, you've never asked. If there's anything you want to know, I'll be happy to explain."

"No, I don't care to hear the sorry details of your relationship with another man, and in return I expect the same courtesy."

Her hand on the back of the sofa steadied her. All these weeks, she'd been kidding herself, living in a dreamer's world. As Glenn's wife, she would fill the void left when Angie married Simon, but now she knew she would never be anything more than a substitute. These glorious days in Charleston had been an illusion. She had thought they'd traveled so far and yet they'd only been walking in place, stirring up the roadway dust so that it clouded their vision and their perspective. Oh, she would cook his meals, keep his house and bear his children, and love him until her heart would break. But she would never be anything more than second best.

"All right, Glenn," she murmured, casting her eyes to the carpet. "I'll never mention her name again."

His eyes narrowed as if he didn't believe her. But he had asked her not to, and she wouldn't. She had swallowed her pride, and come to him when he must have known how difficult it had been for her. That meant nothing to him, she realized. It didn't matter what she said or did; Glenn wasn't going to tell her anything.

Purposefully, Maggie moved into the kitchen and started to prepare their evening meal. She was hurt and disillusioned. She realized that Glenn hadn't been angry, not really. The displeasure he had shown had been a re-action to the fact that he'd been unable to deal with his feelings for Angie. But he must, and she prayed he re-alized it soon. Only when he acknowledged his feelings and sorted it out in his troubled mind would he be truly free to love her.

It took Glenn several minutes to analyze his indig-nation. Of all the subjects in the world, the last thing he wanted to discuss was the past. He had handled it badly. Maggie was upset, and he regretted that, but it was nec-essary. The farewell party was responsible for this sud-den curiosity; Maggie had said so herself. He should have realized earlier the repercussions. Glenn made his way to the kitchen and pretended to read the evening paper, all the while studying Maggie as she worked, tearing lettuce leaves for a salad. *Someday soon he'd make it up to her and she'd know how important she was in his life...how much he loved her and needed her.*

In bed that night, the entire Alaska tundra might as well have lain between them. Glenn was on his side of

the bed, his eyes closed, trying to sleep. He had wanted
to make love and reassure Maggie, but she had begged
off. He did his best to disguise his disappointment. Other
than polite conversation, Maggie hadn't said a word to
him all evening. She cooked their dinner, but didn't
bother to eat any of it. For his part, he could hardly
stomach the fresh crab salad, although generally Maggie was a good cook and he enjoyed their meals together.
Cleaning the kitchen afterward seemed to take her hours,
and when she returned to the living room he had guiltily
searched her face for evidence of what she was thinking. For a full ten minutes Glenn was tempted to wake
Maggie and tell her he would answer any questions she
had. Maggie was right. She did deserve to know and it
was only his pride that prevented him from explaining
everything. But she was asleep by then and he decided
to see how things went in the morning. If Maggie was
still troubled, then he'd do as she had asked. But deep
down, Glenn hoped that Maggie would put the subject
out of her mind so they could go on with their lives.

Maggie lay stiffly on her side of the bed, unable to
sleep. That stupid comment about having a headache had
been just that—stupid. Now she longed for the comfort
of Glenn's body and the warmth of his embrace. He had
hurt her, and refusing to make love had been her way
of getting back. But she was the one who suffered with
disappointment. She needed her husband's love more
than ever. Her heart felt as if a block of concrete were
weighing it down.

The more she thought about their conversation, the
more angry she got. She was his wife and yet he with-
held from her an important aspect of his life. Glenn was
denying her his trust. Their marriage was only a thin

shell of what it was meant to be. If Glenn wouldn't tell her about his relationship with Angie, then he left her no option. Maggie decided she would find Angie and ask her what had happened. From the pieces of information she'd gathered, locating the other woman wouldn't be difficult.

In the long, sleepless hours of the night, Maggie mentally debated the pros and cons of such an action. What she might discover could ruin her marriage. Yet what she didn't know was, in essence, doing the same thing. The thought of Glenn making love with the other woman caused such an intense physical pain that it felt as if something were cutting into her heart. Unable to bear it, she tried to blot the picture from her mind, but no matter how she tried, the fuzzy image stayed with her, taunting her.

By the early hours of the morning, Maggie had devised her plan. It worked with surprising ease.

Two days later Charlotte Lambert dropped Maggie off at the airport for a flight scheduled for San Francisco. As Glenn had agreed earlier, Maggie was going to fly ahead and take care of necessary business that awaited her. From the wistful look Glenn gave her that morning when she brought out her suitcases, she realized that he regretted having consented that she return before him. Some of the tension between them had lessened in the two days before the flight. With Maggie's plan had come a release. Glenn wouldn't tell her what she wanted to know, but she'd soon learn on her own.

The Delta 747 left Charleston for San Francisco on time, but Maggie wasn't on the flight. Instead, she boarded a small commuter plane that was scheduled to land in Groves Point. The same afternoon she would take another commuter plane and connect with a flight to Atlanta. If everything went according to schedule, Maggie would arrive in California only four hours later than her original flight.

Groves Point was a charming community. The man at the rental car agency gave her directions into town, and Maggie paused at the city park and looked at the statues of the Civil War heroes. She gazed at the drawn sword of the man standing beside the cannon and knew that if Glenn ever found out what she was doing then her fate would be as sure as the South's was to the North.

The man at the corner service station, wearing greasy coveralls and a friendly smile, gave her directions to Simon Canfield's home. Maggie drove onto the highway past the truck stop, as instructed. She would have missed the turnoff from the highway if she hadn't been watching for it. The tires kicked up gravel as the car wound its way along the curved driveway, and she slowed to a crawl, studying the long, rambling house. Somehow, having Angie live in an ordinary house was incongruous with the mental image Maggie had conjured up. Angie should live in a castle with knights fighting to protect and serve her.

A sleek black dog was alert and barking from the front step and Maggie hesitated before getting out of the car. She wasn't fond of angry dogs, but she'd come too far to be put off by a loud bark. Cautiously she opened the car door and stepped out, pressing her back against the side of the compact vehicle as she inched forward.

"Prince. Quiet." The dark-haired woman wearing a maternity top opened the back door and stepped onto the porch.

Instantly the dog went silent and Maggie's gaze riveted to the woman. Maggie stood, stunned. The photos hadn't done Angie's beauty justice. No woman had the right to look that radiant, lovely and serene. Angie was everything Glenn's silence had implied—and more. Her face glowed with her happiness, although she wasn't smiling now, but was regarding Maggie curiously. Maggie had been prepared to feel antagonistic toward her, and was shocked to realize that disliking the woman would be impossible.

"Can I help you?" Angie called from the top step, holding the dog by the collar.

All Maggie's energy went toward moving her head in a simple nod. Angie's voice was soft and lilting with an engaging Southern drawl.

"Bob phoned and said a woman had stopped in and asked directions to the house."

Apparently Bob was the man at the gas station. Putting on a plastic smile, Maggie took a step forward. "I'm Maggie Lambert."

"Are you related to Glenn?"

Again it was all Maggie could do to nod.

"I didn't know Glenn had any sisters."

Forcing herself to maintain an air of calm, Maggie met the gentle gaze of the woman whom Glenn had loved so fiercely. "He doesn't. I'm his wife."

If Angie was surprised she did an admirable job of not showing it. "Please, won't you come inside."

After traveling so far, devising the plan behind her husband's back and, worse, following through with it— Maggie stood cemented to the spot. After all that, without allowing anything to dissuade her from her idea, she was suddenly amazed at the audacity of her actions. Wild uncertainty, fear and unhappiness all collided into each other in her bemused mind until she was unable to move, struck by one thought: *it was wrong for her to have come here.*

"Maggie?" Angie moved down the steps with the dog loyally traipsing behind. "Are you all right?"

Maggie tasted regret at the gentleness in Angie's eyes. No wonder Glenn loved her so much, she thought. This wasn't a mere woman. Maggie hadn't known what to expect, but it hadn't been this. Angie was the type of woman a man yearned to love and protect. More disturbing to Maggie was the innate knowledge that Angie's inner beauty far surpassed any outer loveliness. And she was gorgeous. Not in the way the fashion models portrayed beauty, with sleek bodies and gaudy cosmetics. Angie was soft and gentle and sweet—a madonna. All of this flashed through Maggie's mind in the brief moment it took for Angie to reach her.

"Are you feeling ill?" Angie asked, placing a hand on Maggie's shoulder.

"I... I don't think so."

"Here," she said softly, leading her toward the house. "Come inside and I'll give you a glass of water. You look as if you're about to faint."

Maggie felt that a strong gust of wind would have blown her over. Mechanically, she allowed Angie to direct her through the back door and into the kitchen. Angie pulled out a chair at the table and Maggie sank into it, feeling more wretched than she had ever felt in her life. Tears were perilously close and she shut her eyes in an effort to forestall them. Maggie could hear Angie scurrying around for a glass of water.

She brought it to the table and sat across from Maggie. "Should I call the doctor? You're so pale."

"No, I… I'm fine. I apologize for putting you to all this trouble." Her wavering voice gained stability as she opened her dry eyes.

A few awkward seconds passed before Angie spoke. "I'm pleased that Glenn married. He's a good man."

Maggie nodded. Everything she had wanted to say had been set in her mind, but all her well-thought-out questions had vanished.

"How long have you been married?" Angie broached the subject carefully.

"Five weeks." Holding the water glass gave Maggie something to do with her hands.

"Glenn must have told you about me?"

"No." Maggie took a sip of water. The cool liquid helped relieve the parched feeling in her throat. "He won't talk about you. He's married to me, but he's still in love with you."

A sad smile touched the expressive dark eyes as Angie straightened in the chair. "How well do you know Glenn?"

"We grew up together," Maggie said. "I… I thought I knew him, but I realize now that I don't."

"Do you love him?" Angie asked, then offered Maggie a faint smile of apology. "Forgive me for even asking. You must. Otherwise you wouldn't be here."

"Yes, I love him." Words felt inadequate to express her feelings for her husband. "But that love is hurting me because I don't know how to help him forget you. He won't talk about what happened."

"Of course he wouldn't," Angie said with a sweet, melodic laugh. "His pride's at stake and as I recall, Glenn is a proud man."

"Very."

The dark eyes twinkled with encouragement. "First, let me assure you that Glenn isn't in love with me."

Maggie opened her mouth to contradict her, but Angie cut her off by shaking her head.

"He isn't, not really," Angie continued. "Oh, he may think he is, but I sincerely doubt that. For one thing, Glenn would never marry a woman without loving her. He holds his vows too sacred. He could have married me a hundred times after I first saw Simon again, but he wouldn't. Glenn was wise enough to recognize that if we did marry I would always wonder about Simon. Glenn's a gambler, and he gambled on my love. At the time I don't think I realized what it must have cost him to give me the freedom to choose between the two of them."

"You mean you would have married Glenn?"

"At the drop of a hat," Angie assured her. "Glenn Lambert was the best thing to come into my life for twelve years and I knew it. I cared deeply for him, too, but that wasn't good enough for Glenn. He wanted me to settle my past, and heal all the old wounds before we made a life together. It was Glenn who led me by the hand back to the most difficult days of my life. Glenn's love gave me back Simon and I'll always be grateful to him for that. Both Simon and I will. We realize how dearly it cost Glenn to step aside so I could marry Simon."

Maggie grimaced at Angie's affirmation of love for Glenn and briefly closed her eyes to the pain. So this was the sacrifice Angie had mentioned in the letter.

"Knowing this, Maggie, you couldn't possibly believe that Glenn would take his vows lightly."

She made it all sound so reasonable and sure, Maggie thought uncertainly. "But…but if he was so strongly convinced that you should settle your past, then why is he leaving his own open like a festering wound?"

"Pride." There wasn't even a trace of hesitation in Angie's voice. "I doubt that Glenn continues to have any deep feelings for me. What happened between us is a painful time in his life he'd prefer to forget. Be patient with him."

Maggie realized that she had rammed heads with Glenn's pride when she'd asked him to tell her about Angie. His indomitable spirit had been challenged, and admitting any part of his pain to her went against the grain of his personality. Logically, knowing Glenn, it made sense.

"Glenn deserves a woman who will give him all the love he craves," Angie continued. "I could never have loved him like that. But he's found what he needs in you. Be good to him, Maggie, he needs you."

They talked nonstop for two hours, sometimes laughing, other times crying. Angie told Maggie of her own love story with Simon and their hopes and dreams for the child she carried. When it came time for Maggie to leave, Angie followed her to the airport and hugged her before she boarded her flight.

"You're a special lady, Maggie Lambert," Angie stated with conviction. "I'm confident Glenn realizes that. If he doesn't, then he's not the same man I remember."

Impulsively Maggie hugged Angie back. "I'll write once we've settled. Let me know when you have the baby."

"I will. Take care now, you hear?"

"Thank you, Angie, thank you so much. For everything."

Maggie's throat filled with emotion. There were so many things she wanted to say. Glenn had given Angie her Simon, and in return Maggie now had Glenn. She could leave now and there would no longer be any doubts to plague her. Angie would always be someone special in Glenn's life, and Maggie wouldn't begrudge him that. She would leave him with his memories intact, and never mention her name. Angie was no longer a threat to their happiness. Maggie understood the past and was content to leave it undisturbed.

The flight from Groves Point to Atlanta and the connection from Atlanta to San Francisco went surprisingly well. Although before Maggie would have worried that each mile took her farther from Glenn, she didn't view the trip in those terms anymore. She was in love with her husband and the minute she touched down in San Francisco she planned to let him know her feelings.

A smile beamed from her contented face when she landed in the city of her birth. She took a taxi directly to the beach house, set her bags in the entryway and headed for the kitchen and the phone. She had to talk to Glenn; she burned with the need to tell him of her love. In some ways she was concerned. There was a better time and place, but she couldn't wait a second more.

His phone rang and she glanced at the clock. With the time difference between the East and the West Coast it was well after midnight in Charleston. Discouraged, she fingered the opening of her silk blouse, wondering if she should hang up and wait until morning.

Glenn answered on the second ring. "Maggie?" The anger in his voice was like a bucket of cold water dumped over her head, sobering her instantly. Somehow, he had found out that she'd gone to Groves Point and talked to Angie.

"Yes," she returned meekly.

"Where the hell have you been? I've been half out of my mind worrying about you. Your flight landed four hours ago. Why did you have to wait so long to call me? You must have known I was waiting to hear from you." The anger in his voice had lessened, diluted with relief from his worries.

Maggie sagged with relief onto the bar stool positioned by the phone. He didn't know. "To be honest, I wasn't sure if you wanted me to phone or not."

"Not phone?" He sounded shocked. "All I can say is that it's a good thing you did." His voice grew loud and slightly husky. "It's like a tomb around here without you."

Maggie tried to suppress the happiness that made her want to laugh. *He missed her.* He was miserable without her and she hadn't even been away twenty-four hours.

"Whose idea was it for you to leave early anyway?"

"Mine," she admitted ruefully. "But who agreed, and said I should?"

"A fool, that's who. Believe me, it won't happen again. We belong together, Maggie." He made the concession willingly.

From the moment she had left that morning, he'd been filled with regrets. He should never have let her go, he had realized. He'd tried phoning an hour after her plane touched ground in California. At first it didn't bother him that she didn't answer her cell and when he tried the house, she didn't pick up there either. He figured she'd probably gone to Denny's, Glenn assured himself earlier. Later, when he hadn't been able to get hold of her, Glenn assumed she had unplugged the phone and taken a nap. After a time his worry had grown to alarm, and from alarm to near panic. If she hadn't called him when she did—he hadn't been teasing—he would well have gone stir crazy. His feelings were unreasonable, Glenn knew that. His reaction was probably part of his lingering fear that he'd lose Maggie, he rationalized. But there was no denying it: the past few hours had been miserable.

Glenn said they belonged together with such meaning that it took a moment before Maggie could speak. "Glenn," she finally whispered, surprised at how low her voice dropped. "There's something you should know, something I should have told you long before now."

"Yes?" His voice didn't sound any more confident than her own.

"I love you, Glenn. I don't know when it happened, I can't put a time to it. But it's true. It probably embarrasses you to have me tell you like this, there are better times and places—"

"Maggie." He interrupted her with a gentle laugh. "You don't need to tell me that, I already know."

"You know?" All these weeks she'd kept her emotions bottled up inside, afraid to reveal how she felt—and he'd known!

"Maggie, it was all too obvious. You're an artist, remember? You don't do a good job of hiding your emotions."

"I see." She swallowed down the bitter disappointment. Although eager to tell him of her feelings, she had wondered how he'd react. In her mind she had pictured a wildly romantic scene in which he'd tenderly admit his own feelings. Instead, Glenn acted as if she were discussing the weather.

"Well, listen, it's late here, I think I'll go to bed." She tried to make her voice light and airy, but a soft sob escaped and she bit into her lower lip to hold back another.

"Maggie, what's wrong?"

"Nothing. I'll talk to you tomorrow. Maybe. There's lots to do and—"

"Maggie, stop. You're crying. You never cry. I want to know why. What did I say?"

The insensitive boor, she silently fumed, if he couldn't figure it out, she wasn't going to tell him. "Nothing," she choked out in reply. "It doesn't matter. Okay?"

"No, it's not all right. Tell me what's wrong."

Maggie pretended she didn't hear. "I'll phone tomorrow night."

"Maggie," he shouted. "Either you tell me what's wrong or I'm going to become violent."

"Nothing's wrong." Her heart was breaking. She'd just told her husband she loved him for the first time, and he'd practically yawned in her face.

"Listen, we're both tired. I'll talk to you tomorrow," she finished. Before he could argue, she gently replaced the receiver. The phone rang again almost immediately and Maggie simply unplugged it, refusing to talk to Glenn again that night. For a full five minutes she didn't move. She had left Atlanta with such high expectations, confident that she could create a wonderful life with Glenn. There was enough love in her heart to build any bridge necessary in their marriage. A half hour after landing in San Francisco, she was miserable and in tears. Maggie slept late, waking around eleven the next morning. She felt restless and desolate. Early that afternoon, she forced herself to dress and deal with her mail. By evening her desk was cleared and she phoned

Denny. She was half-tempted to paint, but realized it would be useless with her mind in turmoil. Glenn would be furious with her for disconnecting the phone, and she had yet to deal with him. He might not have appreciated her actions, but it was better than saying things she was sure to regret later.

By early evening she had worked up her courage enough to dial his number. When he didn't answer she wasn't concerned. He was probably at the health club, she thought. An hour later she tried phoning again. By ten, Pacific Coast time, she was feeling discouraged. Where was he? She toyed with the idea of phoning his family and casually inquiring, but she didn't want to alarm them.

A noise in the front of the house alerted her to the fact that someone was at the door. She left her office and was halfway into the living room when she discovered Glenn standing in the entryway, setting his suitcases on the floor.

He straightened just in time to see her. Time went still as he covered the short space between them and reached for her, crushing her in his arms. "You crazy fool. If you'd given me half a chance I would have told you how much I love you."

"You love me?"

"Yes," he whispered into her hair.

With a smothered moan of delight, Maggie twined her arms around his neck and was lifted off the floor as his mouth came down hungrily on hers.

Ten

"Why didn't you say something earlier?" Maggie cried and covered Glenn's face with eager kisses, locking her arms around his neck.

"Why didn't you?" She was lifted half off the ground so that their gazes were level, his arms wrapped around her waist.

Maggie could hardly believe he was with her and stared at him in silent wonder, still afraid it could all be part of some fanciful dream. She couldn't very well admit that it had been her conversation with Angie that had convinced her that Glenn needed to know what was in her heart. The time had come to quit playing games with each other. The shock had come when he'd already known how she felt. Well, what did she expect? She'd never been good at disguising her feelings and something as important as love shouldn't be concealed.

"I take it you're pleased to see me?"

Happiness sparkled from her eyes as she raised her hands and lovingly traced the contours of his face. "Very."

His hold on her tightened. He hadn't slept in thirty

hours. The first ten of those hours had been spent in complete frustration. He had tried countless times to get her to answer her cell until he realized she must have turned it off. The only thing that made sense was that she'd turned it off for the flight and then forgot to turn it back on, which was why he'd tried the house countless times. He needed to talk to her; to explain his reaction to her confession of loving him. It wasn't a surprise. He'd known almost from the first even if she hadn't verbalized her feelings. He'd been at a total loss to understand why she'd resorted to tears. He relived every word of their conversation and as far as he could see she was behaving like a lunatic. She announced she loved him and immediately shocked him by breaking into sobs. Maggie wasn't a crier. Several times in the first weeks of their marriage he would have expected a lot more than tears from her. He'd certainly given her enough reason. But Maggie had proudly held up her head unwilling to relinquish a whit of her pride. With startling clarity it had come to him in the early-morning hours. Maggie had expected him to declare his own love. What an idiot he'd been. Of course he loved her. He didn't know why she could ever question it. He had realized he felt something profound for Maggie the minute she had walked down the aisle at Steve and Janelle's wedding. She'd been vulnerable, proud and so lovely that Glenn went weak with the memory. He had originally assumed that his friends' wedding followed the lowest point of his life, but one look at Maggie and he'd nearly been blown over. She'd lived next door to him for most of his life and he'd blithely gone on his way not recognizing what was before his own eyes. Maggie shared his name and his devotion and, God willing, later she would bear his children. How could she possibly think he didn't love her? Just as amazing was the knowledge that he'd never told her. Glenn was astonished at his own stupidity. He would phone her as soon as she would talk to him, he had decided, and never again in her life would he give her reason to doubt.

In theory, Glenn felt, his plan sounded reasonable, but as the hours fled, and a rosy dawn dappled the horizon, he began to worry. In her frame of mind, Maggie might consider doing something stupid.

The first thing the following morning, Glenn decided not to jeopardize his marriage more than he had already. He would fly to Maggie on the first plane he could catch. When he tried phoning several times, and there wasn't any answer, he fretted all the more. For caring as much as he did he'd done a good job of messing things up.

Now that he was looking at her face flushed with a brilliant happiness, Glenn realized he'd done the right thing.

"Do you have to go back?"

"I probably should, but I won't." Her smile was solidly in place, he noticed. He adored that smile. "I don't deserve you, Maggie."

"I know."

Tipping back her head, she laughed and his heart was warmed by the sound. Maggie made his heart sing. Being around her was like lying on the sunny beach on a glorious day and soaking up energy. She was all warmth and vitality, both springtime and Christmas, and he couldn't imagine his life without her. Twisting her around in his embrace, he supported her with an arm under her legs and carried her down the long hall that led to the master bedroom.

"My dear Mr. Lambert, just where are you taking me?"

"Can't you guess?"

"Oh, yes," she said and her lips brushed his, enjoying the instant reaction she felt from him when her tongue made lazy, wet circles outlining his mouth.

"Maggie," he groaned. "You're going to pay for that."

"I'm looking forward to it. Very forward."

She couldn't undress fast enough. When Maggie's fingers fumbled with the buttons of her blouse in her eagerness, Glenn stopped her, placing her hand aside. Slowly, provocatively, he unfastened each one. As the new area of her skin was exposed, Glenn's finger lovingly trailed the perfection until he finally slipped the smooth material of her blouse from her shoulders and down her arms, letting it fall to the carpet. Maggie felt an exhilarating sense of power at the awe reflected in her husband's eyes. Impatience played no role in their lovemaking. Glenn had taught her the importance of self-control. The excruciating wait seemed only to enhance their pleasure; the disciplined pauses heightened their eagerness. Maggie was a willing pupil.

As if he couldn't deny himself a second longer, Glenn wrapped her in his arms and in one sweeping motion buried his mouth over hers.

What had begun with impatient eagerness slowed to a breathless anticipation. When they moved, it was with one accord. They broke apart and finished undressing, then lay together on the thick, soft quilt.

"I love you," she whispered, raising her arms up to bring him to herself. "Please love me," she cried, surprised to hear her own voice.

"I do," Glenn breathed. "Always."

Afterwards, blissfully content, Maggie spread eager

kisses over his face. Briefly she wondered if this exhilaration, this heartfelt elation would always stay with them. She wondered if twenty years from now she would still experience a thrill when Glenn made love to her. Somehow, Maggie doubted that this aspect of their marriage would ever change.

Glenn shifted positions so that Maggie was lovingly cradled in his arms and his fingers lightly stroked the length of her arm. Her fingers played at his chest, curling the fine dark hairs that were abundant there. A feeling of overpowering tenderness rocked him. He reveled in the emotion of loving and being loved, and knew what they shared would last forever. He was tired, more than tired—exhausted. He looked down and discovered Maggie asleep in his arms. Everything was going to work out, he thought sleepily. He wasn't going to lose her.... Slowly, his eyes drifted closed....

Maggie was his.

The following morning Maggie woke and studied her husband as he slept. A trace of a smile curved his mouth and her heart thrilled with the knowledge that she had placed it there. He must have been worried, terribly worried, she thought, to have dropped everything and flown to her. Surely, he couldn't believe that she'd ever leave him. A woman didn't love as strongly as she did and surrender without doing battle. Glenn's arrival had proved that Angie was right.... Glenn took his vows far too seriously to have married her or anyone when he was in love with another woman. Maggie didn't know what Glenn felt for the other woman anymore, but it wasn't love. Utterly content, she silently slipped from the bed and dressed, eager for the new day.

Glenn woke with a smile as Maggie's lips brushed his in a feather-light kiss. "Morning," he whispered, reaching up to wrap his arms around her waist.

"Morning," she returned brightly. "I wondered how long it'd take for you to join the living."

Glenn eased upright, using his elbow for support. "What time is it?"

"Noon."

"Noon!" he cried, rubbing the sleep from his face as he came fully upright. "Good grief, why didn't you wake me?"

Giggling, Maggie sat on the edge of the mattress and looped her arms around his strong neck. "I just did."

"You've been painting," he said, noticing that Maggie was in her smock.

"It felt good to get back to it. Charleston was wonderful, but it's great to be home and back into my regular schedule."

A light knock against the bedroom door attracted Maggie's attention. "Phone for you, Maggie," Rosa, the older Hispanic woman who was Maggie's housekeeper and cook, announced from the other side. "It's your brother."

"Tell him I'll be right there," Maggie said, and planted a tender kiss on Glenn's forehead. "Unfortunately, duty calls."

"Maggie." Glenn's hand reached for her wrist, stopping her. His eyes were questioning her as though he didn't like the idea of releasing her even to her own brother. "Never mind."

"I shouldn't be more than a few minutes. Do you want to wait for me here?"

He shook his head, already tossing aside the blankets

as he climbed from the bed. "I'll be out of the shower by the time you've finished."

True to his word, Glenn leaned his hip against the kitchen counter, sipping coffee and chatting easily to Rosa when Maggie reappeared.

"I see that you two have introduced yourselves," Maggie said, sliding her arms around Glenn's waist.

"Si," Rosa said with a nod, her dark eyes gleaming. "You marry good man. You have lots of healthy *muchachos*."

Maggie agreed with a broad grin, turning her eyes to her husband. "Rosa is going to teach me to cook, isn't that right?"

"Si. Every wife needs to know how to make her man happy," Rosa insisted as she went about cleaning the kitchen. "I teach Maggie everything about cooking."

"Not quite everything," Glenn whispered near Maggie's ear, mussing the tiny curls that grew at her temple. "In fact you wouldn't even need to go near a kitchen to keep me happy."

"Glenn," she whispered, hiding a giggle. "Quiet, or Rosa will wonder."

"Let her." His hold tightened as the housekeeper proceeded to chatter happily in a mixture of Spanish and English, scrubbing down already spotless counters as she spoke.

The lazy November day was marvelous. They took a dip in the heated pool and splashed and dunked each other like feisty teenagers at a beach party. Later, as they dried out in the sauna, Glenn carefully broached the subject of Maggie's brother.

"Was that Denny this morning?"

"Yes. He and Linda have invited us to Thanksgiving dinner. I didn't think you'd mind if I accepted."

"That'll be fine. How's Denny doing?"

Maggie wiped a thick layer of perspiration from her cheeks using both hands, biding time while she formed her thoughts. "Fine. What makes you ask?"

"He seems to call often enough. Didn't you get a couple of calls from him when we were in Charleston?"

"Yes. He's been through some rough times lately."

"How rough?"

Wrapping the towel around her neck, Maggie stood and paced the small enclosure while the heavy heat pounded in around her. "As you probably know, Denny and my parents inherited a portion of Great-aunt Margaret's money. Denny made some bad investment choices."

"What happened?" As a stockbroker, Glenn felt his curiosity piqued.

"It's a long, involved story not worth repeating. Simply put, Denny invested heavily in what he felt would be a good investment, trusting friends he shouldn't have trusted and lost everything. The case is being decided in the courts now, but it looks like he'll only get a dime back on every dollar invested."

"So you're bailing him out?" The statement was loaded with censure.

Maggie had to bite her tongue to keep from lashing out at Glenn for being so insensitive. He should know that litigation and lawyers were expensive. She was only doing what any sister would do in similar circumstances. "Listen, what's between my brother and me is private. You don't want to talk about certain things in your life, and I don't, either. We're both entitled to that."

"Don't you think you're being overly defensive?"

Maggie looked at him sharply. "So what? Denny's my brother. I'll give him money any time I please."

Glenn was taken back by her bluntness. "Fine." He wouldn't bring up the subject again…at least not for a while.

Thanksgiving arrived and Maggie's parents flew out from Florida. The elder Kingsburys had reacted with the same pleased surprise as Glenn's family had when Maggie phoned to announce that she and Glenn had married. The gathering at Denny and Linda's was a spirited but happy one. Neither of Maggie's parents mentioned how brief her and Glenn's courtship had been, nor that they were shocked at the suddenness of the ceremony. The questions were in their eyes, but Maggie was so radiantly happy that no one voiced any doubts.

The traditional turkey was placed in the oven to be ready to serve at the end of the San Francisco 49ers football game. They ate until they were stuffed, played cards, ate again and watched an old movie on television until Maggie yawned and Glenn suggested they head home. The day had been wonderful and Maggie looked forward to Christmas for the first time since moving to the beach house.

Glenn's days were filled. He started work at Lindsey & McNaught Brokerage the Monday after his arrival in San Francisco, and continued to work long hours to build up his clientele. More often than not, it was well past seven before he arrived home. Maggie didn't mind the hours Glenn put in away from home. She understood his need to secure his position with the company branch. The competition was stiff and as a new boy on the block, the odds were against him.

"How are things going at the office?" she asked him one evening the first week of December.

"Fine," he responded absently as he sorted through the mail. "How about a game of tennis? I need to work out some of my frustrations."

"Everything's fine at the office, but you want to use me as a whipping boy?" she joked lovingly.

Glenn raised his gaze to hers and met the teasing glimmer mingled with truth in her eyes.

"Are you sorry we're here?" she asked on a tentative note. In Charleston, Glenn had held more than a hundred million dollars in assets for his firm, a figure that was impressive enough for him to have quickly worked his way into a managerial position. In San Francisco, he was struggling to get his name out and establish himself with new clients. Some of his previous ones had opted to stay with him but others had decided to remain with the same brokerage. From the hours he was putting in during the day and several long evenings, the task must be a formidable one.

"I'm not the least bit sorry we're living in San Francisco," he said. "Where you and I are concerned, I have no regrets. Now," he added, releasing a slow breath, "are we going to play tennis or stand here and chat?"

Just as he finished speaking the telephone rang. "Saved by the bell," Maggie mumbled as she moved across the room to answer it. "Hello."

"Hi, Maggie," Denny said in the low, almost whiny voice she had come to know well.

"Hi. What's up?" She didn't want to encourage Denny to drag out the conversation when Glenn was in the room. Denny was a subject they avoided. She knew her husband disapproved of her handing over large sums of money to her brother, but she didn't know what else she could do—Denny needed her. The money wasn't doing her any good, and if she could help her only brother, then why not?

The argument was one Maggie had waged with herself countless times. As long as she was available to lean upon, the opposing argument went, then Denny would be content to do exactly that. He hadn't accomplished anything worthwhile in months. From conversations with her sister-in-law, Linda, Maggie had learned that Denny did little except decry his misfortune and plot ways of regaining his losses. Maggie could understand his circumstances well enough to realize he was in an impossible position. He didn't like it, she didn't like it, but there was nothing that either of them could do until the court case was settled.

"I just wanted you to know that I'll be meeting with the lawyers tomorrow afternoon."

"Good luck," she murmured.

A silence followed. "What's the matter? Can't you talk now?"

"That about sizes up the situation." Glenn was studying her and Maggie realized her stalling tactics weren't fooling him. He knew exactly whom she was talking to and did nothing to make the conversation any easier by leaving the room.

"Maybe I should phone you tomorrow," Denny suggested.

"That would be better." Maggie forced a carefree note into her tone. "I'll talk to you tomorrow then."

"Okay." Denny sounded disappointed, but there wasn't anything Maggie could do. She wanted to avoid another confrontation with Glenn regarding her brother.

Replacing the receiver, she met her husband's gaze. "You said something about tennis?" Her voice was remarkably steady for all the turmoil going on inside her.

"You're not helping him, you know," Glenn said calmly. "All you've done to this point is teach him to come to you to solve his financial problems."

It was on the tip of her tongue to tell him that she was aware of that. She had seen it all herself, but she was caught in a vicious trap where her brother was concerned. "He needs me," she countered.

"He needs a job and some self-worth."

"I thought you were a stockbroker, not a psychologist."

Maggie could tell by the tightness in his jaw that she had angered Glenn. "Look, I'm sorry, I didn't mean to snap at you. Denny's in trouble. I can't let him down when he needs me the most. If you recall, I did ask you to stay out of it."

"Have it your way," he mumbled and handed her a tennis racket.

Their game wasn't much of a contest. Glenn overpowered her easily in straight sets, making her work harder than ever. Maggie didn't know if he was venting his frustrations from the office or if he was angry because of Denny. It didn't matter; she was exhausted. By the time he'd finished showering, she was in bed half-asleep. Glenn's pulling the covers over her shoulders and gently kissing the top of her head were the last things Maggie remembered.

With the approach of the Christmas holidays, Maggie felt a renewed sense of rightness. She was in love with her husband, they were together and her world seemed in perfect balance. Glenn worked hard and so did she, spending hours in her studio doing what she enjoyed most—painting. With her marriage, Maggie had discovered that there was a new depth to her art. She had once told Glenn that color was mood and brushwork emotion. Now with Glenn's love, her brush painted bold strokes that revealed a maturity in her scenes that had been missing before their wedding. She was happy, truly happy, and it showed in ways she'd never expected.

Maggie didn't mention Glenn's grandmother's antique ring, confident that he'd gift her with it on Christmas morning. And she would react with the proper amount of surprised pleasure.

She wore her wedding ring continually now, even when she worked. Glenn glanced at her hand occasionally to be sure it was there. It was an odd quirk of his, but she didn't really mind. The ring meant as much to her as their marriage vows and that was all he wanted. They had come a long way from the night she'd arrived in Charleston.

For their first Christmas, Maggie wanted to buy Glenn a special gift, something that would show the depth of her love and appreciation for the good life they shared. But what? For days she mulled over the problem. She could give him one of her paintings for his office, but he had already asked her for one. She couldn't refuse him by telling him that that was what she planned to give him for Christmas. He took one of her seascapes and she was left without an idea. And she so wanted their first Christmas together to be special.

For the first time in years Maggie went Christmas shopping in stores. Usually she ordered through the mail or over the Internet, but she feared missing the perfect gift that would please Glenn most. Janelle joined her one day, surprised at the changes in Maggie.

"What changes?"

"You're so happy," Janelle claimed.

"I really am, you know."

"I can tell. You positively glow with it."

The remark pleased Maggie so much she repeated it for Glenn later that evening.

"So you were out Christmas shopping. Did you buy me anything?"

How she wished. Nothing seemed special enough. She had viewed a hundred jewelry display cases, visited the most elite men's stores and even gone to obscure bookstores, seeking rare volumes of Glenn's favorite novels. A sense of panic was beginning to fill her.

"You'll have to wait until Christmas morning to find out," she told him, coyly batting her long lashes.

With so many relatives on their list, Glenn and Maggie were in and out of more department stores the following Saturday than Maggie cared to count. Soft music filled the stores and bells chimed on the street corners, reminding them to be generous to those less fortunate. The crowds were heavy, but everyone seemed to expect that and took the long waits at the cash registers in stride.

While Maggie stood in line buying a toy farm set for Glenn's nephew, Glenn wandered over to the furniture department. Lovingly, Maggie's gaze followed him as he looked over cherry wood bookcases in a rich, deep-red color. Bookcases? Glenn wanted something as simple as bookcases? Maggie couldn't believe it. After days of looking at the latest gadgets and solid-gold toys, she stared in disbelief that he could be interested in something as simple as this. When the salesman approached, Glenn asked several questions and ran his hand over the polished surface.

"Did you see something?" she asked conversationally when he returned to her side. He wanted those bookcases, but she doubted that he'd mention it to her.

"Not really," he replied, but Maggie noted the way his gaze returned and lingered over the cases.

Maggie's heartbeat raced with excitement. At the first opportunity she'd return and buy Glenn those bookcases.

"You're looking pleased about something," Glenn commented over dinner Wednesday evening.

His comment caught her off guard and she lightly shook her head. "Sorry, I was deep in thought. What did you say?"

"I could tell," he chided, chuckling. Standing, he carried his clean plate to the sink. "Do you want to talk about it, or is this some deep dark secret you're hiding from your husband?"

"Some deep dark secret."

"What did you do today?" he asked, appreciating anew how beautiful his wife had become. She was a different woman from the one who'd met him at the airport months ago. He liked to think the changes in her were due to their marriage. He was different too and credited Maggie with his renewed sense of happiness.

"What did I do today?" Maggie repeated, her dark eyes rounding with shock. Swallowing back her unease, she cast her gaze to her plate. "Christmas cards." The truth nearly stuck in her throat. She had written Christmas cards, but in addition she had penned a long letter to Angie, thanking her for everything the other woman had shared the day of their brief visit. In the letter, Maggie told Angie how improved her marriage was now that she'd told Glenn how much she loved him, and was confident that he loved her in return.

As impractical as it sounded, Maggie would have liked to continue the friendship with Angie. Rarely had Maggie experienced such an immediate kinship with another woman. Impractical and illogical. Of all the people in the world, Maggie would have thought she'd despise Angie Canfield. But she didn't. Now, weeks later, Maggie felt the need to write the other woman and extend her appreciation for their afternoon together and to wish her and Simon the warmest of holiday greetings. The letter had been interrupted by Glenn's homecoming and she had safely tucked it away from the other cards she kept on top of her desk.

"I still have several things that need to be done before Christmas," she said in order to hide her discomfort.

Glenn was silent for a moment. "You look guilty about something. I bet you went out shopping today and couldn't resist buying yourself something."

"I didn't!" she declared with a cheery laugh.

Later, in the den, when Glenn was looking over some figures, Maggie joined him. She sat in the chair opposite his desk. When Maggie glanced up she found her husband regarding her lazily with a masked expression, and she wondered at his thoughts.

On the other side of the desk, Glenn studied his wife, thinking that she was more beautiful that night than he ever remembered. Her eyes shone with a translucent happiness and a familiar sensation tugged at his heart. Something was troubling her tonight...no, *troubling* was too strong a word. She was hiding something from him. Which was natural, he supposed. It was Christmastime and she had probably cooked up some scheme for his gift, yet Glenn had the feeling this had nothing to do with Christmas.

Convinced he shouldn't go looking for trouble, he shook his mind free of the brooding sensation. Whatever it was probably involved Denny, and it was just as well that he didn't know. It would only anger him.

Glenn pushed back his chair and stood. "I'll be right back. I'm going to need a cup of coffee to keep these figures straight. Do you want one?"

Maggie glanced up from the book she was reading and shook her head. The caffeine would keep her awake. "No, thanks," she said as he left the room.

The phone rang and Glenn called out that he'd answer it. The information didn't faze Maggie until she realized that he had probably gone into her office since the phone was closer there.

He returned a minute later, strolling into the room with deceptive casualness. "It's your leeching brother," he told her.

Eleven

"Glenn, what a nasty thing to say." Maggie couldn't help knowing that Glenn disapproved of the way she gave Denny money, but she hadn't expected him to be so blunt or openly rude. "I hope Denny didn't hear you," she murmured, coming to her feet. "He feels terrible about the way things have turned out."

"If he honestly felt that, he wouldn't continue to come running to you at every opportunity."

Straightening her shoulders to a military stiffness, Maggie marched from the room and picked up the telephone. "Hello, Denny."

A short silence followed. "Hi. I take it I should call back another time."

"No," she contradicted firmly. She wasn't going to let Glenn intimidate her out of speaking to her own brother. "I can talk now."

"I just wanted to tell you that my lawyer didn't have anything new to tell me regarding our case. It looks like this thing could be tied up in the courts for years. I'm telling you, Maggie, this whole mess is really getting me down."

"But you don't need to worry, I'm here to help you," she offered sympathetically.

"But Glenn…"

"What I do with my money is none of his concern." In her heart Maggie knew that Glenn was right, but Glenn was a naturally strong person, and her brother wasn't to be blamed if he was weak. They had to make allowances for Denny, help him.

"You honestly mean that about helping, don't you?" Denny murmured, relief and appreciation brightening his voice.

"You know I do."

Ten minutes later Maggie rejoined her husband. All kinds of different emotions were coming at her. She was angry with Glenn for being so unsympathetic to her brother's troubles, infuriated with Denny because he pushed all the right buttons with her, and filled with self-derision because she gave in to Denny without so much as a thoughtful pause. Denny had only to give his now familiar whine and she handed him a signed check.

"Well?" Glenn glanced up at her.

"Well what?"

"He asked for money, didn't he?"

"Yes," she snapped.

"And you're giving it to him?"

"I don't have much choice. Denny is my brother."

"But you're not helping him, Maggie, don't you see that?"

"No," she cried, and to her horror tears welled in her eyes. It was so unlike her to cry over something so trivial that Maggie had trouble finding her breath, which caused her to weep all the louder.

Glenn stood and gently pulled her into his arms. "Maggie, what is it?"

"You… Denny…me," she sobbed and dramatically shook her hands. "This court case might take years to decide. He needs money. You don't want me to lend him any, and I'm caught right in the middle."

"Honey, listen." Glenn stood and gently placed his arms around her. "Will you do something for me?"

"Of course," she responded on a hiccupping sob. "What?"

"Call Denny back and tell him he can't have the money…."

"I can't do that," she objected, shaking his arms free. She hugged her waist and moved into the living room where a small blaze burned in the fireplace. The warmth of the fire chased the chill from her arms.

"Hear me out," Glenn said, following her. "Have Denny give me a call at the office in the morning. If he needs money, I'll loan it to him."

Maggie was skeptical. "But why…?"

"I don't want him troubling you anymore. I don't like what he's doing to you, and worse, what he's doing to himself." He paused, letting her take in his offer. "Agreed?"

She offered him a watery smile and nodded.

With Glenn standing at her side, Maggie phoned Denny back and gave the phone over to her husband a few minutes later. Naturally, Denny didn't seem overly pleased with the prospect of having to go through Glenn, but he had no choice. Maggie should have been relieved that Glenn was handling the difficult situation, but she wasn't.

In the morning, Maggie woke feeling slightly sick to

her stomach. She lay in bed long after Glenn had left
for the office, wondering if she could be pregnant. The
tears the evening before had been uncharacteristic and
she'd had a terrible craving for Chinese food lately that
was driving her crazy. For three days in a row she had
eaten lunch in Chinatown. None of the symptoms on
their own was enough for her to make the connection
until this morning.

A smile formed as Maggie placed a hand on her flat
stomach and slowly closed her eyes. A baby. Glenn
would be so pleased. He'd be a wonderful father. She'd
watched him with Denny's girls on Thanksgiving and
had been astonished at his patience and gentleness. The
ironic part was all these weeks she'd been frantically
searching for just the right Christmas gift for Glenn, and
all along she'd been nurturing his child in her womb.
They both wanted children. Oh, she'd get him the bookcases he had admired, but she'd keep the gift he'd prize
most a secret until Christmas morning.

Not wanting to be overconfident without a doctor's
confirmation, Maggie made an appointment for that afternoon, and her condition was confirmed in a matter of
minutes. Afterward she was bursting with excitement.
Her greatest problem would be keeping it from Glenn
when she wanted to sing and dance with the knowledge.

When Maggie returned to the beach house Rosa had
left a message that Denny had phoned. Maggie returned
his call immediately.

"How did everything go with Glenn?" she asked him
brightly. Nothing would dim the brilliance of her good
news, not even Denny's sullen voice.

"Fine, I guess."

"There isn't any problem with the money, is there?"

Glenn wouldn't be so cruel to refuse to make the loan when he'd assured her he'd help her brother. Maggie was confident he wouldn't do anything like that. Glenn understood the situation.

"Yes and no."

Her hand tightened around the receiver. "How do you mean? He's giving you the money, isn't he?"

"He's lending me the money, but he's got a bunch of papers he wants me to sign and in addition he's set up a job interview for me. He actually wants me to go to work."

By the time Denny finished with his sorry tale, Maggie was so furious she could barely speak. Lending him the money—making him sign for it—a job interview. Glenn had told her he was going to help her brother. Instead he was stripping Denny of what little pride he had left.

By the time Glenn arrived home that evening, he found Maggie pacing the floor. Sparks of anger flashed from her dark eyes as she spun around to face him.

"What's wrong? You're looking at me like I was Jack the Ripper."

"Did you honestly tell Denny that he couldn't borrow the money unless he got a job?" she said in accusation. Her hands were placed defiantly on her hips, challenging Glenn to contradict her.

Unhurriedly, Glenn removed his raincoat one arm at a time and hung it in the hall closet. "Is there something wrong with an honest day's toil?"

"It's humiliating to Denny. He's…accustomed to a certain lifestyle now…. He can't lower himself to take a job like everyone else and…"

Maggie could tell by the way Glenn's eyes narrowed

that he was struggling to maintain his own irritation. "I live in a fancy beach house with you and somehow manage to suffer the humiliation."

"Glenn," she cried. "It's different with Denny."

"How's that?"

Unable to remain still, Maggie continued to stalk the tiled entryway like a circus lion confined to a cage. "Don't you understand how degrading that would be to him?"

"No," Glenn returned starkly. "I can't. Denny made a mistake. Any fool knows better than to place the majority of his funds in one investment no matter how secure it appears. The time has come for your brother to own up to the fact he made a serious mistake, and pay the consequences of his actions. I can't and won't allow him to sponge off you any longer, Maggie."

The tears sprang readily to the surface. Oh how she hated to cry. Hopefully she wouldn't be like this the entire pregnancy. "But don't you understand?" she blubbered, her words barely intelligible. "I inherited twice the money Denny did."

"And he's made you feel guilty about that."

"No," she shouted. "He's never said a word."

"He hasn't had to. You feel guilty enough about it, but my love, trust me. Denny will feel better about you, about himself, about life in general. You can't give him the self-worth he needs by handing him a check every time he asks for it."

"You don't understand my brother," Maggie cried. "I can't let you do this to him. I… I told you once that I wanted you to stay out of this."

"Maggie—"

"No, you listen to me. I'm giving Denny the money

he wants. I told him that he didn't need to sign anything, and he doesn't need to get a job. He's my brother and I'm not going to turn my back on him. Understand?"

Silence crackled in the room like the deadly calm before an electrical storm. A muscle leaped in Glenn's jaw, twisting convulsively.

"If that's the way you want it." His voice was both tight and angry.

"It is," she whispered.

What Maggie didn't want was the silent treatment that followed. Glenn barely spoke to her the remainder of the evening, and when he did his tone was barely civil. It was clear that Glenn considered her actions a personal affront. Maybe it looked that way to him, she reasoned, but she'd explained long ago that she preferred to handle her brother herself. Glenn had interfered and now they were both miserable.

When morning arrived to lighten the dismal winter sky, Maggie rolled onto her back and stared at the ceiling, realizing she was alone. The oppressive gray light of those early hours invaded the bedroom and a heaviness settled onto Maggie's heart. She climbed from the bed and felt sick and dizzy once again, but her symptoms were more pronounced this morning. Her mouth felt like dry, scratchy cotton.

Glenn had already left for the office and the only evidence of his presence was an empty coffee cup in the kitchen sink. Even Rosa looked at Maggie accusingly and for one crazy instant Maggie wondered how the housekeeper knew that she and Glenn had argued. That was the crazy part—they hadn't really fought. Maybe if they had, the air would have been cleared.

The crossword puzzle didn't help occupy her mind

and Maggie sat at the kitchen table for an hour, drinking cup after cup of watered-down apple juice while sorting through her thoughts. With a hand rubbing her throbbing temple, Maggie tried to recall how Glenn had been as a youth when he was angry with someone. She couldn't remember that he had ever held a grudge or been furious with anyone for long. That was a good sign.

Tonight she'd talk to him, she decided, try to make him understand why she had to do this for Denny. If the situation was reversed and it was either of his brothers, Glenn would do exactly the same thing. Maggie was sure of it.

Because of the Christmas holidays, the stock market was traditionally slow, and Glenn had been home before six every night for the past week. He wasn't that night. Nor was he home at seven, or eight. He must be unbelievably angry, she thought, and a part of Maggie wondered if he'd ever be able to completely understand her actions. Apparently, he found it easier to blame her than to realize that he'd forced her into the situation. Maggie spent a miserable hour watching a television program she normally disliked.

The front door clicked open and Maggie pivoted sharply in her chair, hoping Glenn's gaze would tell her that they'd talk and clear up the air between them.

Glenn shrugged off his coat and hung it in the hall closet. Without a word he moved into his den and closed the door, leaving Maggie standing alone and miserable.

Desolate, she sat in the darkened living room and waited. She hadn't eaten, couldn't sleep. Leaving the house was impossible, looking and feeling the way she did. Her only companion was constant anxiety and doubt. There wasn't anything she could do until Glenn was ready to talk.

When he reappeared, Maggie slowly came to her feet. Her throat felt thick and uncooperative. Her hands were clenched so tightly together that the blood flow to her fingers was restricted. "Would you like some dinner?" The question was inane when she wanted to tell him they were both being silly. Arguing over Denny was the last thing she wanted to do.

"I'm not hungry," he answered starkly without looking at her. His features tightened.

Undaunted, Maggie asked again. "Can we at least talk about this? I don't want to fight."

He ignored her and turned toward the hallway. "You said everything I needed to hear last night."

"Come on, Glenn, be reasonable," she shouted after him. "What do you want from me? Are you so insensitive that you can't see what an intolerable situation you placed me in?"

"I asked you to trust me with Denny."

"You were stripping him of his pride."

"I was trying to give it back to him," he flared back. "And speaking of intolerable positions, do you realize that's exactly what you've done to me?"

"You... How...?"

"You've asked me to sit by and turn a blind eye while your brother bleeds you half to death. I'm your husband. It's my duty to protect you, but I can't do that when you won't let me, when you resent, contradict and question my intention."

"Glenn, please," she pleaded softly. "I love you. I don't want to fight. Not over Denny—not over anything.

It's Christmas, a time of peace and goodwill. Can't we please put this behind us?"

Glenn looked as weary as she felt. "It's a matter of trust too, Maggie."

"I trust you completely."

"You don't," Glenn announced and turned away from her, which only served to fuel Maggie's anger.

Maggie slept in the guest bedroom that night, praying Glenn would insist she share his bed. She didn't know what she had thought sleeping apart would accomplish. It took everything within Maggie not to swallow her considerable pride and return to the master bedroom. A part of her was dying a slow and painful death.

Maggie couldn't understand why Glenn was behaving like he was. Only once had he even raised his voice to her in all the weeks they'd been married. But now the tension stretched between the two bedrooms was so thick Maggie could have sliced it with a dull knife. Glenn was so disillusioned with her that even talking to her was more than he could tolerate. He wasn't punishing her with the silent treatment, Maggie realized. He was protecting her. If he spoke it would be to vent his frustration and say things he'd later regret.

Instead of dwelling on the negative, Maggie recalled the wonderful love-filled nights when they had lain side by side and been unable to stay out of each other's arms. The instant the light was out, Glenn would reach for her with the urgency of a condemned man offered a last chance at life. And when he'd kissed her and loved her, Maggie felt as though she was the most precious being in the world. Glenn's world. He was a magnificent lover. She closed her eyes to the compelling images that crowded her mind, feeling sick at heart and thoroughly miserable.

In the other room Glenn lay on his back staring at the ceiling. The dark void of night surrounded him. The sharp edges of his anger had dulled, but the bitterness that had consumed him earlier had yet to fade. In all his life he had never been more disappointed and more hurt—yes, hurt, that his wife couldn't trust him to handle a delicate situation and protect her. He wasn't out to get Denny; he sincerely wanted to help the man.

Morning arrived and Maggie couldn't remember sleeping although she must have closed her eyes sometime during the long, tedious night. The alarm rang and she heard Glenn stirring in the other room.

While he dressed, Maggie moved into the kitchen and put on coffee. Ten minutes later, he joined her in the spacious room and hesitated, his gaze falling to her wide, sad eyes. Purposely he looked away. There was no getting around it. He had missed sleeping with his wife. A hundred times he had had to stop himself from going into the bedroom and bringing her back to his bed where she belonged. Now she stood not three feet from him in a sexy gown and his senses were filled with her. He should be aware of the freshly brewed coffee, but he discovered the elusive perfumed scent of Maggie instead. Silently he poured himself a cup of coffee and pulled out a kitchen chair. He tried to concentrate on something other than his wife. He reached for the newspaper and focused his attention on that. But mentally his thoughts were involved in this no-win situation between him and her blood-sucking brother. When he'd learned exactly how much money Denny had borrowed he'd been incensed. This madness had to stop and soon or he'd bleed Maggie dry.

Sensing Glenn's thoughts, Maggie moved closer, wanting to resolve this issue, yet unsure how best to approach a subject that felt like a ticking time bomb.

Propping up the newspaper against the napkin holder, Glenn hid behind the front page, not wanting to look at Maggie yet he struggled to keep his eyes trained on the front page headlines. "Will you be home for dinner?" Maggie forced the question out. Leaning against the kitchen counter, her fingers bit into the tiled surface as she waited for his answer.

"I've been home for dinner every night since we've been married. Why should tonight be different?"

Maggie had only been trying to make idle conversation and break down the ice shield that positioned between them. "No reason," she murmured and turned back to the stove.

A few minutes later Glenn left for the office with little more than a casual farewell.

By noon Maggie was convinced she couldn't spend another day locked inside the confines of the beach house. Even the studio that had been her pride now became her torture chamber. One more hour dealing with this madness and she'd go stir-crazy.

Aimlessly, she wandered from room to room, seeking confirmation that she had done the right thing by Denny and finding none. She took a long, uninterrupted walk along the beach where gusts of ocean air carelessly whipped her hair across her face and lightened her mood perceptibly. Christmas was only a week away, and there were a hundred things she should be doing. But Maggie hadn't the heart for even one.

Recently she had been filled with such high expectations for this marriage. Now she realized how naive she'd been. She had always thought that love conquered all. What a farce that was. She had been unhappy before marrying Glenn; now she was in love, pregnant, and utterly miserable. And why? Because she'd stood by her brother when he needed her. It hardly seemed fair.

A light drizzle began to fall and she walked until her face felt numb with cold. She trekked up to the house, fixed herself something hot to drink and decided to go for a drive.

The ride into the city was sluggish due to heavy traffic. She parked on the outskirts of Fisherman's Wharf and took a stroll. A multitude of shops and touristy places had sprung up since her last visit—but that had been years ago, she realized. She dropped into a few places and shopped around, finding nothing to buy. An art gallery caught her eye and she paused to look in the window at the painting on display. A card tucked in the ornate frame revealed the name of the painting was *The Small Woman*. The artist had used a black line to outline the painting, like lead surrounding the panes in a stained-glass window. The colors were bold, the setting elaborate. The simple woman, however, was strangely frail and pathetic, detached from the setting as though she were a sacrifice to be offered to the gods in some primitive culture. Examining the painting, Maggie saw herself in the tired woman and didn't like the reflection.

A blast of chilling wind whipped her coat around her legs, and to escape the unexpected cold, Maggie opened the glass door and entered the gallery. The room was deceptively large, with a wide variety of oil paintings, some watercolors, small sculptures and other artworks in opulent display.

"Can I help you?"

Maggie turned toward the voice to find a tall, slender woman dressed in a plaid wool skirt and creamy white silk blouse. She appeared to be studying Maggie closely, causing Maggie to wonder at her appearance. The wind had played havoc with her hair and…

"Maggie?"

Maggie blinked twice. She didn't recognize the woman. "Pardon?"

"Are you Maggie Kingsbury?"

"Yes…my married name is Lambert. Do I know you?"

The woman's laugh was light and sweetly musical. "I'm Jan Baker Hammersmith. Don't you remember we attended…"

The name clicked instantly. "Jan Baker." The two had been casual friends when Maggie was attending art school. "I haven't seen you in years. The last I heard, you were married."

"I'm divorced now."

Maggie dropped her gaze, desperately afraid that she would be adding that identical phrase someday when meeting old friends. "I'm sorry to hear that."

"I am, too," Jan said with a heavy sadness. "But it was for the best. Tell me, are you still painting?" Maggie noted how Jan quickly diverted the subject away from herself.

"Occasionally. Not as much since I married."

Jan strolled around the gallery with proud comfort. "I can still remember one of your paintings—a beach scene. The detail you'd put into it was marvelous. Whatever happened to that?"

"It's hanging in our living room."

"I can understand why you'd never want to sell that." Jan's eyes were sincere. "Rarely have I seen a painting with such vivid clarity and color."

"It would sell?" Maggie was surprised. Ridiculous as it seemed, she'd never tried to sell any of her paintings. There hadn't been any reason to try. She gave them away as gifts and to charities for auctions but she didn't have any reason to sell them. She didn't need the money and inwardly she feared they might not sell. Her artwork was for her own pleasure. The scenes painted by her brush had been the panacea for an empty life within the gilded cage.

"It'd sell in a minute," Jan stated confidently. "Do you think you'd consider letting the gallery represent you?"

Maggie hedged, uncertain. "Let me think about it."

"Do, Maggie, and get back to me. I have a customer I know who'd be interested in a painting similar to the beachscape, if you have one. Take my card." They spoke for several minutes more and Maggie described some of her other works. Again Jan encouraged her to bring in a few of her canvases. Maggie noted that Jan didn't make any promises, which was reasonable.

Sometime later, Maggie returned to her car. Meeting Jan had been just the uplift she'd needed. Already her mind was buzzing with possibilities. There wasn't any reason she shouldn't sell her work. Glenn's car was in the driveway when she returned and she pulled to a stop in front of the house and parked there. A glance at her watch told her that it was later than she suspected. Her spirits were lighter than at any time during the past two days, but she didn't hurry toward the house.

"Where have you been?" Glenn asked the minute she walked in the door. Not granting her the opportunity to respond, he continued. "You made an issue of asking me if I was going to be home for dinner and then you're gone."

Carelessly, Maggie tossed her coat over an armchair. "I lost track of the time," she explained on her way into the kitchen. Glenn was only a step behind. From the grim set of his mouth, Maggie recognized that once again she'd displeased him. Everything she'd done the past few days seemed to fuel his indignation.

He didn't say another word as she worked, dishing up the meal of baked pork chops and scalloped potatoes Rosa had prepared for them. Maggie could feel his gaze on her defeated shoulders, studying her. He looked for a moment as if he wanted to say something, but apparently changed his mind.

"I was in an art gallery today," she told him conversationally.

"Oh."

"I'm thinking of taking in some of my work."

"You should, Maggie."

Silence followed. This was the first time they'd had a decent conversation since she'd sided with her brother against him.

Their dinner was awkward, each trying to find a way to put their marriage back on track. Glenn sat across from her, cheerless and somber. Neither ate much.

"Did the mail come?" Maggie asked, setting the dinner dishes aside.

"It's in your office," Glenn answered without looking up. "Would you like me to bring it in to you?"

"Please. I'll finish up here in a minute." Well, at least they were speaking to each other, she thought. It was a start. Together they'd work things out. The situation with Denny was probably the first of many disagreements and misunderstandings they would face through the years. It might take time, she told herself, but they'd work it out. They loved each other too much to allow anything to wedge a space between them for long. They had both behaved badly over this issue with Denny, but if she'd bend a little, Glenn would, too.

When Glenn returned to the living room, he said her name with such fervor that her head came up. Unconsciously Maggie pressed farther back into the thick cushions of her chair, utterly stunned by the look that flashed from her husband's eyes. She could think of nothing that would cause him such anger.

"Explain this," he said and thrust her letter to Angie in front of Maggie's shocked face.

Twelve

Maggie's mind was in complete turmoil. She'd known it was a risk to write Angie, and later had regretted it. She hadn't mailed the card. Yet she'd left the letter on top of her desk for Glenn to find. Perhaps subconsciously she had wanted him to discover what she'd done.

Tension shot along her nerves as she struggled to appear outwardly calm. Lifting the chatty letter Glenn handed her, she examined it as if seeing it for the first time, amazed at her detachment. Whatever she wished, consciously or subconsciously, Glenn had found it and the timing couldn't be worse. They were just coming to terms with one major disagreement and were about to come to loggerheads over another. Only this issue was potentially far more dangerous to the security of their marriage. Going behind Glenn's back had never felt right. Maggie had regretted her deception a hundred times since. And yet it had been necessary. Long ago Maggie had admitted that Glenn had forced her into the decisive action. She had asked him about Angie and he'd refused to discuss the other woman. Maggie was his

wife and she loved him; she had a right to know. But all
the rationalization in the world wasn't going to help now.

"How do you explain this?" His voice went deep and
low, as though he couldn't believe what he'd found. Maggie hadn't trusted him to help her brother, he thought,
somewhat dazed, and now he'd learned that she had betrayed his trust in another situation as well.

Glenn knew he should be furious. Outraged. But he
wasn't. His emotions were confused—he felt shocked,
hurt and discouraged. Guilt was penned all over Maggie's pale face as she sat looking up at him, trying to
explain. There couldn't possibly be a plausible one. Not
one. Feeling sick with defeat, he turned away from her.

Maggie's heartbeat quickened at the pained look in
Glenn's dark eyes. "I met Angie."

"When?" he asked, still hardly able to comprehend
what she was saying. He paced the area in front of her
in clipped military-like steps as if standing in one place
were intolerable.

Maggie had never seen any man's features more troubled. "The...the day I flew to San Francisco... I took a
flight to Groves Point first and then flew from there to
Atlanta before heading home."

If possible Glenn went even more pale.

"I asked you to tell me about the two of you but—"
Maggie attempted to explain and was quickly cut off.

"How did you know where she lived?"

Admitting everything she had done made it sound all
the more sordid and deceitful. She hesitated.

"How did you know where she lived?" he repeated,
his rising voice cold and deliberate. Maggie was pressed
as far back against the chair cushion as possible as dread
settled firmly over her.

"I found her letter to you…and read it." She wouldn't minimize her wrongdoing. The letter had been addressed to him and she had purposely taken it from the envelope and read each word. It was wrong. She knew it was wrong, but given the opportunity, she would do exactly the same thing again.

Shocked, all Glenn seemed capable of doing was to stare back at her. She yearned to explain that she hadn't purposely searched through his drawers or snooped into his private matters. But she could see that expounding on what had happened wouldn't do any good. Reasoning with Glenn just then would be impossible. She felt wretched and sick to her stomach. The ache in her throat was complicated by the tears stinging her eyes. With everything in her, she struggled not to cry.

"What else did you try to find?" he asked. "How many drawers did you have to search through before you found the letter? Did you take delight in reading another woman's words to me? Is there anything you don't know?"

"It wasn't like that," she whispered, her gaze frozen in misery.

"I'll bet!" He moved to the other side of the living room. His anger died as quickly as it came, replaced by a resentment so keen he could barely stand to look at Maggie. She couldn't seem to let up on the subject of Angie. For months he had loved Maggie so completely that he was amazed that she could believe that he could possibly care for another woman. Worse, she had hounded the subject of Angie to death. It was a matter of trust, and she'd violated that and wounded his pride again and again.

"Are you satisfied now? Did you learn everything you

were so keen to find out?" His voice was heavy with defeat. "You don't trust me or my love, do you, Maggie? You couldn't, to have done something this underhanded."

"That's not true," she cried. Glenn wanted to wound her; she understood that. She had hurt him when all she'd ever wanted to do was give him her love, bear his children and build a good life with him. But their marriage had been clouded with the presence of another woman who stood between them as prominently as the Cascade mountain range. Or so it appeared at the time.

With a clarity of thought Glenn didn't realize he possessed, he knew he had to get out of the room...out of the house. He needed to sit down and do some serious thinking. Something was basically wrong in a relationship where one partner didn't trust the other. He loved Maggie and had spent the past few months trying to prove how much. Obviously he'd failed. He across the living room and jerked his raincoat off the hanger.

"Where are you going?" Maggie asked in a pathetically weak voice.

He didn't even look at her. "Out."

Trapped in a nightmare, her actions made in slow motion, Maggie came to her feet. The Christmas card and letter were clenched in her hand. Glenn turned to look back at her and his gaze fell to the brightly colored card. His mouth twisted into a scowl as he opened the door and left Maggie standing alone and heartbroken.

Maggie didn't allow the tears to escape until she was inside their bedroom with the door securely closed. Only then did she vent her misery. She wept bitter tears until she didn't think she could stop. Her throat ached and her sobs were dry; her eyes burned and there were no more tears left to shed. She had hoped to build a firm foundation for this marriage and had ruined any chance. Glenn had every reason to be angry. She had deceived him, hurt him, invaded his privacy. The room was dark and the night half-spent when Glenn came to bed. His movements sounded heavy and vaguely out of order. The dresser drawer was jerked open, then almost immediately slammed shut. He stumbled over something and cursed impatiently under his breath as he staggered to the far side of the bedroom.

Remaining motionless, Maggie listened to his movements and was shocked to realize that he was drunk. Glenn had always been so sensible about alcohol. He rarely had more than one drink. Maggie bit into her lower lip as he jerked back the covers and fell onto the mattress. She braced herself, wondering what she'd do if he tried to make love to her. But either he was too drunk or he couldn't tolerate the thought of touching her.

She woke in the morning to the sounds of Glenn moving around the room. Her first thought was that she should pretend to be asleep until he'd left, but she couldn't bear to leave things unsettled any longer.

"Glenn," she spoke softly, rolling onto her back. At the sight of his suitcase she bolted upright. "Glenn," she said again, her voice shaking and urgent. "What are you doing?"

"Packing." His face, devoid of expression, told her nothing.

He didn't look at her. With an economy of movement he emptied one drawer into a suitcase and returned to the dresser for another armload.

Maggie was shocked into speechlessness.

"You're leaving me?" she finally choked out. He wouldn't…couldn't. Hadn't they agreed about the sanctity of marriage? Hadn't Glenn told her that he felt divorce was wrong and people should work things out no matter what their problems?

Glenn didn't answer; apparently his actions were enough for her to realize exactly what he was doing.

"Glenn," she pleaded, her eyes pleading with him. "Please don't do this."

He paused mid-stride between the suitcase and the dresser. "Trust is vital in a relationship," he said and laid a fresh layer of clothes on top of the open suitcase.

Maggie threw back the covers and crawled to the end of the mattress. "Will you stop talking in riddles for heaven's sake. Of course trust is vital. This whole thing started because you didn't trust me enough to tell me about Angie."

"You knew everything you needed to know."

"I didn't," she cried. "I asked you to tell me about her and you refused."

"She had nothing to do with you and me."

"Oh, sure," Maggie shouted, her voice gaining volume with every word. "I wake up the morning after our wedding and you call me by her name. It isn't bad enough that you can't keep the two of us straight. Even… even your friends confuse our names. Then…then you leave her picture lying around for me to find. But that was nothing. The icing on the cake comes when I inadvertently find a letter tucked safely away in a drawer to cherish and keep forever. Never mind that you've got a wife. Oh, no. She's a simpleminded fool who's willing to overlook a few improprieties in married life."

Rising to her knees, Maggie waved her arms and continued. "And please note that word 'inadvertently,' because I assure you I did not go searching through your things. I found her letter by accident."

Glenn was confused. His head was pounding, his mouth felt like sandpaper and Maggie was shouting at him, waving her arms like a madwoman.

"I need to think," he murmured.

Maggie hopped off the bed and reached for her bathrobe. "Well, think then, but don't do something totally stupid like…like leave me. I love you, Glenn. For two days we've behaved like fools. I'm sick of it. I trusted you enough to marry you and obviously you felt the same way about me. The real question here is if we trust our love enough to see things through. If you want to run at the first hint of trouble then you're not the Glenn Lambert I know." She tied the sash to her robe and continued, keeping her voice level. "I'm going to make coffee. You have ten minutes alone to 'think.'"

By the time she entered the kitchen, Maggie's knees were shaking. If she told Glenn about the baby he wouldn't leave, but she refused to resort to that. If he wanted to stay, it would be because he loved her enough to work out their differences.

The kitchen phone rang and Maggie stared at it accusingly. The only person who would call her this time of the morning was Denny. If he asked her for another penny, she'd scream. It used to be that he'd call once or twice a month. Now it was every other day.

On the second ring, Maggie nearly ripped the phone off the hook. "Yes," she barked.

"Maggie, is that you?" Denny asked brightly. "Listen, I'm sorry to call so early, but I wanted to tell you something."

"What?" Her indignation cooled somewhat.

"I'm going to work Monday morning. Now don't argue, I know that you're against this. I'll admit that I was, too, when I first heard it. But I got to thinking about what Glenn said. And, Maggie, he's right. My attitude toward life, toward everything, has been rotten lately. The best thing in the world for me right now is to get back into the mainstream of life and do something worthwhile."

"But I thought…" Maggie couldn't believe what she was hearing.

"I know. I thought all the same things you did. But Linda and I had a long talk a few days ago and she helped me see that Glenn is right. I went to an interview, got the job and I feel terrific. Better than I have in years."

Maggie was dumbfounded. She lowered her lashes and squeezed her eyes at her own stupidity. Glenn had been right all along about Denny. Her brother had been trapped in the same mire as she had been. Maggie should have recognized it before, but she'd been so defensive, wanting to shield her brother from any unpleasantness that she had refused to acknowledge what was right in front of her eyes. Denny needed the same purpose that Glenn's love had given her life.

The urge to go back to their bedroom and ask Glenn to forgive her was strong, but she resisted. Denny was only one problem they needed to make right.

Glenn arrived in the kitchen dressed for the office. Silently he poured himself a cup of coffee. Maggie wondered if she should remind Glenn that it was Saturday and he didn't need to go to work. No, she'd let him talk first, she decided.

He took a sip of the hot, black coffee and grimaced. His head was killing him. It felt as if someone was hammering at his temple every time his heart beat. Furthermore he had to collect his car. He'd taken a taxi cab back to the house, far too drunk to get behind a wheel.

"Who was on the phone?" he asked. The question was not one of his most brilliant ones. Obviously it had been Denny, but he hoped to get some conversation going. Anything.

"Denny."

Glenn cocked a brow, swallowing back the argument that sprang readily to his lips. If she was going to write WELCOME across her back and lie down for Denny to walk all over her there wasn't anything he could do. Heaven knew he'd tried.

"He…he called because…"

"I know why he phoned," Glenn tossed out sarcastically.

"You do?"

"Of course. Denny only phones for one reason."

"Not this time." Her pride was much easier to swallow after hearing the excitement and enthusiasm in her brother's voice. "He's got a job."

Glenn choked on a swallow of coffee. "Denny? What happened?"

"Apparently you and Linda got through that thick skull of his and he decided to give it a try. He feels wonderful."

"It might not last."

"I know," Maggie agreed. "But it's a start and one he should have made a long time ago."

Her announcement was met with silence. "Are you telling me I was right?"

"Yes." It wasn't so difficult to admit, after all. Her

hands hugged the milk-laced herbal tea and lent her the courage to continue. "It was wrong to take matters into my own hands and visit Angie. I can even understand why you loved her. She's a wonderful person."

"But she isn't you. She doesn't have your beauty, your artistic talent or your special smile. Angie never made up crazy rules or beat me in a game of tennis. You're two entirely different people."

"I'll never be like her," Maggie murmured, staring into the creamy liquid she was holding.

"That's a good thing, because I'm in love with you. I married you, Maggie, I don't want anyone else but you."

Maggie's head jerked upright. "Are you saying...? Do you mean that you're willing to forgive me for taking matters into my own hands? I know what I did wasn't right."

"I'm not condoning it, but I understand why you felt you had to meet her."

If he didn't take her in his arms soon, Maggie thought, she'd start crying again and then Glenn would know her Christmas secret for sure.

He set the coffee cup aside and Maggie glanced up hopefully. But instead of reaching for her, he walked out of the kitchen and picked up the two suitcases that rested on the other side of the arched doorway.

Panic enveloped her. "Glenn," she whispered. "Are you leaving me?"

"No. I'm putting these back where they belong." He didn't know what he'd been thinking this morning. He could no more leave Maggie than he could stop breathing. After disappearing for a moment, he returned to the kitchen and stood not more than three feet from her.

Maggie's heart returned to normal again. "Are we through fighting now? I want to get to the making up part."

"We're just about there." The familiar lopsided grin slanted his mouth.

"Maybe you need a little incentive."

"You standing there in that see-through outfit of yours is giving me all the incentive I need." He wrapped his arms around her then and held her so close that Maggie could actually feel the sigh that shuddered through him.

She met his warm lips eagerly, twining her arms around his neck and tangling her fingers in the thick softness of his hair. Maggie luxuriated in the secure feel of his arms holding her tight. She smiled up at him dreamily. "There's an early Christmas gift I'd like to give you."

Unable to resist, Glenn brushed his lips over the top of her nose. "Don't you think I should wait?"

"Not for this gift. It's special."

"Are you going to expect to open one of yours in return?"

"No, but then, I already have a good idea of what you're getting me."

"You do?"

Maggie laughed outright at the way his eyes narrowed suspiciously. "It wasn't really fair because your mother let the cat out of the bag."

"My mother!"

"Yes, she told me about your grandmother's ring."

His forehead wrinkled into three lines. "Maggie, I'm not giving you a ring."

He couldn't have shocked her more if he'd dumped a bucket of ice water over her head. He wasn't giving her the ring! "Oh." She disentangled herself from his arms. "I...guess it was presumptuous of me to think that you would." Her eyes fell to his shirt buttons as she took a step backward.

"Just so there aren't any more misunderstandings, maybe I should explain myself."

"Maybe you should," she agreed, feeling the cold seep into her bones. It never failed. Just when she was beginning to feel loved and secure with their marriage, someone would throw a curve ball at her.

"After the hassle we went through with the wedding rings—"

"I love my rings," she interrupted indignantly. "I never take them off anymore. You asked me not to and I haven't." She knew she was babbling like an idiot, but she wanted to cover how miserable and hurt she was. All those months she had put so much stock in his grandmother's ring and he wasn't even planning on giving it to her.

"Maggie, I had the ring reset into a necklace for you."

"A necklace?"

"This way you won't need to worry about putting it on or taking it off, or losing it, for that matter."

The idea was marvelous and Maggie was so thrilled that her eyes misted with happiness. "It sounds wonderful," she murmured on a lengthy sniffle and rubbed the tears from her face.

"What is the matter with you lately?" Glenn asked, his head cocked to one side. "I haven't seen you cry this much since you were six years old and Petie Phillips teased you and pulled your braids."

Maggie smiled blindly at him. "You mean you haven't figured it out?"

"Figured what out?"

Glenn's dark brown eyes widened as he searched her expression as if expecting to find the answer hidden on her face. His eyebrows snapped together. "Maggie," he whispered with such reverence one would assume he was in a church, "are you pregnant?"

A smile lit up her face, and blossomed from ear to ear. "Yes. Our baby is due the first part of August."

"Oh, Maggie." Glenn was so excited that he longed to haul her into his arms and twirl her around the room until they were both dizzy and giddy. Instead, he pulled out a chair and sat her down. "Are you ill?"

"Only a little in the mornings," she informed him with a small laugh. "The worst thing is that I seem to cry over the tiniest incident."

"You mean like me packing my bags and leaving you."

"Yes." She giggled. "Just the minor things."

"A baby." Glenn paced the area in front of her, repeatedly brushing the hair off his forehead. "We're going to have a baby."

"Glenn, honestly, it shouldn't be such a shock. I told you in the beginning I wasn't using any birth control."

"I'm not shocked…exactly."

"Happy?"

"Very!" He knelt in front of her and gently leaned forward to kiss her tummy.

Maggie wrapped her arms around his head and held him to her. "Merry Christmas, my love."

Glenn heard the steady beat of Maggie's heart and closed his eyes to the wealth of emotions that flooded his being. She was a warm, vital woman who had made him complete. Wife, friend, lover…the list seemed endless and he had only touched the surface.

"Merry Christmas," he whispered in return and pulled her mouth to his.

* * * * *

YOURS TO KEEP

Shannon Stacey

Thank you so much to my readers.
So many of you have told me you love
the Kowalski family and want more,
so I hope you enjoy meeting Sean Kowalski,
as well as revisiting the rest of the family.
As always, thank you to Angela James
and the Carina Press team, as well as the HQN team,
for your dedication and enthusiasm.
And to my husband, whom I love madly
even though he never lets me drive.

One

"Still as ugly as ever, I see."

Sean Kowalski flipped the bartender the bird and dropped his duffel on the floor next to an empty stool. "Runs in the family, cousin."

Since they both stood a hair over six feet, they were able to exchange a quick hug over the bar, and Kevin thumped him on the back. "Damn glad you made it home."

"Me, too." Sean sat on the bar stool and took a long swig of the foamy beer Kevin put in front of him. "Sorry I missed your wedding. And Joe's, too."

"You were getting your ass shot at in Afghanistan. We won't hold it against you. Much."

"Still can't believe you both found women willing to be your Mrs. Kowalskis. What's wrong with them?"

Kevin flashed him a grin. "It's the dimples, man. Women can't resist them. Too bad for you we got 'em from Ma and all you got are the blue eyes from the old man's side."

"They do me well enough. How are your parents doing?"

"Good. They're looking forward to seeing you, and Ma made lasagna for tonight."

Sean grinned and patted his stomach. "I didn't stop for lunch, so I've got plenty of room. There are a lot of things I miss about my mother, God rest her soul, but her cooking isn't one of them. Aunt Mary, though? Damn, that woman can put a meal together."

Kevin nodded, then stepped away for a minute to grab a water. "So, you've got no job. Gonna mooch food from Ma and bum an apartment from me. The army was supposed to make you a man, not a useless son of a bitch."

"Twelve years was enough. Don't know what I want to do now, but I know it's not more of that."

"No interest in going back to Maine and helping your brother run the lodge?"

Sean shrugged. It had come up—especially when he'd told his brothers and sister he was going to hang out with the New Hampshire branch of the family for a while. But spending the rest of his life at the Northern Star Lodge wasn't something he wanted to do. As a child, he'd hated strangers making themselves at home in his house, and he'd never outgrown it. He just wasn't cut out to be an innkeeper.

"It's a plan B," he said.

Kevin took a swig off the water bottle, then screwed the cap back on. "You know I'm just giving you shit. You can crash here as long as you want."

"Appreciate it. Once I've had my fill of Aunt Mary's cooking, I might go home or…hell if I know." It was one of the reasons he'd decided to leave the army. There was nowhere he had to be tomorrow. Or the day after that.

A tall, busty redhead stepped out from a back room and Kevin waved her over. "This is my cousin Sean.

Sean, this is Paulie Reed, my head bartender, assistant manager and all-around right-hand man. Woman. Person. Right-hand person."

"Nice to meet you," Sean said, shaking her hand. She had one hell of a grip.

"I've heard a lot about you. Welcome home. My fiancé, Sam, and I live in the apartment below yours, so give a shout if you need anything."

"Will do." He watched her walk away because she had a hell of a swing, but—whether it was the mention of a fiancé or the fact she just wasn't his type—it didn't do much for him. "Jasper's Bar & Grille, huh? Interesting name."

"It came with the place and I'm too cheap to buy a new sign. Finish that beer and I'll take you upstairs now that Paulie's off break."

Sean knocked back the rest of the suds and picked up his duffel. He followed his cousin to a back hallway, then up two flights of stairs to the apartment Kevin was letting him use for the duration of his visit. It was a decent place and clean, with an oversize leather couch and a big-screen TV. All good, as far as he was concerned.

"So this is it," Kevin told him when he was done showing him around and had given him the key. "You've got all our numbers, and Paulie's usually in the bar if you need anything."

Sean shook his hand. "See you at dinner, then. Looking forward to meeting Beth and that baby girl of yours."

"Lily's a firecracker. Had her first birthday a week ago and loves terrorizing the shit out of her cousins." He whipped out his wallet, and it fell open to a picture of a feisty-looking little girl with one of those palm-tree-

ponytail things on the top of her head, bright blue eyes
and devilish dimples.

"She'll break some hearts someday," Sean said, because that's what men seemed to say when shown pictures of other guys' daughters.

"And I'll break open some heads. Joe's Brianna looks
a lot like Lily, but without the dimples. She's four and
a half months now and loud as hell." Kevin headed for
the door. "I told Beth I'd be home by three so she can
make something to bring to Ma's without tripping over
Lily, who doesn't stay where we put her anymore. I'll
see you about six."

When he was gone, Sean dropped onto the couch and
closed his eyes. It was good to be home, even if home
was a borrowed apartment. For the first time in twelve
years he could go wherever he wanted. Do whatever he
wanted. The army had given him a good start in life and
he didn't regret the years he'd served, but he was ready
to be his own man again.

The first order of business as his own man? A power
nap.

A knock at the door surprised him, jerking him out of
a light sleep. It wasn't as if he was expecting company.
As far as he knew, the only people who'd be looking for
him were family, and he was meeting them at his aunt
and uncle's. Still, he pulled open the door expecting to
see one of his cousins.

He was wrong. His unexpected guest was definitely
not related to him, which was a good thing considering his body reacted as though it was his first time seeing a pretty woman. She had a big curly mass of dark
hair full of different colors—almost like a deep cher-
rywood grain—and whether she'd be a brunette or a

redhead probably depended on the lighting. Her eyes were even darker, the color of strong black coffee, and just the right amount of curves softened a taller-than-average, lean body.

A body that made his body stand up and take notice in a way the sexy bartender downstairs hadn't. This woman wasn't too top-heavy and the way she took care of her body made him think if they wrestled under the sheets, she'd make it one hell of a good match.

Okay, he really needed to get laid if he was going to start imagining sex with any random stranger who knocked on his door.

"Can I help you?" he prompted when she just stood there and looked at him.

She picked at the fraying wrist of a navy sweatshirt that had Landscaping by Emma written across the front in fancy letters. "Are you Sean Kowalski?"

"Yup."

"I'm Emma Shaw…your fake fiancée."

"Say what?"

Emma Shaw sure knew how to pick a fake man. The real Sean Kowalski was tall, had tanned and rugged arms stretching the sleeves of his blue T-shirt, and dark blond hair that looked as if it was growing out from a short cut. A little scruff covered his square jaw, as if he'd forgotten to shave for a couple of days, and even squinting at her in a suspicious manner, his eyes were the prettiest shade of blue she'd ever seen.

Okay, maybe it wasn't all suspicion. His expression implied he was afraid she was some crazy woman who'd gone off her meds and was going to start speaking in tongues or show him the handmade Sean doll she'd crafted to sleep with.

"Lady, I've never had a fiancée, fake or otherwise," he said in a low voice that made her knees weaken just a little. "And it's been a while since I've gone on a decent bender, so if I'd asked you to marry me, I'm pretty sure I'd at least remember your face."

That would have been hard to do. "We've never actually met."

He stopped squinting at her and snorted. "Let me guess—this is some joke my cousins thought would be a funny way to welcome me home? Okay, so…ha-ha. I've got stuff to do now."

He started to close the door, but she slapped her hand against it. "I'm a friend of Lisa's. Your cousin-in-law, I guess she'd be."

"Mikey's wife?" He pulled the door open when she nodded. "Maybe we should start this conversation in a different place. Like the beginning."

She took a deep breath, then blew it out. "My grandmother's raised me since I was four."

"Maybe not *that* far back."

"She retired to Florida a couple years ago with some friends, and I take care of the house I grew up in. But all she was doing was worrying about me, and when she started talking about moving back so I wouldn't be alone, I told her I had a boyfriend. Then I told her he'd moved in with me. And, because I would only date a super-great guy, after a while he proposed and naturally I accepted."

"And I got dragged into this how?"

"I had just gotten home from having lunch with Lisa and she'd mentioned sending you a care package. Your name just popped into my head when Gram asked what my boyfriend's name was."

He shook his head. "Let me get this straight. You told your grandmother that a guy you've never met is your boyfriend?"

"I just wanted her to worry less."

"Maybe she's right to worry about you."

Ouch. "I'm not crazy, you know."

He folded his arms across his chest and looked down at her. "You made up an imaginary boyfriend."

"You're not imaginary. Just uninformed."

He didn't even crack a smile. "What do you want from me?"

And here came the crazy part—the *more* crazy part, anyway. "Gram's coming home. She wants to check on the house and…she wants to meet you."

As she spoke, Emma made sure none of her body parts were breaking the plane of the doorway, just in case he slammed the door in her face. It was something she might do, if some strange guy showed up on her doorstep and told her they were in a deep, meaningful relationship.

"So…what? You want me to have dinner with you guys? Pretend I'm your fiancé for a few hours?"

"She'll be here a month."

He laughed at her then. A deep, infectious laugh that made her want to join in even though he was laughing at her. Not that she could blame him. Even her best friend had laughed, although that might have been because Lisa thought she was joking. And she had been at the time. But as Gram's arrival grew closer and she still couldn't work up the nerve to tell her she didn't really have a fiancé, the idea didn't seem as funny.

Sean obviously disagreed, since he laughed long

enough so she shifted her weight from one foot to the other before clearing his throat. "Since I know you didn't come here thinking I'd move in with you and pretend to be your fiancé for a month, what is it you want?"

"Actually, I did come here to ask you if you'd move in with me and pretend to be my fiancé for a month." And, no, it didn't sound a whole lot more sane than when she'd practiced saying it in the mirror.

"Why would I do that?"

Good question. "Because you're not really doing anything else. I'd pay you. And you're a nice guy?"

"Lady, you don't know anything about me."

"I know you just got out of the army, so you don't have a permanent home. I know you don't have a job yet. And I know you're a really good guy."

"I know somebody in my family has a big mouth."

"Lisa's proud of you. She talks about you a lot."

He sighed and ran a hand over his hair. "Look, I'm not an actor for hire. I think, if you're not willing to tell her the truth, you should just tell your grandmother you broke up with your…me."

She wanted to argue with him—to make him understand she just wanted her grandmother to be happy—but it had been such a long shot, anyway, and she didn't have the heart to keep at it.

"Well," she said in a voice that only trembled a little, "thanks for your time. And welcome home, too."

"Thanks. Take care of yourself."

Even after he'd disappeared back into the apartment and closed the door, Emma managed not to cry.

It wasn't the end of the world. She'd have to tell Gram they'd broken up, and that would be the end of it.

It wouldn't be the end of the worrying, though. If

anything, it would be worse. Now Gram would not only worry about Emma being alone and taking care of the house and a business, but she'd think her granddaughter was nursing the heartbreaking loss of a broken engagement, too. Even if Gram could bring herself to return to Florida, she'd do nothing but fret again—the very thing Emma was trying to put a stop to.

Emma crossed the street and happened to glance up as she climbed into her truck. Sean Kowalski was watching her from his apartment window, and she forced herself to give him a friendly smile and wave before she closed her door and slid the key into the ignition.

It was too bad, she thought, and not just for Gram's sake. That was a man any woman would want to be pretend-engaged to, even if only for a month.

It was a good ten minutes after walking through the Kowalskis' front door before Sean could even get his coat off. The whole gang was there, but his aunt could throw some mean elbows and got to him first.

"Sean!" She threw herself at him and he caught her up in a big bear hug.

He'd missed her more than he'd imagined he would while he was overseas. After his mom died unexpectedly the year he was nine, Aunt Mary had managed—from a state away and with four kids of her own—to step up and be a mother figure to her four nephews and one niece. It had been good to see his siblings, but being squeezed by his aunt while her tears burned his neck was like coming home.

He got a little choked up himself when Uncle Leo pulled him into his arms and gave him a few solid thumps on the back. Though Leo was shorter than his brother,

Frank, he was close enough in looks and mannerisms to remind Sean of his dad, who'd passed away nine years ago.

"Your old man would have been proud," Leo barked and Sean nodded, not trusting himself to speak.

Then came a gauntlet of cousins and their families. Joe, with his pretty new wife, Keri, who was holding rosy-cheeked baby Brianna. Terry and Evan with Stephanie, who, at thirteen, was growing into a pretty young woman. Kevin introduced him to Beth, who only managed a quick "nice to meet you" since she was wrangling Lily.

Mike and Lisa's family was a lot taller than the last time he'd seen them. He managed to find out Joey was now fifteen, Danny twelve, Brian nine and Bobby seven, before Mary started hushing the kids and herding them all toward the dining room.

"Dinner's ready to come out of the oven," she said. "Let's eat while it's hot."

As he'd expected, the massive dining room table was practically groaning under the weight of his welcome-home feast. She'd even made garlic bread that was soft and buttery on the inside and crusty on the outside. A far cry from his own pathetic efforts to re-create it by sprinkling garlic salt on a buttered slice of white toast.

"I swear, Aunt Mary, the whole time I was in Afghanistan, the only thing I could think of was your lasagna. Except for when I was thinking about your beef stew. Or your chicken and dumplings."

She gave him a modest *tsk,* but he could tell by the slight blush on her cheeks she was pleased by the compliment. "You always did have a good appetite."

The company was as good as the food, and stories

flowed like the iced tea as they plowed through the lasagna. He told a few watered-down tales of Afghanistan. Joe told the story of blackmailing Keri into joining the entire Kowalski family on their camping trip. Mike told him about Kevin fainting like a girl the day Lily was born.

He laughed at the description of his cousin going down like a cement truck that blew a hairpin turn and crashed through the guardrail, holding his stomach because he hadn't been able to resist the third helping his aunt had pushed on him.

"It's game night," nine-year-old Brian told him when the talk had died down and they were clearing the table. "Are you going to stay and play?"

"Sure." It wasn't as if he had anything better to do. "Just give me a few minutes to let my dinner settle, okay?"

"Sean's playing," the kid bellowed as he raced back to the others. "He's on my team!"

"We don't even know what we're playing yet," Danny pointed out.

"Don't care. He's on my team."

While the family debated which board games to drag out with the ferocity of a cease-fire negotiation, Sean stepped onto the back deck for a little fresh air. When he closed the sliding door and stepped to the left—out of view of people in the house—he almost bumped into Lisa.

Sean had always liked Mike's wife. She was on the shorter side of average—maybe five-three—but she had six feet of attitude and didn't let anybody push her around.

"Ran into a friend of yours today," he told her.

"Oh, yeah?"

"Tall. Hot. Batshit crazy?"

It was a few seconds before understanding dawned in her eyes, followed by a hot blush across her cheeks. "She didn't."

"Oh, she did. Knocked on my door and told me she was my fiancée, and that you knew she was throwing my name around."

She put her hand on his arm. "It was harmless, Sean. Really. She was just trying to make her grandmother feel better about being in Florida."

"Did she tell you her grand plan?"

The flush deepened. "Oh, no. Tell me she didn't."

"She did."

"I thought she was only joking."

"I thought it was a prank your husband and his cohort brothers cooked up, but she was serious."

Lisa shook her head, but he could see the amusement tugging at the corners of her mouth. "What, exactly, did she tell you the plan was?"

"What did she tell *you* it was?"

"She was kind of hinting around that maybe you could pretend to be the boyfriend."

"That almost sounds sane." He gave a short laugh. "The plan's now evolved into me moving in with her and pretending to be her fiancé for an entire month."

She didn't meet his eyes. "Maybe she did mention that, too, but she laughed, so I thought she was kidding."

"Nope." Sean folded his arms across his chest and leaned against the house. He should go back in and see if there was any blueberry cobbler left. Emma Shaw was nothing but a weird blip on his radar and he should forget her. But it didn't seem she was a forgettable woman. "So what's her deal, anyway?"

"Her grandmother kept talking about selling the house because she's afraid it's too much for Emma. Emma doesn't want a different house, so she made up a guy."

"Making up a guy would almost be normal. She made up an imaginary life for *me*. That's not normal."

"It's a really nice house." He just looked at her until she laughed and shrugged. "Okay, it's crazy, but—"

"But it's all out of love for her poor, sweet grandmother. Yeah, I got that part."

The look she gave him let him know she hadn't missed his less-than-flattering tone. It was a look that probably would have cowed him if he had to live with her, sleep beside her and depend on her for a hot meal. But he didn't, so he grinned and gave her a wink.

She blew out a breath and then her face grew serious. "Emma's parents were killed in a car accident when she was four, on their way to do some Christmas shopping. Her grandmother, Cat, and her grandfather, John—who died about ten years ago—were watching Emma. When the state police gave them the bad news, they didn't even consider giving her up. They were all she had, and as their friends enjoyed their empty nests and started traveling and retiring, the Shaws started all over with a grieving four-year-old."

"I'm sure they're nice people, Lisa, but come on."

"Cat tried to hide how much she wanted to go down to Florida with her friends, but Emma knew. And it took an entire year for Emma to convince her grandmother it was okay to go. And even then, every time they talked on the phone, Cat talked about moving back to New Hampshire because Emma was alone and the house was too big for one person and there was too much lawn to mow and this whole list of stuff. So Emma made up a man around the house and Cat was free to enjoy her book clubs and line-dancing classes."

Sean was going to point out the rather significant difference between lying about having a boyfriend and asking a stranger to move in for a month, but at that moment his aunt stepped outside and closed the slider behind her.

"I knew I'd find you out here." She smiled to let him know she wasn't offended he'd try to sneak a few quiet minutes away from his own welcome-home dinner. "What are you two talking about?"

"I ran into a friend of Lisa's today," he told her, enjoying the way Lisa's eyes got big and she started trying to communicate with him by way of frantic facial expressions behind her mother-in-law's back. "Emma Shaw."

"Emma Shaw… Oh! The one who does the landscaping, right?" Lisa nodded. "She's such a nice girl, but I haven't seen her in ages. Not since I ran into you two at the mall and overheard you talking about her engagement. How are she and her fiancé doing?"

Lisa opened her mouth, but closed it again when Sean folded his arms and looked at her, waiting to see how—or even if—she was going to get out of the conversation without lying outright to Aunt Mary.

"I…think they're having some problems," she finally said. Nice hedge, if a bit of an understatement.

"Oh, that's too bad. What's her fiancé's name? I meant to ask that day, but you started talking about some shoe sale and I forgot."

It was a few seconds before Lisa sighed in defeat. "Sean."

"Isn't that funny," Mary said, smiling at him before

turning back to her daughter-in-law. "What's his last name? Maybe I know his family."

That was a pretty safe bet.

"She told her grandmother she was dating our Sean," Lisa mumbled.

When his aunt pinned him with one of those looks that made grown Kowalski men squirm, Sean held up his hands. "I had nothing to do with it. I didn't even know."

"How could you not know you were engaged?"

"I was in Afghanistan. And I met her for the first time a few hours ago."

Her eyebrows knit. "I don't understand."

"It's nothing, really," Lisa said. "She didn't want her grandmother to worry about her, so she told her she had a boyfriend, and Sean's name was the first one that came to mind."

"That's crazy."

Sean grinned at Lisa. "Told ya."

The slider opened and Joey's head popped out. "Sean, you got drafted for Monopoly, and they're going to start cheating if you don't get in here and take your turn."

Since he'd rather go directly to jail and not pass go than listen to Lisa try to explain Emma Shaw to Aunt Mary anymore, he gave the women a whaddya-gonna-do shrug and followed Joey to the family room. He was late to the game, so he got stuck being the stupid thimble, but he just grinned and pulled up some floor next to the oversize coffee table.

He then proceeded to have his ass handed to him by his cousins' kids. A guy's attention couldn't wander to a mass of dark curls and pleading brown eyes for a few minutes without hotels popping up all over the damn place. One moment of distraction, remembering the way his body had responded to hers, and he found himself promising Bobby a trip to Dairy Queen in exchange for the loan of a fistful of paper money.

He didn't fare any better at Scattergories, though he did come up with *landscaper* when the letter was *L* and the category was occupations. Stephanie smoked them all, managing to find alliterative adjectives to go with her answers. *Prissy professor.* For an *F* fruit, she came up with *fresh figs.* Sean's answer space for that one was blank.

After the scores were tallied, he scratched down a few adjectives for his occupations pick. *Lovely landscaper. Lush landscaper.* Or maybe…*lusty landscaper?*

"The grown-ups are breaking out the cards for some five-card stud," Kevin told him. "We don't take checks."

Shit. At the rate he was going, he'd be bankrupt by the third hand.

Two

A cleaning service, Emma thought as she attacked another nest of rapidly procreating dust bunnies with the vacuum wand. That's what she wanted the birthday fairy to bring her.

Actually, she really wanted Sean Kowalski for her birthday, but he'd scratched himself off her wish list, leaving her with nothing to do but take out her frustrations on the dark, dust-bunny-breeding recesses of her house. No. Her grandmother's house.

Should she tell Gram over the phone that she and Sean had broken up, or wait until she got there?

It was a question she'd been asking herself since leaving his apartment the day before, but she still didn't have an answer. Gram would be heartbroken for her. And she'd want to fix it, which she couldn't do from 1,531 miles away.

Her phone vibrated in her back pocket, so she slapped the off button on the vacuum and tugged the phone free. A picture she'd taken of Lisa at Old Orchard Beach the previous summer filled the screen and she seriously considered hitting the ignore button. Lisa never called her in the morning because Emma was usually working and, as far as she knew, didn't know she'd rescheduled some appointment to free up time to obsess about the house before Gram arrived. That meant something was going on, and she had a gut feeling that something was Sean Kowalski.

After a bracing deep breath that didn't do much to brace her, she hit the talk button. "Hey, Lisa."

"Did you seriously ask Sean to move in with you?"

Emma groaned and sank onto the couch. "I really did."

"Did he shut the door in your face?"

"No, he was very polite and careful not to make any sudden moves."

"I think the phrase he used was 'batshit crazy.'"

Ouch.

"But hot," Lisa said. "'Tall, hot and batshit crazy' was his exact description."

The hot part made her feel a little better, but in re-membering his expression, she didn't think hot meant hot enough to overcome the batshit-crazy part. "I guess I'll wait until Gram gets here to tell her my fiancé and I called it quits."

"That sucks. If you say it just happened, she'll won-der why you're not broken up about it. But if it happened long enough ago so you're over it, she'll be upset you didn't tell her."

"Last week, when she said she was looking forward to meeting him, I said he felt the same way." She needed something hard to beat her head against. "How did I get myself into this?"

"Your mouth's quicker than your brain."

"Gee, thanks."

"So what did you think of him?" Lisa asked, her voice dropping down into the "let's dish" range.

It should have been an easy question to answer since she'd been thinking about him pretty much nonstop—except when she was obsessing about Gram—since she left his apartment yesterday. "I don't know. Tall, hot and, unfortunately for me, not batshit crazy. But it's not like I haven't seen his face before."

"Pictures don't do that man justice. Even a very happily married woman like me can see that."

No, they didn't, Emma thought, her gaze drawn to the ridiculous photo of Sean hung above the wingback chair. It was ridiculous because he'd had his arm around Lisa's niece Stephanie at a family barbecue, but, in response to a request from Gram, Lisa had helped her insert herself into the picture instead. She didn't even want to imagine what Sean would think of that.

"I wouldn't throw him out of bed," she admitted when Lisa waited for her to say something.

Maybe it was for the best that he'd said no. Her sleeping on a couch a few feet away from Sean Kowalski sleeping in her bed had seemed like a fine idea in theory. But, after meeting the man, being that close to him when the lights went out and not being *in* the bed with him wasn't a fine plan at all.

Work kept her pretty busy. She wasn't one for hanging around in bars, and none of the guys she already knew really got her motor running, so she'd been in a bit of a drought. Based on her reaction to simply meeting the man, Sean had the potential to rev her engine as if she was nosed up to the start line of a quarter-mile run.

"Crap, I've gotta run," Lisa said. "The boys all have

dentist appointments in an hour and I just saw my youngest run by with a handful of Skittles."

"Have fun with that." Emma wasn't sure how her friend did it. If Emma had four boys, she'd spend her days in the bathroom, taking nips off the bottle of Ny-Quil in the medicine cabinet.

"If I don't talk to you again before your grandmother arrives, good luck."

"Thanks." She'd need it.

After shoving her phone back in her pocket, Emma dragged the couch away from the wall, revealing a new nest of dust bunnies to vent her frustrations on.

She used her toe to turn on the vacuum, hoping the drone of the motor would drown out the no-longer-quiet purr of her own neglected engine.

Sean matched the number on the directions to the middle of nowhere Lisa had given him to the number on the mailbox—it had daisies painted on it, of all things—and turned his truck onto Emma Shaw's driveway.

The massive, traditional New England farmhouse at the end of the driveway was a thing of beauty. White siding—painted clapboards, not vinyl—with dark green shutters painted to match the metal roofing. A farmer's porch wrapped from the front around one side to what he assumed was the kitchen door, and hanging baskets full of different-colored flowers hung on either side of every support post.

There was an eclectically painted grouping of wooden rockers and side tables on the porch, inviting him to sit and chat awhile, and flower beds surrounded the sides of the house he could see. Not surprising, he guessed, as he parked alongside a pickup bearing magnetic signs with the same Landscaping by Emma logo she'd had on her sweatshirt.

After climbing out of his own truck, he climbed the steps to the front door, and after taking a deep breath—which didn't help because oxygen didn't cure insanity—he rang the doorbell.

It was almost a full minute before Emma opened the door. She looked cute as hell, with her hair scraped into a sloppy ponytail and a streak of dust down her nose. He stuck his hands in his pockets so he wouldn't reach out and wipe it away.

Her eyes widened when she saw him. "Hi."

"Got a minute?"

"Sure." She stepped back and let him into the foyer. Immediately to the left was a good-size living room, and all the furniture was dragged to the center of the hardwood floor. The air was thick with the scents of Murphy Oil Soap and Lemon Pledge. "Getting ready for the white-glove inspection?"

She grimaced and swiped at her face, but she only made it worse. "Gram's not like that. I just have a lot on my mind, and when that happens, I clean. It's a sickness."

He wasn't sure where to start. "I had dinner at my aunt and uncle's last night."

"How are they doing? I haven't seen Mrs. K. in ages."

"They're good. Got a chance to talk to Lisa, too. She says you're not crazy."

"I already told you I'm not crazy."

"Crazy people don't always know they're crazy."

She blew an annoyed breath at the wisps of hair escaping the ponytail. "Trust me, I know the *circumstances* are crazy. But I'm not. Do you want a drink or something? I have lemonade. Iced tea. I think I'm out of soda, which explains the frenzied, caffeine-fueled cleaning spree."

"I'm good, thanks." He didn't expect to be there long enough to drain a glass. "So let me see if I've got this straight. This all came about because your grandmother moved to Florida and couldn't have a good time because she was too worried about you?"

She nodded and perched on the arm of the couch. "Instead of enjoying herself, she was constantly worrying about me. About me being alone in this big house. Worrying that I won't remember to change the batteries in the smoke detectors or that I'll fall off a ladder trying to clean out the gutters. It seemed harmless at the time to tell her there was a man around the place."

"Why not tell her you'd hired a handyman or something?"

She laughed and he tried to ignore how much he liked the rich sound of it. "And have her frantic I'd managed to hire some transient serial killer? No, a boyfriend was better. Especially one whose family I know so well. You're my best friend's husband's cousin. How bad could you be?"

"What did you tell her I did before I became your imaginary boyfriend?"

"I told her you were in the army and that we met when you came home on leave to visit your family." She shrugged. "And that when you came home for good, we started dating. It was easier to remember if I tried to stick close to the truth. The timeline's off, of course. She thinks you got out of the army before you really did."

He shoved his hands in his pockets, pretty certain he must be losing his mind. "What would I get out of the deal?"

She looked as startled as he felt at the possibility he might actually be considering the plan. "A temporary job—landscaping, not just living here—and a place to stay."

"I have a place to stay. And guys like me can always find a temporary job."

"Guys like you?"

He smiled and raised an eyebrow at her. "Guys with strong backs who aren't afraid to get their hands dirty. What else?"

"Nothing, I guess. There's really nothing in it for you." Her shoulders slumped for a moment, but then she straightened her back and laughed. "It was crazy, anyway. I just wanted Gram to stop worrying about me and get on with her life. She loves it there—I can hear it in her voice—but she's torn."

"Did you think she wouldn't come home for your wedding?"

"I didn't think it would get that far. I assumed at some point I'd meet a nice guy—you know, one who actually knew I existed—and we'd start dating. I'd tell her you and I broke up, and after a little while tell her about my new boyfriend. The real one."

"But you haven't."

She shrugged and shook her head. "No. To be honest, I haven't really been looking. I want to grow my company enough so I can leave the heavy lifting to somebody else and do the design part-time before I get married and have kids."

He should get in his truck and drive away. He had his own life to sort out, and spending a month playing house with Emma would be a weird detour to take. Staying over Kevin's bar and finding a job pounding nails somewhere would give him everything he needed, but without the soap opera.

But she really did seem like a decent woman who'd gotten herself into one hell of a situation. Not to gain anything for herself, but so her grandmother could relax and enjoy her bingo games. Lisa liked her, of course, but so did his aunt Mary, and she was a pretty shrewd judge of character.

He cleared his throat. "Between graduation and signing my name on the army's dotted line, I wrecked a motorcycle. I messed myself up pretty bad, but when Aunt Mary called because she never went more than a few weeks without talking to us, I told her I just had a little road rash and a bruised elbow. I made my family lie for me, too."

Emma nodded. "Because there was nothing she could do and the truth would have worried her sick."

"Yeah. So I get it, I guess. Where you're coming from, I mean, and how you got to this point."

"It started out a harmless white lie, but then it got away from me. And I'm afraid if she comes home and I'm alone, she might not go back. She loves it down there and both of her best friends are there now."

He must be as crazy as she was. "If I do this, what's your endgame?"

"My endgame?" She shrugged. "I'm hoping before she leaves she'll agree to sell me the house. And then I'll wait awhile and tell her we broke up."

"Wait a minute. You're going to get her to give you her house under false pretenses?"

She shook her head, the ponytail swinging. "Not give. *Sell.* Her reasons for not selling to me are ridiculous, and before you proposed to me—" He tried not to react to her words, but it was damn weird when she talked about him like that. As if he had a double life he couldn't recall. "—she kept talking about putting it on the market because she didn't want this big old house tying me down and holding me back."

He looked at her, and her dark-coffee eyes met his with an intensity that almost made him take a step back. It sure seemed as if she was telling the truth. "If I start thinking you're just some deadbeat looking to scam Granny out of her house, I'm done."

"Are you seriously going to do this for me?"

"I guess I am." He pulled the cheap department-store diamond he'd picked up that morning from his pocket and held it out to her.

"Wait." There was a faint thread of panic in her voice. "What are you doing?"

"There's hedging and then there's outright lying. I'd like to keep the latter to a minimum, so I'm going to propose to you, and you're going to accept."

"Oh. Okay."

"So how about it? Wanna be my fiancée?"

When she blushed and nodded, he slid the ring on her finger. He had to wiggle it a bit to get it over her knuckle, but it fit better than he'd expected. It got a little awkward then, because it seemed as if *something* should follow a marriage proposal. A kiss. A hug. Hell, even a handshake.

Then she shoved her hands, ring and all, in the front pockets of her jeans. "Thank you. For doing this, I mean. And for the ring. I can pay you for it."

"Don't worry about it." False intentions or not, no woman of his—more or less—would pay for her own jewelry. "So, do we share a bedroom in this fairy tale of yours?"

He liked the way a slow blush burned her cheeks and had an urge to brush his thumb over the spot, to see if her skin felt as heated as it looked. "She knows we live together. Theoretically, of course. So she probably assumes we're sleeping together, yes."

Now, *that* was a plan he could get behind. "And how would you propose to handle that?"

"I put a sofa in the bedroom. For reading and watching TV…and for me to sleep on. You can have the bed."

They could discuss that later. "So what now? When does she get home?"

"In three days."

"Wow. Short notice."

"Maybe we should have dinner or something so we can talk and get to know a little about each other. I've got a full day tomorrow, but I could grab a pizza on the way home if you want to come over."

A first date with his fiancée, Sean mused. Life after the army wasn't turning out to be quite as boring as he'd feared it might be. "Sounds good. I like anything on my pizza that's not classified as a vegetable. What time?"

"About six? I'll be knee-deep in fertilizer tomorrow, so I'll need to shower first."

Since that was a visual he didn't need any more detail on, Sean nodded, then turned toward the door. "I'll see you at six, then."

He was almost free, when she called his name. "You won't change your mind, will you?"

"Like I said, if I think you're scamming her for anything but her emotional welfare, I'm gone. Otherwise, I gave you my word and I'll see it through."

He could almost see the tension easing from her body. "Thank you."

"Before I go, you need any help putting this furniture back?"

"No, but thanks. I'm not done scrubbing the baseboard trim yet."

He lifted a hand in farewell and let himself out. They had three days to become intimately acquainted enough to pass themselves off as a cohabitating engaged couple.

Mentally, he backspaced out the word *intimately.* There wouldn't be anything intimate about their relationship, despite the close quarters. They'd be playing a role, with stage kisses and fake affection. Once the curtain dropped—or the bedroom door closed, as the case may be—so would the act.

"You're going to what?"

It wasn't anything Sean hadn't asked himself every five minutes or so since getting sucked into Emma's plan, but it sounded different when his cousin said it. Or maybe it was Kevin's subsequent pointing and laughing his ass off that changed the tone.

"It's only a month," Sean said, maybe a little defensively. The shorter, dark-haired waitress—Darcy, he thought her name was—put a beer in front of him and he took a long pull. He'd been looking forward to it all day.

Kevin looked skeptical. "A month of living with a total stranger, pretending you're so madly in love with her you're going to marry her? For real?"

"No, not for real, moron. For pretend. That's the point."

His cousin laughed some more, then pulled out his cell phone and started texting. Sean craned his neck, but couldn't see the screen.

"What the hell are you doing?"

Kevin chuckled. "Telling my wife."

"You could have waited until I went upstairs."

"No, I really couldn't."

Kevin shut his phone, but it was only a few seconds before it chimed. He looked at the screen, chuckled, then was texting again.

Sean pulled out his phone and opened a new message to Kevin. I'm still here, asshole. Send.

A couple minutes later, Kevin grinned and slid his phone back in his pocket. "Beth wants to know the sleeping arrangements since there's no way even a grandmother will buy a separate-bedrooms story."

"Beth wants to know, huh?"

"Trust me, by now the whole family wants to know."

Sean was tempted to bang his head against the bar, but he wouldn't be able to knock himself out, so he didn't waste the effort. "There's a sofa in the bedroom. She'll sleep on it and I get the bed."

"Chivalrous."

"I'm too tall for a sofa."

"I don't know Emma well, but I seem to recall she's not exactly short." Kevin gave him a knowing look. "Not exactly hard on the eyes, either."

That she wasn't. But the last thing Sean wanted to do was get tangled up with a woman. Tangled up in the sheets? Usually okay, but that, along with playing house, could give Emma the wrong idea. Permanence wasn't in his current vocabulary. Not that it was necessarily in hers, either, but no sense taking any chances.

"When does your future grandmother-in-law arrive?" Kevin asked when he finally caught the hint Sean wasn't going to discuss his fake fiancée's easiness on the eyes.

"Saturday. We're supposed to have dinner together tonight and get to know each other, I guess."

"You think you're going to get to know each other well enough over a meal to fake out her grandmother?"

"She thinks we can do it."

"What do *you* think?"

Sean shrugged. "I told her I'd do it, so I'll do my best to make sure we pull it off."

"Does Ma know about this yet?"

"Not yet," he said, grimacing. He wasn't looking forward to telling her, either. Assuming Beth wasn't on the phone with her already, giving her the big news.

Sean stood and picked up his beer, intending to take it upstairs with him. He could return the empty mug later. "I know as soon as I walk away you're going to call Joe and Mike, so I'll just leave it to you to spread the word."

Kevin laughed. "Don't forget Mitch. And Ryan and Josh and Liz."

Sean froze, beer halfway to his mouth. Shit. He hadn't even thought about his brothers and sister and what they might think. Thinking he'd lost his mind was a given, but if one of them got to thinking he needed saving from himself and made the drive over, it would blow everything all to shit.

"Do me a favor," he said, "and let me give them the heads-up. And try to keep your half of the family in check."

"I'll try, but don't put off calling them too long. Once Ma hears about it…"

Yeah, that's what he was afraid of. He'd have to talk to Aunt Mary soon, and as much as he didn't want to, he'd have to have that discussion in person. Hopefully, her wooden spoon wouldn't be close at hand. That sucker hurt.

He went up to the apartment that was supposed to

be a temporary home, but was now going to be nothing more than a motel stop, and sank onto the couch. He hadn't unpacked much yet—not that he had a lot to unpack—so the physical act of moving into Emma's house wouldn't be difficult.

And he didn't think he'd have too hard a time pretending to be attracted to her. Batshit crazy or not, she was tall—which he liked in a woman—and hot, which he *really* liked. And that hair… She had the kind of hair a man could bury his face in or plunge his hands into, capturing the thick, dark cloud in his fingers.

Sean shifted on the couch, muttering some choice words under his breath. It had been a long time since he'd buried his face in any woman's hair, and now he'd be stuck sleeping in the same room with a woman it would be a bad idea to touch. He'd be close enough to smell her shampoo. To hear the whisper of breath and skin as she sighed and shifted in her sleep. But too far away to run his hand down the long, warm curve of her back and turn that sigh into his name on her lips.

Groaning, he hit the TV power button on the remote control next to his leg, looking for some distraction. A movie. An old fight rerun. Hell, a Three Stooges marathon would do. Anything to get his mind off sex. He couldn't be thinking those kinds of thoughts.

He was an engaged man now.

Three

Emma changed her mind about Sean Kowalski at least a dozen times over the course of her workday, but she never got as far as calling Lisa to ask for his cell-phone number—which she'd stupidly forgotten to get—before she remembered what was at stake.

Peace of mind for Gram. Freedom from worrying about losing her home for herself. Pretty much everything, as far as she was concerned.

So at six o'clock, she opened the door to Sean with her hair still damp from the shower and a smile on her face. "I wasn't sure you'd come."

He shrugged and held up a six-pack of bottled Budweiser. "I told you I would. I wasn't sure what kind of wine you'd like, or even if you like it at all, so I brought beer."

"Sounds good. Come on in. The pizza's in the kitchen. I'm starving, so I got a Meat Lover's."

"Beer was probably a better choice than wine, then. Not sure if you serve red or white with pepperoni, ham, sausage, hamburger and bacon."

She laughed and led him into the kitchen, but the

amusement died in her throat when he reached for the fridge door, presumably to keep the beer cold, then stopped. He frowned and leaned closer. Peered at the photograph held in place by a brown-eyed-Susan magnet. This one showed Emma at a Red Sox game with Sean's arm draped around her shoulder and the green field of Fenway Park behind them.

He was still frowning. "This creeps me out a little. Isn't that supposed to be Lisa? I'm pretty sure I was at that game with Mikey and his wife."

"It was Lisa who did the manipulating, not me, if that makes it any less creepy."

"Not really. Just how many of these fake pictures do you have?"

"A couple dozen, I guess, that Lisa's done for me over time. We're not really photograph happy, which helps, but I've got enough so it looks like we're a couple, at least. And I needed some to take with me when I flew down to visit her."

"Where was I when you went to Florida?"

"You couldn't get away."

"From what?"

She shrugged. "You happened to have a family wedding going on during the only weekend I could spare from work. You're a busy guy, really."

He looked as if he was going to say something else, but then he shook his head and stuck the six-pack in the fridge, pulling out two bottles before closing the door. After twisting off the caps, he set one down by each plate.

"Anything I can help you with?"

She shook her head. "Everything's on the table. Go ahead and dig in."

It didn't escape her notice that he placed a slice on her

plate before serving himself, and it gave her hopefulness
a little boost. Obviously he'd been raised with good manners, which would not only help him win Gram over, but
make him more apt to stick to his word.

Before she sat, she grabbed the spiral-bound journal
she'd been jotting down notes in since she'd first joked
about her plan to Lisa, and set it on the table. "I wrote
down a few things. You know, about myself? If you skim
through it, it'll help you pretend you've known me longer than two days."

Instead of waiting until they were done, he set down
his slice, picked up the notebook and opened it to a random page. "You're not afraid of spiders, but you hate
slugs? That's relevant?"

"It's something you would know about me."

"You graduated from the University of New Hampshire. Your feet aren't ticklish." He chuckled and shook
his head. "You actually come with an owner's manual?"

"You could call it that. And if you could write something up for me to look over, that would be great."

He shrugged and flipped through a few more pages
of the journal. "I'm a guy. I like guy stuff. Steak. Football. Beer. Women."

"One woman, singular. At least for the next month,
and then you can go back to your wild pluralizing ways."
She took a sip of her beer. "You think that's all I need to
know about you?"

"That's the important stuff. I could write it on a sticky
note, if you want, along with my favorite sexual position.
Which isn't missionary, by the way."

It was right there on the tip of her tongue—*then what
is your favorite sexual position?*—but she bit it back. The
last thing she needed to know about a man she was going

to share a bedroom with for a month was how he liked his sex. "I hardly think that'll come up in conversation."

"It's more relevant than slugs."

"Since you'll be doing more gardening than having sex, not really."

"Wait a minute." He stabbed a finger at one of the notes in the journal. "You can't cook?"

"Not well. Microwave directions help."

"I'd never marry a woman who can't cook."

"I'd never marry the kind of man who'd never marry a woman who can't cook, so it's a good thing we're just pretending."

He closed the journal and set it aside to return to his pizza. But before he bit into it, he looked across the table at her. "You told her we met while I was home on leave, but did you tell her *how* we met?"

"It's on page one of the journal."

"Paraphrase it for me."

She really didn't want to. Somehow the idea of him reading her lies seemed less directly humiliating than her reciting them out loud. But he cocked an eyebrow at her as he chewed, clearly waiting for her to tell the story. "We met at Jasper's Bar & Grille."

"Kevin's bar?"

"You were home on leave and he hadn't owned the place long, so you stopped in to check it out. Lisa and I had been shopping in the city and stopped in for a Jasper burger." She felt her face flush and stared down at her plate. "It was love at first sight."

She heard him chuckle and wanted to glare at him, but she had a feeling that would only turn his chuckle into a full-fledged laugh. "So you wrote to me and I wrote back and then I left the army and here we are."

"In a nutshell." She let him swallow his mouthful of pizza, then asked, "You have plans for tomorrow?"

He shook his head. "Not really."

"Want to start work? Just a half day, over on the big lake. And then we could do some shopping. Stock up on food and get some stuff so it looks like you actually live here."

"Sounds good. What time?"

"I usually leave here at seven-thirty. I can probably meet you somewhere so you don't have to get up even earlier to drive over here."

"I'll be here. I never sleep past six, anyway."

"Never?" She was up at six on weekdays, but on weekends she liked to sleep in a bit.

"Never. And I like a big breakfast, so I hope you're a morning person."

He kept a straight face, but Emma could see the amusement in his eyes. "You can get two doughnuts at the coffee shop drive-through, then."

When the amusement spread to his mouth, Emma took a long swig of beer and looked anywhere but at the curve of his lips. He had a nice mouth. A *really* nice mouth that looked as if it knew its way around a kiss, and since the thought of kissing Sean gave her a need to squirm in her chair, she looked at the clock over the stove. And at the grocery list stuck to the fridge.

But, dammit, right next to the grocery list was the picture of her and Sean, and the grin didn't lose its potency in two dimensions. Thank goodness he had those good manners and wasn't the kind of guy to plant one on her in front of her grandmother.

The discussion turned to first-date small talk while they ate. They both liked cheesy action movies and preferred home-style diners to fancy restaurants. Emma read romance and Sean read horror and biographies. They both preferred half-hour sitcoms to hour-long dramas or reality shows, and they both hated shopping for clothes.

It was a start, she told herself as she walked him to the door. Hopefully, he'd look through the notes she'd written for him, and she knew a lot about him already, thanks to Lisa. It would have to be enough.

As soon as Emma opened the door at twenty after seven, Sean could see she had spent as much time tossing and turning the night before as he had. She looked tired and her mouth was set in a way that made her look a little cranky.

"I'm running a few minutes behind," she said. "You want a coffee?"

"Sure." He followed her into the kitchen, and when she waved in the direction of the coffeemaker before sitting at the table, he assumed he was on his own.

Maybe it was a test, he thought as he opened the cabinet over the coffeemaker in search of a mug. Luckily, she organized her kitchen in a way that made sense to him, so he didn't have to rummage through drawers looking for a spoon. He could almost pass for somebody who lived there.

Once he'd put the half-and-half back in the fridge, he pulled up a chair across from her. She ignored him, sipping her coffee while she flipped through an enormous leather-bound organizer. Then she pulled out her phone and hit a button.

"Hey, it's Emma," she said after a pause. "The Duncans decided they don't like the black mulch, after all. Or

Mrs. Duncan did, rather. She thought it would be artsy, but it—and I quote—'swallows up the accent lighting.'"

Another long pause while she rubbed her forehead. "I can use most of it to touch up for my other clients with the black, but I'll need three yards of the gold cedar for the Duncans. And, yes, she knows how much it will cost."

Sean tuned her out, then picked up his coffee mug and wandered out of the kitchen. It seemed a little rude to go roaming around her house, but her grandmother might suspect something was up if Sean had to ask her for directions to the bathroom.

In the living room he found another picture of himself and Emma. It took him a few minutes to figure out it was Stephanie who'd been replaced that time, and only because a balloon was barely visible along one edge. He'd been home on a short leave and took the time to drive over from Maine for Stephanie's birthday because her long, funny letters meant the world to him during deployment.

Besides a half bath and a boring formal dining room, he found her office on the ground floor. It wasn't a big room, but bookshelves full of romance novels lined the walls. In one corner, a fat easy chair begged to be relaxed in and a gas parlor stove stood across the room. A desk sat under the window, holding a fairly new computer and piles of paper threatening to slide off in every direction. He wondered if the filing cabinet next to the desk was full or if she just ignored it.

He could still hear her voice coming from the kitchen, so he set his coffee down on an end table and made his way up the stairs. All the doors stood open, so he peeked his head in each room as he walked down the hall.

The first room he looked in had to be her grandmother's, judging by the photos and decor. A lot of crocheted things, too. Not the room he was looking for, so he kept going.

He found what looked like a combination guest room and storage closet, so he guessed she didn't have a lot of overnight company. The bathroom was big and had been updated in the last decade or so. Hiding behind a set of louvered doors was a state-of-the-art washer-and-dryer set, which wasn't surprising considering what Emma did for a living.

Finally, at the end of the hall on the right, he found what had to be Emma's bedroom. His bedroom.

Judging by the long arch meant to disguise a weight-bearing beam, it had started life as two smaller bedrooms, but at some point the wall had been removed to make a master suite. Besides a bed that looked queen-size and the usual bedroom furnishings, there was a sitting area. End table with a lamp surrounded by more books. A small flat-screen TV mounted to the wall. And the couch she'd be sleeping on for the next month.

Even with the room's expansion, he figured there was only about ten feet between the bed and the couch. Despite the fact he'd learned over the years to sleep through any conditions, this arrangement was going to be a little awkward. Intimate.

There was a door to the left of the sitting area, and he poked his head through to find a three-quarter bath—toilet, sink and a shower. It'd do.

Aware of how many minutes he'd burned exploring, Sean went back down to the kitchen, grabbing his coffee along the way. He could see by the tension in her shoulders she didn't really care for him being so free with her home, but she'd probably come to the same conclusion he had.

"I just want to finish this coffee," she said. "Rough night."

He splashed the little bit of hot coffee left in the pot into his mug and leaned against the counter, watching her make a few more notes in her organizer.

"So…landscaping, huh?" He'd pushed a few mowers in his time. "Don't you think having *Emma* in the business name's a bad idea, though?"

She set down her pen and narrowed her eyes at him. "What? Girls can't be landscapers? You've heard we're allowed to vote now, right?"

"I just think if I want my lawn mowed or my weeds whacked, I'm more likely to call Bob or Fred."

"And that's fine. If you want somebody to mow your lawn or whack your weeds, call Bob or Fred. But if you want an artist to design the beautiful, virtually maintenance-free landscaping for your summer cottage or lake house, you call Emma."

Her defensive tone made him want to chuckle and poke at her some more, but he stifled the urge. "So you specialize in design, then?"

"Yes, but I do the labor, too." She smiled. "Except for the next month, of course. I'll have you to do the heavy lifting."

"Not afraid of a little hard work." He was looking forward to it, actually. His body was accustomed to a little more physical activity than it was currently getting. If he got too soft, his cousins would wipe the grass with him during the annual Fourth of July family football game.

Emma looked at her watch and then stood to rinse her coffee mug. "Time to hit the road."

It wasn't until she'd climbed behind the wheel of her truck and was watching him expectantly that Sean realized he couldn't remember a time he'd ever ridden shotgun to a female driver. Call him old-fashioned, but he liked to be the one in control.

But she'd be signing his paychecks for the next few weeks, so she was the boss. He slid in on the passenger side and closed the door, only to find himself white-knuckled by the time they reached the highway. She didn't drive any better than she claimed she cooked.

They spent the morning at a three-million-dollar summer home on the shores of Lake Winnipesaukee, where he had the joy of turning a pile of rocks dumped next to the house into stone walls outlining what would be the perennial beds, whatever the hell that meant.

It was good physical labor that worked up a sweat, but it didn't make him nearly as hot and bothered as watching Emma work. She didn't whine. Didn't worry about breaking a nail. She just worked alongside him, humming country tunes under her breath, and he found out the hard way how attractive a hardworking woman could be.

Ten feet, he thought. Ten feet between his bed and hers. A few steps.

Then she bent over in front of him to adjust a rock, and he dropped the one he was holding onto his toes, which made a dozen curses echo through his head, though he managed not to say them out loud.

Thirty days with Emma was shaping up to be one hell of a job.

Four

"It's not Walt Disney World, Sean. You get in, you get what you need and you get out." If Emma had known shopping with him was going to be like this, she would have hidden a cattle prod in her purse.

"I'm shopping."

"No, you're meandering."

He stopped the cart—again—to look at something on the shelf and then resumed walking at a snail's pace. "I might see something I need."

"I have a list. See?" She held it up. "I know what we need."

"That's *your* list. Do you have salt-and-vinegar chips on it?"

"No. I don't like salt-and-vinegar flavor. Makes my tongue burn."

"See? If we sprint through the store, just getting what's on your list, I won't have any salt-and-vinegar chips."

"Maybe if you'd written down a few notes about yourself, I would have put them on my list."

He shook his head. "*I* don't come with an owner's manual. Sorry."

She pulled on the end of the cart, trying to make him move a little faster. "The store closes in six hours. You might need to pick up the pace."

He stopped so abruptly the cart jerked her arm. "You need to relax."

"No, I need to get the shopping done so I can move on to the next thing." She glared at him, willing him to shut his mouth and move his feet.

"You know, for a long time I've had what Uncle Sam saw fit to issue me and what my family could send in a care package," he said quietly, and her impatience fizzled and died like a match dropped in a puddle. "When I got back stateside, I bought some necessities, but not a lot because I was on the move. I'd like to browse a little bit."

"I'm sorry." She let go of the cart and blew out a breath. "Here you are doing me a huge favor and I'm being all...intense."

"Bitchy," he muttered, not quite under his breath.

"I prefer *intense*."

"Intensely bitchy."

Between the amusement lurking at the corners of his mouth and the fact he was right, Emma decided to let it go. Not only his less-than-flattering assessment of her mood, but the stress of her grandmother's impending arrival. What was the worst that could happen if this plan didn't work? Gram would be angry and see this little escapade as proof it was all too much for Emma. She'd sell the house and Emma would rent an apartment and life would go on.

And that thought made her want to cry, so she shook it off and tried to be patient as they very, very slowly made their way up and down the aisles.

"What the hell is this?" Sean picked up a box from the

shelf and showed it to her. "It looks like a cheese grater for your feet."

"Women like having smooth heels."

"Do you have one of these?"

"Hell, no. It looks like a cheese grater."

They laughed as he put it back and moved on to the next thing that caught his fancy. Between the department store and the grocery store, they managed to almost fill the bed of his truck, but an hour later when everything was all put away, it didn't seem to make much of a difference.

"It still doesn't look like you've lived here for a year," Emma said.

Sean shrugged and sat backward on a kitchen chair, folding his arms across the back of it. "She won't think much of it. Single, former army guys aren't really known for dragging around domestic clutter."

"It just seems like you should have more…stuff. Pictures and sports trophies and stuff like that."

"It's all in boxes in the attic back home. If she says something, which she won't, I'll just tell her I haven't gotten around to getting them yet."

She grabbed a couple of sodas out of the fridge and set one in front of him. "Lisa told me a little bit about your family. She said you're all really close to Leo and Mary, even though you were all in Maine."

"My mom died when I was nine. It was an aneurysm, so we didn't even see it coming, and everything would have gone to shit, including my dad, if not for Aunt Mary and Rosie. Rosie's the housekeeper at the lodge, but really she's more than that. On top of raising her own daughter, she stepped up and helped my dad raise the five of us. He died nine years ago, but Rosie's still there, helping Josh run the lodge. But without Aunt Mary backing her up, I don't know how we would have turned out."

She loved the way his face softened when he talked about his family. And the way the muscles in his arm flexed as he lifted the soda to his mouth. And the way his throat worked as he swallowed. And...

And nothing, she told herself. She needed to think of him as an employee...kind of. Except for the whole sharing-a-bedroom thing.

"So tomorrow's the big day," he said, and she wondered if he was just trying to change the subject away from his family. "Are you ready?"

"As ready as I can be, I guess. I can't wait to see Gram, of course. I've missed her so much, but a month is a long time."

"It'll fly by once we settle in and you two start catching up on lost time."

She twisted the ring on her finger, watching the stone catch the last rays of the late-day sun. "For something I've obsessed about right down to the last detail, I can't help but think I should have thought it through a little more."

"You can still change your mind."

She shook her head. "No, we're committed."

"Or we should be," he said, and they both laughed.

Then he drained the last of his soda and stood. "I'm going to hit the road. Gonna relax and get a good night's sleep before the big show starts."

"Okay. If you bring your stuff over by ten, you'll have time to put it away before I have to leave for the airport."

"I'll be here."

After he was gone, Emma collapsed on the couch in a bundle of raw nerves. Starting tomorrow, she was going to have to start convincing her grandmother she was in love with Sean Kowalski. And tomorrow Sean would be moving into her house. Into her bedroom. Into her life.

A good night's sleep was out of the question.

After a few hours of hard deliberation, Sean decided to call his oldest brother, Mitch. He was a rolling stone, too, never staying in one place too long or spending too much time in one woman's bed. He, of all the siblings, was the least likely to think Sean had left his marbles overseas and needed an intervention.

"Hey, little brother," Mitch said after the third ring. "How's it going?"

"Good." Weird, but good. "You got a minute?"

"Five or six, even. I'm in Chicago, getting ready to drop an old office building, but we're waiting on paperwork right now." Mitch's childhood obsession with wrecking balls had led to his being one of the more respected controlled-demolition experts in the country. "What's up?"

"I've got myself into a little situation here, and since I don't have time to explain it over and over, I thought maybe you could spread the word."

"In other words, you don't want to tell Liz."

"Pretty much." *Fierce* was a good word to sum up the only girl of the five kids. "I don't want to be the one to tell Rosie, either."

"Does it involve bail money?"

Sean laughed. "No."

"A shotgun wedding?"

"Um…not exactly."

He told Mitch the story, starting with Emma knocking on his door and leading up to the present—him at

Kevin's apartment to grab his few belongings and make the dreaded phone call.

"Holy shit," Mitch said when he was done talking. "That definitely qualifies as a *situation*. Is she hot?"

"Very. But she can't cook worth a damn."

"That's what takeout's for." His brother was quiet for a few seconds, then chuckled. "So this hot chick's going to pay you to be her man for a month. Is that legal in New Hampshire now?"

"Screw you, Mitch. She's paying me to do landscaping. The fiancé thing is…whatever. She'll be sleeping on the couch in the bedroom. I'll be in the bed. It's strictly hands-off."

"My money's on a week."

His brothers would have the betting pool in place by the end of the day, no doubt. "Throw me in for making the whole month. Got no problem taking your money."

"She's hot and single. You're a guy. Sleeping in the same room? You're as good as half in the sack already."

Not a chance. "Look, I've got to get going. Get my toothbrush in her bathroom before we head to the airport and all that."

"I think I'll call Liz first," Mitch told him. "I might even record the conversation."

"The important thing is that you get the story straight. If any of you come over for the Fourth of July, you need to have your shit together."

"Oh, I'll be there. You can bet your ass on that. And speaking of the Fourth, what do Uncle Leo and Aunt Mary think of all this?"

Sean winced. "I don't think they know yet. The rest of them do, though, so it's only a matter of time before Aunt Mary comes after me. I've been putting it off."

"That only makes it worse."

"I know. But if it's already a done deal by the time she finds out, maybe she'll go along."

That made Mitch laugh out loud again. "Sure, buddy. You keep telling yourself that."

"I'm hanging up now."

"Good. I've got phone calls to make."

Sean shoved his phone in his pocket and made one last trip around the apartment. Since everything he owned fit in his duffel and he'd only been there a few days, it didn't take long to make sure he had everything.

Five minutes later, he was on the road, and it wasn't long before he was turning in to the driveway. He glanced at the mailbox and shook his head as he parked in front of his temporary home. The one with daisies on the mailbox and Emma under the same roof.

It was just a month, he reminded himself. One month and then he'd be on his way, with his brothers' money and a few paychecks in his pocket and no strings trying to hold him back.

Emma knew a few things about Sean Kowalski. She knew he was tall and outrageously handsome and liked salt-and-vinegar potato chips. She knew he had a body designed to trigger female double takes everywhere he went. She knew he'd served his country, wasn't afraid of a day's work, loved his family, played with his cousins' children and was, no doubt, though she hadn't seen it yet, kind to animals.

What she hadn't known was how much impact seeing him stretch out on her bed and tuck his hands under his head would have on her. And she certainly hadn't anticipated the heat that curled through her body and settled in a place she'd been neglecting for a while.

"A little soft," he said, squirming against the mattress in a way that made her hips want to wiggle along for the ride. "I like it harder."

Emma coughed to cover the little squeaking sound she made, as if announcing her hormones' state of libidinous distress. "I like to nestle."

"It's a girlie bed."

Not with him sprawled across it, it wasn't. "I'm a girl."

"I noticed." When he turned his head and winked at her, she swallowed hard and glanced at her watch in what she hoped was an obvious gesture. She just wanted him off her bed.

Which wasn't going to help, of course, because he was going to be sleeping in that bed for the next month. And she'd be about ten feet away, tossing and turning on the couch. Great plan. Inspired, really.

"Time to go?" he asked.

"Yeah." They'd done everything they could. What little he owned had been moved in. The biography of Ulysses S. Grant he was reading was tossed on the coffee table in the living room. A battered and oversize coffee mug emblazoned with the army logo was upside down next to her favorite mug in the dish rack. She'd found it at the Salvation Army store, along with a few other things that might help give the illusion he'd been living there for a year. It was showtime.

"Okay. Gimme a few minutes and I'll meet you outside."

"Wait. You're going, too?"

He snorted and swung his feet to the floor. "Of course I'm going with you to pick up your grandmother at the airport. What kind of jerk did you think you were marrying?"

"This is insane."

"Pretty sure I already told you that." His eyes grew serious. "This is your last chance, you know. I can be out of here in a half hour. You can still tell her we broke up and you must not have loved me as much as you thought because you're not all broken up about it. She'll be so thankful you came to your senses before marrying me, she won't even ask too many questions."

She knew he was right. It was insane. And this *was* her last chance to back out. Once she introduced him to Gram at the airport, they were all in. For a month.

Then she shook her head. "No. We can do this and then Gram's mind will be at ease and she can finally enjoy her retirement so I can move on with my life."

Sean walked over to her, so close she wondered if he was going to try to shake some sense into her. "Then there's just one more thing to do."

"Oh, crap. What did I forget?" Considering how much time she'd spent going over everything in her mind instead of sleeping, she couldn't imagine what it would be.

When he rested his hand at her waist for a few seconds before sliding it around to the small of her back, she felt her muscles tense and her cheeks burn.

"You can't be doing that," he said in the same low, husky kind of voice a man would use to tell a woman he wanted to take off her clothes.

Her mind was frozen, all of her attention on that warm pressure against her T-shirt, and it took a few seconds to form a coherent sentence. "Doing what?"

"You're as jumpy as a virgin at a frat party." He ran his fingers up over her spine until he reached the small bump of her bra strap, and then back down to her waist. "We've been dating a year and a half, and living together for a year of it, but you still blush and tense up when I touch you?"

He had a point, but there was no way to fix that before Gram got off her plane. "Maybe you're just that good."

It was the wrong thing to say if she was trying to back him off and settle her overheating nerves. The grin he gave her would have been potent enough to get her out of her clothes if the situation was different.

"That's a story I can get behind," he said.

"Thought we were trying to keep the lies to a minimum."

The grin only widened. "Who says it's a lie?"

She rolled her eyes and tried to step back—really needing to put a little space between them—but he held her close. "We're going to be late."

"No, we're not. But don't you think we should at least have a practice kiss first?"

Almost against her will, her gaze focused on his mouth. Yes. Yes, they should. "If Gram asked, I was going to tell her you have a thing about public displays of affection."

"This isn't public. This is your—*our*—home."

"Public as in with an audience." She needed to look away from his mouth, especially since it was getting closer, but she couldn't.

When his face got close enough so she registered his intent, she raised her gaze to his, but it was too late. Before she could react, his lips met hers, his hand still on her back to hold her close, and she closed her eyes.

Practice. That's all it was. And if her body started tingling and her fingers itched to run through his hair and her body wanted to melt against his…well, that just boded well for a month of pretending they were into each other, didn't it?

The jolt of heat that ran like an electrical shock through her body could be an unwelcome complication, but she'd worry about that later. Like maybe when she wasn't too busy thinking about pushing him back onto that soft, girlie bed he'd complained about and proving women liked it a little harder, too.

It took every ounce of self-control she could muster not to whimper in protest when his lips left hers. She wanted to take his head in her hands and drag his mouth in for another kiss. Maybe slip her hands under the back of his T-shirt so she could glide them over the warm flesh of his back and feel his muscles twitch under her fingertips.

"Not bad for a practice kiss," he said in a casual voice that pissed her off. No way could he have felt nothing while her senses sizzled like a drop of water on a hot, oiled skillet.

"And the Oscar goes to," she muttered when he winked and walked out of the room.

She was about to swear and take a kick at the coffee-table leg when she spotted him in the full-length mirror on the closet door standing ajar. He'd stopped just outside in the hall, and she watched his reverse image as he pulled at the fly of his jeans, no doubt adjusting for the evidence he wasn't as unaffected as he wanted her to think he was. Then he rolled his shoulders and kept walking.

Despite the fact both of them being affected would be an even greater complication, Emma was smiling when she met up with him again in the front hall.

"We can take my truck," he told her in a terse voice that made her have to smother a bigger and much more smug smile.

"No, we can't. I have the extended cab and it might rain. We can't throw Gram's luggage in the bed to get wet."

"I'm driving."

She paused halfway out the front door. "Excuse me?"

"You drive like a girl." He held out his hand, presumably for her keys.

"You're an ass."

"We can stand here and argue about it. I'm sure your grandmother will understand."

"A sexist ass, no less."

He grinned and snatched her keys out of her hand before she could react. "Next time, you might want to actually meet the man you're going to marry before you tell your family about him. Get in the truck. *Honey.*"

Five

Catherine Shaw, who preferred to be called Cat, stepped
off the plane in Manchester and quickly retrieved her
luggage. It was good to be back, if only temporarily.
There was a time she might have thought it was good
to be *home,* but she considered herself a Floridian now.

It had cost her a little extra to fly into New Hampshire,
rather than to Logan Airport, but Emma was picking her
up and she didn't want her granddaughter bothered with
Boston, even if her fiancé was driving.

They'd arranged to meet by the small food court and
she spotted Emma immediately, standing next to a tall,
good-looking man who was scanning the airport, watching people. A year and a half of civilian life hadn't taken
much of the edge off the soldier.

Emma hadn't seen her yet, and she took a few minutes
to give her granddaughter a good looking over.

She was thinner, which wasn't surprising since the
girl couldn't cook worth a darn. Her work was so physical she was burning through her steady diet of takeout
and microwave meals. She'd have to put some meat on
the girl's bones while she was there.

Emma looked so much like her mother at first glance, but it was mostly the hair. In the lines of her nose and mouth and the dark brown of her eyes, Cat could see glimpses of the son and husband she'd lost. As always, she felt the pang of grief like a constant and unwelcome companion, but it was overshadowed by her gratitude for the blessing that was her granddaughter.

Then Sean's eyes met hers and he obviously recognized her—no doubt from the photos she sometimes remembered to email from Florida. He touched Emma's arm and Cat didn't miss the way she jumped, her cheeks flushing pink.

Then Emma was running across the lobby and Cat opened her arms for a fierce hug. "Gram!"

She squeezed Emma, rocking a little, until she caught sight of her future grandson-in-law through the corner of her eye. He looked anxious, shifting his weight from foot to foot while he watched their reunion.

Cat let go of Emma and turned to him, extending her hand. "You must be Sean."

He had a decent grip. She didn't trust men with weak handshakes. "It's nice to meet you, Mrs. Shaw."

Lovely manners, too. "Please, call me Cat. Being called Mrs. Shaw makes me feel old."

He grinned, a naughty grin that probably weakened her granddaughter's knees. "Anybody can see you're anything but that… Cat."

"I think you and I will get along just fine."

"How was your flight?" Emma asked as Sean relieved Cat of her luggage and began herding them toward the exit.

"Uneventful, which is never a bad thing."

When they made their way through the parking lot,

the first light drops of rain were falling, so Sean put her luggage in the backseat of the truck and Emma climbed in after it. Cat was impressed when he took her elbow to help her into the passenger seat before closing her door and going around to his own side. He was a nice boy.

"So you have family around here, Sean?" she asked when they were on the highway, heading north.

"Yes, ma'am, I do. My aunt and uncle live about fifteen minutes from…home, and I've got four cousins and their families nearby."

"Oh, good. I can't wait to meet them all."

He turned his head and gave her a quick glance before looking back to the road, and she wondered why it would come as a surprise his fiancée's grandmother would want to meet his family.

"They're always pretty busy," he said, "what with all the kids and everything, but I'll see what I can do. Maybe a barbecue or something soon."

It was a little over an hour's ride, giving Cat plenty of time to not only listen to Emma's constant chatter about the house and work, but to feel the anxiety in the truck. Her granddaughter's voice was a little too chipper. Sean's fingers kept tightening on the steering wheel, then he'd flex them and relax, but they'd tighten again. She'd almost think they'd had a fight before her arrival, but there wasn't any anger simmering between them. Just nervousness.

Cat stopped worrying about them when Sean turned onto the driveway and drove up to the beautiful old house she'd called home since she was a young bride of nineteen. She and John had borrowed down-payment money from his father to buy it when she got pregnant, expecting to fill it with a large and noisy, but loving, family.

They had no way of knowing at the time Johnny would be their only child or that the two of them would end up spending several years rattling around the place alone until tragedy gave them Emma. The girl had not only brought joy back into their lives, but had breathed life back into the house.

It was the joy Cat chose to remember as Sean hopped out of the truck and jogged around to open her door. She smiled when he offered his hand to help her down. And she watched as he did the same for Emma.

Her granddaughter hesitated for only a second, but Cat didn't miss it. Then she put her hand in Sean's, clearly flustered, and hopped out of the truck. Her feet had barely hit the ground before she pulled her hand away and turned to grab the luggage.

It was going to be an interesting month. Cat wasn't sure exactly what was going on, but she knew one thing for sure—whatever they were up to, Emma and Sean hadn't been sharing a bed and a bathroom for the past year.

Sean didn't think it was going too badly...until Emma set a steaming glass dish on a trivet in the middle of the table. It was a casserole. One with tufts of little green trees sticking up out of some kind of sauce.

Broccoli. He hated broccoli. Loathed it.

"Chicken Divan," Emma said, and only an idiot could have missed the note of pride in her voice as she put her hands on her hips, oven mitts and all. "It's my best dish—okay, my only real baked dish—so I made it as a welcome-home meal."

Cat smiled and Sean forced his lips to move into what he hoped was a similar expression. A woman who was sleeping with and living with and planning a future with a man would know he didn't like broccoli. And it was his own damn fault for laughing off her suggestion he write an owner's manual of his own.

She served him first, maybe because he was the fake man of the house, plopping in front of him a steaming pile of perfectly good chicken and cheese ruined by the green vegetable. He smiled at her—or maybe grimaced—and took a sip of iced tea.

He could do this. He'd survived boot camp. He'd survived combat and the harsh weather of Afghanistan. He could survive broccoli. Probably.

"It looks wonderful," Cat practically cooed, and Sean's stomach rumbled. Whether in hunger or protest he couldn't say.

Emma, of course, flushed with pleasure at the compliment. With a few wisps of hair framing her pink cheeks and her eyes sparkling, she was beautiful. Not beautiful enough to merit eating broccoli, but beautiful enough so he watched her for a minute as she served herself and sat down across from him.

Then he made himself look back to his own plate. He'd given his word he'd make this charade work, and Cat wanting to know why Emma fed her fiancé his least favorite food wasn't a good way to start.

He put it off as long as he could—picking out mouthfuls of cheesy chicken that weren't too bad—but he couldn't leave behind a pile of uneaten broccoli.

Suck it up, soldier. The broccoli's tree trunk or stalk or whatever people called it squeaked between his teeth, a little undercooked. Or maybe it was supposed to feel like that. Either way, he didn't like it, so he chewed and swallowed as fast as he could. Then he dug up another forkful and did it again.

He'd gotten through basic training by putting one reluctant foot in front of the other, and that's how he got through Emma's Chicken Divan. One squeaky, nauseating bite after another.

"Sean, you said your aunt and uncle live near here," Cat said in between a bite, "but Emma told me you have two older brothers and a younger brother and sister in Maine?"

Silently thankful for any excuse to put down his fork, Sean gulped down some iced tea and wiped his mouth. "That's where we're from, but only Josh still lives in Whitford. He runs the lodge for the family."

"A lodge for snowmobilers, I think Emma said?"

"Any winter activities, actually, but primarily sledders." He was trying to get used to it, but it was bizarre how much these two women knew about him. "My great-grandfather started the Northern Star Lodge as an exclusive hunting club, but by the time my dad took it over, nobody was doing that much anymore and the clientele changed. It's right on the sled trails, so it does okay."

"What do the rest of them do?"

He might have resented the Twenty Questions game if not for the fact it gave him an excuse to ignore the green tree trunks left on his plate. "The oldest, Mitch, runs a controlled-demolition company. It's based out of New York, but he hotel hops mostly. Then there's Ryan, who builds custom homes in the Boston area. I'm in the middle and then there's Liz, who lives out in New Mexico, of all places. Josh is the youngest."

"Do you see them often?"

It was pretty benign, as questions went, but Sean took

another sip of his drink to buy himself a few seconds. He'd seen them all but Liz a few days ago, when they'd gathered at Ryan's place in Mass for a welcome-home party. With the lodge a five-hour drive from Boston's Logan Airport on top of the flights and busy schedules, it had made more sense to gather at Ryan's. And since he wasn't quite ready to settle down and commit to anything, Sean had decided to spend some time in New Hampshire before heading home.

But, as far as Cat knew, he'd been out of the army for two years, not less than two weeks.

"I see them often enough to not miss them too badly," he said, "but not so much we get on each other's nerves."

Emma cleared her throat. "Do you want some more Chicken Divan, Sean? There's plenty."

Hell, no. "No, thanks. It was good, though."

Her smile brightened, causing him a pang of guilt for the lie. Or maybe the pang was the broccoli. "I have an apple pie for dessert. Store-bought, of course, since I wanted it to actually taste good."

Cat laughed. "I did everything I could to teach her how to cook. Lost cause, I guess. She'd rather play in the dirt. Do you cook, Sean?"

"I grill. We grill a lot." He didn't miss the way Emma's eyes widened.

"At least you won't starve. I've taken to grilling a lot in Florida because it's better than heating up the house. More often than not, we end up gathering at one person's grill and throwing something on it, like a potluck. Maybe tomorrow I can make you my famous honey-ginger grilled salmon."

Emma gave him a quick shake of her head, panic in

her eyes. Shit. She didn't own a barbecue grill. "It's… uh. We had to scrap it."

Cat's eyebrows rose. "Scrap it?"

"I blew it up," Emma said in a rush. "And we haven't bought a new one yet. I mean, not a big explosion, of course, but I did something wrong with the propane tank and… I broke it."

"And you wonder why I worry about you."

Sean smothered a chuckle with his napkin. Way to convince somebody you can be left unattended, he thought.

"Of course, I worry a lot less now that you have Sean."

The look she gave him—all sweet and trusting and gooey with gratitude—made him feel like a heel. No. Wrong body part. He felt like an ass and he had to grit his teeth to keep from spilling everything.

Then he looked at Emma and the urge receded. She was watching her grandmother and it seemed as if some of the tension eased out of her body. Her expression was full of love and relief, reminding him of why they were in this position—to ease Cat's mind so she could enjoy her retirement. At least it seemed to be working.

The store-bought apple pie went a long way toward making him more comfortable, but at the first opportunity, he excused himself. "I need to make a few phone calls, so I'll leave you ladies to catch up."

It was a lie, but, hell, what was one more? On his way out, he ducked into Emma's office and grabbed one of the umpteen pads of sticky notes she had scattered on the desk and rummaged around until he found a Sharpie marker.

Once upstairs, he went straight into their shared bathroom. He peeled the top sticky note off the pad and stuck it to the mirror, and then pulled the cap off the Sharpie.

Emma stared at the note stuck to the mirror, her fingers curled over the edge of the sink. Her face was washed. Hair and teeth brushed. It was time to go out and curl up on the couch and try to sleep.

I hate broccoli. And peas.

Great. So he wasn't a fan of green vegetables. Where was the information she really needed to know—namely, whether or not he wore pajamas? It hadn't occurred to her to worry about it before, but, holy hell, she was worrying about it now.

She was wearing pajamas, of course. Or what passed for them in her world. A well-worn and oversize University of New Hampshire T-shirt over soft flannel boxers. She'd considered buying something prettier and a little more feminine, but she didn't want to send mixed messages to the man who'd be sleeping in her bed.

All she could do was hope Sean had put the same consideration into his sleeping attire. He probably didn't sleep in the buff, despite the deliciously vivid visual of that her imagination had no trouble conjuring. He'd been in the army for twelve years—a good chunk of that deployed overseas—and surely they weren't in the habit of sleeping nude.

Flannel would be nice. And not battered shorts, like hers. Long pants and a long-sleeved shirt buttoned up to his throat would be nice, like something Ward Cleaver would have worn to bed in his 1950s sitcom.

When she finally dropped the curtain on the mental drama and left the bathroom, she was a little disappointed he was already asleep. Clearly he wasn't struggling to hold back the reins of runaway sexual attraction the way she was. He'd dimmed the overhead light, but she could hear him softly snoring and make out the sheet pulled halfway up his stomach. His *naked* stomach, which led her gaze to his naked chest and then to his naked shoulders, the muscles nicely highlighted by the way he slept with his arms raised over his head.

Was the rest of him naked, too?

"When you stare at somebody who's sleeping," he mumbled without moving or opening his eyes, "they usually wake up."

Busted. Her face burned as though his words were a blowtorch and she rushed across the room to slap the light switch off. In the faint glow of moonlight penetrating the curtains, she went to the couch and tried to get comfortable. It wasn't quite long enough, but she curled up under the light cotton blanket and closed her eyes.

Getting caught staring on the first night was embarrassing, but at least he wasn't a mind reader. There was no way he could guess she'd been wondering what he wore from the waist down.

"Good night, Emma."

The quiet, husky voice in the darkness made her shiver. "Night, Sean."

A little less than seven hours of tossing and turning later, Emma's question was answered—much to the detriment of her recently revived libido.

At some point during the night, Sean had thrown off the sheet. Probably right around the time he rolled onto his stomach. With his hands shoved under his pillow and one knee drawn up a little, she had a clear view of his ass—showcased perfectly in dark blue boxer briefs.

Even though she was careful not to look directly at

the ass in question, Sean stirred. He shoved his face a little deeper into the pillow and stretched one of those not-quite-awake stretches that made his entire body—and hers—vibrate and the muscles of his back ripple.

Since there was no way she couldn't stare directly at that view, but she didn't want to get caught looking again, Emma scrambled off the couch. Grabbing the stack of clothes she'd put out the night before, she went into the bathroom and closed the door against temptation.

When she emerged a while later, refreshed and dressed and ready to face the day, Sean was sitting on the edge of the bed, scrubbing his face with his hands. He'd thrown on a pair of jeans, but she noticed immediately he hadn't done up the fly.

"Good morning," she said, injecting a little more cheer into her voice than she felt.

"Morning."

So, not a morning person, then. Since, unlike her, he hadn't had any problem falling asleep, she didn't think he was still tired. "If I know Gram, she's already working on breakfast, and I didn't get my lack of cooking ability from her."

"I'll be down in a few minutes."

He didn't seem inclined to make conversation, so she left the room and followed the heavenly scent of coffee and bacon to the kitchen. "Morning, Gram."

Cat paused in stirring a big batch of scrambled eggs in her favorite cast-iron skillet, which had been sadly neglected in her absence. "Morning, sweetie. Is Sean up?"

"He'll be down in a few minutes." Figuring it was something a domesticated woman would do, she fixed him a cup of coffee along with her own. "You didn't have to go to all this trouble for us."

"Don't think I didn't see the boxes of doughnuts and instant oatmeal in the pantry. And cooking for one isn't any fun."

Emma didn't think cooking for any number of people was fun, but she wasn't going to turn down a homemade breakfast. "I was able to rearrange a few things to get a couple of days off, but Wednesday I have a job I have to do. And Sean, of course."

"I knew you'd be busy this time of year, so I wasn't expecting you to keep me company every minute. I'll probably go into town and see some old friends."

Emma smiled, but a slight tremor racked her insides. The nearest town, where they'd always gone and Emma had attended school, wasn't a small town, but it wasn't big, either. Knowing Gram was probably in contact with old friends, she'd been pretending she was engaged there, too. Her own friends knew the truth, but anybody in Gram's circle was convinced Emma was engaged, even though they'd never met the lucky fellow.

It had been a careful balancing act. Sean tended to travel to the town where his family lived so he could visit them at the same, she told people. And sometimes they'd just missed him. Or he'd gone back to Maine for a visit but work had kept her from accompanying him.

Hopefully, all her groundwork wouldn't crumble under Gram's scrutiny.

"Something smells good," Sean said as he walked into the kitchen. And like any good fiancé, he slid an arm around Emma's waist and leaned in for a quick morning kiss, smelling of shampoo and shaving cream and toothpaste.

It was over almost before she registered his intention,

but she managed not to jump back like…how had he put it? A virgin at a frat party?

"You're in for a treat," she said in a surprisingly normal voice. "Gram's scrambled eggs are to die for."

"So what's the plan for today?" Gram asked while dishing up the eggs and bacon.

"Whatever you want to do." Emma handed Sean his coffee cup.

"We should go buy a new grill," Gram said. "And I'll see if there's any decent salmon to be had."

Emma nodded. At least grill shopping meant going to the city rather than into town. One step at a time. One day at a time. That's how they'd get through the month.

And, God help her, one kiss at a time.

Six

Sean got the summons he'd been dreading in the form of a voice mail left on his cell phone while they were struggling to get the new grill out of the back of the truck.

"Sean, it's Aunt Mary." As if any other woman in his life ever used that tone of voice with him. "I don't know what kind of game you're playing, but I want to see you. Today. Alone. Don't make me come looking for you, young man."

Yeah, he was in trouble. And it was his own damn fault because he should have known his cousins couldn't keep their mouths shut. They never had. Especially Mikey. He was always the rat growing up.

He gave Emma and Cat a song and dance about promising his uncle he'd give him a hand changing the oil in his riding lawn mower and made the drive over like a criminal being marched into the courtroom to face the judge. This judge, though, would whack the shit out of him with kitchen utensils if she didn't like his answers.

He was already exhausted and a confrontation with his aunt was the last thing he wanted. The clock on Emma's bedside table had read one in the morning when

a sound had penetrated his sleep. A sleepy, sexy and definitely feminine moan wasn't a bad thing to wake up to,
except when the female was sleeping on a couch across
the room. Alone.

She'd quieted after that single sound, but his body sure
as hell hadn't. As a result, he'd drifted in and out of a tor-
tured sleep and woken up on the wrong side of the bed.

Aunt Mary was in the kitchen—as usual—when he
arrived, and right after pointing him in that direction,
Uncle Leo disappeared into the den and closed the door.
Chicken.

She started in on him the second he crossed the threshold from the living room. "I was wrong about you all
these years. I always thought you were a smart boy, but
you don't have the brains God gave a jackass."

"Aunt Mary, I—"

"Don't you Aunt Mary me, Sean Michael Kowalski.
I should go get my wooden spoon and thunk some sense
into that thick head of yours."

Sean sighed and tried to school his expression into
something closer to contrition than belligerence. Not that
she wouldn't see through it, but he made the effort regardless. "I'm just helping her out for a few weeks so that—"

"Helping her lie to her grandmother, you mean."

"I know it sounds bad, but—"

"Because you were raised better than that."

He'd known this wouldn't be easy, but he'd been
hoping to at least finish a sentence or two. "Can I talk?
Please?"

"When you have something sensible to say."

He gave himself a few seconds so none of his frustration would show in his voice. Hopefully. "Remember

after high school when I dumped my bike and I told you I had a bruised elbow and a little road rash?"

She pinned him with a look that made him want to squirm. "Yes."

"Well, I dumped my bike because a truck hit me. I also had a bad concussion. And four broken bones."

Her expression froze for a few seconds, but then he saw the comprehension in her eyes, followed by an unholy gleam of pissed off. "You little bastard. Why would you do that?"

"I didn't want you to worry. You wouldn't have believed I was okay without leaving your family to come take care of me, and Lisa was so pregnant she was going to pop any day."

"You're my family, too, and don't you forget it."

"You would have been stressed out for no reason, because there was nothing you could do. I didn't want that for you, so I talked the others into lying for me. It's the same situation Emma found herself in, more or less."

She glared at him, her arms folded across her chest. "Protecting weak old women from the truth, you mean?"

Oh, hell, no. "You are not weak or old, Aunt Mary, and neither is Emma's grandmother, Cat. I know you're upset about this, but I bet you've hedged around the truth a time or two to keep somebody you love from being unhappy."

When she didn't respond right away, he thought maybe she was softening. "I don't like this at all, Sean."

"I gave Emma my word." That was the bottom line.

Her mouth tightened. "And?"

"And…" He took a deep breath. "If you can't back me up on this, I'll have to keep Cat away from here. And she knows you're nearby, which means I'll have to say we had a falling-out."

"Don't threaten me, young man," she said, but her tone was a little softer. She, of all people, knew Kowalski men were stubborn and meant what they said.

But the last thing he'd ever want to do was have conflict with this woman. He loved her too much. "I've seen them together and Emma was right. Cat's a lot happier now, thinking we're engaged, and that's all Emma's trying to do. Please, Aunt Mary. I gave her my word."

She sighed—the deep, meaningful sigh only a mother could really master. "What is it you want me to do?"

"Cat wants to meet you. Maybe have dinner. I was thinking...*hoping* you and Uncle Leo could have a barbecue."

She was still considering the idea when Joe walked into the kitchen and stopped. Sean watched him take in his mother's body language and turn to retreat.

"Joseph, did you know about this craziness Sean's involved with?"

The guy gave him a look promising retribution in the near future and turned back to his mom. "Yes, I did."

"And you didn't tell me?"

"It wasn't my place, Ma. And they're not hurting anybody."

"It's wrong."

Joe smiled what was probably supposed to be a placating smile, but his obvious amusement at Sean's predicament was ruining it. "It's wrong that Emma wanted her grandmother to enjoy her new life in Florida?"

"Don't get wise with me, Joseph. That's not the issue here."

"It *is* the issue," Sean said, drawing his aunt's gaze back to him. "Her grandmother's peace of mind is exactly the issue."

She stared at his face intently, for what seemed like forever, and he hoped like hell none of his own doubts showed there. "Saturday. Anytime after three and we'll fire the grills at five."

"Thank you, Aunt Mary."

"I'll keep my mouth shut and play along, but if she asks me outright if you two are up to no good, I won't lie."

He couldn't see why Cat would ask a question like that. "I'll make it up to you. I promise."

"Go before I change my mind."

He went, Joe on his heels, and didn't stop until he was safely in the driveway. "Your mother can be a scary lady sometimes."

Joe leaned against the fender. "How the hell did you talk her into it?"

"I told her I'd have to stay away—claim we had a falling-out—if she didn't."

"Ouch. But I hope you realize Ma was the easy part."

That was the easy part? He didn't think so. "What do you mean?"

"What are you going to do about the five kids who know that not only were you not engaged last week, but that they haven't been writing letters for Lisa to send to you at Emma's house for the last year and a half?"

"Shit." Every time he thought he had his eye on the ball and could smack it out of the park, it curved on him again. "I didn't even think of them. Dammit."

Joe laughed and slapped him on the back. "We'll take care of the kids. Don't worry."

"Thanks, man." He started to climb into his truck, then stopped. "Look, I know this is funny to you guys, but don't forget it's not a joke to Emma and Cat. If we blow this, her grandmother's going to be really upset."

Joe grinned and slapped the side of the truck. "Come on, cousin. You know we've always got your back."

"Yeah, that's where you usually stick the kick-me sign." His cousin was still laughing when he backed out of the driveway.

"I never would have guessed something with orange juice *and* soy sauce in it could taste so good," Emma said, leaning back in the lawn chair with a sigh. They'd demolished Gram's honey-ginger grilled salmon in record time and she had no desire to move.

"I'll write the recipe down for you."

"I'll just screw it up, anyway."

Gram laughed. "All you do is mix the ingredients together, pour it in a bag with the salmon and half an hour later give it to Sean to throw on the grill. He cooked the salmon to perfection tonight."

Of course he did. As he'd told her earlier, she had nothing to worry about because the Y chromosome came with an innate ability to master the barbecue grill.

"The salad was good, too," Sean said.

"Thanks," Emma muttered. "Even I can't screw up shredding lettuce."

The man looked incredibly relaxed for somebody who'd probably been raked over the coals by his aunt and was now relaxing with two women he barely knew. She, on the other hand, felt as if she was detoxing. Jumpy. Twitching. A trickle of sweat at the small of her back.

Sean stood and started gathering dishes, but held out a hand when Emma started to get up. "You ladies sit and visit. I'll take care of the cleanup."

Once he was inside, Gram smiled and raised her eyebrows. "He does dishes, too? No wonder you snapped him up."

It was tempting to point out a few of his less attractive traits, like the fact he was a sexist baboon who wouldn't let her drive. But he was doing a good job of convincing Gram he was Emma's Prince Charming, which was the whole point, so she bit back her annoyance with the Saint Sean routine. "He's a keeper."

"Something's bothering you. Tell me what it is and you'll feel better."

Emma really doubted that. She made a conscious effort to relax her face. "It's nothing, really. Work stuff."

"Really, Emma, I won't be bothered if you and Sean have to work tomorrow. I understand you're very busy. And I'm proud of the fact your business is doing so well."

"It *is* going well." Emma gave her grandmother a genuine smile. "The summer people love to show off my work, and then all the other summer people just have to have me, too."

"That's wonderful, dear." Gram took a sip of her iced tea, then set the glass on the patio table. "But I want to hear more about Sean."

"Um…like what?" She knew he didn't like broccoli or peas.

"Oh, I don't know. How does he like working for you? Since you're the owner, will he be a stay-at-home dad once you have children?"

Emma was pretty sure Sean's ideal wife would be barefoot and pregnant in the kitchen with a baby on one hip and a laundry basket on the other, but she didn't say so. "His working for me isn't really long-term. He's just not sure what he wants to do yet. And we'll figure out the baby thing when the time comes."

In other words, she had no clue, but she hoped Gram wouldn't figure that out. Maybe if she was vague enough, whatever Sean said about the subject wouldn't contradict her. She sipped her iced tea and concentrated on not looking stressed-out.

Gram reached over and touched her hand. "Are you happy?"

And there it was—the million-dollar question. Everything she and Sean were going through was meant to convince Gram the answer to that question was a resounding *yes*.

"I'm happy, Gram. I really am. My company's thriving and I…have Sean. And, even though I miss you, I love knowing you're having a great time in Florida with your friends."

"You should see us down there. That warm sunshine does wonders for the body, and we feel ten years younger, at least. You should see Martha line dance! That woman can shake and shimmy like a twenty-year-old."

Emma laughed, trying very hard not to visualize Martha—who could only be described as stout—shaking and shimmying. "I loved the pictures of you swimming with the dolphins."

"That was amazing! You wouldn't believe how friendly they are." And, as Gram started telling her the story, Emma felt the tension easing out of her body.

At some point Sean joined them, bringing a fresh pitcher of iced tea with him, and they sat on the deck listening to Gram talk about frolicking in sunny Florida until long after the sun had set. And then, once Gram had gone up to bed, Emma and Sean faced each other across the patio table.

"I like Cat," he said, once her grandmother was safely

out of earshot. "This isn't quite as hard as I thought it would be."

"It's going better than I thought," she agreed. "I'm still having a hard time believing the ploy might actually work."

"She sure does love Florida."

"I could tell that even over the phone. When she started talking about moving back, I knew I had to do something."

He smiled, his eyes warm. "Even if it was crazy."

"I think the words you used were *batshit crazy*." She watched his brow furrow for a moment, as though he was trying to remember saying it. "But Lisa also told me the tall-and-hot part of it, so I didn't take it personally."

"Maybe we shouldn't talk about the hot part right before we go to bed."

Good point. "You think you can stick this out for a month?"

"Told you I would."

"And you've got Gram wrapped around your little finger already. I'll have to start complaining about you once in a while, or when it comes time to tell her I broke up with you, she'll never believe it."

"True. Maybe you should tell her *I* broke up with *you*."

Emma tossed a balled-up napkin at him. "Funny."

"You can worry about that later. For now, your grandmother believes you're madly in love with me and that's all that matters."

"So you're telling me Emma's grandmother actually fell for it?" Kevin dredged a fry through a puddle of ketchup and popped it in his mouth. "I don't believe it."

Sean shrugged. "I'm tellin' you. She doesn't give us funny looks or anything."

He'd taken off midmorning to give Emma and her grandmother some time alone, since he and Emma would be working the next day, and because, after three days of pretending, he needed a break. He'd done some errands and then showed up at Jasper's Bar & Grille to see what was going on. He'd gotten there just as Kevin's wife and daughter had arrived to visit him during his lunch break, and they'd invited Sean to join them.

Beth slid Lily's high chair closer to her seat and farther from Kevin's. The tot was trying to trade her cut-up banana for her daddy's fries, not that Sean blamed her. "I have to admit, I didn't think it would work."

"Neither did we," Sean told her and they all laughed.

"Isn't it weird?" Beth gave Kevin one of those wifely looks when he slipped Lily a fry, then looked back at Kevin. "I can't imagine living with somebody I don't know."

"Yeah, it's weird. Maybe being in the army helped. I'm used to living with whoever came along. And it's not so bad. Cat's a wicked-good cook."

"Takes so little to make a Kowalski man happy," Beth mused.

Her husband smiled and leaned across the high chair to kiss her cheek, slipping the kid another fry. "I seem to recall winning your heart with my Jasper burgers."

"Among other things. And when Lily has a bellyache later, you're dealing with it."

Sean turned his attention from the domestic bliss to his fish-and-chips basket. He was happy for his cousins—all paired off and doing the parent thing—but it wasn't for him. Maybe in a few years when he'd found a place he wanted to stay in and a woman he wanted to stay there with. But for now, he wasn't even looking.

When Lily decided she'd had enough of her high chair and started making her displeasure known rather loudly, Beth packed up all her baby debris and kissed her husband goodbye. "Good luck, Sean. I'll see you Saturday."

"So," Kevin said when they were alone, "how are those sleeping arrangements going?"

"She's still on the couch."

"I think Josh took two nights for the pool. He's out."

Sean shook his head, a little disgusted by his youngest brother's lack of faith in his self-control. "You'll all be out when the month's over. Out money, that is."

He said it as though he believed it, but he was on shaky ground. Three nights of sleeping in the same room as Emma was playing hell on his sleep cycle. And when he'd dreamed of her last night—naked and hot for him, with her dark cloud of hair tickling his chest—and woken sweaty and hard and aching, not crossing that ten feet of bedroom had almost killed him.

Going to work tomorrow would be a good thing, he thought. Even though he'd be alone with her, a little physical labor would do his body good. Maybe if he tired himself out, he could sleep through the night without his dick trying to lead the way to her like some kind of damn dowsing rod.

"I've gotta get back to work," Kevin said, breaking into thoughts he was better off not having, anyway. "Your lunch is on the house today."

"Thanks, man." He stood and shook his cousin's hand before polishing off the rest of his lunch.

On a whim, he took the scenic route to Joe and Keri's

house, and since both their vehicles were in the driveway, he pulled in and got out.

Keri answered the door, looking frazzled and not having the best hair day he'd ever seen. "Hi, Sean. I was just thinking, gee, I need more Kowalskis in my life right now."

He laughed and stepped into the big foyer. "Baby acting up?"

"I thought the Kowalski men were royal pains in the ass—no offense—but you guys have nothing on the girls."

"Joe writing?"

She blew out a sharp breath and put her hands on her hips. "No. Joe is *pretending* to write so I won't dump Brianna in his lap, but he's probably playing some stupid game."

From the other room came a pissed-off howl that Sean hoped was their daughter and not a wild animal foraging for table scraps. "So he's in his office?"

Keri nodded and waved a hand in that direction before making a growling sound and heading off to appease her daughter. Welcome to the jungle, he mused before heading to Joe's office. He rapped twice on the door, then let himself in.

Joe looked up with a guilty start and Sean knew his wife had him all figured out. "She knows you're only pretending to write so you don't have to deal with the kid."

"You know what *really* sucks? Everybody keeps saying to just wait till she's older. Like it gets worse. How can it get worse?" Sean lifted his hands in a "don't ask me" gesture. "For years I've been writing about boogeymen and the evil that lurks in the hearts of men. I had no idea there's nothing scarier than a baby girl."

Sean laughed. "She can't be that bad. What does she weigh? Ten pounds?"

"Fifteen. But it's fifteen pounds of foul temper and fouler smells. Trust me."

"I'll take your word for it."

Joe leaned back in his leather office chair and sighed. "Let's talk about your life. She still on the couch?"

"Yes, she is."

"Good. I said you'd last three weeks."

Maybe, but Sean wouldn't bet on it. Or he *shouldn't* have bet on it, anyway. Especially a whole month. His balls ached just thinking about it. "You guys come up with a plan for the kids for Saturday yet?"

"Yeah, but it's going to cost you."

"Not a problem. I'll just take it out of all the money I'm going to collect from you idiots at the end of the month."

Joe grinned. "You keep telling yourself that, buddy."

He was. With as much oomph as he could muster. And he'd probably keep telling himself that right up to the minute he got Emma naked.

Seven

"If I'd known we were just going to sit around and watch the plants grow today, I would have brought my book."

Emma jerked her attention from the columbine plants she'd been checking on and back to Sean. "Sorry. Zoned out for a minute. Did you get the weed blocker done?"

"Yeah. I don't get why they want the pathway to the beach done in white stone. Don't you usually walk back from the water barefoot?"

"Not this couple. It doesn't matter how practical it is. All that matters is how it looks."

"Whatever. It's going to take the rest of the day to get all that stone down, so stop mentally tiptoeing through the tulips and let's go."

Emma wanted to tell him to shove his attitude up his ass, because she was the boss, or at least flip him the bird behind his back, but she didn't have the energy. Living a fake life was a lot more exhausting than she'd anticipated.

She didn't even want to think about what it was like trying to sleep every night with her boxer-brief-clad roommate sprawled across the bed only ten feet away, so she thought about Gram instead. Gram, who was, at that very moment, on her way into town. The town that had heard the rumors of her engagement, but never actually seen her fiancé.

If Gram returned from town still believing Emma and Sean were headed to the altar, it would be a miracle.

"You look beat," Sean said, and she barely managed to restrain herself from whacking him with the shovel. He, of course, looked delicious with his muscles rippling and a light sheen of sweat making his tanned arms gleam as he shoveled stone.

"The couch is shorter than I thought. But I'm getting used to it."

"There's room in the bed."

She forced herself to keep shoveling stone into the wheelbarrow. If she didn't look at him, she didn't have to see on his face whether or not he was serious. If he wasn't, she might whack him with the shovel, after all. If he was...

"That's a bad idea."

He laughed. "So is filling your wheelbarrow so full you can't move it, but you did it, anyway."

"Crap." She'd mounded the stone so high she'd have to dump half of it out to budge the damn thing.

"I'll wheel it down for you." He winked at her. "This time."

Her mouth went a little dry when he stepped between the handles and hefted the wheelbarrow as though it was a sack of groceries, but she followed him to the area he'd already prepped with weed-blocking fabric, where she'd be spreading the first batch of white stone chips. And she managed to make most of the walk without ogling his backside.

"How have you managed to do this on your own for

so long?" he asked once he'd set the wheelbarrow in place for her.

"I don't usually fill the wheelbarrow all the way to the top."

He pulled off his leather work gloves and shoved them into his back pocket. "I'm serious. This is…"

He let the sentence trail away and Emma rolled her eyes. "Not women's work?"

"I was going to say it's pretty demanding, physically."

"It takes me a little longer than it would a man, but I chip away at it. And sometimes I'll pay Joey and Danny to give me a hand."

"So Mike and Lisa's kids know you pretty well, then?"

"Yeah. If I didn't have you today, I probably would have brought all four boys. Brian and Bobby can spread mulch and stone and they make a few bucks under the table. It usually takes me longer to fix what they did than to do it myself, but they get jealous if it's only the older two all the time."

"Do you think they can really handle a secret like this?"

Emma sighed and leaned on her shovel. "I don't know. I hope so."

It was a two-part plan, though shaky at best. Part one was to keep the kids away from Cat Shaw as much as possible. Part two of the plan was to make it a game. With prizes. Terry's daughter, Stephanie, and Lisa's four boys had been given the backstory and issued the challenge. All children who didn't blow the secret would earn cash and video-game time at the end of the month, with hefty bonuses going to teens who helped coach the younger kids.

From what Sean said, it was surprising Mrs. Kowalski's head hadn't exploded, but she seemed reluctantly willing to comply. For now.

"I can't tell you how much I appreciate what your family's doing for me," she said, pulling her gloves back on. "I know they must think I'm crazy."

"A little." But he smiled, which kept her from focusing too much on his words. "But they're trying."

Because he'd asked them to, she thought. And she knew it wasn't just a matter of asking them to. He'd probably had to fight for their cooperation, trying to convince them to go along with something he himself wasn't sure about. Or hadn't been sure about.

There had been another sticky note on her bathroom mirror that morning. *I think you're doing the right thing.*

It wasn't a lot, but it was enough to get her through one more day. And, assuming Gram didn't come home from town demanding answers, another after that.

Cat took her time wandering down the main street of town, enjoying a perfect New England early-summer day.

She had some old friends to look up and a few groceries and other things to buy, but for now she just walked. Walking helped clear her mind, a state she hadn't achieved since arriving back in New Hampshire.

Something just wasn't quite right about Emma and Sean's relationship. She'd felt it in the airport and the feeling had only grown stronger after living under the same roof with them for a few days.

At first she'd tried to excuse Emma's reaction to Sean's touches as the embarrassment a well-raised young woman would feel about public displays of affection in front of one's grandmother. But really, it was so obvious to her they hadn't been dating for the past year, never mind living together, that she wondered if she should be offended by their drastic underestimation of her intelligence.

What she couldn't wrap her head around was the why of it.

A banner advertising a going-out-of-business sale caught her eye and she stopped on the sidewalk. Walker Hardware had been selling household, gardening, animal and building supplies since Isaiah Walker first hung out the sign in 1879, and Russell Walker had been the guy behind the counter since 1983 when his father had passed away. Actually, he'd been behind the counter helping his dad since he was barely tall enough to see over it, and she couldn't imagine how hard losing the store would be for him.

He'd lost his wife about six years before. Flo Walker had a heart attack hanging out the laundry and she'd lain in the grass until she didn't show up for knitting club. A friend had called the house and then Russell. He'd called out the rescue squad, but he'd beat them there only to find she was already gone. Cat had had just a passing acquaintance with Flo, who was originally from Connecticut, but she'd gone to school with Russell. They'd never been chummy, but they'd known each other their entire lives.

She walked up the wooden steps and smiled as the familiar bell jangled to announce her entrance. No annoying buzzers for Walker Hardware.

Russell was behind the counter, studying a newspaper through reading glasses perched on the end of his nose, but he looked up when the bell sounded. He took the glasses off as a smile warmed his face, which was still handsome under a full head of silvery hair.

"Cat! I heard you were coming home for a visit." He

rose to his feet and closed the newspaper with a snap. "Florida obviously agrees with you."

He'd always been a charmer, but at sixty-five she thought she'd have built up an immunity. She was wrong. "Thank you, Russell. How have you been?"

He shrugged, waving a hand at the nearly empty shelves bearing red going-out-of-business discount signs. "I still have my health."

"I'm sorry."

"Bound to happen. Can't compete with the big-box stores. People tried, of course. If they just needed a roll of tape or a fuse or a pair of garden shears, they'd come here. But times are tough and I can't begrudge them wanting to save what money they have. Glad now I didn't fight too hard when my daughter wanted to go off and be a vet instead of taking over the place."

"What will you do?"

"The building's for sale to help pay off some debt, so I'm on the waiting list for an apartment in senior housing." He paused, sorrow shadowing his features. "A hundred and thirty–some odd years my family's kept this place going, and a couple months from now, I won't have a pot to piss in."

She didn't know what to say. There really wasn't much she *could* say. "Let me take you out to lunch. We'll have something full of fat and cholesterol and sodium because why the hell not?"

The invitation appeared to take him by surprise, but he recovered quickly enough. "I had to let my part-timer go last year. I can't leave."

"What are the customers going to do if you take an hour for lunch? Take their business elsewhere?"

His laugh was rich and echoed through the barren

store. "I guess you're right about that. And I sure could use a smiling face right now."

"Then stick a sign in the door, lock up and let's go."

They walked down to a café at the end of the street, which happened to be the only one in town, and snagged a table in a relatively quiet corner. They both ordered coffee and Russell got the fried-chicken special while Cat ordered a hash-and-cheese omelet.

"How's Emma doing? I haven't seen her in a few weeks, but you must be happy she's finally heading toward the altar."

"She's doing great. And Sean's a very nice young man." She took a sip of her coffee, considering. "Have you met him?"

Russell frowned for a few seconds, then shook his head. "No, I don't think I have. I guess she keeps him pretty busy, and when she shops, he usually heads down to the city so he can visit his family at the same time."

"Have you heard of anybody meeting him?"

"That's an odd question. You just said yourself he's a nice young man, so he must exist."

It did sound crazy, but she couldn't let go of it. "Oh, he exists. But I don't think he's been dating my granddaughter for a year and a half, or living under the same roof for a year."

He looked confused. "Why would they lie?"

"That's the question I can't answer." She took another sip of her coffee. "But you can tell when two people are in love. And when they've…well, you know."

His slow smile warmed his eyes, which were the same blue as his shirt. Funny how you could know a man sixty-odd years and never know what color his eyes were. "It's been a while, but, yes, I know."

When Russell looked at her like that, she could remember so clearly how she'd felt during that headlong rush into love with her husband and how much she missed him. But sometimes she wondered if she was missing him so much as just missing having somebody, and she wondered if Russell ever felt the same way.

She smiled back at him, trying to think of something to say, but coming up empty. It had been a long time since she'd had a flirtatious conversation with a man.

That thought brought her up short. Was that what was going on? Was he flirting? Or was he simply being kind and she was latching onto it as though it was the last lifeboat off her AARP-eligible sinking ship?

Thankfully, the waitress—who was a young woman Cat didn't recognize—brought their meals and she was saved by digging into her forbidden feast.

"I don't think I've had real fried chicken since I turned fifty and Flo dragged me in to have my cholesterol numbers checked," Russell said.

"We've only got so many years left, so I intend to enjoy them. If I can't have eggs and hash and cheese once in a while, I might as well lie down and start decomposing."

"I like that about you."

"But only once in a while," she said again. "If you eat like this all the time, you won't have enough life left to worry about it."

Russell set down his fork to wipe his mouth, then took a sip of coffee. "I remember being at the store when I still needed a stool to reach the cash register, ringing up a customer. I knew from the time I could walk that hardware would be my whole life and that if Dani hadn't been so stubborn, it would have been hers, too. But I've got to admit, there's a little part of me that's not sorry to see the store go. And, sitting here with you smiling at me, and a pile of fried chicken on my plate, I guess I've still got enough life left in me to try to enjoy myself."

For the first time in her sixty-five years, Cat decided to be forward with a man. "You got enough life in you to take an old woman dancing?"

"Well, if I should come across any old women, I'll have to give that some thought. But in the meantime, I'd like to dance with you."

When she blushed like a schoolgirl, Cat supposed she should at least be grateful she didn't giggle like one. "You're a charmer, Russell Walker. I think I'll have to keep an eye on you."

He just grinned and bit into a big, greasy hunk of fried chicken.

Sean jogged past the mailbox, glancing at the daisies, and turned down Emma's driveway. He'd have just enough time for a quick shower before Emma's alarm went off and another day of crazy started.

When four in the morning rolled around and he'd spent more time tossing and turning than sleeping because his aching body was keeping him awake, he'd eased out of bed and sneaked out of the house for a run. It worked in boot camp—crush disobedience and rebellion with grueling physical punishment. He wasn't sure if the same principle would work on his dick, but it was worth a shot.

Slick with sweat and slightly winded, he crossed the porch and sneaked back into the quiet house. After kicking his sneakers off, he went up the stairs— remembering just in time where the squeaky spot was— and let himself back into Emma's room. *Their* room.

She was still snoring, so he went into the bathroom and closed the door.

He ran the shower hot, washing the sweat away, and then slowly turned the dial toward cold until he was wide-awake and his body was beaten into submission. Then he toweled as much of the water out of his hair as he could, dried himself off and wrapped the towel around his waist.

He had a mouth full of toothpaste when the door opened and Emma walked in, rubbing her face. She was carrying a bundle of clothes and squinting against the light, even though in her half-asleep state she still slapped her hand at the wall switch—and almost walked into him before she noticed his presence.

"Oh." She stopped and blinked at him. "I thought you were still in bed."

He spit out the toothpaste and grabbed the hand towel to wipe his mouth. "I usually make a bigger lump."

"I don't look, because you throw the covers off and—" She broke off as her eyes drifted south to the towel, where *bigger lump* took on a whole new meaning. He'd thrown miles of punishment at his body for no reason. "Oh."

Rather than dwell on deciphering the tone of that *oh,* he took her by the shoulders and guided her far enough to the left so he could get by her. Once he was free, he closed the door behind him and swore under his breath.

The only way that could have been more awkward was if his towel had slipped off in front of her.

After getting dressed in record time, he flopped back onto the bed and stared at the ceiling. This was the kind of story a woman would share with her best friend. And her best friend was married to his cousin. His cousin had a big mouth. The story would be embellished. It was only a matter of time before one of his brothers called, asking why he was naked with the woman he wasn't supposed to be naked with.

With a sigh, he pushed himself off the bed and headed downstairs. One, he wanted coffee. And, two, he didn't want to be sprawled on the bed when Emma got around to leaving the bathroom. The only thing more awkward than being caught in a towel that didn't do much to hide an erection was talking about it.

Cat was sitting at the table, sipping tea, when he walked in. "You beat Emma down this morning."

"It doesn't happen often." He poured two mugs of coffee and then froze. He had no clue what Emma took in her coffee. He knew she took some half-and-half, but he wasn't sure about the sugar. Putting his back between Cat and the cups, he dumped two teaspoons in each cup.

"How do you like working with my granddaughter?"

Since he'd only worked with her for a day and a half, he couldn't really say. "It's not too bad. She works hard. Has a good head for business."

"And she has excellent control skills," Cat added.

He laughed, thinking of their trip to the grocery store. "That she does."

"I guess you know her pretty well."

She was watching him, so he concentrated on looking honest. Whatever that looked like. "She's a complicated woman. I'm not sure anybody really knows her well. Except you, of course."

She laughed as the complicated woman in question walked into the kitchen. "Morning, Gram. What's so funny?"

"Just chatting with Sean, and now that you're up, I'll start some French toast."

Sean watched Emma take the first sip of her coffee,

and when she didn't shudder or make faces, he figured he'd done okay. He also noticed, as Cat started hauling things out of the refrigerator, that Emma wasn't making eye contact with him.

He shouldn't have walked out, because now the awkwardness was going to fester until she felt a need to talk about the incident in the bathroom. He could have laughed it off as morning wood, making it clear the pronounced lump had nothing to do with her. That would have been a lie, of course. He'd been up for several hours and it most definitely had something to do with her. But she might have bought the story and not had to talk about it.

The kitchen felt claustrophobic all of a sudden, what with the two women he barely knew and the elephant in the room, so he took his coffee and muttered about catching the morning news. He turned on the TV in the living room and sank onto the couch with a sigh of relief. It would take a few minutes to make the French toast, so he had a few minutes of normal.

"Can I talk to you for a second?" It was Emma, of course, and there went his normal.

He sighed and moved over on the couch. "Knock yourself out."

She sat down, far enough away so none of their body parts touched. "I get the whole guy thing. Morning...you know, and I don't want this to be weird."

"It's no big deal."

"Okay." She took a sip of her coffee, then wrapped both hands around the mug. "We'll probably have more moments like this if we're going to live together for a month. Probably best to just laugh them off."

He raised an eyebrow at her. "Actually, when a guy's

standing in front of you, fully hard and wearing nothing but a towel, laughing might not be the *best* way to handle it."

"True." Her cheeks turned a pretty shade of pink and she laughed softly. "If we were in a movie, the towel would have fallen off. Could've been worse."

"With my luck, I'm surprised it didn't."

"Breakfast," Cat called from the kitchen. They both stood and Sean hoped this would be the last time they had to discuss his erections.

"Make sure you fill up," Emma told him as they went toward the kitchen. "We'll be planting trees today and that'll take the piss out of you."

Physical exhaustion? He was looking forward to it. Desperately.

Eight

Emma didn't want her grandmother to ever leave. Gram had cut some chicken breasts into pieces and rolled them in a bowl of some kind of spices, then skewered them with sticks. A few minutes on the grill and Emma was in heaven.

It couldn't be too hard, she thought. Of course, the last time she'd tried to cook something as simple as burgers on the grill, flames had started shooting out the side and she'd ended up with blackened lumps with raw meat in the middle even her grandfather couldn't choke down. But this was chicken on a stick. How hard could it be?

"This is delicious, Cat," Sean said, licking juices off his fingers in a way that made Emma's spine tingle. "Aunt Mary makes something like it, but the spices don't pack quite as much of a punch."

"I can't wait to meet her on Saturday. From all that you've said, she's quite a woman."

Emma's spine stopped tingling and she picked up another skewer of chicken. She didn't even want to think about how stressful Saturday was going to be, what with everybody having to be careful and watch every single word they said. And, regardless of what Sean had told her, she wasn't sure Mrs. Kowalski would back them up when the time finally came.

"She's looking forward to meeting you, too," he said. "And Emma's been so busy they haven't seen her in a while."

No, she wasn't looking forward to seeing them Saturday. Lisa, yes. But it was going to be hard to look Mrs. Kowalski in the eye, no matter how many times Sean told her it would be okay.

"I rented a movie while I was in town today," Gram said. "Some action movie the girl said was very good."

Emma was all for a relaxing movie. Something mindless that she could lose herself in and stop obsessing about her body language and every word she said. A mental break was just what she needed.

She felt differently about the movie plan an hour later when Gram sat in the armchair and set her knitting basket at her feet, leaving the couch for her and Sean.

Crap. They couldn't very well sit at opposite ends of the damn thing. A happy couple would snuggle, maybe sneaking a quick kiss here and there when they thought Gram wasn't looking. Two hours of up close and personal with Sean Kowalski was about as far from relaxing as she could get.

He got there first, sitting in one corner and propping his feet on the coffee table. Putting in the DVD and getting it ready to play bought Emma a couple of minutes, but then she had to walk to the couch. He seemed to realize at the last second she wasn't going to sit on the far end, and after glancing at Gram, he lifted his arm and rested it on the back of the couch.

Since her back was momentarily to the armchair, she

gave Sean an apologetic "whaddya-gonna-do" smile and sat down in the curve of his arm. He dropped his hand onto her shoulder as she hit Play on the remote control.

She tried to pay attention to the movie. She watched as a woman dropped a cookie sheet of burned cookies in the sink, and then a man walked into her kitchen. He had a gun and he told her he'd kidnapped her son. Emma followed along at first.

But Sean's body was putting off enough heat to melt marshmallows, and a whole lot of his body was touching her body. His arm around her shoulders. His thigh pressed to hers. Their feet sometimes brushing. It was distracting.

"You watch," Gram said. "The man she has to deliver to the kidnappers is going to end up being the father of her son and I bet he doesn't know."

Emma managed to keep enough focus on the television to see that she was right, but Sean was relaxing, which meant even more of his body was touching hers. And minute by minute she was becoming a marshmallow, melting against him. He smelled good and felt good and…she was in so much trouble. This wasn't her man to lust after. Well, technically, she could. She just couldn't act on it.

Sean was temporary. There was no sense in getting used to having a man to snuggle on the couch with or to open stubborn jars or to do her heavy lifting, because as soon as Gram was gone, so was he. And that's the way she wanted it. It would probably be another five years before Landscaping by Emma was ready for her to do the husband-and-babies thing.

And when she did go husband shopping, she wasn't going to settle for a guy whose entire life revolved around football, steak, beer and women. Or a guy who thought only Bob or Fred could mow lawns. Sean wouldn't even let her drive her own truck.

Halfway through a scene in which the mom and dad were rappelling out of a helicopter with guns blazing to rescue their kidnapped son, Sean's hand shifted and his fingertips started tracing circles against her shoulder. His attention was on the screen, as was Gram's, so Emma wasn't sure he was even aware he was doing it.

She was aware of it, though, that was for damn sure. Aware of the warmth of his touch through her T-shirt and very, very aware of the way her body reacted as if he were stroking parts of her a lot farther south than her shoulder.

When his fingers worked their way down to the end of her short sleeve and touched bare skin, she totally lost track of the plot unfolding on the television screen. Temporary or not, it sure was nice being touched by a man. It had been…a long time.

"Can you pause it for a minute?" Gram asked. "Intermission."

When Emma leaned forward for the remote, Sean withdrew his arm and let his feet fall to the floor. "Sounds like a plan."

Gram left in the direction of the kitchen and Emma stood, intending to get out of Sean's way, but when he stood, he grabbed her elbow and spun her around.

His mouth met hers, hot and hungry, and she wrapped her arms around his neck as she responded in kind. So what if he was temporary? She'd enjoy it while it lasted. His hands were on her hips and he pulled her closer— close enough so she could feel he wasn't pretending to want her.

The kiss was incredible and she stood on tiptoe, reaching for more. Her fingertips found the back of his neck and she stroked him from the knot at the top of his spine and up into his hair and back.

Sean pulled away from her so fast she almost fell over. "Shit."

"Flattering." Her senses were still so overwhelmed by him she didn't trust herself to say more.

He ran his hand over his hair, shaking his head. "That was…"

Wonderful, Emma thought. Amazing. Toe-curling. "That was what?"

"A mistake." He pushed by her and a few seconds later she heard his footsteps climbing the stairs.

"Jerk," she muttered, but the word didn't have a lot of oomph behind it. She was still too breathless from being kissed so thoroughly by a man who knew what kissing was all about.

No doubt about it—she was in trouble.

Sean had to get out of the house or he was totally going to lose it. He wasn't sure if that meant punching a hole in the wall or tossing Emma over his shoulder and carrying her off to bed caveman-style, but either was a bad idea.

Time to go for a ride and get some space, but first he stuck another sticky note to the mirror and uncapped the Sharpie.

You can hold my hand or pat my head or scratch my belly, but don't rub the back of my neck again unless you want to get naked.

He went back downstairs and grabbed the keys to his truck off the hook by the door. Cat was back in her chair when he popped his head into the living room.

"I have to bail, ladies. Kevin called while I was up-stairs and needs a hand with something."

"But the movie," Cat said.

"You'll have to tell me how it ends." He forced him-self to look at Emma, who was doing a pretty poor job of hiding her annoyance. "I might be late, so don't wait up."

"Have fun" was all she said.

He jumped on the highway and drove a little too fast with the music a little too loud, hoping to leave no room in his thoughts for remembering the taste of Emma's lips.

Even before he'd spun her around, he'd known kissing her was a big mistake. He hadn't realized the mistake was actually colossal, though, until she started stroking the back of his neck and his body reacted with an urgency that led nowhere but to bed. Together. Hot and sweaty and breathing hard between the sheets.

He got lucky and found a parking spot near Jasper's Bar & Grille and breathed a sigh of relief as he walked through the door. Men drinking beer. Pretty waitresses. Sports on the big screens. Sanity.

It was a little slow, which wasn't surprising for a Wednesday night, so there were plenty of open seats at the bar, where Kevin appeared to be holding down the fort.

"Didn't think I'd see you here tonight," he said as his cousin set a beer in front of him.

Kevin shrugged. "Terry's having one of those parties where the women all get together and one of them sells the others a bunch of shit they don't need so she can earn a free salad bowl or whatever. Paulie wanted to go and I sure as hell didn't, so here I am. How's fake almost-married life treating you?"

"I kissed her." He chugged down a quarter of the mug.

"Yeah, so? Engaged people do that sometimes."

"I kissed her *after* Cat left the room. I didn't kiss her because we were pretending. I kissed her because… Hell, I don't need to draw you a map."

"When did that happen?"

Sean looked at his watch. "About a half hour ago."

Kevin gave a low whistle. "She still sleeping on the couch?"

"Yes. And she's staying there, too, goddammit."

"Did she punch you in the face? Knee you in the balls?"

"No."

Kevin grinned. "So what's the problem? You want her. She can at least tolerate you. Get it out of your system."

He was afraid sleeping with Emma wouldn't get her out of his system, but get her a little further under his skin, instead. "Bad idea."

"Call it a fringe benefit."

"She's already pretending she's in love with me. Throwing real sex on top of that could get it all mixed up in her head."

"You worried about her mixing it up…or you?"

That was ridiculous, so he snorted and swallowed some more beer. He had no interest in settling down—signing his life over to somebody else so soon after getting it back from Uncle Sam—and he sure as hell wasn't planting flowers until retirement age. Assuming he didn't lose his mind and suffocate himself in a mound of mulch before then.

"You ready for Saturday?" Kevin asked.

"Hell, no." He didn't even want to think about that.

Kevin had to move on down the bar, so Sean sipped

his beer and stared at the television without really seeing what was on.

Emma had felt way too good tucked up against his body on the couch. She was warm and her body fit perfectly against his, and the viewing angle had let him appreciate all too much how long and perfectly shaped her legs were. And the heat of her thigh pressed against his...

Sean knocked back the rest of his beer and set the mug out on the far edge, looking for a refill.

Kevin came back and refilled it. "Nurse this one if you're driving home. If you have another, you're staying upstairs."

"I'll nurse it. Why don't you throw in an order of chili-cheese fries for me, too."

He watched the game and ate his fries, making the beer last. Emma would probably be asleep by the time he got back, those amazing legs peeking out from the worn flannel shorts that wouldn't have been sexy on anybody else.

Hopefully, the long, icy-cold shower he was going to need wouldn't wake her up.

Emma ripped the sticky note off the bathroom mirror and tossed it in the trash.

Sean didn't have to worry about her rubbing the back of his neck again anytime soon. And he certainly didn't have to worry about her wanting to get naked. Not with him.

If they were a real couple, she'd throw his pillow onto the couch and let *his* feet dangle over the edge for a change. It was pathetic how fast he'd come up with a lame excuse to run away just because he'd kissed her.

It was just a kiss. A great kiss, yes, but still just a kiss.

She hadn't asked him to marry her—to *really* marry her, of course—or told him she wanted to have his baby. A hot, steamy, toe-curling, bone-melting kiss between two single adults was nothing to run from.

But now he'd made a big deal out of it and everything was going to be even more awkward than it had been for the past few days.

She'd been curled up on the couch, fuming, for almost an hour when she heard Sean's truck pull in to the driveway. It was another ten minutes before he crept into the bedroom and closed the door behind him. Since she was facing the back of the couch, she didn't have to make much of an effort to ignore him.

He was in the shower so long she must have fallen asleep to the drone of running water, because the next thing Emma knew, her alarm was going off and it was time to face another day in the hell she'd created.

But first she had to face Sean. She got first crack at the bathroom, and when she came out, he was sitting on the side of the bed, fully clothed. Thank goodness.

He scrubbed his hands over his face. "We should talk about last night."

"How's Kevin?"

"He's good. And I meant before that."

"You should have stayed for the end of the movie. It was good."

"Dammit, Emma, you know that's not what I'm talking about."

"Oh, you mean the practice kiss?" She clipped her cell phone onto her front pocket. "We're getting better at it. That was almost convincing."

"Practice kiss?" He stood, probably so he could look

down at her, but she was tall enough it didn't make much of an impact. "Almost convincing?"

"Yeah," she said, though she turned her back on him, heading toward the door to avoid eye contact, because that was no practice kiss and it could have convinced even the CIA's finest.

He was muttering when she left the room, but she shut the door on him and went downstairs. She didn't want to talk about it. And she didn't want to think about the fact he wasn't happy she called it a practice kiss.

That meant he considered it a real kiss. And not only a real kiss, but one that had shaken him up. The only reason kissing a woman should bother a man like him was if he was trying to fight being attracted to her.

Hopefully, he'd win, she thought as she headed toward the kitchen, because she was waging that battle herself and didn't appear to be headed for a victory. Maybe he had enough willpower and self-control for both of them.

Other than a little morning chitchat with Gram, neither of them spoke as they ate breakfast and headed off to work—with him driving her truck again. But after ten minutes on the road with fifteen more to go, she couldn't take it anymore. "Why are you mad at me?"

He didn't look at her. "I'm not mad."

"You're not happy."

His fingers tightened on the steering wheel. "That was no practice kiss."

"I know it wasn't. I was trying to give us a reason not to talk about it."

"Oh. So you don't think we should talk about it?"

"I thought guys hated talking things out."

He drummed his fingers on the wheel. "I just don't want you getting any ideas, that's all."

Getting any ideas? Emma was speechless for a moment, unable to believe he'd actually said that. "Since I was walking away from you when you spun me around and kissed me, I'd say *you're* the one getting ideas."

"Of course I'm getting ideas. You're hot and I'm not dead. But I know enough not to confuse lust with anything else."

She snorted and looked out her window. "Oh, yes, Sean Kowalski. Your amazing kisses have made all rational thought fly out of my besotted brain. If only you could fill me with your magic penis, I know we'd fall madly in love and live happily ever after."

The truck jerked and she glanced over to find him glaring at her. "Don't ever say that again."

"What? The 'madly in love' or the 'happily ever after'?"

"My penis isn't magic." His tone was grumpy, but then he smiled at the windshield. "It does tricks, though."

"The only trick your penis needs to know for the next three and a half weeks is *down boy*." How the hell had she gotten herself into this conversation? "To get back to the point, if you think I have any interest in a real relationship with a guy who thinks he's a better driver than me just because I have breasts, you're insane."

"It's not because you have breasts. Women don't drive as well because they lack a magic penis."

She turned toward the passenger door, letting him know with her body language she had no interest in talking to him anymore. "Why didn't I tell Gram I was dating Bob from the post office?"

He laughed at her. "You've met the Kowalskis. You were doomed the minute you said the name out loud."

Doomed, she thought, glaring at the passing scenery. That was a good word for it.

Nine

"Oh, what a lovely home!"

Sean pulled into his aunt and uncle's driveway and killed the engine. "Thanks, Cat. My cousin Joe bought it for them after his horror novels started landing on the *New York Times* bestseller list on a regular basis."

"It's big, which must come in handy with all those grandchildren."

All those grandchildren she was about to meet, Sean thought, resisting the urge to beat his head against the steering wheel. He wasn't too worried about Steph, Joey and Danny, but Brian and Bobby were loose cannons. To say nothing of Aunt Mary.

The introductions didn't go too badly. His uncle's gruff humor put Cat at ease, and his aunt was warm and welcoming, even though Sean knew she had serious reservations about the whole thing.

"I'm Bobby," a young voice piped up, and it seemed as if everybody but Cat sucked in a breath at the same time. "Guess what?"

"What?" Cat said, seemingly oblivious to the frantic hand gestures being waved in Bobby's direction.

"Sean's my cousin. He got out of the army a long time ago and he lives with Emma and he's going to marry her."

Joey, Mike's oldest boy, laughed and put his arm around his little brother to not so subtly start dragging him away. "They have telephones in Florida, dummy. Mrs. Shaw already knows that."

Lisa stepped forward before Bobby could argue. "Now that you kids have all said hello to Mrs. Shaw, you can go to the basement and play your game."

Bobby jumped up and down. "Sean bought us 'Rock Band' for the Wii and all the instruments, so we're going to have a 'Rock Band' Tournament of Doom."

Sean hadn't known he'd bought the kids a bunch of video-game crap, but he couldn't very well argue the point. No doubt Mike and the rest would just put it on his tab.

Luckily, Cat and Aunt Mary seemed to hit it off pretty easily and—since Cat didn't seem in imminent danger of asking Mary outright if his and Emma's engagement was real—Sean started to relax.

They all went out to the backyard, where the women took over the chairs on the deck and the men gathered around the grill. It wasn't time to start cooking yet, but gathering around the cold grill was better than sitting with the women.

"Mary's been a wreck about this for days," Leo said, for once managing to lower his voice so the whole neighborhood wouldn't hear him.

"I know she didn't want to do this." Sean watched the women laugh at something Cat said. Or, more specifically, he watched Emma laugh. "I'll make it up to her somehow."

They talked about the usual stuff. The Red Sox. How

deep into summer vacation they'd get before Lisa's grip on her sanity started slipping. Evan's new truck, which he'd bought in white because Terry said not to buy a white one because they were impossible to keep clean. How Evan and Terry's marriage counseling was going.

Joe nudged Sean's arm. "I swear, I could tell time by how often Emma looks at you just by counting off the seconds."

Sean resisted the urge to turn and look. "She's nervous, that's all."

"That's not nerves."

"I think I know her better than you do."

Joe laughed. "You've known her a week."

"Ten days."

"Hate to burst your bubble, but I've known her longer than ten days. Not well, but I've run into her at Mike and Lisa's. Not that it matters. That look on a woman's face is pretty universal."

"There's no look."

"Oh, there's a look," Kevin said.

"There might be a look," Leo added.

"Mike and I can't see," Evan added. "We're facing the wrong way. We could turn around, but she might wonder why we're all staring at her."

Even though he figured his cousins were pulling his leg, Sean angled his body a little so he could see her in his peripheral vision.

Okay, so she was looking at him. A lot. But Joe and Kevin were still full of crap because there was no *look*. The glances were too quick to read anything into, never mind the kind of message they were implying she was sending.

He watched her watching him for a while, and then

Aunt Mary told them to get the meat ready so they could fire the grill. Since his cousins made for more than enough chefs stirring the soup and he needed a break from the visual game of tag he and Emma were playing, he grabbed a beer and made his way to the big toolshed. It was the unofficial Kowalski man cave, where females feared to tread. Even Aunt Mary would just stand outside and bellow rather than cross the threshold.

It smelled of the old motor oil that had dripped onto and soaked into the wooden floor, and the stack of wood next to the old woodstove meant to ensure that even in the cold months, there was a place a man could go for a few minutes of peace and quiet. The walls were lined with shelves of old mason jars containing nuts and bolts and screws and washers and all the other debris a good toolshed collected over time.

Sean cracked open his beer, flipped on the ancient radio and perched on one of the bar stools somebody had probably lifted from Jasper's. He was too wound up to sit still, though, so he set down his beer and got up to investigate the current project, which appeared to be rebuilding the snowblower's engine.

He was in the process of using gasoline and a wire brush to clean some gunked-up bolts when the door opened and his uncle walked in. "Hey, Uncle Leo."

"Thought I might find you out here." He inspected Sean's work and nodded in approval. "I've been teaching the boys to turn a wrench here and there. Steph used to help me out sometimes, too, but now her thumbs are too busy with that texting crap to twist a bolt."

"I should ask her how to run this damn phone I bought. I can do phone calls with it, but that's about it."

Leo grabbed another brush and pulled up a milk crate next to Sean. "So how you doing?"

"Not bad, I guess, considering what I let myself get dragged into."

"No, son. How are you *really* doing?"

Sean shrugged and grabbed a rag to wipe off some diluted gunk. "I'm doing okay. Lot of guys—and women—had it worse than me over there. I was lucky and now I'm out, no worse for wear."

"Thought about what you're going to do when this charade of yours is over?"

"Probably the same thing I planned to do before this charade started. Get a job pounding nails somewhere until I figure out where I want to land."

"Your aunt's got it in her head you and Emma have chemistry."

Sean snorted and stood to stretch his legs and reach his beer. "Between deployment and being sucked in by Typhoon Emma, I haven't had a chance to sow my wild oats in a good long time. Trust me, right now I've got chemistry with a telephone pole."

The last thing he wanted was chemistry with Emma Shaw—especially chemistry strong enough for other people to notice.

"Leo?" Aunt Mary yelled from outside. "Are you in that damn shed again? Is Sean in there with you? It's time to eat."

"Oops." Sean wiped his hands the best he could on a semiclean rag. "Busted."

"Listen, if you need to talk about…anything, you know where to find me."

"Thanks, Uncle Leo." He put out his hand, but instead

of shaking it, Leo used it to pull him in for an awkward hug and a slap on the back.

"I'm proud you served, but I'm damn glad to have you home."

Sean would have said something, but his throat had tightened up on him, so he just gave the old man's shoulders a squeeze and nodded.

"Sean Michael Kowalski!"

"You better go," his uncle said, releasing him, "before she gets her wooden spoon and storms my castle."

It was almost the end of the evening before Cat managed to get Mary alone in the kitchen. If she didn't know better, she'd almost think Sean's aunt was avoiding her.

"Wonderful meal, Mary."

The other woman spun around, clutching a box of aluminum foil. "Oh! You startled me. And thank you, though the boys did most of it."

"I'll have to beg that marinade recipe from you." Cat leaned against the counter and crossed her arms. "So, why are my granddaughter and your nephew pretending to be engaged?"

Clearly caught off guard, Mary was silent for a few seconds. Then her expression cleared. "They're not pretending. He asked her to marry him and she said yes. That's engaged."

Mary went back to dividing up leftovers and Cat narrowed her eyes at the woman's back. The question hadn't surprised Mary at all. She hadn't wanted to know why Cat would think that or what would possess her to ask such a thing. Obviously there was a conspiracy afoot.

"Okay," she said after a moment's thought. "Why are

they pretending they've been in love and living together for over a year?"

Mary practically flinched and Cat watched the tips of her ears turn a darkish pink. "Sean's been a part of your granddaughter's life for a long time."

Though it was artfully done, Cat could tell Mary was skirting the truth. "How long ago did Sean get out of the army?"

"Oh, he's been out awhile. Would you care for more cobbler? I swear I made enough to feed the entire neighborhood."

"No, thank you. Have Sean and Emma been living together for a year and a half?"

"It's been…oh, I don't know. I can barely keep track of my own four kids and all the grandkids."

She was good. Very good. "We hadn't even left the airport yet and I knew they weren't a couple. Or if they were, they hadn't even been dating long enough to get to second base. What I haven't been able to figure out is…why?"

Mary turned to face her and leaned back against the counter with a sigh, her arms crossed. "If Emma felt a need to invent a relationship with Sean—and I'm not saying she did—maybe she thought *you* couldn't be happy until *she* was happy."

"That doesn't make any sense." Or maybe it did.

Thinking back on their many telephone conversations, Cat realized she may not have done a very good job of hiding how much she worried about Emma. She was always asking her about the house and if she'd had the furnace checked, and admonishing her not to clean the gutters alone or climb a ladder or…a hundred other things. And she'd probably said the big old house was too much for Emma more than once.

And, looking back, maybe she *had* relaxed a little when Emma told her she was dating a really nice guy. Once Sean had supposedly moved in, she'd probably stopped using their time on the phone to fret and had talked about herself and how much she was enjoying Florida instead.

Cat sighed and shook her head. "You must all think I'm a pathetic, doddering old woman for my granddaughter to feel a need to put everybody through this."

"No, we don't think that at all." She looked sincere. "Emma loves you and she didn't want you worrying about her. Obviously it got out of hand. But for what it's worth, I think Sean's very attracted to her."

Cat thought about that for a minute. "Emma's definitely attracted to him."

"They make a lovely couple, and I wouldn't mind seeing Sean settle down. I'm tired of worrying about that boy."

"If I tell them I know they're lying, Sean will leave and go back to whatever he was doing before."

"He hadn't had a chance to do anything yet. He hasn't been out of the army very long and he was going to stay over Kevin's bar until he figured out what to do with his life." Mary paused and then smiled. "I think it's a very good idea not to let on you know."

"This could be fun."

Mary Kowalski's smile spread into a grin that rivaled her sons'. "Oh, it will be."

"Have you two set a date yet?"

Mrs. Kowalski's question sent Emma's iced tea rushing down the wrong pipe and she coughed until Sean pounded her on the back—maybe a little more enthusiastically than was required.

"No, we haven't," Sean answered while she attempted to clear her throat. "Nothing wrong with a long engagement."

"But not too long," Gram said. "I'm ready for some great-grandchildren."

"I wouldn't mind a grandnephew or -niece, either," Mrs. Kowalski added.

Emma wasn't sure, but she thought Sean might have stopped breathing. "We'll think about it."

"Hey," Mike interjected, "you could get married while Mrs. Shaw's home from Florida! A justice of the peace and a big, rented canopy. Couple of barbecue grills."

Emma was afraid Sean was going to chuck his glass at his cousin—who was obviously enjoying himself—so she laid her hand on his arm. It twitched under her fingers, but she turned her attention to Mike. "I don't really want a burgers-in-the-backyard kind of wedding."

"What kind of wedding do you want?" Mary asked.

"A big one," Emma said. "They take a long time to plan."

"And to save up for," Sean added.

"I bet Stephanie would love to be a bridesmaid," Terry said with an angelic smile.

Emma squirmed on the inside, though she did her best to hide it. Sean's family was brutal. They were doing their part in the deception, but they were having way too much fun with it, too.

They were all on the back deck, watching the kids play a very unstructured, rules-free game of badminton. It should have been a relaxing end to a fabulous meal, but all Emma could think about was getting the hell out before she had a total nervous breakdown.

"I still have a stack of bridal magazines and catalogs," Keri said. "We'll have to get together and have a wedding-planning party."

They were diabolical, every last one of them. "Maybe. This is my busy season at work, but...maybe."

"Of course she'll make time," Gram assured Joe's wife, while reaching over to pat Emma's knee. "Weddings are so exciting!"

"You know what's exciting? The Red Sox bull pen," Leo said in that loud voice of his, and Emma wanted to jump up and kiss him for changing the subject as the women rolled their eyes and the men started talking over each other.

Twenty minutes later, Gram yawned and Emma jumped on it like a starving woman jumping on a cheeseburger. "It's been a long day. We should probably get going."

Cat chattered about Sean's family all the way home, while Emma slumped in her seat, thankful the ordeal was over. They'd survived and now she was exhausted.

When they finally parked in front of the house, Gram went in while Emma and Sean took their time gathering the army's worth of leftovers Mary had sent home with them.

"That went pretty well," he said.

She laughed. "Your family has a twisted sense of humor."

"That they do, and they're going to give us both shit whenever they can. But nobody spilled the beans."

As they crossed the porch, Emma shifted her leftovers so she could touch his arm. He turned and looked at her in the fading sun. "Thank you, Sean. For doing this even though your aunt's not very happy about it and your family's never going to let you live it down."

"Don't worry about it. And that was the biggest hurdle, so it'll only get easier from here."

Somehow, she doubted that.

Ten

A knock on the door jerked Emma awake and she blinked at the clock across the room, next to the bed where Sean was now sitting up straight. Six twenty-five.

"Are you both decent? I can't wait to show you what I found!"

Oh, crap. Gram wanted in. She scrambled off the couch. "Just a second!"

After draping the blanket in a half-assed way over the back of the couch, she grabbed her pillow and crossed to the bed in a tiptoe jog, dodging the squeaky spot in the floor. Sean pushed his pillow back to one side and lifted the covers for her, and even though she tried not to look, she caught a glimpse of a gray boxer-brief-clad bulge as she slid between the sheets. She wouldn't mind waking up to that every morning.

Instead, she was waking up to an impromptu visit from her grandmother. She gave Sean an apologetic glance and he flopped backward onto his pillow, throwing his forearm over his eyes. "Come on in."

Gram opened the door and stepped in, carrying an old shoe box decorated with bits of lace and pink hearts cut out of construction paper. She smiled at them and held it up. "Your wedding box!"

Emma's stomach dropped. She'd forgotten about the wedding box. For years she'd been obsessed with weddings—maybe because the only pictures she had of her parents together in the same shot were wedding photos. She'd cut pictures out of magazines and drawn primitive sketches of whatever she couldn't find in the colorful pages. She'd written notes about her future wedding in a crayon scrawl and then penciled block letters. She'd even done a few in cursive with a hot-pink pen before she finally outgrew the box. She hadn't thought about it in years, and she certainly hadn't expected to see it at the crack of dawn on a Monday morning.

"It was in the back of my armoire, way down at the bottom," Gram said. "I was going to start breakfast, but I remembered it Saturday night while we were talking about what kind of wedding you want. I finally found it this morning and I just couldn't wait to show you and I knew you'd be getting up for work."

Emma rubbed her face, wishing the friction could jump-start her brain. "You don't have to make breakfast."

"For the last time, I'm not a fan of instant oatmeal and I don't mind doing it." She walked over to set the wedding box on Emma's lap and headed for the door. "I'll see you downstairs in a few minutes."

She was almost to the door when Emma's alarm went off. The alarm from her cell phone, which was across the room and plugged in next to the couch where she had been sleeping only a few minutes before. Emma watched Gram stop and look at it, frowning.

"I keep it over there because it's too easy to hit Snooze when it's next to the bed. If I get up to shut it off, I stay up."

"Makes sense." Gram smiled and left, closing the door behind her.

Emma groaned and climbed out of her bed—her wonderful, comfortable bed that she missed very much—and crossed the room to shut off the alarm and unplug her phone. When she turned around, Sean was sitting up, rummaging through the box.

He held up a small piece of paper she recognized with a pang as being from the pink stationery set her grandfather had bought her for her tenth birthday.

"'I want to marry a man who will wear pink shirts because it's my favorite color,'" he read aloud, and then he looked up at her. "Really? That's your criteria?"

"It seemed important when I was *ten*."

"'Bouquet—pink gladioli tied with white ribbon,'" he read from a torn piece of school notebook paper. "What the hell is gladioli? Sounds like pasta."

"Glads are my favorite flower." She grabbed her clothes and went into the bathroom, closing the door none too softly behind her.

When she emerged, he was still in bed and still rummaging through her childish dreams for her future. She watched him frown at a hand-drawn picture of a wedding cake decorated with pink flowers before he set it aside and pulled out another piece of pink stationery.

"'If the man who wants to marry me doesn't get down on one knee to propose,'" he read in a high-pitched, mock-feminine voice, "'I'll tell him no.'"

"My younger self had very high standards," she snapped. "Obviously *that's* changed."

He just laughed at her. "Were you going to put all this into spreadsheet form? Maybe give the poor schmuck a checklist?"

"Are you going to get up and go to work today or are you going to stay in bed and mock a little girl's dreams?"

"I can probably do both."

When he put the lid back on her wedding box and set it aside, she bolted before he could throw back the covers to get up. One glimpse of his boxer-brief-clad body was all she could take in a day.

Gram was making blueberry pancakes, which improved Emma's mood drastically. She fixed two coffees and set Sean's army mug in his spot before sipping her own.

"Thanks for finding my box, Gram."

"You used to work on that box for hours. You were so little when you started, your grandfather had to help you cut the pictures out of the magazines because you cried if you cut into the pretty dresses."

She'd had such big dreams. Prince Charming was going to charge into her life with his white horse and his pink shirt and sweep her off her feet. There would be romance and roses and champagne every day, and he'd write poems about his love for her.

Things had definitely changed since then. If and when she finally reached a point when settling down and starting a family was an option, she'd settle for love, reliability and respect over romance and roses.

She was on her second pancake by the time Sean finally appeared, his hair damp from his shower, and he dug in with relish after making a fuss over Gram.

"I'm going to cry when you go back to Florida and I'm back to instant oatmeal and fast-food drive-through windows," he said.

"Kiss ass," Emma muttered against the rim of her coffee mug, but he just grinned at her.

Gram plopped another pancake on Sean's plate. "Mary invited us all to their big Fourth of July bash on Saturday. They have a party and then go watch the fireworks over the lake. I told her we'd be there, of course. She said your family sometimes comes, too, Sean."

And there went Emma's appetite. "You didn't tell me that."

He shrugged. "Mitch said he'd be there. I haven't heard from the others yet."

Banging her head against the table wasn't an option, so Emma shoved another bite of blueberry pancake into her mouth and chewed slowly to buy herself time to stop screaming on the inside.

Not only were more people getting dragged into the mess she'd made, but his brothers and sister would be even worse because she'd have to pretend they weren't total strangers. Just thinking about it gave her a headache.

She shoved back from the table and rinsed her plate. "I've got a few phone calls to make before we leave. And we'll be working in the sun all day, Sean, so you might want to take it easy on the breakfast."

"Are you okay, honey?" Gram asked, her eyes full of concern. "You looked fine before, but now you're a little pale."

She forced herself to smile. "Just trying to sort my schedule in my head, Gram. I'm not sure about Saturday. I might need to work."

"Don't be silly. Nobody's backyard is more important than your family. If Sean's family can make the time, so can you."

"Okay, Gram. I'll make it work." She kissed her grandmother's cheek and escaped to her office for a few minutes of peace.

Sean hadn't mentioned the upcoming family bash or the fact his aunt would expect them to be there. Or the fact some of his siblings might show up.

Emma rested her forehead on the cool surface of her desk and sighed. Just what she needed. More Kowalskis.

Sean still didn't have much of a plan for what he'd do when the month was over, but he was pretty sure of one thing he *wouldn't* be doing—landscape design for finicky people with too much damn money.

They were spending the day on the shores of Lake Winnipesaukee again, at one of those little summer cottages that were really mansions, adding to landscaping Emma had previously done.

"Is she going to make you take these all out after?" he asked, making sure the mulch he was spreading was level enough to satisfy his boss's insane control freakishness when it came to her work.

"She might. But she'll pay for it, so I'll do it. But these are mostly annuals, anyway, so she can leave them for the rest of the summer without ruining the overall landscaping plan."

Mrs. Somebody-or-other was hosting a baby shower for her spoiled princess at the cottage the following week and the much-heralded first grandchild was reportedly a girl. Emma's job—and therefore Sean's, as well—was to turn the beachfront property into an explosion of pink.

There were tall, skinny pink flowers and short, bushy pink flowers and all different kinds of pink flowers he knew nothing about. There were even some of those gladioli things she'd been talking about that morning. But he wasn't likely to learn anything about them since she didn't trust him to do more than carry over whichever pot she pointed to and then spread mulch when and where she told him to.

Being surrounded by so much pink made it impossible to put the morning out of his mind because every flower made him think of a ten-year-old Emma wanting to marry a guy wearing a pink shirt.

That thought invariably led to thoughts of a very grown-up Emma sliding between the sheets, her long leg brushing against his thigh and making him think all kinds of naughty things. Luckily, the steamy thoughts of pulling her body, still warm from sleep, up against his had fled when her grandmother walked into the room. Residual desire had remained, though, even while they went on about that stupid box, so it was a damn good thing Emma had jumped out of bed to shut off her alarm.

The whole thing seemed wrong to him somehow, though, the more he thought about it. Cat didn't seem like the kind of woman to work herself into such a tizzy over finding a box that she had to burst in on them before they were out of bed. Excitement at the breakfast table, sure, but she'd been too respectful of their fake need for privacy for her actions to make any sense.

"I think Cat's onto us."

Emma sat back on her heels and brushed dirt off her gloves. "What makes you think that?"

"Just a feeling." He couldn't really explain it. "The way she watches us sometimes. And coming into our room at twenty after six? That didn't seem suspicious to you?"

"She was excited." But that excuse was weak and she knew it. "Gram would say something if she thought I was lying to her."

"Maybe not. Maybe she wants to figure out what we're up to."

She seemed to consider his comment for a moment, then she shook her head. "I don't think she could keep quiet about it. But, just in case she's suspicious, we'll have to step it up."

Step it up? If they stepped it up any more, his balls were going to explode. "What do you mean by that, exactly?"

"I don't know. Maybe…more touching or something?"

"No." He hadn't meant to say that out loud, but he meant it. He couldn't take any more touching. "I mean, I don't think that's the problem."

Actually, touching was exactly the problem, but not in the way she was thinking. He was horny, plain and simple, and the constant touching and looking and pretending was killing him. Slowly and seemingly without end.

The nights were the worst. Emma was a restless sleeper and he was a light sleeper and the combination made for a constant state of low-grade sleep deprivation. The sight of her dark curls spread across her pillow and her long legs kicked free of the blanket made for a constant state of high-grade lust.

"What do you think *is* the problem, then?"

He shook his head. "Forget it. Probably just my imagination."

When she pushed herself to her feet and stretched, he tried not to watch, but he couldn't look away. He knew being bent over the garden was hell on the muscles, but the way she put her hands to the back of her waist and arched her back—which pushed out her breasts—was hell on his self-control.

"How come you didn't tell me about your aunt and uncle's big holiday bash?"

"Because you'd just worry about it and stress, and

it's only Monday. I thought I'd wait until Friday to bring it up."

"Gee, thanks."

"Have you talked to Cat about the house yet?"

She shook her head. "I keep hoping she'll bring it up, but she hasn't. And it never seems like the right time."

"If you let her go back to Florida without selling you the house, this was all for nothing, you know."

"Yes, I know," she snapped. "I know it doesn't seem that way, but I don't *like* lying to my grandmother this way, and now that the time has come, I'm finding it hard to bring up the house."

His phone rang and he pulled it out of his pocket to look at the caller-ID window. "Shit."

"Who is it?"

"My sister. Sorry, I have to take it or she'll keep calling back." He flipped open the phone as he put a little space between him and Emma. "Hi, Liz."

"You're an idiot."

"I miss you, too."

"Tell me Mitch is full of shit."

"He usually is."

Her sigh practically vibrated his phone. "Are you living with some woman you just met and pretending to be her fiancé?"

"Yup."

"Does that seem normal to you?"

"I never claimed it was normal. It's pretty crazy, actually, but we're making it work." More or less. Other than an unexpected case of blue balls, it was going better than he would have guessed it would.

"And Aunt Mary's going along with this?"

"Reluctantly, but yes."

"I can't make it, but Mitch is going to be there for the Fourth. If he tells me he thinks this woman's up to no good, I'm going to sic Rosie on you."

"Nobody's up to no good, Liz, and we're not hurting anybody. I promise."

"We'll see what Mitch has to say." He heard a voice in the background and what sounded like a door slamming. "I have to run. I'll call you next week, after I talk to Mitch."

"Thanks for the warning," he said, but she'd already hung up.

He shoved his phone back in his pocket and smiled at Emma. "She sends her regards."

"I bet. She's not coming here, is she?"

"Not for the party. If Mitch reports back that I've fallen into the clutches of an evil, scheming temptress, she'll be here. Otherwise, she doesn't come home much."

Emma knelt in front of the garden bed and went back to planting pink flowers. "You said she lives in New Mexico. What does she do?"

"She waits tables at a truck stop to support the deadbeat artist wannabe who swept her off her feet and talked her into dropping out of college when she was nineteen."

"Oh. I guess that's not a happy story."

"No. But she's as stubborn as all four of us boys put together and I think she stays with him just so she won't have to admit our old man was right."

"Even though he passed away almost a decade ago? That's...stubborn."

"That's Liz." He scowled at the mulch she pushed in his direction. "We've all tried to talk some sense into her and we've had a few chats with him, too, but she won't leave him."

"Are they married?"

He snorted. "No. Asshole's too much of a free spirit to embrace government regulation of their relationship."

"One of those, huh?"

"Yeah. She'll get tired of his shit eventually. I hope."

"So none of you are married?"

"Nope. Liz has been wasting her time with her deadbeat for thirteen years. Ryan's divorced. And Mitch, Josh and I are too hard to pin down."

"You mean you haven't found women willing to put up with *your* shit yet."

He laughed. "Pretty much."

Of course, he hadn't been looking too hard, either. But he imagined when it was time to look—way down the road—he'd probably fall for somebody like Emma. She was smart and funny and loyal to her family. And, unlike a lot of women, she didn't take any of his crap.

Sure, she had some annoying habits. Like those little moaning sounds she made in her sleep. And she could be a bit of a smart-ass. The cleaning thing, of course. She'd taken a toothbrush to his sneakers the other night and they weren't even really broken in yet.

But, overall, if the urge to settle down ever struck him, he wouldn't mind a woman like Emma.

"It's all a sham?" Russell leaned against his counter, shaking his head. "The living together? The engagement? All a lie?"

"Yes." Cat sighed. It was a little embarrassing to admit Emma would resort to such an elaborate scheme to protect her peace of mind. But she'd told him the whole thing, anyway, including her conversation with Mary Kowalski, while he chuckled.

"She must really love you to go to all that trouble," he said when she was through, and Cat smiled.

"I guess you're right. She's a good girl, even if she did think I'd fall for this." But she hadn't worked up her courage and come into town to talk about Emma. "You owe me a dance, Russell Walker."

He gave her a sheepish smile. "I'm keeping my eye out for a nice place to take you. Heard there's a chem-free graduation fundraiser dance Saturday after next at the high school for the older crowd. It won't be fancy, but it's close and for a good cause."

"That might be nice."

"So it's a date, then?"

A date? What the heck was she doing dating at her age? "It's a date."

"Good. Are you and the kids doing anything for the Fourth?"

"We're going to spend the day with the Kowalskis and then all go over and watch the fireworks go off over the big lake."

He nodded. "Dani and her husband, Roger, always do that, too."

Cat picked up the bag of clearance gardening tools she'd bought just to have an excuse to stop at the hardware store. "If you go with them, maybe I'll see you there."

"Maybe you will. Where are you off to now?"

"I'm driving down to Concord to meet Mary Kowalski for lunch."

"Those poor kids don't stand a chance, do they?"

She laughed. "Nope."

Mary was already waiting at the fancy café they'd chosen because it was unlikely to attract any of the other family members and they could have a friendly lunch. Cat was older than her, of course, but not by much. She'd had Johnny young, and Johnny and his wife had been young when they had Emma.

Mary had gotten them a pitcher of water, but they both asked for tea to go with the salads they reluctantly ordered. With all the barbecuing going on, they had to be good when they had the chance. Cat still had guilt over the hash-and-cheese omelet and it had been almost a week.

They chatted about family and the weather until the salads arrived, and then Mary broached the subject of Sean and Emma. "How are things going between them?"

"I found out she sleeps on the couch in the bedroom. When I knocked on the door, I could hear her crossing the room to get into the bed before she called me to come in. And her phone, which she uses as an alarm clock, was plugged in next to the couch, too."

"I'm surprised they've managed to resist each other this long."

Cat nodded and drizzled a low-calorie dressing over her salad. "Me, too. I'm not sure why they're trying so hard, actually. Did you tell anybody I've figured out their little scheme?"

"No. I can't be sure none of them will tell Sean. Or that Lisa won't tell Emma. I haven't even told Leo, so it's just between us."

"It's going to be fun watching my granddaughter pretend Mitch isn't a total stranger to her."

"Having him here this weekend will help push Sean over the edge."

"You think so?"

Mary smiled. "Mitch is quite the ladies' man. There's

also a betting pool they think I don't know anything about, and they don't want Sean to win. Once Mitch starts flirting with Emma, we'll find out in a hurry how Sean really feels about her."

"I hope you're right. They definitely need a nudge."

"Trust me. I know my boys."

Eleven

Saturday rolled around and Emma knew she was in trouble when a slightly taller and older version of Sean spotted her across the Kowalskis' big backyard.

He grinned and started toward her. "Emma!"

When he picked her up off her feet—which was no easy feat considering how tall she was—and spun her around, she clutched his shoulders. "Mitch…hi."

Thank goodness only one of his brothers could come. Not only because there were fewer people to keep track of, but because there was a much better chance this actually *was* Mitch.

"Laying it on a little thick?" she heard Sean mutter.

"Can't help it," Mitch said, setting her back on her feet. "My future sister-in-law's quite the looker, you lucky bastard."

Sean made a snorting sound, but she couldn't tell if it was directed at the fact he'd called her his future sister-in-law, that she was a looker or that he was a lucky bastard, so she ignored him.

She'd noticed right off Mitch was a little taller and older than Sean, but his eyes were a little darker shade of blue and his hair was longer and scruffier. And he was leaner, too, though still pretty well built.

She jumped when Sean slid his arm around her waist and put his face close to hers. "Stop ogling my brother."

"He's taller than you."

"Older, too."

"Maybe, but what's a few years?" When he made a growling sound, she laughed and elbowed him in the side. "You're not jealous, are you?"

"Of Mitch? Please."

"I could totally take you, little brother," Mitch said. "Now, introduce me to your future grandmother-in-law so I can go back to my beer."

Emma mingled and laughed and ate too much and laughed some more as the day went on. Everybody was relaxed and nobody seemed particularly interested in watching her and Sean—or in pushing his buttons with wedding talk—so she relaxed, too.

She was licking a Fudgsicle stick clean when her grandmother dragged a chair close to hers and sat down. "Hi, Gram. Having fun?"

"I'm having a blast. Sean has a very nice family. And they really like you."

"I like them, too," she said, and it wasn't a lie. It was hard not to like them, even when they were giving her and Sean a hard time.

"I've been thinking about it and I'm going to give you the house as a wedding present."

All the food and the cookies and the chips and the ice cream she'd eaten turned over in Emma's stomach. "No, Gram."

"Yes. It's pretty clear you've made it your home, and

I want you to have it. Your grandfather wanted you to have it, too. We'd talked about it before he passed away."

"I want it, too, Gram, but I want to *buy* it. It's worth too much for you to just give it to me."

Gram scoffed at her words. "That monster's been paid off forever. There's no sense in putting another mortgage on it now. I've got enough money to keep me happy, and you've got a business to keep going."

Emma struggled not to cry. She wanted the house. And she'd been willing to buy it under iffy circumstances. But she couldn't let Gram give it to her as a wedding present when there wasn't going to be a wedding.

She took a deep breath. "Gram, I—"

Bobby ran up on the deck and skidded to a stop in front of them. "It's time for the Kowalski Fourth of July Football Game of Doom!"

Cat laughed and pushed herself out of her seat. "We'll talk about this some other time, Emma. Go have fun."

"I'm not sure I want to play football. Especially if there's doom involved," she said, but Bobby grabbed her hand and dragged her off the deck.

They were divvied up into teams roughly by size, each with an assortment of men, women and children. Emma was on Sean's team, which was good. She'd just hide behind him, because the only thing she knew about football was that it involved a lot of hitting.

It only took a few plays to see that the Kowalskis played by their own rules and the few they had were fluid. Mostly they served to ensure the smaller kids didn't get plowed over, victims of the adults' competitive streak.

Five minutes into the game, Emma somehow ended up with the ball. She squealed and looked around for somebody—anybody—to hand it off to, but there was nobody. Well, there was Danny, but he was doubled over in laughter.

"Run, Emma," Lisa yelled.

She ran in the direction her friend was frantically waving her hand, but she only went a few feet before two very strong arms wrapped around her waist and then she was falling. Luckily, she landed on a body instead of the ground.

"I love football," Mitch said, grinning up at her.

Emma grimaced and managed to get one of her knees on solid ground so she could push herself to her feet. He was quicker and freed himself to stand and help her up.

"They should give you the ball more often," he said, his blue eyes sparkling and the grin so like Sean's—but not quite as naughty—in full force.

"Hands off my girl," Sean told him, pulling on Emma's elbow.

"You should do a better job of blocking for her."

"Let's go," Brian shouted.

The very next play, Mitch intercepted Mike's pass to Evan and turned to run toward the other end zone. He was halfway there when Sean took him down hard. They hit the ground with a bone-jarring thud that made Emma wince, and came up pushing and shoving.

When Sean drew back his arm to throw the first punch, Mary blew her whistle from the sidelines. "Boys! Enough!"

Instead of heading straight for the huddle, Sean walked to Emma and pulled her into his arms for a hard, almost punishing caveman kiss that made her skin sizzle and her knees go wobbly. Then he glared at his brother for a few long seconds and went back to his team, leaving Emma standing there breathless and discombobulated.

Lisa was staring at her. So were Terry and Beth and Keri. All with raised-eyebrow speculation that made her want to bolt for a hiding place. So what if Sean had gone all Neanderthal on her? It didn't mean anything. It wasn't as if he'd staked a claim. It was probably just an instinctual reaction to his older brother flirting with the woman he'd brought to the party. That had to be it.

A few plays later, Emma ended up with the ball again. There seemed to be some kind of unspoken rule that everybody got a chance to make a play, even if they sucked. She was going to run, but then she saw Stephanie bearing down on her with that killer Kowalski spirit in her eyes and tossed the ball up in the air.

Mitch—who hadn't touched her since his first misguided tackle—snatched it out of the air and ran it back for a touchdown, much to the vocal dismay of her teammates.

"You play football even worse than you drive," Sean muttered.

"Clearly, it's my lack of—"

He yanked her back against his body and wrapped his arms around her so he could whisper in her ear. "Don't you dare say it."

She laughed and leaned back against his chest. "Don't say what?"

"If you mention the magic penis in front of these guys, I'll never hear the end of it. Never. Hell, fifty years from now when our dicks are shriveled up and useless, they'll still be cracking magic-penis jokes."

"What's it worth to you?"

He tightened his arms around her and nuzzled her hair. "What are you looking to get?"

She turned her head so her lips were almost touching his cheek and dropped her voice down into the sexy bedroom range. "I want…to drive home."

He snorted. "Figures."

"Just imagine Mike all old and decrepit and toothless and leaning on his walker cackling and shouting, 'Hey, Sean, how's the magic penis hanging?'"

"Okay, you win. You can drive."

"You gonna play or what?" Leo shouted at them.

Sean let go of her and headed back toward the ball, but as Emma looked over at the sidelines and debated making a break for it, she saw Mary watching her with what looked like a rather smug smile curving her lips.

Emma wasn't sure exactly what that could mean, but she wasn't sure she wanted to know, either, so she forced herself to rejoin her team. They were in a huddle, discussing a play that, thankfully, didn't seem to include her, but she listened, anyway. And jumped when the huddle broke up and Sean slapped her on the ass.

His brother flirting with her had really brought out the touchy-feely in him, she mused as Terry ran past her with the ball.

"Emma, take her down," Terry's husband shouted, but it was too late. And she wasn't stupid. Tackling Terry would hurt.

The score was either twenty-one to forty-two or tied at thirty-five, depending on who you asked, when Mary blew the whistle. "Time to clean up and get ready for the fireworks. Kids, make sure you go to the bathroom *before* we leave this year."

Maybe it was only because Mitch was nearby and Mary had her eye on them, but Emma didn't pull away when Sean took her hand in his for the walk into the house.

* * *

It was almost dusk before the horde of Kowalskis got themselves settled on a patchwork island of old quilts. Cat staked her claim on one corner by setting down her bag and the straw hat she'd worn earlier to keep the sun off her face. Then she wandered away to see who she could run into.

She stopped here and there, saying hello to a few friends, but when she saw Russell Walker sitting on one of the park benches, she was forced to admit to herself she'd been looking for him. He was alone, so she took a deep breath to steady her ridiculous schoolgirl nerves and walked over.

"Is this seat taken?"

His face brightened when he saw her and he patted the empty bench next to him. "I was sitting on a blanket with Dani and her husband, but I'm a little old for that."

"Emma and I are with Sean's family, but I thought I'd go for a walk and put off sitting on the ground for as long as possible."

"Would they be upset at all if you stayed here with me?"

With the number of people on the Kowalskis' acre of blankets, they probably wouldn't even notice she was gone. "Probably not."

"Do you care if they are?"

She smiled and shook her head. "Not really, no."

And speaking of Emma, there she came, obviously looking for her. She waved her hand to get her attention and didn't miss the surprise that crossed Emma's face.

"Hi, Mr. Walker. We were starting to think Gram got lost."

"I think I'm going to watch the fireworks with Russell."

"Oh." Cat watched Emma try to wrap her mind around that. "Okay."

"You look lovely tonight," Russell said. "Clearly, love agrees with you."

Because she was looking for it, Cat saw the flash of guilt in Emma's eyes before she smiled and couldn't resist poking at her. "Russell tells me he hasn't met Sean yet."

"No. He…uh… Sean's not much of a shopper. And he goes down to the stores in the city when he needs stuff so he can visit his aunt and uncle at the same time."

At least the girl was consistent. Cat wondered if she'd made up cue cards. "You'll have to bring him over after the fireworks."

"Yeah. Maybe. So…have fun."

She walked away, but Cat caught her looking back with a frown, as if trying to puzzle out why her Gram was choosing to watch the fireworks with the guy who owned the hardware store instead of with her family.

Then they fired a test shot, and Cat put Emma out of her mind as the burst lit up the darkening sky.

They oohed and aahed along with the rest of the crowd, and as the show built toward the grand finale, Russell's hand bumped hers. It rested there for a moment and then he threaded his fingers through hers.

"Where's Cat?"

Emma sighed and looked toward where she'd found Gram and Russell Walker, even though it was too dark to see them. "She ran into a friend. She's sitting on the bench with him, over by the trees."

"Him?"

"Yeah. Russell Walker, who owns the hardware store."

Sean shrugged. "Probably beats sitting on the ground."

With her grandmother watching the fireworks with Russell, Emma was free to put a little space between her and Sean on their part of an old, gaily colored quilt. Not too much space, of course, because there were a lot of Kowalskis and they had to keep the kids spread farther apart than jabbing elbows could reach.

"Need a Valium?" Sean leaned over to ask in a low voice.

"No. Why?"

"You spin that engagement ring around on your finger when you're stressed, and right now, it looks like you're trying to generate electricity with it."

Emma locked her fingers together and hooked her clasped hands over her drawn-up knees. Stressed? Why would she be stressed? Her body was still humming from that caveman kiss during the football game, her grandmother had ditched her for Mr. Walker from the hardware store, and she couldn't make sense of either event.

It wasn't for lack of trying. Her mind raced, trying to sort it all out, as colors burst above her in the dark sky. Maybe Sean was right and Gram had simply taken a seat on the bench next to Mr. Walker because she didn't want to sit on the ground. And maybe Sean had only kissed her because he thought that's what a man in love would do when his older brother was flirting with his fiancée. All very innocent.

But she'd been watching Sean pretend to be in love with her for two weeks, and while he didn't do too badly, she didn't think he had the acting chops to fake the primal, possessive gleam in his eye right before he'd claimed her mouth.

Sean scooted a little closer, probably so his mouth could be near her ear. The discretion, she appreciated. His warm breath against her skin, not so much. "You're not even trying to enjoy this, are you?"

"I am, too." She enjoyed the feel of his shoulder pressing against hers. And the way he smelled. And the way the fireworks kept lighting up his face.

He didn't seem inclined to say any more, but he didn't move away, either, so they watched the fireworks and laughed at the kids, who were oohing and aahing with exaggerated exuberance. They were all decked out in glowing neon bracelets and necklaces, and they were as lively and vivid as a Vegas show.

After a while, Emma shifted her weight, trying to find a reasonably comfortable position on the hard ground. It wasn't easy, until Sean pulled her close and she rested against his chest. It was very comfy…physically. Played hell on her senses, though, and she was surprised—and not in a good way—to find herself wishing Gram was with them on the blanket so Sean would have an excuse to wrap his arms around her and kiss the back of her neck.

She was starting to wish Sean had excuses to do a *lot* of things to her. Especially things he couldn't do in front of Gram.

They were only halfway through the month, and she'd spent so much time wondering what sex with Sean would be like, she was afraid someday soon he was going to touch her and she'd burst into spontaneous orgasm. The trip from the bathroom to the couch every night was the worst, requiring her full concentration. She didn't trust her body not to hang a right and climb into bed with him.

"What are you thinking about now?" Sean whispered

against her ear, and she cursed under her breath. She really had to stop thinking about sex near him.

"I'm thinking about all those cakes and pies waiting at your aunt's house," she lied.

He chuckled, the sound almost masked by the fireworks. "I had no idea desserts had that effect on you. I'll have to remember that."

Rather than deal with the implied promise in those words and the husky bedroom voice it was implied in, she turned her face away and ignored him. But she couldn't ignore the aching need he'd brought back to the surface. *I'll have to remember that.*

When the last loud and colorful bursts of the grand finale lit up the sky over the lake, the Kowalski family clapped and cheered, then started gathering their things. In just the short time they'd been on the quilts, it looked as if the family had taken up residence, with drink bottles and snack wrappers and toys spread all over the place. Sean pushed himself to his feet and then held out his hands to her.

She hesitated to touch him, which was dumb. He was a gentleman, so of course he'd help her up. The fact she was still all shivery and freaked out on the inside from the kiss earlier was her problem, not his.

Once on her feet, she withdrew her hands as quickly as she could, then looked down at her grandmother's hat and bag. "Gram wanted me to bring you over after the fireworks. To introduce you to Mr. Walker, I guess."

"Does it bother you?"

"Introducing you?"

He shook his head and pulled her off the quilt because Terry was trying to fold them up. "That she watched the fireworks with him."

The mature thing to do would be to scoff at the suggestion she was bothered by her grandmother having a friend, but she couldn't quite pull it off. Not with him watching her so intently. "I don't know. I didn't see it coming, that's for sure. Where did Mitch go?"

"Blonde. Over by the grandstand."

She turned to look and saw Mitch talking to a pretty blonde woman in a skimpy yellow sundress. She had the kind of primped and polished look that implied she'd shown up alone solely for the purpose of finding a man to take her home. "He doesn't waste any time."

Sean snorted, and she couldn't tell if the look he gave his brother was annoyance with the ladies'-man routine or annoyance he wasn't free to find his own sure thing in a skimpy sundress.

Before she could figure it out, Gram showed up with Russell Walker in tow and behind him a couple who looked younger than what her parents would have been, but not by much.

"Emma," Gram said, "this is Russell's daughter, Dani, and her husband, Roger. This is my granddaughter, Emma, and her fiancé, Sean."

Emma smiled and shook hands, and then kept smiling as the introductions continued around her. Inside, though, her brain was going numb. Performance exhaustion, she told herself. It was tiring, all this pretending, and she wanted to go home and make Sean crash on the couch so she could curl up in her bed and sleep. But at least this night was almost over.

"If you're not doing anything," Mary said to Russell and the others, "you should come back with us and have dessert."

Or maybe not.

Twelve

Sean was going to kill his cousins. Slowly. Painfully. And he'd kick the crap out of both of them first.

They'd all gone back to his aunt and uncle's after the fireworks, as expected. What wasn't expected was Cat introducing Russell and his daughter, Dani, and her husband, Roger, to the Kowalskis, who then invited them along for post-fireworks decaf and dessert.

After the pies and cakes were demolished, Mike and Lisa had taken their boys home and the two babies, Lily and Brianna, were asleep, so the older generation decided on some card game nobody under forty knew how to play. So the under-forty crowd had retreated to the rec room in the basement, except Mitch, who'd said his goodbyes before he left the fireworks with the gorgeous blonde in the barely there sundress.

Joe had a perfect game to pass the time, he'd said. Kevin had smirked and agreed. And there were four couples, so it was perfect. Sean should have known better.

The reason having four couples was perfect, he found out too late, was because the game was a kind of demented adult version of *The Newlywed Game*. And now

Joe and Kevin were laughing their asses off on the inside because Dani and Roger's presence meant Sean and Emma had to keep up the pretense or Dani would tell her dad, who would in turn rat them out to Cat.

"'What's the first place you had sex?'" Roger read from a card.

Dani hit the timer and six of them bent over their notepads, furiously scribbling down answers. Sean looked down at his blank page and decided to keep it simple. Hopefully, Emma would do the same.

When the timer dinged, he tossed his pencil down. Joe and Keri scored the first point by both writing, *In the backseat of Joe's 1979 Ford Granada.* For Kevin and Beth it was the hotel where Joe and Keri's wedding reception was held, and Dani and Roger both wrote, *Dani's dorm room.*

Emma grimaced at Sean and then held up her notepad. "'On a quilt, under the flowering dogwood.'"

The other women made sweet *awww* noises, but Joe and Kevin were already snickering. That wasn't keeping it simple. Under a flowering dogwood?

"We need your answer," Roger said.

Sean held up his paper. "'In a bed.'"

His cousins' snickers became full belly laughs, while Dani and Roger just looked a little confused.

"Oh," Emma said. "You meant sex with *each other?*"

It was a nice save, but Sean had a gut feeling it was only going to go downhill from here. And since he and Emma would be lucky if they got out of there with their secret intact, never mind having a snowball's chance in hell of winning, he might as well have some fun with it.

Then came Dani's turn to read a question. "'Who's in charge in the bedroom?'"

Much to the group's amusement, none of them got a match, and Sean didn't think they would either as he held up his notepad. "'I am, since I carry the big stick.'"

Emma read hers with a remarkably straight face. "'Sean, because he has a magic penis.'"

"Wow. Um…so Sean and Emma have a point," Dani said as the men nearly pissed themselves laughing.

No way in hell was he leaving that unpunished, and he winked at Emma when Kevin read the next question. "'Where's the kinkiest place you've had sex?'"

The fact that Joe and Keri had done the dirty deed on the back of his ATV led to a few questions about the logistics of that, but then it was Emma's turn. "'In bed, because Sean has no imagination.'"

Roger threw an embarrassed wince his way, but his cousins weren't shy about laughing their asses off.

Sean just shrugged and held up his notepad. "In the car in the mall parking lot. Emma's lying because she doesn't want anybody to know being watched turns her on."

Her jaw dropped, but she recovered quickly and gave him a sweet smile that didn't jibe with the "you are so going to get it" look in her eyes.

Beth asked the next question. "'Women, where does your man secretly dream of having sex?'"

Keri knew Joe wanted to have sex in the reportedly very haunted Stanley Hotel, from King's *The Shining*. Dani claimed Roger wanted to do the deed on a Caribbean beach, but he said that was her fantasy and that his was to have sex in an igloo. No amount of heckling could get him to say why. And when it came to Kevin, even Sean knew he dreamed of getting laid on the pitcher's mound at Fenway Park.

Then, God help him, it was Emma's turn to show her answer. "'In a Burger King bathroom.'"

The room fell silent until Dani said, "Ew. Really?"

"No, not really," Sean growled.

"Really," Emma said over him. "He knows that's the only way he can slip me a whopper."

As the room erupted in laughter, Sean knew humor was the only way they'd get through the evening with their secret intact, but he didn't find that one very funny, himself.

It was the final answer that really did him in, though. The question: "If your sex had a motto, what would it be?"

Joe and Keri's was, not surprisingly, *Don't wake the baby.* Kevin and Beth both wrote, *Better than chocolate cake,* whatever that was supposed to mean. Dani wrote, *Gets better with time, like fine wine,* and Roger wrote, *Like cheese, the older you get, the better it is,* which led to a powwow about whether or not to give them a point. They probably would have gotten it if they weren't tied with Keri and Joe, who took *competitive* to a cutthroat level.

When they all looked at Sean, he groaned and turned his paper around. They'd lost any chance of winning way back, but he was already dreading what the smart-ass he wasn't really engaged to had written down. "'She's the boss.'"

The look Emma gave him as she slowly turned the notepad around gave him advance warning she was about to lay down the royal flush in this little game they'd been playing.

"'Size really *doesn't* matter,'" she said in what sounded to him like a really loud voice.

Before he could say anything—and he had no idea what was going to come out of his mouth, but he had to say *something*—Cat appeared at the top of the stairs.

"I hate to break up the party," she said, "but it's getting late, so we're calling it a night."

Maybe Cat was, but Sean was just getting started.

If Gram wasn't in the truck, Emma would have given Sean a ride home he'd never forget. As it was, she pushed it a little, enjoying his sucked-in breaths and the way his foot kept reaching for a brake pedal he didn't have.

Because it was so late, Gram went right to bed, and Sean followed her up the stairs. By the time Emma was done locking up, she heard snoring coming from her grandmother's room as she paused on her way by.

Sean wasn't snoring, but he was already in bed. He was on his back with his hands tucked under his head, scowling at the ceiling. Rather than give him time to grumble at her for driving like a girl, she went straight into the bathroom to clean up and get ready for bed.

In her hurry, though, she'd forgotten to grab her pajamas, which was a dilemma. She could either go out and get them and return to the bathroom to change, or she could go out there and put them on. If Sean didn't like it, he didn't have to watch.

After leaving the bathroom, she turned off the overhead light in the bedroom, but it didn't do much good. The night was clear, the moon was bright, and she knew she was all too visible when she undid her jeans and shimmied them down over her hips.

"What the hell are you doing?"

"Changing into my pajamas."

"You always do that in the bathroom." His voice was low and rough, but she noticed he didn't look away.

"I forgot them, and there's no point in going back in there." She kicked off the jeans and was going to pull on the shorts before changing shirts, but then she remembered his stupid answers to the stupid questions in that game and changed her mind.

"The point is that you don't do it in front of me."

"Oh, did you forget? Being watched turns me on." And she pulled her T-shirt over her head.

She had to bite down on a surprised yelp once she was free of it because suddenly Sean was standing in front of her, wearing nothing but blue boxer briefs and a scowl. "You said I had no imagination."

"And having no imagination is *so* much worse than your best friend's family thinking you're an exhibitionist."

"And we're not ever going to talk about the other thing you said. Ever."

He was crowding her personal space, so she put her hands on his chest to push him back, but he caught her wrists. Standing there with her palms pressed against his naked skin, she could feel his heart beating at a quickened pace that matched her own and she knew she had two choices. Walk away or end up in bed with him.

She leaned her body a little closer and splayed her fingers across his chest. "Which thing aren't we talking about? The fast-food-joint bathroom or—"

"Don't push me too far, Emma. It's been a long time for me."

"How long?"

"Too damn long." He lifted her hands from his chest,

but didn't let go of her wrists. "And I never even got to scope out the dating situation here before you showed up at my door with this half-assed scheme."

"And since we… You haven't…"

"The last thing I need is to get caught cheating on a woman I can't tell anybody I'm not really in a relationship with." His gaze dropped from her face to her lacy white bra and he sighed. "You're killing me."

"Lying awake on the couch every night, wondering what it would be like to slide into bed with you has been killing me for two weeks."

"Yeah." He let go of her wrists and slid his hands up the back of her neck and into her hair. "I've thought about that, too. A lot. Pretty much constantly, actually."

"We're two single adults. There's no reason we have to suffer."

He was pulling her slowly closer, his fingertips still massaging the back of her skull, and she was starting to lose patience with the talking. She wanted more doing.

Sean apparently hadn't turned that page yet. "This won't change anything, Emma, so I don't want you getting any ideas. The day we drive Cat to the airport, I'm moving on. This isn't…real."

"The orgasms will be real, right?"

"Very real. And numerous."

"I'll take it."

With a deep, guttural groan, Sean pulled her face to his and claimed her mouth. It was a hard and demanding kiss, the way he'd kissed her on the makeshift football field earlier, but there was nothing quick about it. His tongue flicked across hers as one hand tightened in her hair.

With the other hand, he pulled her hips against his,

and she felt hard evidence she'd been so very, very wrong to imply he wasn't blessed below the waist.

Her hands slid from his chest to his shoulders and then to his back, holding him to her because she never wanted him to stop kissing her. Then she squeezed him, holding tight as he reached down the backs of her thighs and lifted her so she could wrap her legs around his waist.

A moment later he had her on the bed, his body covering hers and his erection nestled between her legs. She lifted her hips, urging him to get on with it, but he didn't seem to be in much of a hurry for a guy who said it had been a long time.

Then he lifted his head and looked down into her face. "Before we go any further, one more thing."

She groaned. "Seriously?"

"One wisecrack about a magic penis," he warned, "and I don't care if I have to dump ice cubes down my pants, I'll walk away. Bowlegged, probably, but I'll walk."

She laughed and slid her hands under her back to undo her bra. "I'll try to contain myself."

Sean slid the straps free of her arms and flung the bra aside before lowering his mouth to her breasts. When he drew her nipple into his mouth and sucked gently, she moaned and ground her hips against his.

He gave the same attention to her other breast, then lifted his head so he could see her face. He was panting a little—they both were—and he gave her a sheepish grin.

"As much as I'd love to wow you with my stamina and imagination, maybe we could do that tomorrow night."

She wrapped her legs around his calves, running her foot up his leg. "Tomorrow night? You're not getting any ideas, are you?"

"I have ideas about what I'd like to do to you tomorrow night. Right now there's a little…urgency, if you know what I mean."

"I know exactly what you mean." She tugged down on her panties, and Sean moved so he could pull them all the way off before reaching into her nightstand drawer and pulling out a condom.

"Hey. You put condoms in my nightstand?"

"I'm an optimist." Then he stood and dropped his boxer briefs and Emma got optimistic, too.

When he lowered himself over her again, Emma wrapped her legs around his hips, urging him forward. He resisted, lowering his head to give her another blistering kiss before settling between her thighs.

And, holy hell, he was everything she'd thought he'd be during the last two weeks' worth of restless nights. He filled her with excruciatingly slow strokes until her nails dug into his back and she was whimpering, begging for more in barely coherent, fractured sentences.

When he hooked his arm under her right knee and then drove even more deeply into her, she sucked in a hard breath and moaned his name.

"Shh," he whispered, and then he did it again.

There was no way she could be quiet. Not when she wanted to yell at him to do it faster and harder, so she twisted her body around and he caught the hint pretty quickly. Then she was on her knees, her weight resting on her forearms as she buried her face in his pillow.

Sean's fingers bit into her hips as he drove into her, each stroke a little harder than the one before. She moaned into the pillow, clutching the pillowcase in her fists as the very real orgasm shook her body.

Sean groaned, his hand squeezing her hips as he shuddered and drove into her a few final times. Then he collapsed on top of her, stretching her body out flat against the mattress.

Turning her head so she wouldn't suffocate in the pillow, Emma sucked in air and basked in the heat of his heavy, trembling body. He kissed the back of her neck and started to lift himself, but then he collapsed again.

"Just another minute," he murmured into her hair.

"Mmm." She didn't have words yet, but if she did she'd tell him she didn't want him to move. She was content just the way they were.

He got up after a minute to go into the bathroom, and on his way back, he grabbed her pillow off the couch and tossed it onto the bed. "Get over. You're on my side of the bed."

"It's my bed," she muttered, already half-asleep. "You don't have a side."

"Get over."

She got over, but only because she didn't want to ruin the glow with bickering. And once he'd gotten in on *his* side of her bed and pulled her close again, she didn't really care.

"That was amazing," he whispered.

"Magic."

She yelped when he slapped her ass, but he was chuckling when he wrapped his arm around her and nuzzled his face in her hair. She was still smiling as she fell asleep.

Sean woke to the sound of a phone going off. For a few seconds he was confused because it was Sunday, so Emma's alarm shouldn't go off. Then he realized his cell phone was ringing on the nightstand.

At the same time he also realized Emma had rolled to face him during the night and the blankets had slipped down, and, damn, she had nice breasts. But she was stirring, probably because his phone was ringing, so he stopped staring and answered it.

"What?"

"I'd say I hope I didn't wake you, but I'm guessing I did." It was Mitch and he didn't sound too sorry about it.

"It's seven o'clock on a Sunday, asshole. Of course you woke me up."

And he'd also woken Emma up, and Sean sighed in disappointment when she slid out of bed, grabbed her clothes and went into the bathroom. Not the way he'd envisioned their waking up when he'd been drifting off to sleep last night.

"I need a favor," Mitch said.

"Call Triple-A."

"You're my brother."

Sean swung his feet to the floor and scrubbed at his face. "What's up?"

"My rental car has a dead battery and they can't do anything about it until midafternoon. And April doesn't have a car."

"April. Oh, wait…is that the blonde's name?"

"Yeah. I need you to come get me and drive me to the airport."

"Call a cab."

"I tried. This ain't Boston, dude. The soonest I can get a taxi here that'll take me to Manchester is ten minutes after I have to *be* in Manchester. I just need a ride. The rental company's going to come get their shitbox."

"Fine. How do I get to April's house?"

By the time he'd scrawled directions on a sticky note and promised his brother he was as good as on his way, Emma was on her way out of the bedroom, leaving flower-scented shower steam in her wake. He thought about calling her back, but he didn't have a clue what he'd say, so he went into the bathroom to see if she'd left him any hot water.

Before he went downstairs, he pulled out his Sharpie and stuck a fresh sticky note on the mirror. *Btw, THAT was my favorite sexual position.* He almost added a happy face to it, but decided just in time that would be lame. It was a slippery slope that led nowhere but to dotting his *i*'s with hearts.

When he went into the kitchen and found a plate of scrambled eggs and bacon at his seat, he looked at the clock and decided Mitch could cool his heels for a few more minutes.

Emma was an unusual flurry of activity, all of it seeming to require she not look at him. She buttered toast and put the juice away and spent a few minutes wiping up an invisible coffee spill, from what he could tell. Maybe it was the fact her grandmother was in the room, but she seemed a little embarrassed that they'd had sex last night.

Great sex. Sex he wasn't embarrassed about at all and hoped to do again as soon as bedtime rolled around. Only, an extended version this time, like a director's cut. He could add back in all the parts of his performance he'd had to cut to fit the time slot his long-neglected sex drive had given him.

For now, he had to deal with Mitch. After shoveling down his breakfast in record time, he rinsed his plate and kissed Cat's cheek. "I hate to eat and run, but my brother needs a ride to the airport."

When he went to kiss Emma goodbye, as he always did because that's what a fiancé would do, he half expected her to shy away. Instead, when his mouth met hers, she flicked her tongue over his bottom lip and gave him a look that promised they'd be putting his imagination to good use later.

He found April's house with no problem and sat in his truck while Mitch kissed her goodbye in the doorway. And then kissed her goodbye again, and so thoroughly Sean finally tapped on the horn to break up the party.

The blonde was smiling and waving as they pulled out of sight, and Sean shook his head. Not only would she never see Mitch Kowalski again, but she knew she wouldn't. His oldest brother had an amazing ability to love and leave women without them bearing him any ill will at all.

It didn't take long for Mitch's good mood to get on his nerves. "If you keep whistling, you're going to walk."

"Hey, it's not my fault you hooked up with a woman who's only pretending to like you."

Sean's fingers tightened on the steering wheel. It was tempting to tell Mitch Emma hadn't been pretending last night, but he kept his mouth shut until the urge passed.

For one, there was money on the line. If he confided in Mitch, he'd tell Ryan and Josh before he even got on the plane so they could determine who'd won the pool. But that wasn't a big deal. There were always betting pools, and sometimes he won and sometimes he lost.

What *was* a big deal was the possibility—no, probability—that Mitch would also tell one of their cousins, who would tell the other cousins, who would then tell their spouses and…it was only a matter of time before the news reached Aunt Mary. And if Aunt Mary got it in her head he and Emma were becoming a *real* couple, she'd jump on him in a second, pushing him into settling down.

Better to keep his mouth shut because, no matter how much Emma had rocked his world last night, settling down was the last thing on his mind.

Thirteen

As soon as Emma and Sean left in separate trucks—Emma having been called not five minutes after Sean left by an upset customer whose new garden had been ravaged by some nocturnal creature—Cat did a victory dance in the kitchen. It couldn't have been more obvious they'd had sex if they'd had T-shirts made to mark the occasion.

They'd barely said two words to each other and they'd avoided eye contact at all costs, but they weren't fighting. Anger wasn't the vibe filling the kitchen with tension. No, it was morning-after awkwardness and she couldn't be happier about it.

By the time she was done puttering around the kitchen, it was a decent enough hour to call Mary. She brewed herself some tea and took it into the living room to get comfortable.

"You were right about Mitch making a difference," she said after they'd exchanged hellos.

"Sean didn't like him touching her. I swear, that kiss almost set the grass under their feet on fire."

"Guess who *didn't* sleep on the couch last night?"

"And the plot thickens," Mary said, and they laughed.

"Speaking of thickening plots, I told Emma I want to give her the house as a wedding gift, and I thought she was going to throw up in my lap."

"That's interesting."

Cat took a sip of her tea. "I think, besides worrying about me, she was also afraid I'd sell the house."

"So making up a relationship with Sean put your mind at ease, but also made you stop telling her the house was too much for a woman alone."

"Exactly."

"What did she say?"

"She kept insisting she wanted to buy it from me, not have it given to her. I know my granddaughter. I don't think she'll accept the house as a gift under false pretenses."

"I'd like to think you're right. What are you going to do?"

Cat sighed. "I'm going to leave it alone for now. If I push, she might decide to tell me the truth. Since they've only just…discovered each other, so to speak, I'd rather leave things as they are for a bit longer."

"Good point." Mary dropped her voice a little. "Speaking of discovering each other, what's going on between you and Russell Walker?"

"We're friends," she said, but her friend only laughed. "Okay, *friends* might not be a strong enough word."

"What *would* be a strong enough word?"

"I don't know. It's so silly. When I'm away from him I tell myself I'm too old to be flirting with a man. But when I'm with him, I don't feel old at all."

"He's smitten with you. Anybody can see that."

"Smitten." Cat chuckled. "I like that word. But I'm

going home in less than two weeks and his whole life is here."

"You said his store was going out of business."

"Yes, but he's still a part of the community and his daughter's here."

"Like your granddaughter's here?" She heard Mary's *tsk* clearly across the line. "That's not an obstacle."

"Maybe not, but I'm also set in my ways. He's charming and I enjoy his company, but I'm not sure I want to spend my remaining years unballing another man's socks. It's been a long time since I've had to do that."

"I unball Leo's socks. Leo rubs my feet. It works for me."

Cat sipped more of her tea, then sighed, wondering if Russell would rub her feet. "It's ridiculous."

"I bet that's what Sean and Emma said, too."

And the conversation circled back to the kids, which was just fine with Cat. She hadn't yet sorted out how she felt about Russell, so she didn't want to talk about it.

Maybe it was infatuation. They'd both been alone a long time. But that didn't mean either of them wanted to pack up and start a new life together. That was a big commitment and she wasn't sure she had the energy or the desire for that at this point.

It was much easier to meddle in Sean's and Emma's lives than dwell on her own.

Once he'd dumped his brother off at the airport, Sean had nothing to do but kill time until it was time to get Emma back in his bed. Or *her* bed, actually. He tried out the sound of *their* bed, but his mind shied away from it. Made them sound too much like a real couple.

As long as Emma was naked in it, he didn't really

care whose bed it was. He'd been quick on the trigger last night, and while he didn't have anything to prove, he intended to take his time with her tonight. If tonight ever came. The only time he'd ever seen clocks move so slowly was during his flight back to the States.

Emma's truck wasn't in the driveway when he pulled in, and at first, he thought the house was empty. But then he heard laughter and looked out the window to find Cat in the backyard swing, the cordless house phone pressed to her ear. Since he wasn't about to interrupt her conversation to ask her where Emma had taken off to, he grabbed his book and stretched out on the couch to read.

He must have dozed off because the next thing he knew, the sun had shifted and he could hear Emma's voice coming from the direction of the kitchen. He stretched and sat up to set his book on the coffee table. That wasn't a bad way to kill some time. After a detour upstairs to take a leak and kill the nap breath, he went looking for the women. They were on the deck, but they had the windows and the back door open to let in the light breeze, so he could hear them clearly as he opened the fridge to grab a beer.

"So Lisa as your matron of honor and Stephanie as bridesmaid," Cat was saying. "Do you know who Sean wants as best man?"

"No. We haven't gotten that far yet." He didn't hear any tension in Emma's voice, but he guessed she was feeling it. Planning a wedding that wasn't going to happen was weird, to say the least.

"Maybe he could ask Mike's oldest son—Joey, right?—to be a groomsman so he can escort Stephanie."

"I don't know," Emma said. "I don't think it's very fair to ask one of the boys and not the others."

"True. Maybe they could be ushers and then join their parents once everybody's seated."

Sean had just decided to beat a fast retreat back to the living room, when he heard a chair scrape back. "We can talk about that later, Gram. Right now I should go wake Sean so he's not still groggy when we ask him to fire up the grill."

He didn't have time to escape, so he leaned against the counter and twisted the top of his beer. Emma paused when she saw him, and then grabbed his hand and dragged him down the hall to the living room.

"Where did you disappear to?" he asked.

"What? Oh, a client had an emergency. But—"

"There are gardening emergencies?"

She blew out an exasperated breath. "Yes. When you're rich, everything's an emergency. But did you hear what Gram was saying?"

"Yeah. How the hell are guys supposed to pick a best man, anyway? I've got three brothers and I like them all. And what about Mikey? Or Kevin or Joe? It seems easier to pick a stranger off the street so you don't have to play favorites. I guess maybe I'd ask Mitch. He's the oldest, so most of what the rest of us know about catching a woman we learned from him."

"In case you've forgotten, you haven't actually caught a woman yet. And it doesn't really matter who you choose, because there *is* no wedding."

She was wound up like an eight-day clock, so he didn't dare laugh at her. Her cheeks were bright and she kept spinning her ring around and around on her finger. Since there was nothing he could say to make her feel better about Cat wanting to plan their fake wedding, he slid the hand not holding his beer around her waist and hauled her close.

"You worry too much," he told her.

"And you—"

He kissed her to shut her up. And because all he'd been able to think about since the last time he'd had his hands on her was getting his hands on her again. And, most of all, because he liked kissing her. A lot. Maybe too much, if he thought about it.

So he didn't think about it. Instead, he lost himself in the taste of her mouth and the softness of her lips and the way her hands slid over his lower back, holding him close.

"Oh," Cat said from behind him. "I didn't mean to interrupt."

"No," Emma said. "We were just…talking."

"I can see that."

Since it was going to be at least a couple of minutes before he was fit to turn around and face anybody, never mind her grandmother, Sean sidestepped around Emma and grabbed the television remote. "I'm going to see if I can catch tomorrow's weather and then I'll start the grill."

Fortunately, they made it through the evening without any more talk of bridesmaids and ushers thanks to Emma and him steering the conversation toward Florida and television and anything else they could think of that didn't involve weddings. But if he'd thought the minutes were slow to tick away before, the seemingly endless time between dinner and bedtime was excruciating.

Finally the time came for him to crawl naked between the sheets and wait for Emma to come out of the bathroom. He didn't really care if she was naked or not. It would only take a few seconds to get her out of what she wore to bed.

When she finally came out, wearing her usual sleepwear, he grinned and flipped back the covers for her.

She arched an eyebrow at him, then went over to shut off the light. "Pretty cocky, don't you think? Just assuming I'll sleep with you again?"

"Last night was a little quick. I think we can do better."

By the time Emma reached the bed, she was naked, leaving behind her a trail of clothes. "Are you saying you can do better? Because you set the bar pretty high, you know."

He didn't waste any more time with words. Once she was in the bed, he rolled onto his side and cupped her face in his hand. Her eyes were dark pools he wanted to drown in, so he moved his gaze to her mouth. She was worrying at her bottom lip with her teeth and he kissed her to make her stop. And then he kept kissing her because even the promise of the good feelings to come didn't intrigue him more than her mouth.

"You're very good at that," she said a little breathlessly when he reluctantly broke it off.

"I'm very good at many things."

"Oh, really? And you can back that up?" When he nodded, she stretched her body like a cat's, offering herself to him. "Take your time."

Even though his blood was practically boiling, he flicked his tongue over her lip and smiled. "I intend to."

He explored every inch of her, definitely taking his time as he learned where and how to touch her to make her crazy. He kept touching her, with his hands and with his mouth, until she was panting and squirming under him. Then he slid his finger into her wet heat and rubbed her clit with his thumb until her hips bucked and she pounded his shoulder with her fist because she couldn't scream.

And then he did it all again.

He lost track of time. Lost track of everything but Emma and the way he wanted to make her feel, until she grabbed him by the hair and dragged him up her body.

"Whatever you were trying to prove, you proved," she said between panted breaths. "I want you inside me. Now."

He slipped on a condom in record time and settled between her legs. She lifted her head, kissing him fiercely as he entered her, and then dropped her head to the pillow. He watched her eyes, letting them drag him under as he thrust into her. They were both too far gone for finesse, and it wasn't nearly long enough before the pleasure hit him and knocked him for a loop as Emma bit her knuckle, trying to be quiet as the orgasm racked her body.

Oh, yeah, that was better. When he'd finally caught his breath, Sean disposed of the condom and then pulled the covers up over them. He tried to nudge her over a little, but she was as limp as overcooked spaghetti, and when he told her to move over, she mumbled something he couldn't hear into the pillow.

Curling up around her, Sean grinned as he closed his eyes. Maybe tomorrow night he'd make her do all the work.

"Do you think if you stare at those trees long enough, they'll shrivel up and disappear?"

Emma struggled to refocus her attention on Sean and away from the problem at hand. "What?"

"You've been staring at that spot for half an hour now."

She was sitting on the summer cottage's back steps, looking over a piece of property she'd been invited to bid on. "I'm not looking at the trees. It's the exposed roots that are the problem. And the overall drainage."

He was leaning against a tree, one hand holding a soda and the other hooked in his pocket. "And staring helps?"

"Yes, it does." She stood and brushed off the seat of her jeans. "See those places where the dead leaves are thick and decomposing? That means the water was collecting there during the snowmelt and spring rains. The drainage sucks, party because of these exposed tree roots, and standing water's a problem I need to deal with *before* I get hands-on with the landscaping."

"Does the home owner want the shade or can you rip the trees out?"

She shook her head and slid her phone out of her pocket. She'd already taken a dozen photos of the property, but she snapped a couple more from that angle. "Can't take the trees out. This shoreline's more regulated than nuclear waste."

"Even the tree roots?"

"Huge erosion factor. I have to work around them." But there was nothing else she could do on-site. She had the photos and the measurements to plug into her software, so she'd be spending several hours with her computer to generate prints and estimates for the home owner to consider. "We're done here."

"Okay, boss," he said, winking at her as he pushed away from the tree.

"Oh, sure. Now I'm the boss. How come I'm never the boss when I want to drive my truck?"

He didn't answer her, but she could see the smirk flirting with his lips as he disappeared around the corner of the cottage. After tucking her phone and memo book back into her pockets, she followed him and wasn't surprised at all to find him already in the driver's seat.

"Where to now?" he asked once she was in and buckled up.

"Take a right and then a left when we hit the main road. The Johnsons think they've got some tree limbs about to come down and they want me to look. They don't want to pay a tree service if they don't have to."

"I thought your clients didn't mind throwing their money around."

"If they have it. The Johnsons were one of my first clients. Their kids all moved away and they were moving into a smaller house. Mrs. Johnson didn't want to leave her peonies behind, so I transplanted them for her. They're far from rich."

"We can take care of the tree limbs." She gave him a doubtful look, but he was serious. "I grew up in a lodge in the middle of the woods. I've limbed a few trees in my time."

They reached the main road and she pointed left as a reminder even as he turned his blinker on. "How come you came to New Hampshire when you left the army instead of going home?"

"Wanted to see Uncle Leo and Aunt Mary. Hang out with my cousins."

After a few moments passed, she realized he wasn't going to say anything else. And that made her think about how most of what she knew about him, she'd actually learned from Lisa before she'd even met him. "What was it like, growing up in a snowmobile lodge?"

"It was…okay. The Northern Star's a big place and has

a lot of land, so we had room to run. Our bedrooms were separate from the guest rooms, and we had our own family room and bathroom. But it's weird having strangers in your house every weekend and I never got used to it."

"So you don't want to go back there, then?"

He turned his head to look at her, an unreadable expression on his face. "Not really, no."

"Take your next left," she said after a few miles of silence. "After Gram leaves, are you going to go back to the apartment over Jasper's?"

He didn't say anything for a few seconds, but he was drumming his fingers on the steering wheel. "Don't know."

"Okay." She directed him through a few more turns. "It's the last house on the right. Beige, with cranberry shutters."

He pulled into the driveway and killed the engine, but didn't make a move toward getting out. "What's with the questions? We have sex and all of a sudden you're interested in my childhood?"

Too stunned to respond, Emma stared at him for a minute. Then she laughed. "You are *so* paranoid. It's called making conversation."

"So you're not getting ideas now that we're sleeping together?"

Still laughing, she opened her door and slid out of the truck. "No, I'm not getting any ideas about you and me."

She had a few ideas an hour later, though, when Sean was sweaty and all sexy and in charge. Ideas about him getting sweaty with her. Ideas about him naked and soapy in the shower. She even had a few ideas about finding someplace secluded to park the truck and not waiting until they got home.

After giving the Johnsons' tree limbs a good looking over, Sean had grabbed some rope and the chain saw out of toolboxes in the back of her truck and gone to work. He was about halfway through the job now, and so far, she hadn't had to do anything but guide a few of the smaller limbs away from the house with the rope after he tied them off.

Once he dropped a main limb, he made quick work of cutting off the smaller branches before cutting it into chunks of wood Emma, along with the home owners, could set off to one side. It would be a while before it would be any good in a woodstove, but Mr. Johnson was going to stack it and let it dry out. She didn't normally let her clients work alongside her, but it made her feel better about the fact she was going to charge them next to nothing. But after a while, Mrs. Johnson brought out lemonade for Emma and Sean, then fussed at her husband to get in out of the sun for a few minutes.

"I was out of line before," Sean said when they were alone.

"When before? Not letting me drive? The sticky note on the bathroom asking me to never make pasta salad again?"

"Before, when I assumed you were picking out white picket fences just because you asked me about my childhood."

"I already have a white fence. Which I installed all by myself, by the way." She took a sip of her lemonade. "I'm not sure what kind of women you've dated before, but I don't hear wedding bells during sex."

"I guess I've dated some women who do, then. Just wanted to make sure things aren't getting messy." He drained his glass, then he pulled up the hem of his

T-shirt and mopped the sweat off his face, baring the abs she loved running her hands over. And, of course, he caught her looking. "Speaking of sex, maybe you should—"

That thought was cut off by the reappearance of Mrs. Johnson, and Sean flashed Emma a naughty grin. "I'll tell you later."

She'd look forward to it.

Fourteen

On Wednesday they only worked half a day, leaving Sean free to pay a visit to his aunt and uncle while Emma caught up on some paperwork. Emma's truck wasn't in the driveway when he got home, but he could hear music, so he knew somebody was home.

Sean found Emma in the kitchen and he almost turned around to go anywhere else. She had the refrigerator pulled away from the wall and was cleaning the baseboard trim behind it with a toothbrush. While the view of her ass was sweet since she was on her hands and knees, it didn't bode well for his frame of mind.

But when he got closer and saw the coils on the back of the fridge had not only been vacuumed, but were actually gleaming, he got a little worried. A person whose refrigerator coils could pass a military inspection couldn't be right in the head.

"You okay?" he asked.

She didn't stop scrubbing. "Sure."

"Liar."

"Whatever."

"Emma, stop for a sec."

Much to his surprise, she listened. Tossing the toothbrush into a bucket, she sat back on her heels and turned her head to look at him. "What's up?"

"Where's Cat?"

"Said she had some errands to do, so she took my truck and went into town. She's probably just sneaking off to see Russell."

Clue number one. "She's sixty-five years old. I doubt she needs to sneak off if she wants to see a man."

Her jaw tightened. "Then why didn't she tell me that's where she was going?"

"Maybe she's not. Maybe she has errands to do." When she rolled her eyes, he had to bite the inside of his cheek to keep from laughing at her. "Why don't you let me push the fridge back and I'll take you out to lunch."

"Why?"

"Because you clean when you're upset and taking a toothbrush to the back of the fridge means you're on the ragged edge. I'll take you down to Concord for a Jasper burger. They can fix anything."

She laughed, but it was on the bitter side. "Yeah, 'cause I need more Kowalskis in my day."

"Hey, whatever it is, I didn't do it."

"I'm just not in a good mood today."

He grinned and rocked back on his heels. "This is because of my magic penis, isn't it? Four nights of it too much for you?"

"Ha. Don't flatter yourself, Kowalski. I'm only having sex with you so I can sleep in my own bed again."

The renewed color in her cheeks let him know she was full of crap. "So if I offered to do you right here on the kitchen floor, you'd say no?"

"I'd have to say no just to prove my point now."

"Damn."

Emma sighed and pushed herself to her feet. "You know what? A Jasper burger sounds really good, actually. It seems like it's been forever since I had one."

After she wiped down the baseboard and retrieved the bucket, he pushed the fridge back into place for her, then waited for her in the truck.

She was distracted on the drive down, staring out her window and sighing a lot. Figuring she'd feel better after a burger and a beer, he let her stew in silence.

Kevin's bar was quiet and he was nowhere to be seen, much to Sean's relief. He didn't really want to get any crap for taking his fake fiancée out to lunch, though he hadn't thought of that until *after* he suggested Jasper burgers.

Paulie, the stacked redhead, was behind the bar, but other than a casual wave, she didn't show much of an interest in them. Sean found a table in a dimly lit back corner and ordered a couple of beers and Jasper burgers for each of them.

Once their waitress set their glasses down and went to place their food order, Emma seemed to relax a little, but her mouth was tight and she was tapping the toe of her sneaker against the table leg.

"So what are you upset about today?" he asked when he got tired of the silence.

"Nothing."

"You afraid Cat's going to fall madly in love with Russell Walker and want her house back?"

With the way her head jerked back and the expression on her face, he was afraid for a second the other patrons would think he'd slapped her. "You're an asshole."

He shrugged. "I've been called worse."

"No doubt."

"If you just tell me what's bugging you today, I won't have to guess."

She looked for a second as if she was going to lash out with something bitchy, but then her body slumped in the chair and she sighed. "I want Gram to be happy. I want that more than anything. But seeing her with Mr. Walker was…weird. And I always miss Gramps, but it just hit me especially hard, I guess, seeing her with somebody else."

Tears shimmered in her eyes and he reached across the table to hold her hand. "I think that's pretty normal, Emma."

"And they've known each other forever. Just because she watched the fireworks with him doesn't mean she's going to run off and marry him. They're friends."

"Have you asked her?"

"No."

"You should talk to her."

She sighed and he knew there was more. "At the Fourth of July party, she told me she wants to give me the house as a wedding present."

"Isn't that what you want?"

"No," she snapped, pulling her hand away. "I want her to *sell* it to me. I told you that."

"Okay." He took a second to think about what to say next. In his experience, talking to a woman in this kind of mood was like sitting on a keg of gunpowder to smoke a cigarette. It was only a matter of time before your ass got burned. "Did you tell her that?"

"Of course I did. But she said it doesn't make any sense to put another mortgage on the house when it's been free and clear so long. And she doesn't need the money."

He was going to ask her what the problem was, then,

because getting a house free wouldn't bother most people. But he already knew. If at any time over the past two years Cat had offered to give her the house, she probably would have taken it. But the fact it was being offered as a gift for a nonexistent wedding was going to keep Emma up at night.

"Can you tie it in to the business somehow? You have your equipment and your office and shit there. Maybe tell her the bank thinks you should build credit by having a loan for a business location or something?" He didn't know jack about such things.

She shook her head. "Maybe if I was buying a nursery or something, but that's pretty shaky."

That left him fresh out of ideas. "You've got a couple more weeks. Maybe you can talk her into selling it."

"And how am I supposed to convince her that going two hundred thousand dollars or so into debt makes more sense than accepting as a gift the house that's been more or less mine now for two years, anyway?"

"I...don't know." He saw the waitress approaching with two plates. "But here come our burgers. That'll help."

"Jasper burgers are good, but even they can't help me out of this."

He grinned. "No, but they'll make you feel better about being in it."

Jasper burgers were better than sex, Emma thought as the first bite made her taste buds stand up and happy dance. She had the same thought every time she ate at Jasper's, but the past few times she hadn't had sex recently enough to call it a fair comparison.

Technically, *nothing* was better than sex with Sean,

but the burger had the edge right now because it wasn't complicated. It tasted amazing and it didn't screw up her life beyond her having to make a half-assed promise to herself to eat more salads to make up for it.

Sex with Sean was screwing up her life. As promised, the orgasms were very real and very numerous, but there should have been fine print. By accepting the orgasms, she'd also agreed to accept a level of intense intimacy she didn't think either of them had expected.

With mind-blowing sex came the tender touches. The way he'd capture her gaze with his and she couldn't look away. And he was a talker, always murmuring to her about how good she felt and how he never wanted to stop. And there was the life-screwing-up part—she never wanted him to stop, either.

"You're thinking about my magic penis again, aren't you?"

She almost choked on a fry. "No, I am not. And stop saying that."

"You started it." He leaned across the table. "And, yes, you were. I see that flush at the hollow of your throat and the way you're looking at me. You're all hot and bothered, right here in the bar. I was right about you."

"I am *not* an exhibitionist," she hissed.

"Oh, shit." She followed his gaze and saw that Kevin and Beth had just walked in and Kevin had spotted them. "Just be cool."

"Be cool?" She laughed. "We're having lunch, not planning a bank robbery."

"I just mean… Forget it."

"You don't want your cousins to know we're having sex," she said flatly.

"It complicates things."

He had that right. She was saved from further comment, however, by Kevin and Beth approaching the table. Kevin had Lily in his arms, but she clearly wanted down and they looked like a walking wrestling match.

"Hey, guys," Beth said, giving Emma a warm smile. "Couldn't resist the siren call of the Jasper burgers? I ate so many of those while I was pregnant, Kevin said Lily's first word would be *moo*. Thankfully, he was wrong."

"It was *da-da*," Kevin informed them in an exaggerated stage whisper that made Beth roll her eyes. "I was going to call you later. Me and Joe and Evan and Terry are going four-wheeling Saturday. You guys want in?"

"Hell, yeah," Sean said, but then he seemed to remember Emma was sitting across the table. "Maybe. If I can."

"I should ask Gram if she minds. But if she doesn't, I'd love to go if Lisa will let me steal her machine again. I haven't ridden since last summer."

"We'll hook you up." Lily was squirming like a fish out of water and Kevin was losing the battle. "She wants to see her aunt Paulie. Call me and let me know. By Thursday night would be good so we can figure out which trailers we need to load up."

After they left, Emma returned to her Jasper-burger consumption with gusto. She'd asked Lisa once to find out the recipe for their seasoning mix, but Kevin wouldn't give it up. Plus, as Lisa had pointed out, it wouldn't do Emma any good to have it since she couldn't cook worth a damn, anyway.

"So about what I said before," Sean said after he'd wolfed down his food, "about not wanting them to know we've had sex. It's not that I'm trying to hide it, I just…"

"Don't want them to know."

"Yeah."

"That makes sense."

His face brightened. "Really?"

"No."

"Damn." He'd finished his beer, so he took a swig off the glass of water she'd requested with her meal. "Under normal circumstances, I'd want everybody to know we're sleeping together. Trust me. I'd put a sign on my front lawn."

"But these aren't normal circumstances."

"Not even in the ballpark. I have this bet with my brothers I'd last the whole month and I don't want to listen to them gloat." Of course he had a bet with his brothers. Such a guy thing to do. "But it's more about the women."

"The women?"

"In my family, I mean. Aunt Mary, especially. They might start thinking it's more than it is. Getting ideas about us, if you know what I mean."

Emma ate her last French fry and pushed her plate away. "So we have to pretend we're madly in love and engaged…while pretending we're not having sex."

"Told you it complicates things."

"I'm going to need a color-coded chart to keep track of who thinks what."

He grinned and pulled his Sharpie out of his pocket. "I could make sticky notes."

The man loved sticky notes. He stuck them on everything. A note on the front of the microwave complaining about the disappearance of the last bag of salt-and-vinegar chips. (Emma had discovered during a particularly rough self-pity party that any chips will do, even if they burn your tongue.) A note on the back of the toilet lid telling her she used girlie toilet paper, whatever that meant.

He liked leaving them on the bathroom mirror, too. *Stop cleaning my sneakers. I'm trying to break them in.* Her personal favorite was *If you buy that cheap beer because it's on sale again, I'll piss in your mulch pile.* But sometimes they were sweet. *Thank you for doing my laundry.* And… *You make really good grilled cheese sandwiches.* That one had almost made her cry.

"Not to change the subject," she said, intending to do just that, "but I'm going to bid on a landscaping job tomorrow. The home owner wants to extend the deck out and add some built-in seating. It's a rush job because they're spending the last week of July there and want it done. I thought maybe you could do up a bid for that and we could submit it as a package. You know, if you're interested and think you can get the work done in time."

"Are you going to stand over my shoulder and double-check all my measurements and cuts?"

She felt her face blush and rolled her eyes. "No. Pounding nails is your thing, not mine."

"Then I'm interested. We could make a good team, you and I."

The words pierced some part of her heart she didn't want to think about, but she laughed. "Yeah. Just don't tell anybody."

Watching Sean flip ham steaks on the grill through the window, Emma tore up lettuce for salad. Her grandmother was cutting the tomatoes, which was probably good since she shouldn't use a knife and watch Sean cook at the same time.

"Hey, Gram, would you mind if Sean and I disappeared for a few hours on Saturday?"

"Of course not."

"A few of the Kowalskis are going four-wheeling and

Kevin invited us to go. But if you want to spend the day with us, I can go—*we* can go—another time."

"I had plans of my own, actually."

Something in Gram's voice drew her attention away from admiring the way Sean wielded a meat fork. "Oh, really?"

"Russell's going to take me out for an early dinner and then we're going dancing at the high school. They're having a fundraiser for chem-free graduation."

"Oh." Emma realized she was tearing the lettuce into confetti and dropped it into the bowl. "That sounds fun."

"Do I need to have the talk with you about how going on a date with Russell doesn't change the fact I still love your grandfather very much and miss him every day?"

"No." She shook more lettuce out of the bag, just to give her hands something to do. "Maybe."

"It's the truth. Nobody will ever replace John Shaw in my heart. But I'm lonely and it's been a long time since I've had a warm body to rub my cold feet on under the covers."

Emma didn't want to think about Gram under the covers with anybody, never mind Russell Walker. "Fourteen years."

It occurred to her *after* she said the words that just because it had been fourteen years since her grandfather died didn't mean it had been fourteen years since her grandmother had rubbed her cold feet on a warm body under the covers. She propped her elbows on the counter and rested her chin on her hands, hoping she looked attentive, but mostly wanting to hide the heat she could feel in her cheeks.

"But it's more than that," Gram continued. "When I read something interesting in the paper, I don't have anybody to share it with. And when I'm watching a murder mystery, I don't have anybody to tell who I think dunnit."

It was on the tip of Emma's tongue to tell Gram she should move back home and they could figure out the plot twists together, but she bit it back. Not only because Gram was happy in Florida, but because she knew it wouldn't be the same. Gram didn't just want somebody else to make conversation with. She wanted a companion to share her life with.

"He seems like a nice man," Emma said, which sounded lame, but she couldn't think of anything else to say.

"He is, and I enjoy his company."

"That's good, Gram." She meant it and she hoped Gram could see that she did.

Sean walked in with a plate of ham steaks and then stopped, as if his man radar had just pinged on the level of feminine drama in the room. "Everything okay?"

"Of course." Gram dumped the diced tomatoes into the salad bowl. "Emma was just telling me you're going four-wheeling Saturday."

"Only if you don't mind," he said, setting the plate on the table.

"Of course not."

"Gram's going dancing with Russell."

"Oh." He searched Emma's face for a moment, then turned to Gram. "He seems like a nice guy. Hope you have a good time."

"I haven't been dancing in ages, but I'm sure I will. Let's eat before the ham gets cold."

"Sean and I have to give an estimate on a job tomorrow, but then we can drive down to Concord and find you a dress, if you want."

Gram beamed. "I'd love that. I think the last time I bought a new dress, shoulder pads were still all the rage."

They all laughed, putting an end to any lingering tension in the room. And later, when Sean slipped between the sheets and asked her if she was really okay with her grandmother dating, she could honestly say she was.

"I want her to be happy. If dancing with Russell makes her happy, she should go for it."

He stretched out against her body. "I agree. Know what would make *me* happy?"

"If I buy a more manly brand of toilet paper?"

"No. Well, yes. But we can talk about that when we're not naked."

She draped her arm over his shoulders and ran her fingertips over the sweet spot at the back of his neck. "What should we talk about while we're naked?"

He groaned and rolled onto his back, but he took her with him so she was straddling his hips. "Let's talk about how you look working in the sun, with your skin all shiny and a smear of dirt on your nose."

"Does me being all grubby and sweaty turn you on?"

"Watching you work turns me on. You work hard and you're not afraid to get your hands dirty. I like that in a woman."

"Flattery will get you—" she swiveled her hips, brushing over his erection and making him suck in a sharp breath "—everywhere."

He reached up and cupped her breasts, rubbing his thumbs over her nipples. "Don't wanna be anywhere but here."

The man knew all the right words. He definitely had all the right moves. And he was a quick learner, so he already knew all the right ways to touch her to drive her out of her mind. He had a way of looking at her with those intense blue eyes that made her feel as though he'd been waiting his entire life just to make love to her.

And, as long as she wasn't stupid enough to imagine she could see forever in those eyes, she'd take it.

He ran one fingertip down her forehead to the bridge of her nose. "You're frowning. What are you thinking about?"

She shoved the word *forever* out of her mind and ran her hands over his rippled abdomen. "I was wondering why you're not inside me yet."

"Because you're frowning at me. Gives me confidence issues."

Reaching between their bodies, she stroked the hard length of him. "Confidence is never an issue for you."

He grinned and flipped her onto her back. "I'm confident I can have you whimpering my name into your pillow in five minutes or less."

"I don't know," she said as his hand brushed over her stomach and kept going south. "I'm not an easy woman to please."

His mouth followed the trail his hand had marked against her skin. "I never could resist a challenge."

Fifteen

Saturday turned into an awesome day for riding. Warm enough for T-shirts, Emma thought, but not too hot under the helmet and goggles.

At the last minute Joe had bailed. Brianna had been fussy with a low-grade fever all night and he knew better than to abandon Keri, so it was Emma and Sean, along with Kevin, Evan and Terry.

She started up the ATV Kevin had borrowed from Lisa for her and backed it off the trailer, leaving it to warm up while she put on her helmet and adjusted her goggles. Sean was riding Mike's four-wheeler and he parked beside her to do the same.

"You think you can keep up?" she asked, tightening the strap under her helmet.

He snorted. "You drive like a girl and sleep in a girlie bed. I bet you ride like a girl, too."

"You know, saying that's going to make it so much more embarrassing when I leave you in the dust."

"We'll see about that."

She started to step closer to him—to maybe press up

against him and ask what kind of wager he'd like to bet on that—but she remembered the others just in time.

With this group, they were just friends. Nothing more. And definitely not friends with benefits, since Sean didn't want them to know she wasn't sleeping on the couch anymore.

Instead, she turned her back on him and yanked on her riding gloves. It was ridiculous, trying to keep all these stories straight, and she was tired of it. She just wanted to relax and be herself, but she couldn't really complain since she was the one who'd gotten them into the mess to begin with.

When it was time to hit the trail, she took her frustration out on the throttle. Throwing her weight backward, she hit the gas hard and wheelied out of the parking area. When the front wheels dropped, she laughed and settled back on her seat. Let Sean chew on *that* dust for a while.

They were all experienced riders and keeping a fast pace, so she stopped dwelling on her current situation and gave all her attention to the trail ahead. Kevin was leading, with Evan and then Terry behind him, and Sean was pulling up the rear behind Emma, so there was a lot of dust. Dust meant poorer visibility, which meant paying attention and not stewing about the fact Sean was so adamant nobody in his family guess they were sleeping together.

But she couldn't help it. Why was it such a big deal to him? There was the betting pool with his brothers, but that wasn't it. It wasn't as if the guys had all put a hundred grand on when they'd sleep together. It was simply that he didn't want them to know.

He'd said he was worried about his aunt getting ideas, but so what? Didn't mothers—and mother figures—

always get ideas when a guy in his thirties started dating a new woman? Sometimes it worked out and sometimes it didn't, but you didn't hide a new girlfriend in your closet unless the maternal figure in question was a psycho. Mary Kowalski definitely wasn't a psycho.

To Emma it could only mean one thing. Sean was only in it—*it* being in her bed *with* her—for the sex. If nobody knew they were sleeping together, there wouldn't be any questions from his family after he walked away from her. No disappointment on his aunt's part. He wouldn't have to deal with Lisa's torn loyalties. Nobody would know.

She could live with that. It was what she'd agreed to—just sex without getting any ideas it might be more. And she was okay with it, too…mostly. A couple of weeks of the best sex of her life was better than no sex at all. She just wished it didn't feel so much like a dirty secret.

They ate up some miles before Kevin pulled off on the side of a grassy area bordering a pond and they all pulled in behind him. Sometimes, in the early dawn hours or around sunset, there were moose around the pond, but in the middle of the day it was abandoned.

She killed her engine and took off her helmet and goggles, trying to wipe the worst of the trail dust from her face with the back of her arm. It was a lost cause, helmet hair and a dirty face being one of the side effects of four-wheeling, but she made the effort.

Sean walked up beside her, looking as grubby as she knew she looked, but, being a guy, he didn't have the helmet hair. "I guess the next time somebody tells me I ride like a girl, maybe I should thank them for the compliment."

She grinned and leaned forward to set her helmet on the front rack. "At least you're keeping up."

"It's obvious you're not a rookie. How come you don't have your own?"

"I did. Blew the engine summer before last. I've been so busy with work I don't get out enough to justify buying a new one. If I go out with Mike and Lisa, they usually borrow somebody's for me. I'd planned to buy one for work, but then word of mouth got around and I spend most of my time in neighborhoods that frown on ATVs."

Terry was walking toward them with a couple of water bottles, no doubt on a mission to mother-hen them into staying hydrated. Sean took one and then walked away to talk to the guys.

"Thanks," Emma said, cracking the top and taking a long drink. "Dusty today."

"It'll be better once we get more into the woods. Still, it must be nice for you to get away for a few hours. You know, not having to pretend you and Sean are a couple and all that."

Emma forced herself to nod when in reality, it was just as hard pretending they weren't together as pretending they were. "Yeah, it's a little stressful at times."

"I bet the family having a little fun with it doesn't help."

"I'm so grateful everybody went along with it, I don't mind a few laughs at our expense."

Terry laughed. "It's too good not to, really. But Sean's always been a solid, levelheaded guy, so we figure it must all be for a good cause."

"My grandmother's going to go back to Florida without any worries about me, so it's definitely for a good cause." Assuming it didn't blow up in their faces before her plane left, of course.

Kevin gave the signal, and it was time to put the water

away and put the gear back on. Sean winked as he walked past her to his machine, but she just smiled and put her helmet on.

After a half mile or so of dirt road they hit the woods, but Kevin didn't slow down. They crashed and banged along the rough trail, dodging the bigger rocks and low-hanging branches. And when Sean started playing—tapping the back of her machine with the front of his—Emma laughed and gave it a little more gas.

The corner came up fast, but she didn't panic. No brakes. Just goosed it a little to bring the rear end around so it would slide through the corner and she could throttle out.

Then she saw the chipmunk.

All it took was a second's hesitation and the inside wheels lifted and the ass end came up off the ground. *Oh, shit, this is gonna hurt.*

Sean saw Emma's machine start to roll and there wasn't a damn thing he could do about it.

He skidded to a stop, his ATV sliding sideways, and watched as she managed to push herself off, diving for the dirt. She hit the ground, bouncing and skidding until—thank God—she was clear of the four-wheeler as it rolled twice before coming to rest against a tree.

He was off his machine and at her side before the dust even settled. Emma rolled to her back as he dropped to his knees.

"Ow" was all she said.

"Jesus, Emma. Are you hurt?"

"That would be why I said *ow.*"

He resisted the urge to grab her by the shoulders and

shake the smart-ass out of her, but just barely. "Answer the damn question. Are you hurt bad?"

"I don't think anything's broken. Just gimme a minute."

She didn't look too bad. She'd gotten lucky and plowed through a mostly rock-free patch of trail. Her arm was scuffed up a bit and she was winded and filthy, but as long as nothing was broken, she'd made out pretty good.

"Has it been a minute yet?" He wanted her on her feet so he could look her over.

"No." She took a deep breath, exhaling slowly. He watched her closely, but she didn't wince and her breath didn't hitch in her chest at all. "How bad did I muck up Lisa's machine?"

"Don't care. Are you ready to get up yet?"

"I think so."

He moved to kneel behind her head and slid his hands under her back to help her sit up. "Just sit for a couple minutes. Make sure you're not dizzy."

Riding as hard as they were didn't lend itself to looking over one's shoulder, so the group in front had kept going. Sean knew it wouldn't be long before they reached an intersection. Kevin would stop to make sure he had everybody before choosing a direction, and when he and Emma didn't show, they'd come back.

"I think I'm okay," Emma told him.

He slid his hands under her arms, gently hoisting her to her feet. "Take it nice and easy."

"I'm okay, Sean. Really." She pulled off her goggles and then undid her chin strap and lifted her helmet off.

"I shouldn't have been pushing you." She gave him a *look*. It was the kind of look he saw his cousins' wives give them and it made him bristle. "Don't give me that look."

"What, the 'you're being an ass' look? Don't be an ass and I won't give you the look."

"How am I being an ass? Because I'm sorry I was pushing you and almost got you killed?"

"No, you're an ass because you think you were pushing a *girl* to go too fast."

He crossed his arms and scowled at her. "So?"

She scowled right back at him. "So, *you* had nothing to do with it. Believe it or not, I've rolled an ATV before. Today, I was riding the way I always ride when we're dumb enough to let Kevin lead, and I got ambushed by a chipmunk. It could have been any one of us."

He couldn't help it. He stepped close and threaded his fingers through hers. "I wish it hadn't been you."

"Because I'm a girl?"

No, because being helpless to get to her when he thought she was about to be crushed by six hundred and fifty pounds of rolling four-wheeler made him feel... something. Something not good. "Because I don't want to be the one who has to tell Cat we broke you."

That made her laugh. "I'm going to feel like I got hit by a Mack truck later, but I'm not broken."

"I'll run you a hot bubble bath when we get home. That'll help with the aches and pains."

When she smiled and her face relaxed, Sean moved in for a kiss. Not because he was thinking about Emma all naked and soapy with her nipples peeking through the bubbles, but because he was so damn relieved she wasn't hurt.

His lips had barely met hers when she jerked away. First he thought he'd hurt her, and then he thought she was mad. But he realized she'd already heard the sound he was just now registering—an ATV racing toward them.

"Wouldn't want to make you lose your bet," she muttered with a faint thread of bitterness that made him feel guilty, even though he wasn't sure why.

He had no reason to feel guilty. He hadn't done anything wrong. Besides, she knew he didn't take that stupid betting pool seriously and that he didn't want his aunt disappointed when he and Emma parted ways. But he didn't get a chance to explain it.

Kevin came into view, riding fast. He braked when he saw them, and his machine had barely stopped when he jumped off. "What happened? Emma, are you okay?"

She nodded. "Chipmunk. I hesitated and blew the corner."

"You hurt?"

She showed him her scuffed arm. "I'll live. Hoping I can say the same for Lisa's four-wheeler."

Evan and Terry pulled up, and Sean stepped off to the side while they fussed over her. Kevin fired up Lisa's machine and maneuvered it back onto the trail.

"Doesn't look too bad," he said. "Cracked some plastic and scuffed the end of the grip. Pretty sure her front rack was already bent a little. Small tear in the seat. We'll slap some duct tape on it and call it good."

Emma groaned. "Duct tape. That's classy."

Terry laughed. "They have four boys. Half the stuff they own's held together by duct tape."

Sean picked Emma's helmet up off the ground and turned it over in his hands, brushing it off and looking for damage. The way she'd looked hitting the ground still had him feeling a little wobbly inside, he realized as he ran his thumb over a gouge that may or may not have been from this incident.

She could have been seriously injured, and he was having trouble processing just how much that scared him. He didn't want to see anybody get hurt, but the thought of how close they might have come to waiting for a helicopter to come airlift Emma out of the woods had his gut churning.

The feeling didn't lessen when Terry got her first-aid kit out of her cargo box and started cleaning the scrapes on Emma's arm. She was leaning against the front of Terry's machine, smiling at something Kevin and Evan were talking about, but his stomach seemed to clench up even more instead of relaxing.

She was one hell of a woman. Emma was smart and fun and tough and she worked hard, and she turned his world upside down between the sheets. And maybe that was the problem. His world was starting to feel a little upside down when they were fully clothed, too.

"You okay?" Kevin asked him, and Sean swore under his breath. He hadn't even noticed him coming.

"Yeah. Just checking out her helmet."

"You look a little peaked."

Pretty natural look for a guy whose world wasn't right-side up anymore. "Wasn't a fun thing to watch."

"I've been teaching Beth to ride when Ma can watch Lily and I swear I have a heart attack every time she so much as hits a bump."

"But she's your wife." Sean looked at Emma, who was looking back at him. "That's different."

"Is it?"

"Yes." He said it firmly, wondering which of them he

was trying to convince. "Emma's a nice girl and I don't want to see her get hurt, but it's not the same thing at all."

When she raised an eyebrow at him from across the distance, he wondered if she was a better lip-reader than he'd thought. And when she mouthed *nice girl,* with a questioning look, he knew he was busted. She wouldn't like being called that at all.

"You keep telling yourself that and I'll leave you two to make googly eyes at each other while I go check the air in my tires. Think I've got one going soft on me." Kevin slapped his shoulder. "And I don't think that's all that's going soft around here."

His cousin walked away before Sean could tell him he wasn't going soft. The fact he didn't want to see the woman he was and wasn't pretending to have sex with wrapped around a tree didn't mean he was going soft. It just meant…

It just meant he might be *starting* to get a little soft and he needed to get the hell out of there the second Cat's departing flight started its taxi down the runway.

The fruit punch was horrible, the fake disco light looked more like a police light bar and the folding metal chairs were hell on old hips, but Cat was having one of the best nights of her life in the high school gymnasium.

Frank Sinatra crooned from the speakers, her head rested on Russell's chest and his arms wrapped around her as they swayed to the music. Neither of them were particularly snazzy dancers, but they didn't care. It was nice just to dance again.

As the song came to an end, Cat leaned back so she could smile and thank him and suggest they sit for a few minutes, but she could tell he was thinking about kissing her. His gaze flicked to her mouth several times and the butterflies in her stomach panicked.

She hadn't kissed any man but John in…for goodness' sake, it had been forty-six years. That didn't seem right to her, but she'd been nineteen when she fell in love with John Shaw and married him six months later. She hadn't been kissed by another man in almost half a century.

And she could see the hesitation in Russell's eyes, too. He was thinking of his wife, and Cat thought maybe he hadn't kissed anybody but Flo in a long, long time.

"Do you want some more punch?" she asked, hoping to take the pressure off the moment.

He laughed. "I don't ever want more of that punch. I could use a little fresh air, though."

He didn't take her hand as they went through the propped-open gymnasium doors into the cool summer night, but Cat tried not to be bothered by it. While it had been fourteen years since she'd lost her husband, for Russell it had only been six. Maybe when push came to shove, he just wasn't ready to face a new relationship.

They walked across the grass to the small copse of trees in the high school's courtyard, where granite benches sat honoring the graduates who'd lost their lives serving in the military over the decades. Surprisingly, the benches were unoccupied, and Russell finally took her hand as he pulled her down to sit beside him on one.

"I enjoy your company so much, Cat," he said quietly, and she heard the *but* coming from a mile away. "I just… I'm not sure what we're doing here."

"Enjoying each other's company?"

"That we are." He turned his head to smile at her and his gaze fixed on her mouth again. "I'm afraid if I kiss you, I might cry."

She squeezed his hand, though not as hard as his words squeezed her heart. "I might cry, too, but I'd rather cry because I feel something and not just because I'm lonely and feeling sorry for myself."

"Maybe I should do it, then, and stop trying to count how many years it's been since I kissed a woman besides my wife."

Cat tilted her face up and closed her eyes as Russell cupped the back of her head in his hand and kissed her.

She tried not to compare his mouth to John's—Russell's lips were softer and yet more aggressive—but eventually everything and everybody except the man touching her fell away. And, as his tongue brushed hers, the dormant feelings of desire and anticipation fluttered to life.

When he reluctantly broke away—or so it seemed to Cat—there were no tears. Maybe deep down there might have been a few bittersweet pangs of sorrow, but the avalanche of renewed and wonderful feelings had buried them *way* down deep.

He looked her straight in the eye, his face softening as he smiled. "It's been about half a minute since I kissed anybody but you, Catherine Shaw."

And for the second time in her life, Cat thought maybe she'd found a man worth keeping.

Sixteen

Sean watched Emma fumbling with her keys in the darkness. Having left earlier in the day, nobody had thought to turn the outside light on. "I can't believe Gram's out this late."

"We've got the house all to ourselves. Maybe after I run that hot bubble bath for you, I'll help you wash your back."

"As filthy as I am, I'm going to have to make do with the shower or I'll leave two inches of mud in the bottom of the tub."

"We should conserve water and shower together," he said as he followed her into the house.

"Gee, I couldn't do that. I'm a *nice girl,* remember?"

He groaned and bent forward to untie his filthy boots. "There was nothing in your owner's manual warning about your unnaturally good lip-reading ability."

"But then I wouldn't know you think I'm a nice girl, *but...*"

He wasn't even sure what he was in trouble for. "I was trying to make him see the difference between him and his wife, and you and me. I didn't mean anything by it."

"Relax," she said with an impish gleam in her eyes. "I swear, it's so easy to push your buttons."

"You have a really twisted sense of humor."

But he forgave her when she unzipped her jeans and wriggled out of them right there in the hall. She probably didn't want to track trail dust all through the house, so he'd do the same. But he'd watch her first, since he wasn't one to pass up a striptease by a beautiful woman.

She turned and walked toward the kitchen with her T-shirt still on, though, so he sighed and resigned himself to just admiring her legs. Her bruised legs, he noticed. She had an egg-size bruise on the outside of one thigh, along with a few smaller ones. He kicked off his jeans and yanked his T-shirt over his head so he could follow her.

"You took a good whack to the thigh," he pointed out while she filled a couple of frosted mugs with water.

She twisted around so she could see the bruises. "Yeah. It's a little tender to the touch, but nothing major."

"You should let me check the rest of you over." She gave him a cold glass of water and an arched eyebrow. "For bruises, I mean, though you do look sexy as hell with a dirty face, wearing nothing but a T-shirt."

Putting a hand on her hip, which drew the hem of her T-shirt up a tantalizing half inch, she scowled at him. "When I made you my fake fiancé, I had no idea you had this weird dirty-face fetish."

"I didn't have it before I became your fake fiancé." He took a long drink of water. "And it's not a fetish. I told you, it turns me on that you work hard and you play hard. The dirt's just a visual representation of that, I guess."

"That's very deep of you."

"Plus, it means you'll be showering soon and I like you all soaped up and slippery, too."

A slow flush burned up her neck. "Dirty. Clean. Doesn't matter to you, does it?"

He was going to tell her no, it didn't matter—that he'd take her any way he could get her—but he kept his mouth shut. It was true, of course, but nothing good would come of her knowing that. She didn't need to know that sometimes when they were curled up on the couch watching television or arguing about white versus wheat bread at the store, he would sometimes forget they were pretending to be a couple.

And she *really* didn't need to know it sometimes bummed him out when he remembered.

That was bad. Sure, he enjoyed her company—and he sure as hell enjoyed the sex—but in just a week, he'd be leaving. He'd be free to explore the wheres and whats of the rest of his life, as he'd planned to do before being waylaid by Emma's crazy scheme. He hadn't had his freedom back long enough to give it up again, especially to a woman who drove him nuts. He wasn't going to spend the rest of his life deadheading daisies and reading flow-charts on the proper order of household chores.

Emma walked past him, stripping off her T-shirt and giving him a come-hither look over her shoulder.

On the other hand…

Two of them in the shower made for a tight fit, but Sean didn't mind. The more of her skin touching his, the better. They did a quick lather and rinse to get the trail grime off and then Sean took his time, soaping her body inch by inch. He found a few more smatterings of bruises, especially near her right shoulder blade, though none as pronounced as the one on her thigh.

He kissed the ones he could reach standing up and noted the others for later. She winced a little when he carefully cleaned around the scrape on her arm and he kissed her mouth until that little gasp of pain became a moan of pleasure.

When the water started running cold, they dried off and brushed their teeth. She nudged him out of the way so she could spit and the moment hit him like a sucker punch to the gut.

It was so…domestic. They were acting like a married couple. Or like a couple who'd been living together and would be getting married in the near future. And didn't that just confuse the hell out of him, because that's what they were supposed to be. But not really.

He followed her to bed, his mind reeling as she tucked herself against him like she did every night. As if she belonged there. And he pulled her even a little closer because he did every night.

"Penny for your thoughts," she whispered.

"I'm beat. Haven't ridden in a long time, especially like that."

Her hand stroked his chest. "Starting things in the shower you can't follow through on, soldier?"

"The last thing your body needs right now is more action."

She sighed, still stroking his chest. "I don't know if I'll be able to sleep."

He rolled toward her a little so he could cup her breast. "I know a great cure for that."

"I thought you were beat."

"I am." And he wasn't so sure about being *fully* involved with her while still processing the domestic moment in the bathroom. "And you don't need any more roughhousing, but I know a little trick to take care of that."

As he spoke, he slid his hand down her stomach and between her legs. His own body heated up along with hers, but he willed his libido into submission. She had bruises in enough places, so he wasn't going to go groping at her.

Instead, he stroked, watching as her eyelids fluttered closed and her teeth bit into her bottom lip. Her breath quickened as her hips moved against his hand and she whispered his name. Then she opened her eyes and stared into his with such intensity he kissed her just so she'd close them again. He wasn't sure what she'd see.

She moaned into his mouth as she found release and then he wrapped her in his embrace and she sighed in happy contentment.

He shouldn't hold her, he told himself. He should pat her on the ass, roll over and go to sleep. Instead, he nuzzled her hair and closed his eyes. Maybe tomorrow night he'd work on putting some distance between them.

Emma pulled the covers over her face, mentally bargaining with her subconscious. If she could have another hour of sleep, she wouldn't hit Snooze for a whole work-week. Or at least not on Monday.

When Sean climbed onto the bed and stretched out next to her, though, she gave up and rolled over. And... *ouch*. There was that hit-by-a-Mack-truck feeling she'd been waiting for.

She opened her eyes and then frowned. "Why are you dressed?"

"Because I got up and got dressed so I could find some coffee, but I changed my mind and I'm coming back to bed."

"Fully dressed?"

"Yes. No shoes, though."

It was too early to follow along with his crazy bouncing ball of logic. "Did Gram put a pot of coffee on yet?"

He groaned and threw his arm over his eyes. "Not exactly."

"What is *wrong* with you this morning?"

"I just ran into your grandmother. She was sneaking into the house…in the same dress she wore last night."

"What?" Emma sat up, aches and pains forgotten. "You caught Gram doing the walk of shame?"

"Yes, and it was awkward and now I'm going back to bed."

She pushed his arm off his face. "What did she say?"

"She said good-morning and told me she was going to take a quick shower and then start breakfast."

"And what did you say?"

"I muttered something about taking her time and then ran like a girl."

Emma flopped back onto her pillow and stared at the ceiling. "Wow."

"I probably should have broken it to you better, but I'm not sure how I could have."

She didn't know what to say. *Go, Gram,* a part of her was thinking, but another part wanted to hide under the covers with Sean and not deal with the fact her grandmother was currently taking a shower after doing the walk of shame. That was obviously the same side of himself Sean was currently listening to.

"We have to go down eventually," she said. "I need coffee. And food."

"I'll wait here. Bring some back."

She laughed and slapped his thigh. "If I can face her, so can you. She's not *your* grandmother."

"It was awkward."

"I'm sure it's awkward for her, knowing we're having sex, but she's an adult about it."

That just made him cover his face with his arm again. "That's different."

"Why? Because she's sixty-five?"

"No. Because, as you just said, she's a grandmother. *Your* grandmother."

"Come on. We'll go down together." She slid out of bed and walked toward the bathroom. "Stop making it such a big deal."

Gram was still in the shower when they went past the bathroom on their way down the hall. They could tell because she was whistling a very cheery tune that made Sean wince.

Emma grabbed his arm and tugged him toward the stairs. "Coffee."

They got a pot going and sat at the table in silence until enough had brewed to sneak two cups from it. Emma put the kettle on and dropped a tea bag into Gram's mug.

The woman of the hour appeared just as it whistled, looking refreshed and cheerful. "Good morning."

"Morning," they both mumbled.

"Thank you for making my— What happened to your arm?"

Emma looked down at the angry-looking scrape and then tucked her arm behind her back. "I took a little spill yesterday, that's all."

"I told you to be careful."

"I was. There was a chipmunk."

Gram cast an accusing glare at Sean and he held up his hands. "Hey, don't look at me. You've been in the truck with her. You know how she drives."

"Yes, my husband taught her to drive, unfortunately." Emma saw the fleeting shadow cross her face. "I was thinking omelets today. Maybe broccoli and cheese?"

Sean's head slumped over his coffee cup and Emma knew she had to say something…without telling her grandmother she'd fed her own fiancé a food he hated her first night home. "Um…how about mushrooms instead?"

Gram rummaged in the fridge. "I don't see any mushrooms. We still have broccoli, though."

"Sean only eats broccoli once in a while, like for special occasions," Emma said in a rush. "He loves it, but it…it makes him gassy."

Since Gram still had her head over the crisper drawer, Sean was free to give her a what-the-hell look and she gave him an apologetic smile. After three weeks of living a lie—or two different lies—she should have been better at thinking on her feet.

"We can't have that," Gram said. "We still have some leftover ham. How do ham-and-cheese omelets sound?"

"That sounds wonderful," Sean said, still glaring at Emma.

She set the table while Gram cooked, and then refilled the coffee cups. At this rate, they'd need the caffeine.

"So, Sean," Gram said, dropping diced ham into the pan, "how do you like this old house?"

He looked startled by the question. "It's a nice house. Big and homey."

"Lots of room for children."

Emma barely managed to swallow her coffee before it went down the wrong pipe. "Gram. We're not ready to have kids yet."

"No, but you will soon, I'm sure. We'll have to get the

calendar out after breakfast and start looking at possible wedding dates."

Sean shifted in his seat and Emma put her hand on his knee so he wouldn't be tempted to go back to bed again. "We haven't even figured out if we want summer or winter. There's no rush."

"Don't you want to get married in the garden? You always did."

Emma shot a desperately pleading look at Sean and he cleared his throat. "If we get married in the winter, we can honeymoon at my family's lodge and…snowmobile and stuff."

"You can do that any winter," Gram insisted. "But it's up to you two, of course."

She used the spatula to cut the omelet and slid pieces onto their waiting plates. Emma wasn't surprised when Sean wolfed his down and then excused himself before disappearing like a superhero blur.

Since the women were eating at a normal pace, Emma was left with her grandmother. "Did you have a nice time? At the dance, I mean?"

Gram smiled at her plate. "I had a lovely time at the dance. And after the dance, as well."

"Oh. I'm happy for you. Really."

"Don't go making more of it than it is. We're just enjoying each other's company for a little while. I'll be going home at the end of the week, so…like I said, we're just enjoying each other's company."

That sounded familiar, Emma thought, moving egg and cheese and ham bits around on her plate. Just temporarily keeping each other's feet warm, as the case may be.

They talked about inane things while they cleaned up, and then Emma went in search of Sean. When she didn't find him downstairs, she went up to their room, but he wasn't there, either. There was, however, a sticky note on the mirror.

Gassy? Payback's a bitch, honey.

She laughed and dropped the note into the bottom drawer with the others she'd collected. They amused her too much to throw away and sometimes she'd pull one out and reread it. But that made her feel like some kind of lovesick teenager, so she closed the drawer and continued the search.

When she looked out the living room window, she finally found him. He was sitting in one of the rockers, his head back and eyes closed. Probably looking for a short reprieve from the craziness she'd dragged him into, so she dropped the curtain and left him alone.

She had a wedding date to pick out, anyway.

And, a half hour later, with her head next to her grandmother's looking at the calendar, she tried not to think about the phone call she'd eventually have to place to Florida, telling Gram she and Sean had gone their separate ways.

When Sean's phone rang, he pulled it out and read the caller-ID screen: Northern Star Lodge. It would be either Josh or Rosie, so he flipped it open and said hello.

"Hey." It was Josh. "Did I win yet?"

He shook his head even though his dumbass youngest brother couldn't see him, and left the rocking chair to move farther away from the house. "Nobody's won a damn thing."

That technically wasn't a lie since he hadn't officially ceded yet and he wasn't sure who'd put money on two weeks. Speaking of which, he had to remember to pick up another box or two or three of condoms. He didn't think he should add them to Emma's list on the refrigerator.

"You're almost done with the whole thing, aren't you?"

"A week," Sean said, not that he was counting. "Cat's flying out Sunday."

"Then what are you going to do?"

He wasn't going to go back to the lodge, if that's what Josh was after. "Not sure yet. Thinking about taking the scenic route to New Mexico and visiting Liz."

There were a few seconds' silence on the line. "She'd probably be glad to see you. She talked to Mitch after the Fourth, by the way. He seems to think you and this Emma woman are serious."

"That's the point." Sean didn't want to talk to his brother about Emma. "People are *supposed* to think we're serious."

"We grew up with you, stupid. Ain't nobody standing in line to give your ass an Oscar."

Sean leaned against the front fender of his truck and tilted his head back to look up at the sky. "I'm not looking for serious, Josh. Not looking for anything right now."

"Just because you're not looking for something doesn't mean you won't find it."

"Well, aren't you quite the fucking fortune cookie."

His brother laughed. "That's me. So, hey, why don't you come home for a few days before you head west?"

Because if he went home for a few days, he might get sucked into staying and he wasn't ready to do that. "I don't know what I'm going to do yet. We'll see."

They talked about the lodge for a few minutes, and then Josh had to run. Sean slid his phone back into his pocket and sighed. Time to go back in the house and see what the women were up to. Probably picking a wedding date.

And knowing Cat, probably making a list of baby names. He supposed it was natural for people to assume that after the wedding bells came the stork, but it had still given him the cold sweats to hear her talking about children. Not that he didn't like kids. Mike and Terry's kids were cool, but first you had to get through the phase Kevin's and Joe's kids were stuck in, and he wasn't ready for that yet.

He paused in the doorway to the kitchen, watching Cat and Emma flip through the pages of the calendar. The wedding box was on the table, too, which meant good old Grams was stepping it up. Emma was smiling and nodding, but he could tell she wanted to be anywhere but there.

He could see the tension in her face and the way she held her shoulders. She was fidgeting with the ring he'd given her, spinning it around on her finger. He could see how uncomfortable she was, because he knew her.

How could he not know her? He lived with her. They worked together and played together and brushed their damn teeth together. He understood her. He loved… *Shit.*

No, he didn't love her. He *pretend* loved her and he was sick of his mind getting that mixed up.

Emma looked up and saw him then, and she frowned. "Is everything okay?"

"What? Yeah." He shook it off and walked to the counter to steal the last dark dregs of coffee. "Josh called and he always annoys the crap out of me."

Emma was watching him, and he guessed his expression had been more horrified than annoyed. And she'd know that because she knew him. Just like he knew her.

"Before you run off again," Gram said, "I don't want to be all mopey and sad Saturday night, so I invited everybody over for a bon voyage party."

"Sounds like fun," he said. "Who's everybody?"

"Your family, of course. And Russell and Dani and Roger. I'm thinking burgers and dogs, and Mary already said she'd bring a dump-truck load of that amazing coleslaw of hers."

"We'll take care of the cooking, Gram, so you can relax." When he and Cat both looked at her, Emma blushed. "Okay, fine. Sean will take care of the grilling so you can relax."

"I was counting on it. And, Sean, why don't you sit down and help us settle on a wedding date."

"I told Emma to tell me when to be there and I'd be there."

"Nonsense. Sit down."

He'd rather be dipped in barbecue sauce and dropped in the desert, but he sat. One more week and it would be over.

Then he wouldn't have to think about Emma anymore. Not think about marrying her or having babies with her or holding her in his arms at night. He'd be gone and she'd be some funny story his brothers brought up sitting around the fire knocking back beer.

"Really, Sean, are you okay?" Cat asked him, putting her hand on his arm.

He realized he'd been rubbing his chest, and he forced himself to lean forward and prop his arms on the table so he wouldn't do it again. "I'm fine. Let's pick a date."

Seventeen

If anybody had asked her, Cat would have said she was at least a couple of decades past having butterflies of nervous anticipation fluttering around inside. But as she put her hand on the door of Walker Hardware and prepared to push it open, a winged *Nutcracker* ballet was being performed in her stomach.

She'd spent a little time talking to Russell on the telephone over the past couple of days, but this would be the first time she actually saw him since kissing him goodbye the previous morning.

Maybe she shouldn't have come. Sure, they'd talked on the phone, but he hadn't asked her out again. Maybe it had been too much, too fast, and rather than tell her he didn't want to see her again, he thought he'd just play along until she went back to Florida.

She pulled her hand back and took a deep breath. She was being silly. It wasn't some grand romance they were embarking on, anyway. They were good friends, that's all. Friends with occasional benefits, as the younger generation would say. With no pressure, there was no reason not to casually drop in and say hello.

There was a tapping on the glass and she looked up to see Russell standing on the other side of the door, watching her. The amusement on his face made her laugh at herself as he pulled open the door and made the bell ring.

"That must have been quite the dilemma you were sorting through," he said as she walked by him. "Maybe I shouldn't have interrupted you."

"I was being ridiculous. I'm glad you did or who knows how long I would have stood out there arguing with myself."

"Were you winning?" The laugh lines around his eyes danced as he smiled at her.

"I was, actually." She looked around at the shelves, which didn't look much more empty than they had the first time she'd been in. "I had to come into town for sugar and I thought I'd stop in and say hello."

"I left a message at the house. Wish I'd caught you before you drove over here."

"The phone started ringing right after I locked the door behind me and it's usually for Emma's business, so I didn't go back."

"I was wondering if you'd want to take a ride down to Concord with me tonight. Get some dinner and see a movie maybe?"

He looked as nervous as she'd felt standing on his front step, she realized, and she smiled back at him. "I'd love to."

"Should I pick you up at your house around five or..."

"That would be lovely. I'm not sure if the kids will be home by then. They had a couple of things to take care of before they could head to the big job for this week. Sean has to get that deck done, so they might work late."

"How's that going?"

"Honestly, if I was just meeting Sean for the first time now, I'd never guess they aren't a real couple."

"So your plan is working, then?"

"It seems to be, which is good because the clock's ticking." She sighed and glanced at the door. "Speaking of ticking clocks, I should move along if I'm going to get everything done before five. I'll probably make up some dinner for the kids before I go. If left to her own devices, Emma would work that poor man into the ground and then give him a grilled cheese sandwich for supper."

"I'll see you at five, then," he said.

She nodded and moved to open the door, but he caught her hand and stopped her. One long, lingering kiss later, the butterflies were dancing again. "I'll be looking forward to it."

"You're not very good at this," Emma said, laughing at the frustration on Sean's face.

He pulled his hand out from under the back of her T-shirt. "You're distracting me."

"How am I distracting you?" She shook the bag at Sean, reminding him to pull two letter tiles to replace the *C* and the *T* he'd used to make *CAT*.

"You look totally hot. And you did it on purpose so I wouldn't be able to concentrate and you'd win."

Emma laughed. Sure, she'd thrown on baggy flannel boxers and an old Red Sox T-shirt after her shower just to seduce him out of triple-word scores. "You not having a shirt on is distracting. And you keep pretending you want to rub my back so you can peek at my tile rack."

"Nothing wrong with checking out your rack." He craned his neck to see better and she shoved him away. It wasn't easy playing Scrabble sitting side by side on the couch, but after a long workday, neither was willing to take the floor.

They'd found a note from Gram on the counter when they got home. She was going to dinner and a movie with Russell and they shouldn't wait up. She'd also left a small casserole in the fridge with *very* specific instructions on how to warm it up. Cleaned up, well fed and facing a long, rainy evening together, they'd hit the game cupboard. And, ironically, Scrabble had been Sean's choice.

"Did you call your brother back?" she asked while looking over the board. Ryan had called while they were intent on obliterating a nasty patch of poison oak for a family with several kids and Sean had sent the message to voice mail.

"Not yet. I'll give him a shout back tomorrow."

"Are you avoiding him?" She dropped an *O* and *T* on the end of *BALL* and noted her points.

"Yup." He rearranged some tiles on his rack, frowning. "They're taking turns calling me to see if anybody's won the bet yet."

And he wouldn't tell them because somebody might tell the women and he didn't want them getting ideas. She was about to tell him it was lame to avoid his siblings over a stupid bet, when he laid down his tiles, adding a *Q, U, A* and an *R* on a triple-word-score space before the *T* she'd put down, and then a *Z* on the end. "You did *not* just use a *Q* and a *Z* on a triple-word score."

"I think that puts me in the lead." He grinned and picked up the pencil and paper. "Never count a Kowalski out. We don't like to lose."

"Obviously I'm not hot enough. Maybe I should have put on some mascara."

He grabbed her arm and pulled her close. "You don't need shit on your face to be hot."

"Just a dirt smudge here and there?"

He laughed and leaned forward to kiss her. She wanted more and threw her leg over his so she was straddling his lap. He moaned against her mouth, his hands going to her hips as she put her hands on his bare chest and pushed him back against the couch.

"Now I know you're trying to distract me," he muttered against her lips.

"I don't like to lose, either."

It was her turn to moan when he lightly caught her nipple between his teeth, the thin T-shirt doing nothing to dampen the delicious sensation. He slid his hands under the fabric, pushing it up until her breasts were bared to his mouth.

She reached down to undo his fly, but his arm blocked hers. He worked his hand into the wide leg opening of her boxers and found…only her. Groaning, he slid his fingers over her slick flesh and her fingers dug into his shoulders.

"Please tell me we don't have to go all the way upstairs for a condom," she said.

"Back pocket." She leaned with him as he fished it out, then tried to help him get his jeans down over his hips. Her foot hit the coffee table, which snagged on the throw rug and sent the Scrabble tiles sliding all over the board.

She laughed as he tore open the condom packet. "Now nobody wins."

"I was ahead." He put one hand on her hip, using the other to guide himself into her. "So I win."

Emma moaned as he filled her, bracing herself against the couch with a hand on either side of his head. "The game wasn't over. It's a draw."

He pulled down on her hips as he drove up into her, making her gasp. "Ties are for pussies. Admit I won."

She looked down into his blue eyes, crinkled with amusement as he grinned at her. God, she loved…having sex with this man. "One good word isn't a victory."

"That's not what the score sheet said." He stopped moving, and when she tried to rock against him, he held down on her hips so she couldn't move, either. Then he had the nerve to chuckle at her growl of sexual frustration. "Admit it. I can sit here all night."

"Oh, really?" She went straight for a known weak spot—nipping at his earlobe before sucking it into her mouth.

He let go of her hips with one hand, intending to push her mouth away, but she rocked her hips. He groaned and put his hand back. She breathed softly against his ear and then ran her tongue along the outside.

"Admit I was going to win," she whispered, "because I can do this all night."

With one leg, he kicked at the table, sending it over and the letter tiles flying. Before Emma could react, she was on her back on the throw rug with Sean between her legs and her hands held over her head.

"I don't lose." He crossed her wrists so he could hold them with one hand, then used the other to pull her leg up over his hip so he was totally buried in her. "Give up?"

She shook her head, but couldn't hold back the sigh as he oh, so slowly withdrew almost completely and then just as slowly filled her again. "You're cheating."

He did it again and again, the slow friction delicious and frustrating, until they were both trembling and on the edge.

Then, as he was pulling out of her once again with

a self-control that made her want to scream, it became a matter of life or death, because she was going to die if she didn't get what her body was looking for. "Okay, fine. You win."

He drove into her hard, his fingers biting into her wrists before he released them so he could lift her legs to her shoulder. She cried his name as his fingers dug into her hips and he gave them what they both wanted.

When he collapsed on top of her, breathing hard against her neck, she wrapped her legs and arms around him, holding him close.

"Another one for the win column," he said once they'd caught their breath.

"It has an asterisk, though, because you totally cheated."

"All's fair in sex and Scrabble, baby." He propped his head on his hand and smiled down at her. "What should we play next?"

"I've still got clothes on. You've still got clothes on. Maybe we should break out a deck of cards."

"You're my kinda girl, Emma Shaw," he said, and thankfully, he was in the process of getting up off the floor, because she didn't think she did a good job of hiding how happy those words made her.

Sean eyeballed the bubble, making sure it was exact dead center in the level, and then drove the last screw home. The stairs were done. Tomorrow he'd lay the seats for the built-in bench seating and the deck would be done.

Just in time, too, since tomorrow was his last day of work. He and Emma were taking Thursday and Friday off to spend with Cat since she was leaving on Sunday.

Which meant he'd be leaving on Sunday, too.

"Nice work," Emma said, startling him because he'd been so lost in thought he hadn't heard her approach.

"I told you it'd be good. If it's treated properly, this deck will outlast the house." And he wouldn't be the one treating it. Either Emma would have to see to the weatherproofing or hire somebody else to do it. He wouldn't be around anymore.

"Are you going to be able to finish the benches tomorrow?"

"Yup." He turned around and looked out at the property Emma had transformed while he built the deck. "They're going to love this place."

She took off her gloves and tossed them down next to his toolbox. "I think so, too. It all came together even better than I thought."

They made a good pair, just as he'd thought they would, but he didn't say it out loud. It was something he'd had to do a lot lately—watching what he said. He'd gone with her the previous afternoon to look at a lakefront property and he'd almost pointed out they really needed to rebuild the owners' boat dock. And when they'd stopped at the grocery store to pick up some steaks, he'd noticed the pot roasts were on sale and almost asked her if she could use a Crock-Pot, because nothing beat slow-cooked pot roast on a chilly autumn day.

Luckily he'd remembered he wouldn't be there for any chilly autumn days before he'd opened his mouth. And, even if he did get a job pounding nails after he left, he shouldn't bid on pounding any nails with her. She'd managed to get under his skin so completely, the only way he was going to get out of there was to walk away and not look back.

"Are you okay?"

He shook off his thoughts and looked at Emma. She was frowning at him. "Yeah, why?"

"You just looked really unhappy for a minute."

"Just hungry. Thinking about those steaks we bought and how good they're going to taste tonight."

She gave him an uncertain look, but didn't argue. "We should start picking up. I didn't realize how late it was, and Gram likes to eat on the early side."

He started gathering his tools, wondering if Emma had moments like that. Moments when she was making plans or thinking about something they were going to do before remembering he wouldn't be there come Monday morning. And if she did, if she cared.

After carrying his tool bucket to the truck, he helped Emma clean her tools and carried them around for her.

"I'm going to miss having you around," she said lightly, carrying nothing but her gloves. "I'll have to do my own heavy lifting again."

Was that the only reason? "You should hire somebody. You can afford to pay me, so you can afford to pay somebody else."

She only shrugged, as if she might think about it, and he let it go. Wasn't his business what she did with her company. Once he had her tools stowed in the diamond-plate lockboxes in the back of her truck, he brushed off his hands and opened her door for her since she was just standing there looking at him.

"What's bothering you?" she asked again. "And don't tell me you're hungry."

What was he supposed to say? He wasn't going to tell her he was moping because she didn't seem too broken up over the fact he'd be leaving soon and wouldn't be coming back. Except for the fact she wouldn't have him around to carry her tools anymore.

Instead, he backed her up against the inside of the open truck door and kissed her. It was a good kiss, too, but apparently not good enough, because she pushed him back. "Don't put me off like that. We've already had the discussion about your kisses not making my brain empty of any intelligent thought."

"Fine. Building a deck alone is hard work and I'm tired. I've also been thinking a lot about what I'm going to be doing next week because being a lazy, unemployed bum isn't really my style."

And there was the opening. If she had any interest at all in keeping whatever was between them going, she'd at least offer to keep him on with her. Not that he wanted to be a landscaper by trade, but she could ask.

"Okay." She sighed. "You'll be back where you started before I knocked on your door, so I'm sure you'll figure it out. And if you let me drive home, I'll give you a massage later."

Back to sex, which was a pretty solid way of reminding him exactly where their non-relationship stood. He could live with sex. Shaking off the mushy-feelings stuff, he smiled and hooked his fingers in her front pockets. "How about I drive and I give you a massage later?"

"You're not going to let me drive, are you?"

"I have the magic penis, so I get the keys, remember?"

She laughed and tried to shove him away. "You're a penis, all right. A big walking, talking penis."

He kissed her again, this time until she surrendered and wrapped her arms around his neck. There were only a few more days of kissing her in his future, so he intended to make it a priority.

"Okay," she whispered when he was done. "You can drive. But I get to pick exactly what part of me you're massaging."

"I can live with that." He slapped her on the butt when she climbed into the truck, and then laughed as he walked around to the driver's side and caught her flipping him off through the window.

He'd make her pay for that later.

Eighteen

"I needed to grab another box of screws, but, when I got to the truck, I realized I'd left my wallet in my tool bucket. When I went back around the house to get it, she had my plans open and was double-checking all my measurements."

Emma's cheeks burned when Gram laughed at Sean's story, but, since she couldn't deny it, she stuck her last bite of the fabulous steak he'd grilled into her mouth.

"That's my Emma," Gram said. "I think her first words were 'If you want something done right, do it yourself.'"

"In my defense," she said when she'd swallowed, pointing her fork at Sean for emphasis, "my name is on the truck, and being able to pound nails doesn't make you a builder. I have a responsibility to my clients to make sure they get quality work."

"I do quality work."

"I know you build a quality deck, but stairs are tricky." She smiled sweetly at him. "I had to double-check."

"It's all done but the seating now and it's good work,

even though I practically had to duct tape you to a tree in order to work in peace."

She might have taken offense at his words if not for the fact he was playing footsie with her under the table. And when he nudged her foot to get her to look at him, he winked in that way that—along with the grin—made it almost impossible for her to be mad at him.

"It's Sean's turn to wash tonight. Emma, you dry and I'll put away."

"I'll wash, Gram. Sean can dry."

"I can wash," Sean told her. "The world won't come to an end if I wash the silverware before the cups."

"It makes me twitch."

"I know it does. That's why I do it." He leaned over and kissed her before she could protest.

"That new undercover-cop show I like is on tonight," Gram said as they cleared the table. "Maybe Sean won't snort his way through this episode."

He laughed and started filling the sink with hot, soapy water. "I'm sorry, but if he keeps shoving his gun in his waistband like that, he's going to shoot his…he's going to shoot himself in a place men don't want to be shot."

Emma watched him dump the plates and silverware into the water—while three coffee mugs sat on the counter waiting to be washed—but forced herself to ignore it. "Can't be worse than the movie the other night."

"That was just stupid," Sean said while Gram laughed.

They'd tried to watch a military-action movie and by the time they were fifteen minutes in, she thought they were going to have to medicate Sean if they wanted to see the end. After a particularly heated lecture about what helicopters could and couldn't do, Emma had hushed him, but he'd still snorted so often in derision she was surprised he hadn't done permanent damage to his sinuses.

"I don't want you to think that's real life," he told them.

"I promise," Gram said, "if I ever want to use a tank to break somebody out of a federal prison, I'll ask you how to do it correctly first."

He kissed the top of her head. "Thanks, Cat. At least you appreciate me, unlike Emma, who just tells me to shut up."

"I'd appreciate you more if there wasn't salad dressing floating in the dishwater you're about to wash my coffee cup in."

"According to the official guy's handbook, if I keep doing it wrong, you're supposed to let me watch *SportsCenter* while you do it yourself."

"Did the official guy's handbook also tell you that if that happens, you'll also be free to watch the late-night sports shows while I do *other* things myself?"

The tips of his ears turned pink as he cast a sideways glance at her grandmother, but Gram just laughed.

Emma couldn't put her finger on exactly when it happened, but at some point the time she spent with just Sean and Gram had become her new normal. And she liked her new normal.

Laughter over the dinner table. Banter during the cleaning up. Then Gram in her chair, knitting while they watched television. Sean stretched out on the couch with his head in her lap. She could stroke his hair or give him a kiss in the kitchen and not feel like a fraud. And without the Kowalskis stirring up trouble, they'd fallen into a comfortable evening routine that felt a little more *real* every day.

It was a tourism commercial for Florida that popped her bubble. It was a too-cheerful reminder that in less than a week, Gram would be flying back to North Fort Meyers. And that meant Sean would be leaving, too.

She'd be alone again. She hadn't minded it before—had enjoyed having the big house all to herself—but now she couldn't imagine sitting alone and watching TV. Or heating up a microwave meal. Not having anybody to talk to or to laugh with.

It wasn't only Gram she couldn't imagine her life without. It was Sean, and that scared her so badly she nudged him and told him she wanted to get up.

"You okay?" He touched her face, clearly concerned.

"Fine. I just need to… I'll be back in a few minutes."

She went upstairs to their bedroom—*her* bedroom—and then locked herself in the little bathroom. Once there, she discovered a possible culprit for her emotional state, but she knew it was far worse than hormones on their monthly roller-coaster ride.

Despite his warnings, she'd gone and gotten ideas about Sean. She was afraid she'd fallen in love with him and there was nothing she could do to talk herself out of it now.

Just great, she thought, pressing the heels of her hands against her eyes in an effort to stem the tears. Now she had to pretend not to the love the man she was pretending to love while pretending she wasn't sleeping with him.

Sean gave Emma twenty minutes before he decided to go after her. Something had obviously upset her, and he suspected it was the Florida commercial. Now that she was in her last week with Gram, it had probably hit her Cat would be going home soon.

"Do you want to pause this?" Cat asked him when he got up off the couch.

"No, go ahead and watch it. I'm going to check on Emma. I think… I think maybe she doesn't feel good, so I'm not sure if we'll be back down or not."

She gave him a warm smile and went back to her knitting, so he went up the stairs and into their room. Emma was curled up on the couch, wrapped in the blanket, and she'd brought her pillow.

"What happened?" he asked, crouching next to her and pushing her hair back from her face. She wasn't crying, but she had been recently.

"Nothing."

"Was it the commercial? The one about Florida?" She hesitated a few seconds, then nodded. "I'll miss her, too. She's a great lady."

A tear spilled onto Emma's cheek and he wiped it away. "Is that all that's bothering you?"

She lifted one shoulder in a half-assed shrug. "I'm just tired."

He tucked her hair behind her ear. "Then we'll go to bed. Why are you on the couch?"

"Because…" She sniffled and her cheeks turned pink. "It's, um…*that* time."

"Oh." Plumbing issues, as his uncle so delicately referred to *that* time, explained a lot. "You'll be more comfortable in the bed."

She shook her head and pulled the blanket up over her face, so he stood and considered his options. He could go back downstairs and finish watching the show with Cat, but he didn't really like leaving Emma alone, not that there was anything he could do to ease her misery. And he couldn't stand next to the couch all night watching her, so he went into the bathroom and got ready for bed.

After turning off the light and punching his pillow into shape, Sean sprawled on the bed and tried to force himself to sleep. He had the whole bed to himself and he didn't have to share the covers, so it should have been all good.

But he was too aware of her across the room and he didn't want her there. He wasn't going to be able to sleep with her there. He wanted her next to him, where she was supposed to be.

His eyes flew open and he flopped onto his back, staring at the ceiling. That was wrong. She wasn't *supposed* to be sleeping next to him. She was *supposed* to be sleeping on the couch, which was exactly where she was. What they had between them wasn't real, so he should be able to do something as simple as fall asleep without her in his arms, dammit.

He'd be leaving in less than a week. He'd probably go back to the apartment over Jasper's Bar & Grille. Or, screw it, maybe he'd go back to Maine and stay at the Northern Star until he figured out what he wanted to do. Or hop in his truck and drive to New Mexico to check on his sister.

No matter what he did or where he went, there'd be no more Emma for him.

When she sniffled and then shifted for what seemed like the tenth time in two minutes, Sean had had enough. She wasn't on the couch because she was more comfortable there. She was there because she didn't think he'd share the bed if there was no sex in it for him. He got up and walked across the bedroom. Then he threw the blanket across the back of the couch and scooped her up, pillow and all, to carry her to the bed.

The look she gave him, all sleepy and questioning, as he crawled in beside her squeezed something inside him. "I can't sleep with you tossing and turning on the couch, that's all."

Only when she'd snuggled against him and drifted off to sleep did Sean close his eyes. He still didn't sleep, though, because that *wasn't* all. There was also the fact having the rest of his life in front of him like an open road, with no obligations or strings, just made him feel empty inside.

He must have slept at some point because her alarm clock startled him awake. Emma was curled up on her side, facing him, and he smiled when she opened her eyes.

"How you feeling this morning?"

"I'd feel better if you got up and shut my alarm off." She'd plugged it in next to the couch, the way she had in the beginning of their nonrelationship.

"Now you're just taking advantage," he said, but he got up and killed the phone.

He turned back to the bed and froze. She was watching him, her eyes sleepy and her hair tumbled across the pillow. A smile curved her lips and he found himself smiling in response.

God, she was gorgeous, bedhead and ratty T-shirt and all.

"I'm starving," she said and then she stretched, which made him turn away so he didn't have to go down to breakfast walking funny.

"Do you want me to bring you up a tray of food?"

"Like room service?"

"I don't know." He shrugged. "I wasn't sure if you were up to going downstairs. Or working."

"I'm okay, and you have two days to get that deck done. You can have dibs on the bathroom and then I'll get dressed."

Cat was flipping the first batch of banana pancakes when Sean hit the kitchen. "Morning, Cat."

"Good morning. How's Emma today?"

"Better. She's, uh…it's *that* time," he said, going with Emma's terminology.

"Huh. It doesn't usually affect her much."

"I think she also realized you're not going to be here much longer." And neither would he.

Emma would probably be relieved to have him out from underfoot. She could go back to driving her truck and sleeping on her side of the bed and washing her dishes in the proper order.

"I'm going to miss her, too," Cat said. "Both of you."

"I'm going to miss your cooking, that's for sure," he said, sitting in front of the pancakes she set down for him. "You sure we can't talk you into staying?"

Then he stopped with the fork halfway to his mouth. He had to stop doing that. There was no *we*.

"I miss Emma when I'm there, but I really enjoy Florida."

He was on his second pancake when Emma came downstairs, looking a hell of a lot better than she had the night before. She kissed her grandmother's cheek and picked at a pancake before disappearing into her office to make a phone call.

"What are you going to do today, Cat?" Sean asked when the woman just stood there staring after Emma, concern in her eyes.

"Oh, I'll probably go into town and see if I can sweet-talk Russell into buying me lunch."

He wondered how that budding romance was going to turn out, since she was leaving in a few days, but it wasn't his place to ask. "I should get my boots on. If I'm not ready to leave before her, she might get the truck keys first."

She touched his shoulder for a moment as she leaned in to take his empty plate, and he felt a pang of…something. Maybe guilt. But also affection and sorrow that she'd be flying out of his life soon and she didn't know it would be for the last time.

On his way to the foyer, he paused to kiss her cheek. "Say hi to Russell for me."

"Try not to let Emma drive you crazy today."

"Fat chance of that," he said, grinning. Then he went off to get to Emma's key ring before she got off the phone.

The bell rang as Cat walked into Walker Hardware and she smiled, anticipating the way he'd look up and see her and his face would light up with a warm smile.

He didn't let her down. "Cat, I was just thinking about you."

"Good thoughts, I hope."

"Of course. I was debating calling you and asking you to lunch, but I wasn't sure if you'd have plans with Emma since…you're leaving soon."

Maybe she was imagining it, but she thought his smile might have dimmed a little when he mentioned her leaving. "They have to work today and then they're taking tomorrow and Friday off. I came to invite *you* to lunch, actually."

She met him at their usual café in town, where she ordered a salad and he told her he'd have the grilled chicken instead of the fried. "It would be a real shame if I went to hell in a handbasket now."

They talked about the store and the liquidation sale. It wasn't going as well as he'd hoped because people weren't too comfortable taking advantage of the bargain prices. "One of my regular customers said she felt as though she was picking at my carcass."

Cat laughed. "That's a horrible visual, but I think I understand what she meant by it. It's nice that people care about how you feel in all this."

"One of the many reasons I love this town." He smiled at her and sipped his water.

She smiled back, though she felt a pang of sorrow deep inside. Russell not only loved the town, but his family was here. His friends. She'd been starting to play with a foolish notion about asking him to come down to Florida. Maybe for a visit or maybe for more.

"Have you figured out what to do about Emma yet?"

Cat sighed. "No. But if I don't do something, we're going to part ways with this silliness between us and I don't want that."

"You're still planning to give her the house?"

"Definitely. John and I both wanted her to have it, and that was before she grew up and made it her home." She took a bite of her salad, at a loss as to what to do.

"You said she got upset at the Fourth of July barbecue when you mentioned giving it to her as a wedding gift. Have you mentioned it again?"

"No. That day I thought she was on the verge of confessing everything and we didn't want that. *We* meaning Mary Kowalski and I. We wanted Sean and Emma to have a little more time together."

He nodded as though it all made perfect sense to him. "But now time's running out, anyway."

"Maybe I'll push her on the subject tomorrow. I need to see a lawyer about it, anyway, so I might as well start the process before I go home."

"And you think she'll confess?"

"I don't think she'll accept the house as a wedding gift knowing it's a lie. I know she won't."

He toyed with the mashed potatoes on his plate, dragging his fork through them in a grid pattern. "And what are you hoping will happen between her and Sean when that happens?"

That was a harder question to answer. "I'm hoping that, when faced with going their separate ways, they'll both realize they don't want to do that. And maybe they'll go on as they are now, only they won't be pretending."

"They do seem like a nice couple."

"They really are good together, though I'm not sure they see it." She chuckled. "Leave it to my granddaughter to accidentally choose her Mr. Right to be her fake fiancé."

Nineteen

Even with her alarm turned off, Emma was up at the crack of dawn. They weren't working these last three days before Gram flew back to Florida, so she slid out of bed without waking Sean and threw on her boxers and T-shirt.

Not surprisingly, Gram was already up. There were no signs of breakfast yet, but she told Emma she'd brewed a pot of coffee along with making herself tea, so Emma poured a cup and sat down at the table.

"I can't believe we only have three days left," she said after the first bracing sip.

"I know. And I'll miss you, honey. You know I will, but I miss being there. My friends and all my activities."

Emma smiled. "I'm glad, Gram. You know I miss you, too, but it's great that you have all that in your life."

"Before I go, I'm going into town to talk to a lawyer about giving you the house."

The little bit of coffee she'd gotten into her stomach did a slow roll. "I told you I want to buy it from you, fair and square. We'll get a fair market value for it and then you can sell it to me."

"That's ridiculous. It's a gift."

"I don't feel right about that. And it'll be good for my business to build credit."

Gram snorted. "Then you buy a new truck and lease a tractor or something. You don't buy an old farmhouse. My mind's made up, Emma."

Crap. Once she said that, it was over. But there was no way she would let Gram give her the house without knowing the truth. She stared down into her coffee for a minute, and then took a deep breath. They'd almost made it, but it was time.

"It's all a lie, Gram. All of it. There's not going to be a wedding."

There. Now it was done and the entire month had been for nothing. Now her grandmother would be angry and maybe sell the house to a stranger, anyway. And Sean would have no reason to stay. She wasn't sure which hurt more.

"Maybe you should explain yourself."

"I made up a boyfriend so you'd stop being so nervous about me being alone. Sean's name just kind of popped out. He was still in the army until a month or so ago. And I met him for the first time four days before you arrived, when I knocked on his door and asked him to pretend to be my fiancé."

Gram actually chuckled. "That must have been an interesting conversation."

Emma was confused. The very last reaction she expected from her grandmother was amusement. She'd been hoping and praying her confession wouldn't fracture their relationship beyond repair. Laughter wasn't something she'd anticipated.

"You're not upset?" She looked into the older woman's eyes and reluctantly recognized the truth. "You already knew."

"Of course I knew. Couples who've lived together for a year are comfortable with each other. There's familiarity. I could tell as soon as I got off the plane you and Sean didn't have that."

She'd known the *entire* time? "Why didn't you say anything?"

"Because I wanted to figure out what you were up to. And then, later, Mary and I decided you two needed a little more time to get to know each other, so we played along."

"Oh, my God." Emma covered her face with her hands. "Mrs. Kowalski knew you knew?"

"I had to practically drag the truth out of her, but once she realized I already knew you two were lying, she gave up. I must confess, though, I was a little put out that you thought I'd fall for this."

"By the time I realized how really crazy it was, I was in too deep to back out. I know it sounds dumb, but I did it because I love you, Gram. I wanted you to let me go so you could enjoy being in Florida."

"I'll never let you go. But maybe I did give you the impression I was worrying more about you than enjoying myself. But you also wanted the house."

Emma's cheeks burned. "Of course I wanted the house. It's my home. But I wanted you to *sell* it to me. I never expected you to just give it to me. You have to believe that."

Gram reached across the table and squeezed her hand. "I knew you wouldn't take it. I told Mary and Russell both you wouldn't accept it as a wedding gift without telling me the truth, and I was right."

"If you'd said something, we wouldn't have wasted the entire month playing games."

"Oh, I don't think it was a waste," Gram said, smiling. "I see Sean's sleeping in this morning. Did you keep him up too late last night?"

When the implication behind her grandmother's words sank in, Emma shook her head. "It's not like that. We're not… It's not real."

"Well, it's certainly not pretend."

"No." Emma really didn't want to have this conversation. "It's like friends with benefits, Gram. Once he knows I told you the truth, he's going to pack up his stuff and go."

"Maybe he won't if you ask him to stay."

"Who says I want him to stay?" she asked, forcing a little attitude into her voice. Maybe if she could convince somebody else she didn't care, she'd believe it herself.

"I think we've had enough lies, Emma."

"We had a deal, Gram. Love wasn't part of it."

"I've spent the last month living with you two and I've watched your relationship change. Don't sell him short, honey."

She got up and rinsed her empty teacup, then walked over to kiss the top of Emma's head. "I'm going to go have a nice bath and get dressed. I'm still going into town and I'm still giving you the house."

"Gram, I—"

"My mind is made up, Emma," she said as she left the kitchen.

Sean was whistling when he hit the kitchen, hunting for coffee, but he stopped when he saw Emma sitting at the table. Her nose was a little blotchy and her eyes still damp from a cry.

"I told Gram the truth," she said. "It's over."

His lungs deflated in a rush, leaving behind an ache he hoped was a lack of oxygen and not the beginning of a heartache. That would be stupid, since it wasn't as if what they had was real. It was all pretend and he'd known the day would come he'd walk away from her without looking back.

But he thought he had three and a half more days before he had to face that.

"Are you okay?" he asked. She nodded, even though she didn't look it. "How did she take it?"

"You were right, that day we were working and you said you thought she was onto us. She knew all along."

That set him back a bit. "She knew?"

"She said she suspected as soon as she saw us together in the airport because we didn't look like a couple who'd…been intimate. And she and Mrs. Kowalski have been in cahoots since the first barbecue."

"I don't understand. Why didn't she say anything? And in cahoots with Aunt Mary to what?"

"She didn't say anything because she wanted to know what we were up to." Her cheeks flushed and she looked down at the table. "And they were in cahoots to make us a real couple."

"Oh." He really didn't know what to say to that. "They thought we'd make a good couple?"

"Crazy, huh?"

That wasn't the direction he'd been heading, but it was probably best she'd said it. It *was* crazy. They were so different. They were in different places in their lives and wanted different things.

"Where's Cat now?"

"Taking a bath. Then she's going into town and—" She had to stop because she was tearing up again, and then she took a deep, shuddering breath. "She's going to talk to a lawyer about giving me the house."

"That's good, then."

"That's why I told her the truth. She was insisting on giving me the house as a wedding gift, so I had to tell her."

"But she already knew."

"And she knew I wouldn't accept it based on a lie. She wanted me to tell her the truth."

Sean poured himself a cup of coffee, hoping the caffeine would help restore some of his equilibrium. Even though he'd been blindsided, this turn of events was a good thing for Emma. She could stop lying to her grandmother. Cat wouldn't be selling the house out from under her. And, while Emma would still be single, maybe the shenanigans would be a wake-up call to Cat that she didn't need to worry quite so much.

"I'm happy for you," he said, and he meant it. What he wasn't sure was how he felt on his own behalf.

She nodded, but she didn't look as happy as he expected her to. With the house soon to be in her name and him soon to be out from under her feet, he was surprised she wasn't dancing across the kitchen.

He took a bracing sip of the coffee, not bothering with cream or sugar. "So… I guess that's it, then."

She nodded again, her hands folded so tightly on the table her knuckles were pale. "I guess it is."

He started for the door, but then stopped and looked back at her. "Are you sure you're okay?"

"I'm sure." She even managed a wobbly smile. "Emotional shock, I guess. So much drama for...no reason. Telling her was terrifying and such a relief at the same time, so it's probably just the letdown."

"Okay, then." He took his coffee into her office and closed the door.

It was over. He was free to go be his own man again, his life revolving around steak, football, beer and women. He could go back to his wild pluralizing ways, as she'd put it during their first dinner together.

Before it could all settle in, he pulled out his phone and hit Kevin's number on the speed dial. He answered on the second ring, sounding groggy, and Sean belatedly remembered that, due to owning a sports bar, Kevin and his family stayed up late and slept late in the morning.

"Shit. I didn't mean to wake you." Sean scrubbed a hand over his face, realizing it was too early to be calling anybody. "Quick question and then you can go back to sleep. Can I still mooch that apartment?"

"Uh-oh."

"Long story short, she told Cat the truth, so my services are no longer needed."

"You okay?"

He wasn't sure yet. "Why wouldn't I be?"

"Okay. You still got the key?"

"Yup."

"It's yours, then. Head on down for a beer later, on the house. You know, when it's not dark o'clock."

"The sun's up, dude. But thanks."

It took him a depressingly short time to pack his stuff. A few minutes to empty his drawer. Less than two to grab his stuff out of the closet. It took him a little longer in the bathroom sorting his toiletries from hers. He'd just retrieved the stash of condoms from the bedside drawer and tossed them in the duffel because he'd be damned if he'd facilitate her sleeping with some other guy in the future, when Emma walked in.

"I'll be out of your way in a few minutes," he told her. "Just have to gather up a few things downstairs."

"You don't have to run out of here, Sean."

"No sense in hanging around," he said, maybe a little more gruffly than he'd intended.

"Oh. Okay, then. Gram wants me to go to town with her and she's ready to go."

"I'll put the key in the mailbox when I leave. Don't forget to grab it later."

"Sean." He shoved a pile of socks into the bag. It was like ripping off a Band-Aid. A clean and fast exit was best for everybody. "Goddammit, Sean, it's obvious you can't wait to get out of here, but she wants to say good-bye to you before you go."

"What about her goodbye barbecue? Or am I uninvited?"

"There's no sense in dragging your family over here now. She'll probably have lunch with your aunt or something."

She tossed something onto the bed and then turned and walked away before he could apologize. He was being a jerk and he couldn't help it. If he showed any weakness and she gave him some indication she didn't want him to go, he might stay, and this wasn't where he'd wanted to end up.

Sean shifted his bag so he could see what she'd tossed onto the bed. It was the small diamond ring he'd put on her finger a month ago when he asked her to marry him, and as the sun hit the stone, it winked at him. Feeling nothing but hollow, he closed his fingers around it, squeezing it in his fist. Then he tucked it into the front pocket of his jeans and took a deep breath.

It was best for both of them if he shut Emma out and walked away. But first he had to get through a moment he'd been dreading.

Cat was waiting for him at the bottom of the stairs. Emma was next to her, but she wouldn't even look at him. He could tell by the way her jaw was set he'd pissed her off.

"I'll wait in the truck," she said, and then she seemed to collect herself. She turned to face him and stuck out her hand. "Thanks, Sean."

A handshake? After all that, he was getting brushed off with a handshake? But he was the one who'd made it very clear to her none of what they had was real.

He gripped her hand in his, running his thumb over hers. "I'll see you around, Emma."

She nodded and pulled her hand back. Sean squeezed her fingers for a second, but he couldn't hold on to her. Before he could say anything else, she walked out of the house.

"You two are going to be stubborn about this, aren't you?"

Sean turned to Cat and chose to ignore her words. "I'm going to miss you. And I mean that."

"Even though Emma thinks a party isn't a good idea now because it would be awkward, I'm sure I'll see you again."

"Don't know where I'm going from here. But you never know. Maybe I'll drive down to Florida and crash one of your wild and crazy beach parties someday."

She opened her arms and he enveloped her in a hug.

"You're welcome to hang out under my beach umbrella anytime."

After extricating himself from her arms, he kissed her cheek. "Take care of yourself, Cat."

"And you...don't be *too* stubborn."

She went out the door before he could ask her what that was supposed to mean. He heard the truck door close and then it was heading down the driveway.

He stood there for a few minutes and then went into the kitchen. Over the past few weeks, he'd actually accumulated a few things, and his belongings didn't fit in the duffel anymore. He grabbed a trash bag because what the hell did he care, then scoured the downstairs, tossing in anything that belonged to him.

Then he finished upstairs and there was nothing left but to get in his truck and drive away. But first he went into the bathroom and pulled the pad of sticky notes out of his pocket. He stuck a pink one to the mirror and pulled the cap off his Sharpie.

And...nothing. What could he say? Something flip like *Thanks for the good times* didn't feel right. Maybe *Goodbye.* Or *Why does it feel so shitty to be leaving right now?*

He stared at the blank note a long time, then put the cap back on the marker and shoved it in his pocket. There was nothing left to say, so he grabbed his bags and walked out of Emma's house.

Cat and Mary met at a coffee shop, the mood pessimistic. The month certainly hadn't ended the way either of them had thought—and hoped—it would.

"She was so cold to him before we left," Cat said, "but about a half hour after we got home, I heard her crying.

I peeked into her room and she was sitting on the floor with a sticky note in her hand, sobbing her heart out."

"Could you read what it said?"

"That's the thing—it was blank. Just a blank sticky note."

Mary frowned. "That doesn't make any sense."

"I don't know what the deal is with the sticky note, but I know she cares about him a whole lot more than she wanted him to know."

"Sean's not answering his phone. I made Kevin go up and knock on his door. He said Sean wasn't in a really sociable mood and we should just leave him alone for a few days."

Cat shook her head and put another sugar cube in her tea just to get the kick. "They're both hardheaded. I'm afraid if they're left alone for a few days, they won't come around at all."

"When I talked to Lisa earlier, she gave me the impression you weren't going to have your goodbye party since we're not all going to be one big happy family. Maybe you should."

"I hadn't even thought about it yet. Emma's knee-jerk reaction was to cancel it but, to be honest, even if she and Sean boycott, I still want to say goodbye to everybody."

"Sean won't boycott." She said it with the certainty of a woman who'd brook no argument from the men in her life.

"Emma won't, either."

"Maybe a little more time together, without the lies, is just what they need."

Cat smiled and took a sip of her tea. The bad part of the plan was the fact she'd have to say goodbye to Sean all over again. She wouldn't look forward to that, consid ering how sad doing it the first time had made her. But it would be worth it if there was a chance of bringing him and Emma together, especially if it happened before she flew back to Florida.

They talked about the party for a few minutes, but then Mary finished her tea and dug a few dollars out of her purse. "I hate to run, but I promised I'd watch Brianna this afternoon. Joe has a writing deadline and Keri has an editing deadline and the baby doesn't really care about either one."

Once she was gone, Cat asked for a tea to go and walked down to the patch of grass that passed for a public park and pulled out her phone.

"Walker Hardware."

Just hearing his voice brightened her day. "Hi, Russell. Are you busy?"

"Nope. Already had my customer for the day. What's up?"

She told him the whole story, starting with Emma's confession and ending with their intention to have the party as planned. "I hope you'll still come. And Dani and Roger, too."

"We'll be there. It sounds like you've had a big day. Do you want me to close up early?"

He was such a good man. "No, but thank you for offering. I'm going to go home and see how Emma's holding up. If I know my girl, she'll have her everything's-okay mask in place by the time I get there. And she'll be scrubbing the crisper drawer runners or reorganizing the junk drawer."

"I'll be thinking of you, Cat. And call me later if you need somebody to talk to."

"I will." She closed her cell phone and took a deep breath.

They had two days to keep the kids on an even keel, and then they'd see how things went at the party. She had her fingers crossed forty-eight hours would be long enough for Sean and Emma to realize how much they missed each other.

Twenty

Sean was going to crack. Or his steering wheel was going to crack if he didn't loosen his grip on it.

He was fourth in the caravan of Kowalski vehicles heading to the house with those stupid daisies painted on the mailbox to eat cheeseburgers and say goodbye to Cat. And it was a damn good thing he was alone in the truck because he needed the time to steady himself so he didn't totally lose his shit in front of his entire family.

It would be a final goodbye to Emma, too. Now that they didn't have to pretend anymore, it should have been easy. A fun barbecue with friends and family. No deception. No trying to remember who was getting which story.

But Sean was still pretending. He was pretending it didn't bother him his fake engagement had come to an end.

The rest of his life stretched before him and the time had come to figure out what he wanted to do with it, but he couldn't see it. Every time he tried, he pictured Emma.

All too soon, they were pulling into the driveway and parking down the sides so nobody got blocked in. He could still make a break for it, he thought. Drive out across the lawn and back out onto the street.

But he wouldn't. He'd man up and see this hellish day through.

Everybody was out back, and he made his way through the crowd to say hello to Cat, and then Russell, Dani and Roger. Emma wasn't in the yard, and when he looked toward the house, he saw her in the kitchen window. She was watching him, and in the seconds before she moved away, he saw that she looked as tired as he felt.

The kids immediately went off to explore Emma's yard, but there wasn't much to hold their interest. Bobby had his Nerf football with him, though, so an impromptu game broke out.

He watched Cat say something to Russell, who went over and fired up the grill. It was a stupid thing, really, but Sean had to look away. That had been his job when he was the man of the house, and seeing Russell do it just brought it home it had all been a fraud.

He'd never been the man of Emma's house. He'd been an actor filling a role.

Mike handed him a beer and pulled up a seat next to him. "Which one of us won?"

Sean looked around, but nobody was paying any attention to them. "Whoever called two weeks."

"So what now?"

Wasn't that the twenty-five-thousand-dollar question? "What do you mean?"

"Kev said you moved back into the apartment over the bar, but are you guys going to keep seeing each other?"

He shook his head and took a long pull on his beer so he wouldn't have to say it out loud.

"Why not?"

"Leave it alone, Mikey," he growled.

Emma came out the back door with an armful of potato-chip bags, which she dumped on the patio table. She smiled at him, but it was a little shaky, and went back inside.

"You should talk to her."

"Thanks, Oprah."

"Whatever. I know sometimes you guys feel sorry for me. Poor Mikey, with the mortgage and the minivan and no life. Well, guess what? I feel sorry for you because I've got an amazing wife and four kids that rock my world every day."

Rather than tell his cousin to pound sand, Sean drained the rest of his beer and dangled the empty bottle between his fingers. "I'm happy for you, but not everybody wants that."

"No, but you do. You're just too chickenshit to go for it."

Sean shook his head. "What the hell do you know about it? We were sharing a room. She's hot. We had sex. End of story."

"If you say so."

"I do." And when Emma came out of the house with a tray of condiments, he turned his head and watched the kids tossing the football.

After a few minutes, Mike got bored with the brooding silence and, after slapping him on the shoulder to let him know there were no hard feelings, got up and walked away. Rather than sit and draw the attention of any more amateur shrinks in the family, he followed suit, forcing himself to be sociable. It wore on him, though, and after a while he wandered around to the front of the house, looking for some peace and quiet.

He found Keri sitting in one of the porch chairs, rocking Brianna. He hadn't seen much of her in the backyard, and the baby was probably why.

Keri smiled when she saw him. "I just fed her. Hoping if I sit here and rock long enough, she'll take a nice nap."

"I'm in the mood to sit for a while and you haven't gotten to visit at all. Hand her over and I'll rock her while she naps."

"Don't offer if you don't mean it," she warned.

"I mean it."

She got up so he could sit down and then she deposited the warm lump of baby in his lap. Brianna squirmed and sniffled a little, but then he started rocking and she quieted down. Keri peeked at her daughter's face, smiled at Sean and then ran, probably afraid he'd change his mind.

The rocking motion soothed his frayed nerves after a while and he leaned his head back and closed his eyes. He was too paranoid about dropping the baby to nod off, but he relaxed and let himself enjoy the summer breeze and the smell of freshly cut grass. The sounds of a happy, boisterous family in the backyard. The squeak of the chair every time he rocked backward.

For a few minutes he could even pretend it was what he'd wanted all along.

"Have you seen Sean?" Emma couldn't find the big spatula and she was hoping he knew where it was.

Joe nodded. "Keri said he's on the front porch, rocking Brianna while she naps."

"That explains why Keri's having a good time," she said, which made him laugh.

Rather than go back through the house, Emma walked around the outside, her feet silent in the grass. And when she turned the corner, her heart did a painful somersault in her chest.

Sean was in one of the rocking chairs, the baby cradled in his arms as he gently rocked. His head was tipped back and his eyes were closed, but it was his mouth that drew her attention.

He was almost smiling. Not quite, but enough to give him a peaceful and contented look that made her ache. They could have had this. They could have had a baby he would rock on the porch on midsummer evenings. She could have had a man like Sean.

Instead, she'd had a performance.

"I told you what happens when you stare at people," he said in a quiet voice without opening his eyes.

"You weren't sleeping."

"No, but same principle." He did open his eyes then, turning his head to look at her. "Were you looking for me?"

"I'm looking for the big spatula and thought maybe you might know where it is."

"Check the pantry. I was putting stuff away and I had it in my hand and my phone rang. I might have set it down in there."

"Okay." She waited a second, but he didn't say anything else. "Thanks."

Bypassing the gauntlet of loved ones, she went in through the front door and walked back to the kitchen. The spatula was on the second shelf of the pantry, and she gripped it in one shaking hand.

It was all wrong. Her Sean would have teased her about his putting something away in the wrong place just to push her buttons. There would have been warmth and humor in his eyes. This Sean was closed off, giving her nothing.

It made sense. Her Sean had never been anything but a lie. Just her luck to choose a man who lied so well she'd almost believed it herself.

"Emma?" It wasn't until she heard Lisa's voice that she realized she was standing in the pantry holding a spatula and crying. "Emma, what's wrong?"

"Nothing," she tried to say, but it got all caught up in a sob and didn't come out right.

Lisa took the spatula out of her hand and tossed it on the table before pushing her toward the stairs.

"The burgers—"

"They'll find the spatula," Lisa said firmly. She pushed Emma up the stairs and down the hall to her room.

It hurt so much to look at the bed. The tears ran freely down her face and there wasn't a damn thing she could do to stop them. "I fell in love with him."

"Oh. Oh, shit." Lisa shook her head. "Kowalski men do that. They show up in your life and drive you so insane you want to slap them upside the head and then—*bam*—all of a sudden you can't live without them."

"That's pretty much what happened."

"Did you tell him?"

She shook her head, mopping her face with a tissue Lisa pulled from the travel pack she always had in her back pocket. "I can't do that to him. He disrupted his whole life to do me a huge favor and I'm not going to repay him by dumping my emotions in his lap."

"I *really* think you should tell him, Emma. Mike told me they all think he's serious about you."

A glimmer of hope flickered to life in her chest, but it fizzled almost instantly. "When I told him it was over, he ran out of here like the house was on fire. He didn't look back. And just now… He doesn't feel anything."

Lisa blew out a breath and crossed her arms. "Sometimes they need a little help."

"It's over, Lisa." The words echoed like a mournful bell tolling in her mind. "But I'll be fine. Really."

"We know Sean almost better than anybody and he does feel something. We've all seen it."

"Hell of an actor, isn't he?"

"No, he's not. He's such a bad liar none of us really thought he could pull this off in the first place."

Emma refused to let herself feel hopeful again. She may as well have been a complete stranger for all the emotion he'd shown her today, and it hurt too much to poke and prod, looking for scraps.

"You should go downstairs," she told Lisa. "If people start looking for us, I'll end up with your whole damn family in here."

"Do you want me to tell them you don't feel good?"

"No. I'm going to take a couple minutes and wash my face, and then I'll be down."

Her friend gave her a quick hug. "I'll save you some Doritos."

She managed to smile, but it faded as soon as Lisa left the room. Throwing herself facedown on her bed and having a good cry sounded like a good idea, but she couldn't. Having an emotional breakdown would ruin Gram's party.

Instead, she doused her face with ice-cold water and did a little makeup magic. She didn't look her best, but maybe she could get through the rest of the day without anybody guessing she was totally coming undone on the inside.

"It's not working," Mary said quietly, and Cat had to reluctantly admit she was right.

Sean and Emma couldn't have had more distance between them if they were in different counties. Cat and Mary were smooshed together in front of the kitchen sink, watching the party through the window. Sean on one end of the yard, Emma on the other.

"Why are they being so stubborn?"

Mary snorted. "He's a Kowalski. I'm not sure what Emma's excuse is."

They sighed in unison. "I know there's something there. I've lived with them for a month. Maybe they're not ready to run off to Vegas yet, but it was more than the sex. I'm sure of it."

"I'm sure of it, too. And would they be so carefully avoiding each other if it was nothing but a breezy fling? It hurts them, seeing each other here."

"Idiots." Cat left the window and started pulling desserts out of the fridge.

"Speaking of stubborn idiots, how are you leaving things with Russell?"

Cat set a bowl of Jell-O salad on the table and stared at it. "I don't know."

"Do you love him?"

"I don't know." She sighed. "It doesn't feel like it did when I fell for John. And we haven't been seeing each other very long."

"I'm not surprised it doesn't feel the same. You're

sixty-five years old, and what's important to you—what you want in a man—is different now."

"I enjoy his company. I know that sounds lame. I'd probably enjoy the company of a golden retriever, too. But I *like* him. I like being with him."

Mary took over, taking the plastic wrap off the Jell-O salad and sticking a spoon in it. "But you're afraid that's not enough."

Cat laughed. "You're very good at this."

"I raised four children, plus had a hand in the raising of four nephews and a niece. Throw in teenage grand-children and I've seen my share of love woes, trust me."

"His life is here."

"A one-bedroom apartment in senior housing? The occasional Sunday dinner with Dani and Roger?"

"Have I known him long enough to ask him to move to Florida with me?"

Mary slid the bowl toward Cat and moved on to slic-ing Keri's store-bought chocolate cake. "I don't know. Have you?"

The door opened before she could answer and Stepha-nie walked in, pulling her earbuds out and shoving them into her pocket. "Mom told me to come in and help."

"You can start carrying things out to the table," Mary told her. "Make sure you keep the dishes away from the edge of the table if Lily's cruising."

They finished preparing the desserts in silence and then it was time to drown her uncertainties in copious amounts of sugar, chocolate and whipped cream. She laughed as Sean and Keri played best out of three Rock-Paper-Scissors for the last blonde brownie, and at Beth, who had her hands full trying to stop Lily from sneaking whipped cream from anybody she turned her blue eyes and dimples on.

They were such a wonderful family, she thought. Having them as in-laws would have been a pleasure.

When she couldn't possibly eat another bite, she threw her paper plate in the trash and headed toward the double-wide swing hanging in the shade of the big maple. John had built it from scratch and she'd spent many an hour there, gently swaying with a four-year-old Emma on her lap. The picture books and stories they'd read together in the swing had helped them both leave their grief behind for a few minutes.

She sat and nudged the ground with the toe of her shoe, giving it a little swing. The wood was warm and smooth under her hand, worn with time but meticulously cared for by Emma.

Russell crossed the lawn to join her and she scooched to one side, making room. "I can't believe how much food you ladies made. I'm going to waddle for a week."

Their hands were on the seat between them and he threaded his fingers through hers. She sighed and rocked her feet against the ground, from heel to toe and back, making the swing sway.

"This time tomorrow, you'll be back in Florida," he said, and it was just a statement. No hint of how he felt about it or whether he was getting around to saying something else.

"Come to Florida with me."

Russell locked his knees and stopped the swing. "What?"

"Well, not tomorrow, of course." Now that she'd made the leap, she wondered if she should have thought a little more about where she'd land. And how much the landing might hurt. "When the hardware store's closed and you get the property sold, don't move into senior housing. Pack up your car and come enjoy my company in the warm sun."

He just kept looking at her, his expression not giving anything away. Taking a deep breath, she forced herself to give him a smile. "It was just a thought."

"When I was a boy, I read a book about the building of the Hoover Dam. I was obsessed with it, really, and if not for the store I might have thought about an engineering degree. I always wanted to see it for myself, but I gave up on that dream a long time ago. Recently, though, I've had a snapshot in my head of you standing in front of Lake Mead, smiling at me. You're making me dream again, Catherine."

Russell blurred as tears filled her eyes and she blinked them away. "Then, when you're ready, you come on down to Florida. We'll relax on the beach for a little while and then we'll borrow Martha's RV and go see the Hoover Dam."

He leaned forward and kissed her. "I won't be far behind you."

"I'll wait for you."

Twenty-one

"For the gazillionth time, Gram, I'm going to be fine."

And for the gazillionth time, her grandmother gave Emma a very skeptical look. "You just don't seem like yourself."

Emma summoned every bit of acting ability she could muster and smiled. "I'm going to miss you, that's all."

"It probably won't be very long until you see me again. Russell thinks it'll take two or three months to wrap things up. I might fly up and then drive down with him when he's ready."

"Maybe you can stop and see a few sights on the way down," she said, careful to keep the smile bright.

The fact was, it hurt a little that Gram had the guts to put her heart and her pride on the line and invite the man she loved to be a part of her life and Emma didn't. She'd let Sean walk away without even taking a shot. Probably for the best, though. Judging by the way he'd shut her out at the barbecue, she would have gotten nothing by confessing her feelings but humiliation to add to her pain.

Gram looked at her watch. "I'm going to have to go

through security in a few minutes. I hate leaving you alone."

"I have so much work lined up, I won't have time to be lonely."

"You can always call me. And make sure you visit Mary. I know she'd like to see you. And feed you."

Somehow she doubted that. "I will. And you call me when you get home."

"I won't forget. Are you sure you don't want me to stay longer?"

"And miss the big bingo tournament? You promised Martha you'd be there."

Gram rested her palm against Emma's cheek. "You're more important to me than Martha."

"And I'm fine." She covered Gram's hand with her own. "You're worrying already and you're not even on the plane yet."

"Maybe you should get a fake dog."

Emma laughed and wrapped her arms around Gram. The laughter turned to a few tears, but everybody cried saying goodbye to loved ones in an airport, so she didn't feel out of place.

Gram kissed her cheek and gave her one last squeeze before picking up her carry-on bag. "I love you, Emma."

"I love you, too." She stood there until she couldn't see her anymore and then she made the long walk back to her truck.

She took the back roads instead of the highway since she wasn't in a rush to get home to her empty house. Nothing waiting for her there but paperwork to catch up on and the echo of her own voice.

Her phone rang as she was unlocking the front door, and her thumbs hovered over the buttons as she tried to gauge whether or not she was in the mood to talk to Lisa. She wasn't, but she hit the talk button, anyway, just because the caller was her best friend.

"Did you get Cat off to Florida okay?" Lisa asked.

"She should be in the air right now."

"Then you should come over tonight for dinner. After the little ones go to bed we can crack open a bottle of wine. Or two."

It was tempting, if only for the company, but there were enough similarities between Mike and Sean in both looks and mannerisms that she wasn't sure she'd make it through the evening. "I think I'm going to throw on some raggedy old sweats and plop myself in front of the TV."

"Uh-oh. A pity party. Do you want me to come over there?"

"It's not a pity party. I'm fine. I swear." Even though she really wasn't, she was afraid if she fell apart over Sean, Lisa might let it slip to Mike and then it would eventually make the rounds and get back to Sean.

A self-pity party was one thing. His pity would be too much.

"Call me if you change your mind," Lisa said.

"Okay. And, hey, see if you can sneak something good out of Mrs. K.'s cookie jar for me."

Lisa laughed. "I will. Call me tomorrow."

Once the conversation was over, Emma stood in the hallway and listened. The house was so quiet. And it was different, too. In the two years before Gram and Sean had descended upon her, the house was always quiet. But now the quiet wasn't the same, as if a joyful song had suddenly been cut off in the middle of the chorus.

Rather than stand around listening to her own thoughts,

she grabbed her iPod and—after making sure the play-list she was looking for didn't have a single sad song on it—she stuck her earbuds in her ears and grabbed the cleanser from under the sink. Maybe cleaning the bath-rooms would wear her out enough to sleep.

Sean put fifty miles on his truck cruising around town, waiting for his aunt and uncle's driveway to be free of miscellaneous vehicles, before he finally pulled in and killed the engine.

He had soft and hazy memories of feeling sick or scared or tired and crawling into his mother's lap. She'd hold him and rub his back until all was well in his world again. He needed that now. But he wasn't a little boy any-more and his mom was gone. He had his aunt, though, and maybe if he looked pathetic enough, she'd wrap her arms around him and give him a good hug.

His uncle opened the door. "You look like hell, boy."

"Thanks, Uncle Leo. That helps."

"Guess you're looking to go mooching around in the Cookie Monster." Back when Danny was little, he'd pleaded with Lisa to buy a Cookie Monster cookie jar for his grammy for her birthday. On any given day, the blue monster was full of delicious, melt-in-the-mouth baked goodies.

"Is Aunt Mary in the kitchen?"

"Have you ever known her to be somewhere else? I'll be out in the shed if you want to talk after."

"Thanks."

His aunt was at the counter, hulling strawberries, when he walked into the kitchen. She gave him a good looking over. "Blonde brownies."

One of his favorites. He grabbed two from the Cookie

Monster and pulled out a chair at the table. She washed her hands and then poured him a glass of milk to go with them.

"What's got you looking like something a dog dug up in a backyard?"

Since she was wearing her apron with the ever-present wooden mixing spoon in the pocket, he swallowed the smart-ass retort that came to mind. "Not sleeping, I guess. After being in the middle of nowhere for the last month, being over the bar in the middle of the city's taking some getting used to."

She whacked him in the back of the head with that damn wooden spoon and he rubbed the spot. That might actually leave a knot. "Ow!"

"You look at me, Sean Michael Kowalski." He looked in the general vicinity of her face, and she took his chin in her hand and jerked his head up. "You look me in the eye, young man, and don't you dare lie to me. Do you love Emma?"

"Yes," he said through gritted teeth.

She released his face and he rubbed his jaw. "Well, that's a start. And I'm going to guess you didn't tell her that before you packed your stuff and moved out."

"I don't know what I'm doing. Other than not getting any sympathy."

"If you're looking for sympathy—"

"I know. It's between shit and syphilis in the dictionary." So they'd all heard. Many times. "The brownies are good, though."

She pulled out a chair across from him and sat down. "What makes you happy, Sean?"

Emma. Emma made him happy. "I didn't even get a chance to figure out what would make me happy. I was going to go do…something. Travel, maybe. Find a place I wanted to call home. And, yes, I love Emma, but she's so…rooted. She has that house and her business and that's *her* life. I want to live *my* life."

"You've been sharing a life for a month now. And you were happy. Don't deny it or I'll whack you again. And now you're not sharing a life and you're unhappy."

"She didn't ask me to stay." There. He'd said it.

"Had you given her any reason to believe you would?"

He felt himself clenching his jaw and forced himself to relax. "How could she not know?"

She leaned forward and covered his hands with hers. "And how could you not see the way she looks at you? How could you look at her at the goodbye party and not see her heart breaking?"

"I… She was sad her grandmother was leaving."

"You two are so busy trying to hide your own feelings because of your stupid arrangement, you're not seeing each other." She got up and pulled out the bar stool she used to sit at the counter when her feet got tired. "I'm too old to bend over and you boys are all too tall, so come here and sit."

He did as he was told and was surprised to find, when she stepped in between his knees, he was at the perfect height for her to wrap her arms around him. Sighing, he locked his arms around her waist and rested his head on her shoulder.

She kissed the top of his head and stroked his back. "If, a year from now, you were stuck on the tracks and a train was coming, what would you regret? Not taking a road trip to the Grand Canyon? Or not spending that year with Emma?"

He gave a short laugh. "Trust me, Emma *is* the train."

"That's love, honey." She squeezed a little harder and he felt some of the crappiness he'd been feeling slip away. "Think about it."

He took a few minutes to compose himself with the help of another blonde brownie, then kissed his aunt goodbye. "Tell Uncle Leo I'll join him in the shed another time, okay?"

It was quiet at Jasper's when he walked in, and Kevin was nowhere in sight, so he sat at the bar and asked Paulie for a beer.

He stared down into the gold liquid, even swirled it in the glass, but no Magic 8 Ball answer popped up.

Shit. He knew the answer. If he was about to become a bug splattered on the windshield of a runaway freight train, his last thought would be of Emma.

So what if she couldn't cook and couldn't drive worth a damn? And she came with a house he didn't help pick out and a business he didn't help her build. He could live with that. The family they'd make together would be *theirs*.

If she even wanted him.

There was a pad of sticky notes in his back pocket, but he had nothing to write with. He checked all his pockets, but the Sharpie was gone. Hopefully, that wasn't some kind of omen.

"You got a pen I could use?" he asked Paulie as she walked by.

She tossed him a ballpoint and he peeled off the first sticky note. Without letting himself think too much, he started to write.

The sight of Sean's truck pulling up her driveway hit Emma like an emotional wrecking ball and she backed away from the window, trying to will her heart into submission.

He'd probably forgotten something, she told herself, even though he'd been pretty thorough in removing all traces of himself from her life and her home. Except for the stupid army mug she couldn't stop herself from using, but she doubted he'd make the drive for an old, second-hand coffee cup.

He rang the doorbell and she stopped in front of the hall mirror to see if she looked as much like a train wreck as she felt. She did, but there was nothing she could do about the puffy eyes and pale cheeks. At least she'd thrown her hair into a ponytail, so there was only so bad that could look.

Emma pulled open the door with what was probably a sorry excuse for a smile on her face and froze.

Sean stood on the porch, his face set in the expression she recognized as the one he used to mask uncertainty. But her gaze only settled on his face for a few seconds before being drawn to his chest.

He was wearing a button-up dress shirt and it was pink. And not a tint of pale blush, either. It was *pink*.

"Hey," he said, handing her a small bouquet of pink-and-white gladioli, the stems tied together with a length of pink ribbon.

Her breath caught in her throat as she took them, her mind racing to make sense of what she was seeing. What did it mean? Why was he here, dressed like the man of her ten-year-old self's dreams?

"I, uh…made some revisions to your owner's manual." She hadn't even noticed the journal in his other hand, but when he held it out, she took it.

"Okay." Her voice was as shaky as her hands.

She opened the cover and found a bright pink sticky note stuck to the first page. *I miss you.*

"I miss you, too," she whispered, and slowly turned the pages.

You don't take any crap from me.

You make me laugh.

Missionary is my favorite position now because I can see your face. That made her laugh, even as the sweetness of the sentiment warmed her heart.

I'll let you drive. She gave him a doubtful look and then turned the page. *Sometimes.*

Yeah, there was the Sean she knew and loved.

When he pulled a small velvet box out of his pocket, one of the tears blurring her vision broke free and rolled down her cheek. And when he got down on one knee, a few more followed. He lifted the lid, and nestled in the box she saw a shimmering ring with a central diamond nestled down between two bands set with smaller stones. It was gorgeous.

"I know I already bought you one of these, but that one was always hanging up in your work gloves. This won't catch on the leather or twist around too much." He tilted his head up to look at her. "This whole month was crazy, with all the pretending, but somewhere along the way it stopped being a lie."

"Did you go getting ideas about me, Sean Kowalski?"

"I did, and it was one hell of an idea, too. I love you, Emma. I think, deep down, that's what I wanted to write on that blank sticky note I left on the mirror, but I wasn't ready yet. I'm ready now. I love you and I want you to marry me. For real."

Words were flying around in her head, but she couldn't

seem to get them into any kind of coherent thought. "I don't... I... Are you sure?"

"I'm wearing a pink shirt."

"I love you, too," she said, because that seemed like the most important thing to get out there. "And I want to marry you. For real."

He slid the ring onto her finger and then stood up so he could kiss her breathless. As a little girl she'd imagined she would shed pretty, feminine tears during this moment, but she was too damn happy to cry.

"I was thinking," he said when he was through kissing her, "that if I do some odd-job carpentry, like that deck remodel, and you do your landscaping, maybe we could coordinate our work so we wouldn't have to wait too long to have kids. We could switch off days, maybe."

"That sounds perfect. But will it make you happy?"

"It will." He kissed her again and a happy sigh escaped her lips when it hit her she was going to get to kiss this man for the rest of her life. "But most important, *you* make me happy."

She threw her arms around his neck and—just to be different—she kissed him this time. And then she reached into the back pocket of her jeans and pulled out the blank sticky note. It was a little tattered now, but she held it out to him.

"Wondering what you were going to say has been killing me."

He took it from her and then pulled out a pen that said Jasper's Bar & Grille from his back pocket. *I love you,* he wrote, and then he stuck it to the front of her shirt.

"So you won't ever doubt it," he said in a husky voice.

"Let's go inside and get started on this for-real thing we having going on." She took his hand and tugged him toward the door. "And, because I love you, I'll start by stripping you out of that pink shirt."

* * * * *

We hope you enjoyed reading

WHITE LACE AND PROMISES

by #1 *New York Times* bestselling author

DEBBIE MACOMBER

and

YOURS TO KEEP

by *New York Times* bestselling author

SHANNON STACEY

They were originally Harlequin® Special Edition
and Carina Press stories!

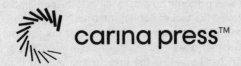

From passionate, suspenseful and dramatic
love stories to inspirational or historical,
Harlequin offers different lines to
satisfy every romance reader.

New books available every month.

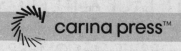
Mitch took a different route out of the city and cruised the back roads, pointing out interesting bits of scenery here and there. The bike was a bit loud and, with their helmets on, talking was difficult, so mostly he just burned up the miles and enjoyed the feel of her behind him.

It took over an hour to reach one of his favorite spots in the area. It wasn't much more than a wide spot in the shoulder, but he pulled the bike in and parked it near the tree line. Bracing his feet, he waited while she put her hands on his shoulders to steady herself and climbed off, then he leaned the bike onto its stand.

"Where are we?" Paige hung her helmet on the sissy bar and pushed at the wisps of hair escaping from her braid.

"Just wait." After hanging his helmet from the handlebar, he led her to a narrow path in the trees and reached out his hand. "It's a little steep."

With Paige's hand in his, he walked along the short trail down a mild slope to the river. A huge slab of rock extended out over a brook and he stepped on it, tugging her along with him.

"A little steep, huh?" Paige asked, amusement in her voice.

"I just wanted to hold your hand."

She didn't pull away, which made him ridiculously happy. Instead she looked around, so he did the same, taking in the way the fading sun shone through the trees and hit the water in splotches of gold. There was just enough current in the water that it gurgled through the rocks, and birds chirped from the cover of full summer foliage.

"It's beautiful." Paige didn't whisper, but her voice was soft and low, as if she didn't want to disturb their surroundings. "I bet you bring all the girls here."

"Nope." He'd never brought a woman there before, though he wasn't sure why. And he wasn't sure why he'd brought Paige. "I don't come here very often. Maybe that's what keeps it special. I came the day after my dad's funeral, though. Lay on this rock and looked up at the sky for a while."

She squeezed his hand. "It seems like a nice place to be alone with your thoughts."

It was an even better place to be alone with her, though he didn't say that out loud. There was a fine line between flirting and getting mushy, and it was bad enough his mind had even gone there. He wasn't about to share it.

"It's peaceful" was all he said, but he was in trouble.

Standing in a place that he was emotionally grounded to, holding hands with a woman he was painfully attracted to, was liable to blow the foundation out from under the wall he'd built between himself and seriousness. He liked that wall. It kept romantic entanglements from creeping in and getting a choke hold on him when his guard was down.

What the hell had he been thinking, bringing her here?

Don't miss **ALL HE EVER NEEDED**,
a Kowalski novel by New York Times *bestselling author Shannon Stacey, available now wherever Carina Press books are sold.*

www.CarinaPress.com

CARSSKOWALSKIEXP

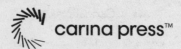